To the Honour of the Kings

By

Wayne Jarman

To the Honour of the Kings

Written by Wayne Jarman

Published by AWL Media
74 Fletcher Street
Edgeworth NSW 2285
Australia
Website: www.ReflectiveBubble.com

First printed August 2011

National Library of Australia Cataloguing-in-Publication entry

Author:	Jarman, Wayne.
Title:	To the honour of the kings / written by Wayne Jarman.
Edition:	1st ed.
ISBN:	9780987093110 (pbk.)

Dewey Number: A823.4

ISBN 978-0-9870931-1-0

Other Books by Wayne Jarman: ***With a Mind to Achieve***
(Personal Development / Success)

Connecting with Wayne Jarman via Social Networks:

Twitter: http://twitter.com/#!/ProfessorWhen

FaceBook: http://www.facebook.com/WayneJarman.Author

FaceBook: http://www.facebook.com/pages/Reflective-Bubble-Creative-Arts-Magazine/178494828865283

To My Loving Parents,
Jean and George,
for providing me with an
education to live a life … rather
than just to earn a living.

Thank You.

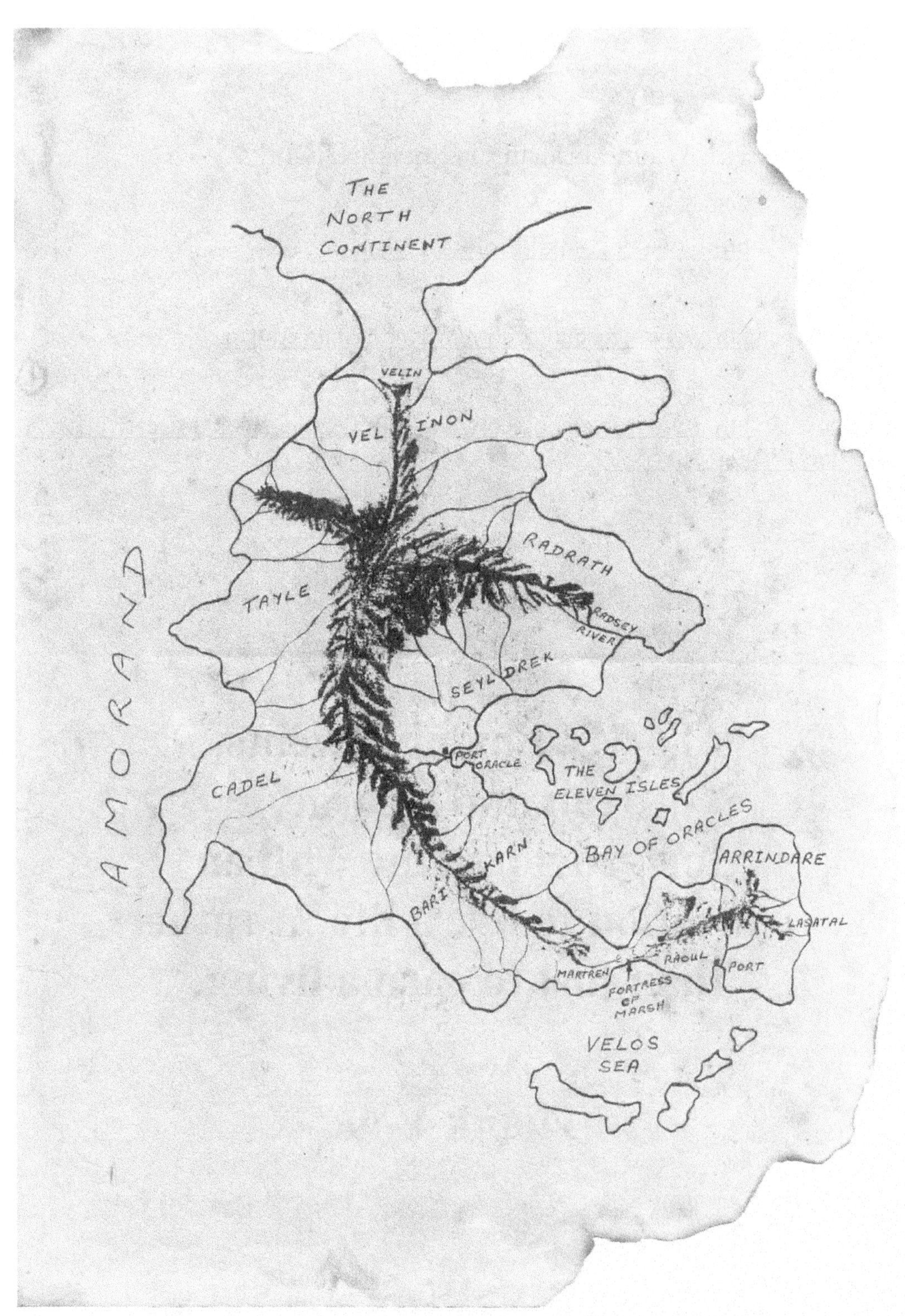
THE
NORTH
CONTINENT
VELIN
VEL
INON
RADRATH
TAYLE
AMORAND
RADSEY
RIVER
SEYL
DREK
PORT
ORACLE
CADEL
THE
ELEVEN ISLES
BAY OF ORRACLES
KARN
BARI
ARRINDARE
LASATAL
RAOUL
PORT
MARTREN
FORTRESS
OF
MARSH
VELOS
SEA

THROUGH THE FORTRESS

The four reined their mounts to a halt.

They had left the fortified city of Martren almost two hours ago and had finally descended out of the early morning mountain mist. After what had seemed an eternity in an unreal world of mist and shadowy forest, the vivid colours that met their eyes seemed just as unnatural.

From the rock outcrop, the travellers could view directly down the heavily forested mountain and out onto the Bay of Oracles, with the greenness of The Eleven Isles. Scanning further south, they looked over their own land of Arrindare, and then out to the Velos Sea and its dangerous reefs and islands.

After months of travelling, they were finally in sight of their homeland and within days of their journey's end. While there was some exaltation in that sight, their feelings were dulled by the failure of their mission.

Indeed, the mocking tones of King Raynor of Barikarn still echoed in their ears. He had scoffed at their suggestions that the Dark Emperor was preparing for war. He had called them 'Alarmists' and accused them of 'going about the countryside frightening women and young children.' His only concession had been to allow the armies of 'weaker Kings from the north to scamper across Barikarn to hide in Arrindare'. At least ***that*** was a worthwhile outcome. King Tyne of Velinon (the most northern Kingdom of the Southern Continent of Amorand) had shown an interest in moving his army south if the Dark Emperor crossed their shared boundary. He was the only King of the six to give any credence to their warning.

Their stop on the outcrop was brief. The four riders had a long, difficult day's travel ahead of them, through the Fortress of Marsh and eventually to the fortifications at Raoul where they could rest for the night. It would be another two days before they reached their final destination, the fortified city of Lasatal, the seat of power of the King of Arrindare.

They moved on in single file with Magnor leading the foursome. He did not look the most likely choice for such a position in this hostile terrain. Although he was well veiled in his brown cloak and hood, the wisps of thin white hair that fell across his face and his long white beard signified a man of great age. He was not large in stature and his face was deeply creviced and weather-beaten. All other facial features were overridden by his deep, green eyes. Apart from his shadowed face, the only visible parts of Magnor were his two thin, bony hands straining to control the massive grey horse that he was guiding down the mountain.

Only those who knew of Magnor knew of the power in those old hands. Magnor had been the King's personal guard in Arrindare for over forty years. He had protected and advised the old King Fenore and now protected and advised that King's son, King Daroyd. He was master of all forms of combat and, even at his present age, was capable of dealing with most adversaries.

Of the four, he was the obvious choice for lead rider.

King Daroyd followed close behind. In his late thirties, Daroyd had assumed the throne on his father's death only two years ago. Even before then, spies had been reporting on the Dark Emperor's preparation for war. To Daroyd, being a King had so far meant nothing more than worrying and planning to repel the assault that he was sure would come. Consequently, he did not look a well man. He was prematurely greying and he always appeared to be overwrought. This situation bewildered the third rider. Prince Stefarne saw no meaning in his father's behaviour. He considered this whole journey to be futile and, in fact, had told them so at every opportunity, between grumbling about the various hardships that they had encountered on the way.

Stefarne was the eldest son and, therefore, heir to the throne. His idea of being King varied greatly from his father's behaviour since assuming the throne. He had often told his parents (during arguments over the perceived threat from the Dark Emperor) how ***he*** would live the life of a noble and powerful King.

The last rider was Prince Gwaine, Stefarne's younger brother. Gwaine, like Magnor, seemed a strange choice for a guard position in a hostile countryside. He was not yet eighteen and of slender build. If anyone looked least like a warrior, it was Gwaine. He was, however, Magnor's pupil and had earned some reputation with the sword and bow and was therefore placed at the rear of the column.

The four rode in silence. After spending so long in each other's company there was very little left to talk about, and the ineffectiveness of their journey had left them depressed and unwilling to talk, even if there had been a subject that had not been exhausted.

An hour later they reached the base of the mountain and found the track that would lead them home.

'Now I'm starting to feel better,' the King remarked, putting on a cheerful show. 'This road leads to paradise.'

'You've got to get through that smelly bog yet.' Stefarne could always be counted on for a deflating comment.

Magnor spun his horse around angrily. 'That ***smelly bog***, my Lord Stefarne, has been the saviour of our land for centuries. It has kept many an army at bay. Without the Fortress of Marsh, you would not have been born a Crown Prince. Some foreign King would be sitting on the throne at Lasatal.'

Stefarne's voice assumed the high and mighty attitude of a Crown Prince. 'I am not disputing the defensive attributes or the historical significance of the marsh, my Lord Magnor. I am merely stating that it is a smelly bog.'

Magnor gave up, shook his head and turned his horse in the direction of the Fortress of Marsh. Magnor and Stefarne had never been able to get along. As Crown Prince, Stefarne should have been trained in defence by Magnor, but Stefarne had considered it below his station to carry arms. Besides, he abhorred violence. After two attempted lessons, all sides had given it up as a dead loss. There had been animosity and general disdain between them ever since.

'Well, regardless of the smell Stefarne,' the King continued undaunted, 'I shall be glad to cross into our lands and I will wash the smell away tonight in Raoul. What say you Gwaine?'

'We have been away too long, father. I would put up with much more than the smell of the marsh to see home again.' Gwaine's answer was sincere. He loved his home and did not care much for the other six Kings of Amorand. Nor was he comfortable in the presence of any of the Princes and Princesses. He would happily return home and never cross his border again, if only the outside world would leave him alone.

At midday they were within two kilometres of the marsh. The ground was sloping down to the low-lying peninsula that was the neck and boundary of their land. Here, three freshwater rivers met the salt water of the sea that shallowly covered the marsh. The resulting expanse of nature was a unique environment that offered more challenges to the traveller than just nasal tolerance.

Where the salt water lay undisturbed by the movement of the freshwater currents, marsh trees and plants grew, brackish putrid mud sucked at every moving muscle, and insects swarmed. Snakes were prevalent in these areas and the occasional shark had been seen in the areas closer to the coast.

Where the freshwater reduced the salinity of the water flow, forests of trees flourished. While this was an easier climate to tolerate, it did provide other hazards, such as large areas of quicksand, snakes and the occasional crocodile.

An army attacking through this terrain would be at the mercy of a defending army of bowmen hiding in the trees and brush. This terrain, combined with the severely cliffed coastline of the remainder of Arrindare, had kept Arrindare impenetrable since the beginning of recorded history.

‘Before the smell becomes too great for Stefarne,’ the King announced, ‘we shall break for lunch.’

All four dismounted and moved to the side of the track.

‘At least King Raynor was courteous enough to have his servants pack us some food.’ Stefarne was already seated and chewing into a piece of meat. ‘The way he stormed out of our meeting last night, I didn’t think he would bother.’

The other three were still getting seated and preparing to unwrap their food parcels.

‘Yes he was rather annoyed,’ remarked Gwaine, with a quick wink at Magnor. ‘I hope it’s not poisoned.’

The coughing and spluttering that erupted from Stefarne brought howls of laughter from Gwaine and Magnor. Even King Daroyd couldn’t hold back a chuckle, though he tried to cover it up with a cough.

‘That’s not funny,’ Stefarne protested, trying to recover some princely composure. ‘When will you grow up, Gwaine?’

Gwaine was still recovering from his laughter. ‘I don’t know, my Lord. I must be a dreadful trial.’ He had intended the statement to have some element of contrition in it, but the uncontrollable humour in his voice spoilt it.

‘You certainly are,’ came the icy, Crown-Princely reply, before Stefarne went into a sulk.

Nothing more was said over lunch, each traveller lost in his own thoughts. When they had finished eating, they all, without command or communication, climbed back into the saddle. It was the discipline of months of pushing to reach a goal, the common urgency of their mission.

They rode on toward the marsh.

Before long the sun had been obliterated by the foliage of a dense forest. The river that flowed from Martren to the Fortress of Marsh was on their right, though it could no longer be recognised as a river. This was a transitional area where river flowed without the constraints of banks and eventually became marsh.

As they moved deeper into the forest, the ground became more saturated with water and a heavy mist that had earlier hung in the trees moved down to almost head height.

The horses sludged on.

A little further on, the travellers met with what was left of the Martren River. The horses were now struggling to stay upright. They were sliding on a slimy, hard surface that was often covered by as much as a metre of water.

'Time to dismount,' announced Magnor. His voice sounded strangely dull in this heavy atmosphere and the command was immediately joined by a chorus of shrill screams from a flock of waterfowl that flew off in fright.

The hackles on Gwaine's neck stood up with the sound. He slowly shifted his weight in the saddle and steadied his mount before lowering himself into the water. It was freezing cold. As he planted his weight onto the slimy ground, he slipped slightly and grabbed his saddle for balance. The horse slipped a little and then they both corrected and took their own weights.

There was an almighty splash.

'***Damnation! ...Vile Bog!***' Stefarne had fallen in and was now coughing and spluttering and cursing all at the one time. '***Putrid, vile bog!*** ...It's freezing! I'll die of the coughing sickness before we reach Raoul.'

Gwaine lowered his eyes toward the water, shook his head despondently and prayed. 'Why God? Why Stefarne? Anybody but Stefarne. I would have happily fallen in myself rather than listen to him moan all the way to Raoul.'

'***Cursed Marsh!*** ...Ridiculous mission anyway.' Stefarne was standing in the water completely soaked and totally out of control. In frustration, he twisted the upper half of his body to slap the water's surface with his hand while he let forth a guttural growl. It was enough to upset his foothold on the slime. He went down for a second time.

Gwaine leant slightly on the side of his horse, folded his arms across the saddle and buried his head in his arms. It had been a long, exhausting journey and there was still a long way to go.

Magnor and King Daroyd stood in silence and watched Stefarne re-emerge from the water.

'Shall we continue now, Stefarne?' the King asked calmly.

The second dunking had quelled the active side of Stefarne's temper. He took a deep breath that heaved his chest up and down to show his pent-up frustration, grabbed his horse's rein and moved off quickly. He passed Magnor and King Daroyd without uttering another sound. Several steps later he slipped again, this time only to his knees. He quickly regained his height, issued forth another deep, frustrated breath, straightened his back and shoulders and moved on much more carefully.

Magnor and King Daroyd moved off side by side, jointly shaking their heads after Stefarne. From his leaning position on the side of his horse, Gwaine could see a wry smile on the face of both men.

'At least they've retained a sense of humour,' he thought to himself.

He allowed them to move off into the mist before motivating himself into following them.

There was no longer any need to retain their formal column defence. They were now in their own land. Anyone following them could not do so quietly in this world of mud and water and noisy birds. And how would they track them anyway? The water and deep mist would prove a successful handicap to the greatest of trackers.

Danger from the front could now be discounted as well. Ahead were the guards of their own army; those poor souls who spent weeks at a time in this terrain, turning back any travellers who were foolhardy enough to enter.

Arrindare was a closed land. No one entered unless they had permission of the King. As few outsiders as possible were allowed to travel any of the tracts that led safely through the Fortress of Marsh. The marsh was indeed their fortress. The secrecy of its safe paths was necessary for the continued survival of Arrindare, particularly if the Dark Emperor was preparing for war.

Gwaine trudged on through the watery expanse. He had always expected to be challenged but, when it finally came, it startled him and stopped him in his tracks.

'Who goes there?'

The voice drifted across the mist from an unknown distance or direction.

Magnor answered the challenge. 'The King of Kings', he shouted into the mist that shrouded their vision.

Magnor would not have used this title outside of Arrindare. It was a particularly touchy subject with the other six Kings of Amorand that, within recorded history, the King of Arrindare had commanded respect and homage from all of the Kingdoms of Amorand. The title of 'King of Kings' had been bestowed upon the King of Arrindare during that golden era and the title had been used within Arrindare for the centuries that followed, regardless of the fact that none of the other Kings acknowledged its validity.

The four now stood motionless in the frigid water, waiting for a response from the mist. Eventually, the watery sound of someone wading toward them disrupted the silence. A short while later, a figure could be perceived through the mist. Taron,

Commander of the Fortress Guard, came into clear view and bowed before the four travellers.

'Welcome home, my King. And my Lords.'

'Thank you, Taron. It is good to be in Arrindare, though I will be much happier when we reach Raoul.' The King gestured at the surrounding mist. 'This is not my favourite part of our land.'

Taron replied with a laugh. He was young for his responsible position, but at the age of twenty-two he was confident of his ability and of his relationship with his King.

'We shall soon have you warm and dry in Raoul, my Lord.' Taron turned his attention to Stefarne. 'I see that Prince Stefarne has tested the Martren waters.'

Stefarne ignored Taron's friendly smile. 'Can we kindly go through these formalities in Raoul. I'm freezing.'

'Of course, my Lord. Your escort is waiting on dry land only a hundred metres from here. We have towels, though...' Taron paused, looking at Stefarne's soaked condition, 'I am afraid that we cannot provide dry clothes until we reach Raoul.'

'Of course not,' snapped Stefarne. 'I wouldn't have expected anything so civilised in this blasted bog.'

Stefarne was walking before he had finished his sentence and was out of sight within seconds, though he could be heard wading through the water for much longer.

Gwaine's temperament had undergone a change for the better the moment that he had recognised Taron. Though there was a difference in their ages, Taron and Gwaine had been close friends for as long as Gwaine could remember. Taron had been raised in the Court and trained as a warrior and commander by Magnor. Under Magnor's caring wing, they had both suffered mental and physical stress, exhaustion, and pain in their efforts to prove themselves warriors.

Outside of Magnor's battle rooms, the two had earned a reputation for causing mischief and calamity wherever they went. Their friendship had been bonded by the cementing force of shared blame and shared discipline as Magnor and the King had both taken their turns at attempting to correct their errant behaviour.

When Taron invited them to follow Stefarne to the dry area of land, Gwaine moved immediately to his side. The two moved slowly, allowing the others to leave them behind in the mist. Finally, Gwaine broke the silence with a whispered question.

'Why is the Commander of the Fortress Guard getting his feet wet?'

Taron smiled. 'I heard a report that the Crown Prince was drowning in the waters of the Martren. Of course, being the loyal subject and soldier that I am, I dashed down here, without any regard for my own personal safety, only to find that he was quite safe ...and all the crocodiles had mysteriously died.'

Gwaine wasn't amused. 'Seriously, what has happened that you are at the front line?'

'Our defences are being probed,' Taron replied in a more serious tone. 'In the last two nights we have frightened off six travellers who would not answer our challenges. An unmarked ship sailed into the Bay of Oracles last night and anchored just out from the marsh. It stayed for less than an hour before leaving again - enough time to put assassins or spies ashore.'

'Have you found anything?'

'No, my Lord. We have found nothing.'

Gwaine studied his friend for a while before commenting. 'It doesn't mean that our defences are being probed. It could all be unrelated.'

'Yes, my Lord.' Taron sounded less than convinced. '...It could.'

They had stepped out of the water onto solid ground. Stefarne, Magnor and King Daroyd were already there, towelling their clothes to extract as much water as possible. Six Arrindare Guards were standing with them. One offered Gwaine a towel and he, too, commenced extracting water from his clothes.

'All a complete waste of time you know,' boomed Stefarne. 'We'll be slipping and sliding in black, smelly mud within half an hour.'

Gwaine felt his spirits fall. Though he hated to admit it, Stefarne's gloomy report was quite correct. There was still a long, demanding journey ahead of them before they reached Raoul.

When they had all given up the attempt to towel dry their clothes, Taron gave the command to mount. The band, now numbering eleven, climbed to the top of the ridge of dry land.

'End of defence number one,' Gwaine mumbled as they reached the summit and started descending the other side.

They were now entering a tract of the Fortress of Marsh that was actually marsh. There was no fresh water here. This was one of many salt water, stagnant wastelands that provided the barrier that kept Arrindare impenetrable.

The smell that struck them was repulsive. Black mud, rotting vegetable and animal tissue, and stagnant water all combined to generate a smell that had to be smelt to be believed.

Taron led the band in single file. For as long as possible he kept them travelling on hard, packed mud so that they could ride. Eventually though, the mud became too deep and they had to dismount and move into the oozing black bog.

During the ride, Stefarne had found a captive audience to complain to, of his wet condition and the freezing cold. Consequently, as they dismounted, Gwaine found himself praying again. 'Please God, don't let him fall over in the mud.'

The mist was lighter in this area, granting greater visibility in choosing a path that could lead, eventually, to firm ground. Taron knew his area well, but the firm mud was rare and he could provide little relief for his weary travellers. They trudged on, the mud gripping and holding their feet and arms and then sticking to them as they struggled free, so that their limbs were never free of its weight. They dragged themselves and their horses through four kilometres of mud and swarming insects before climbing another ridge of dry land.

All eleven fell to the ground, exhausted. Gwaine peered back, over the insect infested pit of mud and then looked wearily across to Taron.

'God save any army that attacks over this terrain.'

Taron scoffed. 'No army should wait to be saved by superstition. Any army attacking through here had better be prepared for eternal darkness.'

Gwaine had forgotten that his beliefs varied from Taron's on the subject of whether there was, or was not, a God.

As they all struggled to their feet, Gwaine peered back once more. 'End of defence number two,' he mumbled to himself.

Taron overheard his comment. 'Only one more defence to go my Lord. It will be easy from here, ...across the freshwater forest of the Raoul Rivers and then on to Raoul.'

Again they waded through icy water, carefully searching for safe footing on the slimy ground. Taron had been correct though. It was easier now. They even took the opportunity to wash away the mud. Apart from their meeting with a lone crocodile, this part of the journey was uneventful. They had managed to frighten it off by yelling and bashing the water with their shields. Stefarne's concerted effort in screaming loudest and jumping up and down in the water provided some jovial discussion to lighten the subsequent kilometres to the edge of the marsh.

Eventually, they climbed out of the Fortress of Marsh and out of the eternal mist in time to see the last rays of light fading on the horizon. They had taken almost six hours to cross the twelve kilometres of marsh.

A firm, dry track lay at their feet, pointing the way to their day's goal. Four hours later they were within the fortifications of Raoul.

LAS BATAL

It was mid-morning when the four met over breakfast. If they had risen early and travelled all day they could have been in Lasatal by nightfall, but they had always planned an easy two-day ride from Raoul. They had known, all too well, how demanding the Fortress of Marsh was to cross and how they would need this rest.

Gwaine left the table and walked to the window. They had arrived last night in darkness and had only taken time for a bath and some food before making their way to bed. By the light of day, Gwaine now studied the city and battlements of Raoul.

This city fortress was set at the junction of two arms of the mountain range that stretched down the centre of Arrindare. The peaceful city spread down the mountains, overlooking two arms of the Raoul River that ran in the valley below. It was a picturesque sight, with views of the Bay of Oracles, The Eleven Isles, and the lands of Barikarn and Seyldrek. The massive stone battlements stood defiant, contrasted against the intense blues and greens of the water and forests that they surveyed.

Gwaine smiled at the irony. The battlements of Raoul had been built, repaired, redesigned and restructured again and again over centuries of recorded history but had never been needed. The fortress that nature had built at the neck of the country, 'that smelly bog', had done its job over those centuries with no maintenance necessary while these man-made walls had cost a fortune and a permanent garrison of soldiers to maintain them in a defendable condition.

'Excellent day, Gwaine.' The King's voice woke Gwaine from his thoughts.

'Yes, Sire. Unusually warm for this time of year. It should be a pleasant ride to Port.'

Conversation resumed at the table, while Gwaine's thoughts turned to Port. He had noticed that other lands had named their shipping ports by using the word 'Port' to prefix another name, such as the large city of Port Oracle in the land of

Seyldrek. To a land such as Arrindare, with its sheer cliff coastline, this was unnecessary. Port was the only land formation on the coastline that could be reasonably used to harbour ships and, therefore, a more distinctive name had been considered unnecessary by those early fishermen who had founded the settlement.

Even in this so-called port, the freight was unloaded from the ships by hoisting mechanisms that dragged the imported goods up the sheer cliff. The reverse process of loading for export was similar, but much more difficult to manage. Like the rest of Arrindare, Port was closed to all but natives of the land. The treacherous Velos Sea, with its unpredictable and sudden temperament changes and its submerged reefs, kept all but the Arrindare captains well clear of their coastline and even they occasionally came to grief.

At Port, even the forces of nature had not been able to make much of an impression on the sheer volcanic rock of Arrindare's coast. The Port River flowed to meet the Velos Sea only by leaping from the cliffs as great waterfalls that made the traffic of ships in the port even more chaotic and dangerous.

'Your escort is ready to leave when you are, Sire.' This time it was Taron's voice that broke Gwaine's thoughts.

'Excellent, Taron. I am refreshed, rested and well fed. I even feel like a King again. Let us move on to Port and one day closer to Lasatal.'

The breakfast party rose with the King. The small gathering of senior members of the court of Raoul followed the King and his companions as they made their way to the courtyard where a carriage and twenty mounted guards were waiting.

Stefarne and the King mounted the carriage while Gwaine and Magnor, preferring to ride, were assisted by attendants into the saddle.

The parade moved through the city to the cheers and greetings of its inhabitants and then down the steep mountain track. To Gwaine's surprise and delight, Taron led the soldiers.

Later, as Magnor was riding beside the carriage, near his King, Gwaine spurred his horse to join his friend at the head of the column. 'How did you wangle a trip to Lasatal?' Gwaine knew his friend's preference for Lasatal over Raoul.

'A Commander of the Fortress Guard has some influence you know.'

'Nonsense. He's just a glorified mudfish.' Gwaine was enjoying himself. It was a glorious day and he had now found good company.

Taron laughed. 'If you could have seen the expression on the half-drowned mudfish that I dragged out of the marsh yesterday, you wouldn't be so cocky.'

'I'll have you know, Commander, that I was in full control of the situation yesterday and I didn't really need your rather trifling assistance.'

Taron merely smiled and made no reply.

Gwaine looked across at his friend, realising that Taron had left the conversation, and searched for a new subject for discussion. 'I hate to be the bearer of bad news, my friend, but you're going the wrong way.'

The column had reached the base of the mountain and was moving along the path that led back to the Fortress of Marsh.

'Yes, it's a nuisance having to travel all this distance in the wrong direction, but some addle-brained Warlord built Raoul on a mountain range that we now have to travel around.'

'Careful!' Gwaine's voice had taken on a pretence of sternness. 'That's one of my ancestors your calling addle-brained.'

'Yes,' replied Taron, 'and I must say that you're carrying on the tradition very well.'

'Oh, thank you very much!'

With light hearted conversation and a friend to share the ride with, it seemed to Gwaine that it took no time to cross the third and fourth arms of the Raoul River and to travel over the flatland that led to Port. Even with a one-hour break for lunch, the column was settled into the royal lodgings at Port well before dinnertime.

There would have been an all-night party that night if the senior members of the court had their way, but the King was determined to be well rested for his last day of travel. A banquet supper with an extremely large number of speeches could not be avoided.

The next morning saw a light-hearted company crossing the Port River on the last leg of the journey. The weather had returned to what was normal for this time of year. The sky was permanently overcast and an icy wind blew from the snow-capped mountain range on their left. But the weather could not dampen their spirits. Even Stefarne, despite his cold, seemed in a good mood.

Magnor rode beside the carriage that carried his King and Stefarne, while Gwaine had taken up permanent residence beside Taron at the head of the column.

The entire trip from Raoul had been uneventful. For his part, Gwaine was sorry that this particular stage of the journey was coming to an end. It had been refreshing to ride the flatland of his own country beside his friend. The last two days had helped to blur some of the worst memories of hardship and despondency of their fruitless mission.

Lasatal was now in sight. Sitting high up the mountain at the very tip of the mountain range, it looked like some giant dog peering out to the eastern sea, out to the fabled eastern land of Parrin.

A garrison of soldiers could be seen forming a guard of honour at the base of the mountain. Five hundred soldiers dressed in black, lined either side of the path that led to the gates of the city of Lasatal.

When the King and his escort were within one hundred metres of the beginning of the guard of honour, a chorus of trumpets echoed across the mountain and the

King's banner was lifted into the air by a mounted soldier as he charged in full gallop toward the King's escort. At the halfway point between the King and the honour guard he suddenly reined his mount and drove the spear end of the banner into the ground so that it stood upright and waved in the icy gusts of wind. The soldier wheeled his horse and rode back toward the guard.

Before Taron had stopped the escort, Gwaine had fallen back several metres behind his friend so that Taron was now alone at the head of the column.

When the banner bearer had returned to the guard of honour and taken his position in the line, Taron moved his horse forward, beginning a ritual whose origins had been lost in time. The motion now was slow and deliberate, in direct contrast to the way the banner had been delivered. Taron stopped his horse beside the banner and scanned the guard of honour, beginning with those soldiers closest to him and slowly advancing up the mountain until he was staring at the giant gates of Lasatal. There was absolute silence. That so many soldiers and horses and an entire population of a city could have been so quiet was a shock to the senses. Only the wind occasionally whistling about his ear kept Gwaine from believing that he had suddenly fallen deaf or into some dreamlike trance.

Only when he was certain that all were totally still and totally quiet did Taron reach out his left hand and grasp the thick carved handgrip of the wooden pole of the banner. The silence combined with Taron's deliberate movements made all to appear to be in suspended motion. The sound of the banner being wrenched from the ground was audible to Gwaine over those forty of fifty metres.

Having taken the weight of the banner, Taron slowly extended his arm upward to raise the banner to its full height. The King's banner fluttered violently in a sudden gust of wind but the sheer material made little sound.

Gwaine watched Taron's rib cage expand as he sucked in air in preparation for his oath. When the words finally came they were loud, slowly deliberate and intended to reach the deepest rooms of the castle of Lasatal.

'To ...the ...Honour ...of ...the ...King.'

His shouted words were immediately echoed by every soldier and citizen on the mountain. The mountain erupted into screams, cheering, applause and the beating of five hundred swords onto five hundred shields. Gwaine's startled horse reared slightly and then trotted backwards. Bringing his own mount under control, he then went to the aid of the King's carriage driver who was having difficulty containing his horses.

Taron trotted his mount back to his column. He had little chance of moving back slowly as his horse, too, was startled and difficult to control. Nevertheless, the banner was passed to a soldier of the column without mishap and he and the banner then led the column up the mountain track between the two lines of the guard of honour.

As they passed the beginning of the guard, two banners, which until now had been touched to the ground, were raised to their full height. These were the regiment's banners and, like the soldiers of the regiment, they bore no other colour than black.

This was the Last Regiment. The ancients of Arrindare, who had planned the defence of this land, had known that if the enemy came to Lasatal then it could only mean that all was lost, that all other regiments had been destroyed and that this was to be the last battle, or 'Las Batal' in the ancient tongue. Hence, the name of their city had been derived from a condensed version of that old tongue. The pledge of the Last Regiment was to die in honour, in order to preserve the honour of those regiments that had perished before them and to defend, to the last man, the King and the Royal Family.

'Not a very cheery prospect,' thought Gwaine. 'No wonder the ancients decided on black as the Regiment's colours.'

The column was well on its way up the mountain. The Last Regiment was at attention. While the cheers echoed from the city walls and from the people who had descended the mountain to greet their King, the men and horses of the Last

Regiment were perfectly still, having recovered from the pandemonium, and were on display for King Daroyd.

Gwaine, for the first time in the whole journey, felt shabby, His brown cape and hood had served as a coverall in forest and King's Court alike. But now, before the shining blackness of these soldiers, he felt the need to change into something that displayed his position in the court and his position in the land of Arrindare.

The column finally halted at the closed gates. Gwaine looked over his shoulder and saw that the two lines of the Last Regiment had moved onto the track and were facing up the mountain ready to move back into the city.

The heavy gates of Lasatal creaked and groaned as they were pushed open.

The first sight to greet Gwaine's eyes were the smiling faces of his mother and younger sister.

After such a long journey, Gwaine looked at his mother as if for the first time and realised why the reputation of her beauty had spread throughout Amorand. His sister, Ellorn, although only fifteen, was obviously going to be just as attractive.

Gwaine was surprised when the King brushed past his horse. His father walked briskly through the gates, threw his arms around the Queen, totally ruining her attempted curtsy, lifted her off the ground and spun her around in circles while kissing her on the cheek.

Laughter and renewed cheering erupted from the crowd.

Queen Lenore laughed and returned her husband's embrace. Ellorn, who had been forced to jump back to avoid injury, was now standing close to her parents looking amused, even if somewhat embarrassed at being so close to the centre of humour.

While Gwaine was enjoying the spontaneity of the moment, he was almost afraid to look over his shoulder at Stefarne. This would, surely, not be acceptable behaviour in Stefarne's eyes. Regardless of the fear that had overcome him, Gwaine decided that he had to look. He slowly leant forward in his saddle, with his folded arms resting across the base of his horse's neck and, as casually as possible, turned his head to peer over his left shoulder. Stefarne had turned to stone. His face was a deathly mask of anger and disdain. He had gone red with what may have been embarrassment, or possibly high blood pressure. Stefarne spotted him and gave an ice-cold stare that wiped the smile from Gwaine's face and turned his head back toward the gate and his parents. He sat up in the saddle.

King Daroyd had released his bear hug hold on his Queen, though he still held her hand, and was now greeting Ellorn. He turned and waved to the crowd and then, placing his arm around Ellorn, started walking up the path through the city, toward his castle.

Gwaine's blood turned cold. His father's unexpected action had taken his guards by surprise. There wasn't a soldier within reach of the King. He threw himself off his horse, grasping his shield in flight, and ran after his parents. When he reached the gate Taron was at his side, sword in hand, and running at top speed. Within seconds, they pulled up on either side of the King, puffing with their sudden uphill exertion.

'I was wondering when you two would turn up.' King Daroyd was smiling and waving as he spoke. 'You know you shouldn't leave a King without a guard like that. It's very dangerous.'

Gwaine and Taron could only shake their heads and gasp for breath.

Gwaine looked over his shoulder and saw one of the soldiers tending to his and Taron's horses. He heard a twanging sound. Instinctively, he dived to his left and threw his shield in front of his father, where it clanged against Taron's shield. Gwaine felt the wind of the arrow as it narrowly missed his neck, passing to his right side. His blood chilled again as he urgently searched for Ellorn while losing his balance and falling against his father. She was unhurt.

By the time Gwaine, Taron, King Daroyd and Queen Lenore had recovered from their tangled heap, the would-be assassin had been slain. He had fired from a risen area, so that the arrow, having missed its mark, had embedded itself harmlessly in the road.

King Daroyd was quite pale and his exuberance and light heart had disappeared. He looked from Gwaine to Taron with a slight nod of his head that was obviously meant to say 'thank you'.

'A King should never be frivolous.' King Daroyd looked unwell as his words came in a gust of despondency.

Gwaine gasped for breath as he tried to think of a response.

'On the contrary, my Lord. If a King cannot be frivolous, then it paints a gloomy outlook for the rest of the world. It was merely your timing that was wrong.'

A faint, forced smile appeared on King Daroyd's lips.

Magnor had taken charge of the situation. Soldiers searched houses and the crowd for any other aliens. The King's carriage was brought forward, with Stefarne still seated, and the guard doubled around it, while Taron's and Gwaine's horses were delivered to them.

The King's carriage, surrounded by soldiers, and carrying the King and Queen, Stefarne and Ellorn, was already out of sight when Gwaine was preparing to mount his horse.

Magnor rode by and then, obviously remembering something, pulled his horse to a halt.

'One hour before sun-up, my Lord Gwaine, I want both you and Taron in my war room.' His manner was not good tempered. 'You both have a great deal to learn.' He spurred his horse after his King's carriage.

Gwaine looked around for Taron, who was giving final instructions to his soldiers. When he had finished, Gwaine waved and signalled for him to ride over.

They rode off together in silence, with six soldiers following, toward the fortified castle. Riding across the massive square, Gwaine turned to Taron.

'We're booked for hell at the usual time tomorrow morning.'

Taron continued looking ahead. 'Oh, shit! Why didn't I stay in Raoul?'

Gwaine veered to the left, to the castle steps, while Taron and his soldiers continued on to the barracks.

TALK OF WAR

Taron and Gwaine met in Magnor's War Room before daylight, as they had been directed. To their surprise, Magnor was not there to meet them.

'This is unusual,' remarked Taron. He was warming up, swinging a large practice sword. The blade was made of a roughly rounded bar of iron. It couldn't cut, but it certainly stung when it contacted, as both Gwaine and Taron knew only too well. 'He's usually here abusing us for being late, even when we're on time.'

'Yes.' Gwaine reached for his practice sword and began his warm-up. 'I have heard that a messenger was allowed through the marsh yesterday and rode all night. There seems to be quite a gathering in the throne room.'

'Doesn't sound good. Perhaps the war has come.'

'Perhaps.' Gwaine's reply was rather absently directed at the ceiling as he reached for a war-shield from the dirty stone wall. Only torches lit the room and cast long shadows and a yellowish glow over the two figures and the strange assemblage of implements of war that littered the walls and floor of the dingy room. 'Nothing to concern mere soldiers. How do you wish to die?'

Gwaine's sudden change of subject was accompanied by a threatening posture as he brought the shield up to his chest and pointed the sword at Taron.

'Ah! The sign of a true friend. One who allows you to choose how he will kill you.' Taron was leaning casually on his sword with his left hand on his hip. 'If you must know, I would rather go quickly with an arrow, but I wouldn't think of choosing such a weapon now that you've gone to the trouble of gathering a sword and shield.

Taron walked to the far wall and chose a shield.

‘You realise, after the way you chattered in my ear all the way from Raoul, I’m going to enjoy hitting you with this stick.’ Taron pointed his roughly shaped sword threateningly at Gwaine.

Gwaine laughed. ‘It only seemed that I was talking a lot because I said everything twice ...in the hope that some of it would penetrate your thick skull.’

Taron was smiling. ‘Come on, Warlord. Let’s see if you can fight as well as you talk.’

With that, Taron jumped forward and threw a massive blow at Gwaine’s shield that sent a deafening clang through the old chamber. Gwaine’s reply was instant. His blow against Taron’s shield joined the echo that was already ringing in their ears. Blow after blow resounded as they fought, defended and dived around the room. Five minutes later, Magnor called a halt as he entered the room. He ignored their sweat soaked condition and their gasping breaths.

‘One of the Dark Emperor’s armies has invaded Velinon.’ Magnor paused for effect. ‘...Six days ago.’

The announcement shouldn’t have come as a surprise. Gwaine had been trained since childhood in preparation for this war. Nevertheless, he was shocked now that the moment had actually arrived.

Magnor walked to a dimly lit table in the corner of the chamber. A plaster model of Amorand, approximately three metres square, had lain here for decades collecting dust. Taron and Gwaine joined him by the table.

‘King Tyne put up a token resistance while his people burnt as much of the crops as was possible in the time allowed. He is now retreating down the east coast. King Daroyd has sent commands to dispatch our fleet and messengers so that we can take the Velinon army aboard at Port Oracle.’

‘He’s unlikely to catch them in time,’ Gwaine interrupted. ‘They will probably be passed Port Oracle by then. King Tyne will come through the marsh.’

‘Yes. I agree. But it is worth a try. It would be better if they came through Port, rather than have fifteen thousand soldiers trudging single file through the marsh.’ Magnor wiped some of the dust off the east coast of Amorand, before continuing. ‘The Kings of Seyldrek and Radrath have joined their armies at their border and intend putting up a fight.’

‘Thirty thousand against seventy? It’s a waste of good soldiers. The doddering old fools.’ Gwaine had little respect for either King Bartak of Seyldrek or King Thale of Radrath. Both were old men who would prefer to fight and die in glory than plan a strategy to win.

‘Nevertheless, Gwaine, it will give us time to get King Tyne within our boundaries and to work on the other Kings. Perhaps, now, they will listen to our plans. Our journey may not have been futile after all.’

‘Why only one army of seventy thousand?’ Taron queried. ‘The Dark Emperor could have dispatched three that size and easily taken Amorand.’

‘He knows that he can take Amorand with one army. Our seven small armies are too dispersed to put up any concentrated opposition. He will take Amorand with one, use another as a second wave to take control of the population, and the third will stay at home to handle his domestic situation. It’s quite a sound plan.’

Gwaine had a great deal of respect for Magnor. At this critical point, he was still very matter-of-fact and totally level-headed.

‘So...’ Gwaine stopped. He was about to ask a question that seemed overly simplistic, but, having stopped and thought, he still couldn’t see the answer. He continued. ‘...What now?’

Magnor grinned. ‘Now, my young warriors, we shall wait for King Tyne to arrive. We shall wait for the response of the other Kings. We shall wait and see how Kings Bartak and Thale fair in their battle ***and***’, Magnor’s voice became emphatic, ‘...we shall continue to practice to be warriors, and wonder why we almost allowed our King to be assassinated in front of five hundred soldiers of the Last Regiment.'

Gwaine perceived that Magnor's temper had settled overnight and his use of the term 'we' meant that he was blaming himself for being caught off-guard as much as anybody else. He twisted his face into a perplexed grimace. 'Yes, that was a little awkward, wasn't it.'

Taron only bowed his head and waited for Magnor's verbal abuse.

'Yes. Very awkward,' Magnor replied dryly as he walked away from the table to the centre of the room. He turned and looked toward the floor in thought for some time before recommencing the discussion.

'Taron has told me of the unmarked ship near our shores, in the Bay of Oracles. Yesterday's attempted assassination proves, quite obviously, that spies and assassins have been put ashore. We must all take greater care.'

'Yes my Lord,' agreed Taron. 'I have increased the guard around the King and emphasised the danger. But, ...someone must also talk to the King. He cannot continue to take the sort of risks that he took yesterday.'

'Yes, Taron. I have already talked to the King. But, I said ***we*** must ***all*** take greater care.'

Silence fell on the room. Taron finally took the initiative. 'I'm sorry, my Lord. I don't understand.'

Magnor ignored Taron and turned to Gwaine. 'What did you think of the bowman's marksmanship yesterday?'

Gwaine smirked. 'Terrible, my Lord. He couldn't have hit the side of a barn.'

'I see.' Magnor looked toward the floor and scratched his hairy chin in thought. He seemed to be searching for, and studying, his own questions as if he had suddenly come across a point that he wasn't sure of but wanted to explore. 'Wouldn't you expect that if an assassin were selected and sent so far to penetrate an enemy territory to dispatch someone who was a threat, ...that the assassin would be selected on his merits as a marksman? I mean, it seems stupid to send someone on such a trek if he lacked the ability to perform the final task.'

'Yes, my Lord,' Gwaine could see the logic in Magnor's words, but yesterday's events made this discussion seemingly useless. 'But ...the proof is in the final outcome. The bowman would have missed even if Taron and I hadn't tripped all over the King.' Gwaine smiled as he saw the mental picture of himself, Taron, the King and the Queen all tangled in a heap on the ground.

'Exactly, Gwaine.' Magnor seemed to have reached an outcome in his own mind. He was now more confident in his speech. 'And where would the arrow have landed if you had not …'tripped all over the King'?'

'Oh well,' Gwaine projected a mental image in his mind's eye as he shrugged and smiled toward Magnor, '...I suppose you would finally be rid of your star pupil.'

'Surely, you're not suggesting,' interrupted Taron with wide eyes, 'that he was aiming at me.'

'Oh don't be ridiculous,' laughed Gwaine. 'Mudfish don't count.'

'It is my belief,' Magnor was talking loudly to regain control of the discussion and bring it back to a serious conclusion, 'that the King may not have been the target yesterday.'

The smile disappeared off Gwaine's face.

'I repeat,' Magnor continued, 'we must ***all*** take greater care. Particularly you Gwaine. The Dark Emperor knows, only too well, the value of the second Prince of Arrindare. The Dark Forces have been repelled countless times over the centuries by the control and authority of the Warlord over the armies of Amorand. Their last defeat, only two centuries ago, by Baradetch, was their greatest route. You are the Dark Emperor's greatest threat. You can do to him what Baradetch has done before you.'

Gwaine saw the opportunity to lighten the conversation and take some of the gravity off his shoulders. 'I must first learn how to fly, my Lord, and to travel faster than a beam of light, and to wield a magic sword, and to...'

'Enough!' Magnor was annoyed. 'You have scoffed at the legends without studying the facts. Yes, the legends boast great feats and what would seem to be miracles. They are simply things that you do not understand. Do not scoff at your own ignorance.' Magnor took a deep breath and quelled his temper.

'I'm glad you mentioned the sword, Gwaine.' Magnor's storm had passed and, as always, he now continued as if it had never happened. 'The sword is not magic, but it is made of a metal and an art that we cannot duplicate. The technology has been lost over the centuries. The legends say that it is sealed in a casket at the base of the Waterfall Hole in the Immortal Gardens. It would be an advantage if you possessed the Sword of Baradetch, ...not so much for the strength of metal as for the respect that it would command from the soldiers of all of the armies of Amorand and ...from the Kings.'

'Yes my Lord. I agree that, politically, I would do well to retrieve the sword. I once tried, but the Waterfall Hole was too deep. I do admit, though, that the legends are correct on that one point. There is a casket of some sort on the rock bottom.'

'Then try again. ...Try again!'

'Yes my Lord. I will.' Gwaine smiled. 'If the legends are correct, we should be able to sail to the magical land of Parrin, where Baradetch still lives, bring him back and make him dive for the sword himself.'

Gwaine thought for a moment that he might have annoyed his teacher again. He wasn't about to find out. Trumpeting resounded through the castle. The King was calling his court to the throne room. Magnor charged out without another word. Gwaine and Taron ran to their rooms to wash and change before joining the court.

IN THE RAOUL WATERS

The King's announcement was that of war. Taron and Gwaine listened to the sobering news for a second time.

After the court had been informed of the new situation in Amorand, there were some decisions made on logistics. An army of fifteen thousand was about to arrive. It was now up to the King of Arrindare to provide shelter, food and weaponry for that army, and for the armies of the other Kings that everyone hoped would soon follow. The Royal Family of Velinon (King Tyne, Queen Kayla, Princess Tanya and Princess Susanne) also had to be welcomed and accommodated within the castle.

The decision that most affected Gwaine was that Taron, as Commander of the Fortress Guard, was to return immediately to Raoul in case the Velinon army came through Barikarn and the Fortress of Marsh.

Gwaine and Taron were not to be separated for long though. Four days later they met on the road to the Fortress of Marsh. Taron was travelling from Raoul, while Gwaine had ridden all night from Lasatal.

'Good morning, my Lord.' Taron was in a cheerful mood. The morning gave every indication of developing into a glorious day.

'Who told you that gibberish?' Gwaine snapped. Some of his response was a mock display of grumpiness, but there was a serious element to his foul mood.

'Aha!' Taron was not deterred. He knew his friend too well to back off. 'I bet you travelled all night, didn't you?'

Gwaine's only reply was a drop-dead look. He wasn't prepared to be trapped into conversation by such an obvious question.

Taron, Gwaine and their escort of twenty soldiers of the Fortress Guard rode on for another quarter of an hour before Taron tried again to improve his friend's humour.

'It looks like I'm the only one who will be smiling today. I know of fifteen thousand poor bastards who won't be very happy. They will soon be wishing that they had taken a nice, cosy sea voyage.'

Taron was referring to the soldiers of the Velinon army, which was sitting on the far side of the marsh, in Barikarn. They had passed Port Oracle before the messengers had reached them and King Tyne had refused to turn his army around.

Gwaine gave a half smile. 'Yes. I wouldn't like to be the fifteen thousandth soldier, trying to stay upright and walk in that mud.' Gwaine shook his head slowly as he pictured the image in his mind. 'Is everything prepared for them?'

'Yes, my Lord. Sections of your Fortress Guard moved into the marsh at midnight. They have formed two columns to mark a route for our guests. By now, the Royal Family of Velinon and their army should be moving into the Martren waters. In six hours time, they should start to emerge from our beautiful swamp.'

'And we shall be at the edge of the swamp in three hours.' Gwaine paused and took a deep breath. He was exhausted, but he'd had enough of being grumpy. 'At least the company will improve.'

Taron didn't understand. He gave Gwaine a quizzical look. 'My Lord?'

Gwaine smiled. 'Crocodiles make better conversation than mudfish.'

Taron laughed. 'And where is your escort my Lord? Surely you haven't travelled from Lasatal alone, after Magnor's warning?'

'No, I have not.' Gwaine felt warmed. It was good to have a friend who was concerned about his safety. Taron was Gwaine's only close friend. Others cared about his safety, but only because of his importance to the war effort. Members of his family were concerned too. But that was different. They were family. 'I travelled with six soldiers of the Last Regiment. Before I caught up with you, I sent them to Raoul to collect what you had forgotten.'

Once again, Taron was having difficulty understanding his friend. 'What have I forgotten?' There was a hint of irritation in Taron's question. Gwaine was doubting his ability to organise.

'Did you remember to pack dry clothes for the Royal Family of Velinon?'

'No, my Lord, but they will be in Raoul within four hours of emerging from the swamp. Surely they can wait that long. They will want to bathe before changing into dry clothes.' Taron was, nevertheless, feeling somewhat remiss ...until he thought of a complication. He carried on in more confident terms. 'Anyway, where would they change?'

'Good question. That's why my escort is collecting the second thing that you forgot. ...A large tent, that will be erected as a change room.'

'I see.' Taron's ire had subsided. 'I'm almost afraid to ask, but how are your six soldiers going to carry this large tent from Raoul to the marsh?'

Gwaine smiled. 'In the third thing that you forgot. ...A closed-in carriage.'

Taron looked bemused. His forehead was knotted in thought. 'The plot thickens. Do you have a use for this closed-in carriage?'

'Oh yes, Commander. I am guessing that King Tyne will want to talk with my father as soon as possible. He will not want to stay in Raoul tonight. He will want to travel directly to Lasatal. ...This could be an extremely long day.'

Both Gwaine and Taron became involved in their own thoughts. It was some time before Gwaine broke the silence again.

'Did you hear the result of the battle in Seyldrek?'

'No my Lord. Though, I believe I could guess the outcome. The messenger came through here yesterday.'

'Actually, King Thale and King Bartak faired much better than I would have expected. They met the Dark Emperor's forces at the Radsey River. The Commander of the Dark Forces is Qarad - a formidable warrior according to reports of the battle, but he unwisely decided that superiority of numbers was going to win the day. He was right in the long run, but he paid a terrible price in numbers.'

'They can afford to throw lives away. They have the numbers,' Taron interjected.

'Only to a point Taron. Our numbers are not too bad, if we can get all of the armies together. Anyway, the story is that Qarad's seventy thousand attacked across the river while the thirty thousand of Thale's and Bartak's stayed on the bank and cut them down with arrows. In the final outcome, Thale and Bartak retreated still with twenty thousand men while only fifty thousand of Qarad's soldiers remained.'

'That is a much better outcome than we expected.'

'Yes, but those ten thousand soldiers would have been better used here than lying dead at the Radsey. ...Anyway, our fleet is still at Port Oracle. They will wait there for Thale and Bartak and bring them and their combined army to Port.'

'That's another twenty thousand to combine with the force to defend the Fortress. We're starting to look healthy, but those numbers will only allow us to defend. We could never counter-attack. The Dark Emperor would win eventually.'

Gwaine did not respond. Again, they both fell into their own thoughts. At one point, Gwaine thought of breaking the silence by asking if everything was in readiness at Raoul for King Tyne's army. He didn't. Taron would have organised tents, bedding and everything else that the Velinon soldiers would require. He decided not to insult his friend by asking the obvious. There was no more conversation until they met with soldiers of the Fortress Guard at the marsh.

'What news?' Taron questioned as he approached the soldiers.

'The trumpets have announced that the front of the column is over half way, Commander.'

‘Excellent. They’re making good time.’ Taron was still riding. He had to shout his next command over his shoulder. ‘Carry on.’

Gwaine smirked. ‘Carry on? ...Carry on what? They’re standing around waiting. Is that an instruction from the Commander of the Fortress Guard? ...Carry on standing around!’ Gwaine laughed.

Taron continued looking ahead with no sign of amusement on his face. ‘Oh, shut up. I’m the Commander. I don’t ***have*** to make sense.’ Only after making that statement did he smile, and then, as if to make amends for telling his Prince to ‘shut up’, he tacked onto the end ‘...my Lord.’

They joined Taron’ subordinate officers in their makeshift camp. An hour and a half later, the six soldiers of the Last Regiment arrived with dry clothes, a large tent and a closed-in carriage. They immediately set-to erecting the tent. All the while, trumpets blared from the swamp, indicating the position of the front of the column - presumably containing the Royal Family of Velinon.

An hour later, the last trumpet blared its signal. King Tyne and his court were within half an hour of emerging from the swamp.

Gwaine gulped down the last of his hot drink and put his cup by the fire. ‘Come on, Taron. It’s time we got our feet wet.’

Taron looked shocked. ‘Pardon, my Lord?’

Gwaine was already throwing his saddle onto his horse. ‘I said, let’s go. We have to greet King Tyne.’

Taron was on his feet and walking toward his horse. He was confused. ‘Why don’t we greet him here? ...On dry land.’

‘Because King Tyne and his family are going to come trudging out of that swamp, ...exhausted, wet, cold and without a doubt, ill-tempered. I’m not game enough to greet them on dry ground, in dry clothes, enjoying myself by a warm fire.’ Gwaine was riding past Taron as he finished speaking. Taron was preparing to mount. A short distance on, Gwaine reined his horse to a halt and looked back as Taron mounted. 'I would rather be a little wet and a little uncomfortable than chewed and spat out by an irate King.'

They rode toward the swamp and the icy waters of the Raoul Rivers. It wasn't long, however, before they were forced to dismount and walk their horses through knee deep water. Taron slid as he dismounted, but quickly regained his footing.

'Easy, Taron,' Gwaine said with a wry smile, 'I only said to get our feet wet. You always try to overdo things.'

'I assure you, Gwaine, that I will not try to overdo this instruction. I am in no mood for a swim.'

Gwaine was pleased that he and Taron were finally alone, if only to hear Taron use his name rather than continually calling him 'my Lord'.

They waded on, toward the point where they would meet the King.

'I have been meaning to ask, Gwaine, ...have you met Princess Tanya or Princess Susanne?' Taron's voice had lowered to almost a whisper.

'Yes. I have been introduced to both of them in the court of Velin.'

Taron waited for more information, but none came. 'Well?'

'Well ...what?'

Taron found Gwaine to be very exasperating sometimes. 'Well ...tell me more. I mean, boy to man, what are they like? Are they pleasant mannered? Are they attractive? You could give me some warning of what we're about to run into.'

Gwaine hadn't missed the 'boy to man' comment. He was quiet for some time, trying to decide whether he would be even more exasperating in retribution. He decided not to push his luck too far.

'They are both attractive. Though, after six hours in this swamp, I wouldn't expect to be knocked over by their beauty. Actually, Tanya is very attractive ...though, pretty stuck up and unapproachable. She's the Crown Princess and she knows it, and, what's worse, she lets you know it. Susanne seems nice, but she's very shy. She doesn't say much.'

Taron was about to pass comment, but a watery sound from up ahead caught their attention. They moved through the mist toward the sound of conversation.

As they moved closer, figures became discernible in the mist. Soldiers of the Fortress Guard, soldiers of the Velinon Army, horses. Gwaine recognised the outline of King Tyne further back. Three female silhouettes were visible. The more mature figure was obviously Queen Kayla, but Gwaine could not tell which of the other two silhouettes was Tanya and which was Susanne.

As they moved closer, detail became clearer. King Tyne's black hair and black bushy beard were the first features that Gwaine recognised. He looked exhausted. Gwaine scanned the party. They all looked exhausted. King Tyne, Queen Kayla and Princess Susanne were all damp, with mud splashed over their clothes and faces and through their hair. Only Princess Tanya was clean of mud. The watery noise that Taron and Gwaine had heard had been Tanya slipping into the cold waters of the Raoul Rivers. She was the centre of attention at the moment, with her family and ladies of the court standing around her, trying to give some comfort. She was totally soaked. Water was running from the loose curls of her long brown hair as she clutched her saturated cloak pathetically around her body in a vain attempt to gain some warmth. Her bottom lip was trembling, probably both with cold and exhaustion, and she was shaking uncontrollably.

Gwaine was sorry for the unkind description he had given of her.

Taron and Gwaine were able to approach without really being noticed. Everyone was preoccupied with Princess Tanya. Gwaine considered interrupting by introducing himself and then thought better of it. In the end, he chose the informal approach. He directed his comment to Tanya. 'We have towels and dry clothes only fifteen minutes from here, my Lady. We will soon have you dry and comfortable.'

The party was surprised by Gwaine's voice. He had their attention. He gave Tanya a comforting smile and turned his attention to King Tyne as Tanya nodded a silent 'thank you'.

'I am Prince Gwaine. I suggest we leave our greetings until everybody is dry. Will you follow me.'

'Yes. Lead on.' King Tyne was keen to get out of this water and to have himself and his family in dry clothing.

Taron and Gwaine led the way back to the camp. Gwaine kept checking, over his shoulder, on Princess Tanya's condition. He didn't think that she was in any real danger, but she was obviously suffering from exposure to the cold and exhaustion. He couldn't help noticing, though, that she seemed much more attractive and more human in her present condition than she had ever appeared in all her court finery in Velinon.

Finally, they came to dry land and to the camp. The officers stood to attention as the party approached. The Royal Family was ushered into the tent and shown to the towels and dry clothing while Taron yelled commands for plenty of hot drinks.

The Royal Family of Velinon were soon seated, in dry clothes, in front of the fire, drinking hot brews. It still took some time for Princess Tanya to stop shaking. The officers had disappeared to exercise control over the soldiers who were now starting to emerge from the marsh.

When King Tyne appeared to be rested and comfortable, Gwaine bowed and re-introduced himself.

'I am Prince Gwaine, second son of King Daroyd of Arrindare. I travelled with my father during his recent visit to your court.' Gwaine paused for some sign of acknowledgement from the group but no glimmer of recognition or interest showed in any of the faces of the Royal Family of Velinon. '…I have been instructed to escort you and your family to Raoul and then...'

‘Is King Daroyd at Raoul?’ King Tyne interjected.

This was the question that Gwaine had anticipated. Taron, standing on the outskirts of the group, marvelled at the accuracy of Gwaine’s prediction.

‘No, my Lord. My father is at Lasatal.’

‘Then you will escort me to Lasatal. I must have urgent discussions with King Daroyd.’

‘Yes, my Lord. If that is your wish, then I will escort you to Lasatal. I must warn you though, that we will not arrive until tomorrow morning.’ The words struck home as Gwaine uttered them. He did not sleep last night and he would not sleep tonight.

‘Then so be it. I must talk to your father urgently.’ King Tyne hesitated and looked down to his family seated near the fire. The realisation had dawned that they would be too weary to ride with him all night, but he was reluctant to leave them.

Gwaine interrupted his indecision. ‘I have arranged a closed-in carriage for your comfort, my Lord. You may even be able to capture some sleep on the journey.’

‘Very good.’ The relief showed on King Tyne’s face. ‘My family and I will travel in your carriage to Lasatal. When can we leave?’

‘As soon as I can organise a fresh mount, my Lord.’ Gwaine looked toward Taron, who immediately bowed.

‘My horse is at your disposal, my Prince. I will rest yours and then ride him back to Raoul.’

‘Thank you, Commander. Will you also organise food and drink for the carriage.’

‘Yes, my Prince. They should be here any minute.’

Gwaine smiled. No one could organise as efficiently as his friend. He would have to remember to apologise for stirring him about the dry clothes.

The Royal Family were soon seated in the carriage, the food and drink had arrived and Gwaine and Taron had said their farewells.

'You will see more of me after my birthday. I shall take up residence at Raoul.' Gwaine was shouting back to Taron as he rode off after the carriage and its escort.

'I will look forward to that, my Lord. ...Try to get some sleep before you return.'

AN EVENTFUL RETURN

Gwaine had already had more than enough of this journey. He was overtired. He looked across at the carriage where the Royal Family of Velinon were sleeping and envied their relative comfort.

'Though,' he thought, 'they have travelled a difficult trail and they have crossed the Fortress of Marsh.'

Gwaine felt guilty at being envious when they had suffered so much. His thoughts turned to the Queen and Princesses. 'It must have been very difficult for them.'

He shook his head in an effort to clear the cobwebs and cursed his wearied mind. His mind was now in that condition of exhaustion where he was no longer in control. Thoughts flowed, seemingly unconnected, with no effort from him and continued to flow regardless of his efforts to stop them. For every thought or feeling there was instantly a counter-thought or feeling that argued against the first.

His thoughts of envy and then of guilt at having felt envious were just a fraction of the chaos that his mind was weaving through. It seemed the more tired he became, the more frantic his mind became to remain active.

He peered around at the column of seventeen soldiers - eleven of the Fortress Guard and the six from the Last Regiment who had escorted him to Raoul.

'At least those six will be as exhausted as I am. That's some comfort.' Hardly had the thought been ushered through the chambers of his mind, than a conflicting thought chased in brisk pursuit as if to run it down and destroy it. 'That's no comfort. It doesn't help me, or them, that we are all exhausted together.'

Gwaine's mind turned to the twelfth Fortress Guard, whom he had sent ahead to Lasatal to warn his father of the imminent arrival of King Tyne. He wished that he could ride just as swiftly toward Lasatal, to be in bed early, instead of riding at this leisurely pace. Gwaine waited. No contrary thought came. He sighed. At least he and his mind were in agreement about wanting to go to bed.

The last rays of daylight had disappeared over an hour ago. There were few clouds in the sky and a full moon was reflecting from the Port River only a hundred metres ahead.

As they moved into the river, Gwaine felt his horse shudder, balk a little and then regain its stride. He patted the animal's neck and smiled. 'What's wrong, O Noble Coward? Can't you take the cold?' As the river deepened, Gwaine leant to his right and stretched down to the water. He cupped handful after handful of the almost frozen liquid across the back of his neck and head.

Temporarily refreshed, he regained his position in his saddle and looked to his right to check that all was well with the carriage. One of the curtains was drawn back, and the amused smile on Princess Tanya's lips proved immediately that she had been watching his antics.

As Gwaine veered his mount closer to the carriage, his mind turned to the question of just how he would have looked; hanging almost upside-down from his horse while throwing water over his head. The decision was that he probably looked totally ridiculous, but he comforted himself with the image of Princess Tanya's ignoble condition after she had fallen into the Raoul River earlier in the day. Gwaine decided that they were now even. He gave Tanya a weary smile.

'Good evening, my Lady. Are you fully rested?'

Tanya's smile was warm and relaxed as she leant her arm on the carriage window and then her chin on her arm. Her eyes were drawn to the moon's reflection in the water as she whispered her reply. (Apparently the others were still asleep). 'I feel better, but I would still like to spend a night in a bed. ...When will we arrive in Lasatal?'

'Not until about two in the morning, my Lady.'

Tanya screwed her nose up at the thought of the long hours ahead. Her brow knotted in a look of tired despair. Gwaine tried to think of something comforting to say but it wasn't easy to find comfort from within his own tired despair.

'I know how you feel, my Lady. It is a long journey from the north, and the trek through the marsh is anything but easy. Just another six hours though, and your journey will be at an end. I am sure that my father will make the reception short and I am sure that my mother will have baths and beds prepared.'

Tanya gave a forced smile. She looked up from the waters of the Port River into Gwaine's eyes. 'You must be looking forward to bed even more than I am. When did you last sleep?'

It was a caring question that Gwaine would have liked to have answered immediately. He felt embarrassed at the delay as he prodded his mind into trying to recall his last sleep. He finally captured the vision of a night some time ago but, when he tried to pinpoint which day it was, his mind ran into a chaos of days and nights and hours upon hours of sleeplessness.

'My Lord...?' Tanya was prompting him, perhaps thinking that he was not going to answer her question.

Gwaine shook his head slowly. 'I'm sorry, my Lady. ...Two nights ago ...I think.'

Tanya studied his indecision for some time. When it appeared that he had settled on that answer, she continued.

'That's a long time without sleep. You should have stayed in Raoul and let someone else escort us.'

Gwaine felt irritated by the suggestion, but he wasn't sure why. He told himself that he was just tired, and anyway, Tanya probably wouldn't have realised his importance in the coming events of war and preparation for war. He tried not to let his irritation show when he spoke.

'No, my Lady. I have been commanded to return with the King of Velinon. I must take part in the discussion of the war.'

Tanya sat up and gave Gwaine a wide-eyed look. 'Why?'

It was not Tanya's question that annoyed Gwaine, but the incredulous tone with which she had asked it. The tone of her question implied that she did not believe that someone like him should be involved in discussions between Kings. Gwaine was too tired to hide his temper. His words flowed in frigid anger.

'Because I am the second born son of the King of Arrindare and because I obey the King's command. Unless, of course, you have any objections to that.'

Gwaine instantly regretted his tiredness and his temper. Tanya was obviously taken aback and hurt by his rebuke, but she did not wilt as Gwaine expected she would. By the moonlight, Gwaine saw her cheeks flush before she leant forward and pulled the curtain closed. He was left staring at a plain blue cloth, feeling like some animal that had just ceased to be of interest to its master.

Gwaine shook his head slowly, rebuking himself for his ill-mannered temper, before prodding his horse forward and ahead of the carriage.

By the time they reached the east bank of the Port River, Gwaine was at the front of the column with six of his soldiers. The other soldiers were riding to the sides and behind the carriage in a protective pattern.

Until Gwaine had joined them, the soldiers had been having some discussion that had kept them all involved for some time, with regular outbursts of laughter interspersed with the conversation. However, all conversation ceased as Gwaine approached.

This had become the norm over the last few years but Gwaine still found it difficult to handle. The same thing had always happened to Stefarne, but Stefarne had accepted this situation as a compliment. 'It's a mark of respect,' he had once told Gwaine, in a time when Gwaine was younger and naive enough to ask questions of his brother. Thinking back now, Gwaine could never remember a time when he was naive enough to believe any of his brother's answers. He knew that he was not accepted by his soldiers. He was just a boy Prince in their eyes, and with the war moving closer by the minute, this was an area of real concern.

The column moved slowly toward Lasatal. Hours passed in silence and in a drowsy semiconscious dream world where Gwaine continued to fight his exhaustion and his frantic mind. He was sorry that he had hurt Princess Tanya. He would have preferred that they had been friends. But, in typical fashion, having thought this thought, his mind immediately put forward the alternative that it really didn't matter anyway. The war was coming. He would soon move to Raoul. There would be no time for friendships, only battles.

Gwaine was jolted out of his stupor. A bugle was sounding only a few hundred metres ahead of them. It was sounding an attack. The thunder of hoof beats and the scream of attacking soldiers froze Gwaine's blood. He turned to his soldiers and screamed at them with all the energy he could muster.

'Turn around. ...Protect the carriage.'

Turning himself, he spurred his horse toward the carriage yelling. 'Turn it around. Run for the mountains.'

The carriage driver began the turn but, even before he had done half of it, Gwaine knew that it was hopeless. His soldiers were now all around the carriage. He drew his sword and tore his shield from the side of his saddle and faced the oncoming assault. His soldiers did the same and joined at his side.

The attackers, in full flight, were now in view. To Gwaine's amazement, they were about fifty soldiers of the Last Regiment. Stefarne was in the lead. In his confusion, Gwaine tried to find an explanation for this turn of events. Perhaps a coup? Perhaps Stefarne had killed his father and taken the throne?

Stefarne and his fifty soldiers reined to a sudden stop. Stefarne was wearing a grin from ear to ear, but the captain of the unit looked distinctly embarrassed. Even before his mount had come to a halt, he was sending an apologetic grimace toward Gwaine.

Now that the fear had gone, Gwaine found himself in a rage. It was just one of Stefarne's stupid stunts. 'Stefarne, you idiot! What the...'

'Ho, little brother. Do you have the Royal Family of Velinon?'

It was King Tyne who replied. 'Who are you, and what do you want?'

Stefarne ignored the rage in King Tyne's voice. He looked past the King, to the Queen and Princesses who had emerged from the carriage. He dismounted and bowed to the King, though obviously taking more interest in Tanya and Susanne.

'I am Prince Stefarne, Crown Prince of Arrindare.'

'Did he say 'Clown Prince'?' It was Tanya's voice. She was looking at her mother but, by the volume of her question, it was obviously meant for Stefarne.

Stefarne was taken aback. He continued in a more subdued tone. 'I have brought this body of soldiers to escort you into Lasatal, in all the glory that is befitting the King of Velinon.'

'Is that any reason to scare my family half to death? What is the meaning of this charge?'

Stefarne smiled and bowed again. Gwaine couldn't help admiring his brother's confidence and bravado.

'The attack is a symbolic tribute to our combined might and to our imminent victory over the Dark Emperor.'

The sting had been taken out of King Tyne's temper. He could hardly roast this young Prince for offering him a tribute. Gwaine felt physically sick. No matter how stupid Stefarne's acts were, he always managed to talk his way out of trouble.

‘I think I’m going to be sick,’ was Tanya’s comment on the proceedings - again loud enough for all to hear. She was obviously furious, and prepared to tell everyone what she thought of events.

In scanning the chaos around the carriage, her eyes met Gwaine’s and she gave him a long furious stare. Gwaine tried to muster some sort of facial expression that would let Tanya know that they were on the same side. She darted a quick look at Stefarne and then returned to Gwaine. ‘You two ***must*** be brothers!’

Gwaine was hurt. Tanya, in associating him with Stefarne’s stupidity and gall, had offered him the greatest insult that he could possibly think of. He straightened himself in his saddle as Tanya turned and walked back to the carriage. As she placed her foot on the step to climb inside, she turned back to Gwaine.

‘And, unless you’re going to put yourself out of your misery, you had better put that sword away. Your little battle is over.’

She disappeared inside the carriage.

It wasn’t until then that Gwaine realised that he was still clutching his sword and shield. He put his sword away and looked for the saddle bracket that held his shield.

‘Well, on the contrary, I think Prince Gwaine was very brave.’

Gwaine looked up in surprise to see Queen Kayla perform a quick curtsy as she threw him a warm smile. Susanne, behind her mother, followed the Queen’s lead as she too curtsied and cast him a smile.

‘Thank you, my Ladies,’ Gwaine responded, with a restricted bow, as he fumbled to place his shield on its bracket.

The ladies turned and walked toward the carriage.

‘Very well, Prince Stefarne,’ King Tyne was getting back to business, ‘You have come here to escort us to Lasatal. Let’s get on with it. How much farther have we got to go?’

‘Less than an hour’s riding, your Majesty.’

‘Excellent. Then let’s go. As quickly as possible, ...seeing we are now all wide awake.’

With that command, King Tyne turned away and disappeared into the carriage.

Stefarne turned his horse and moved off in the direction of Lasatal. Gwaine waited for the command to move the soldiers into position and then on to Lasatal. It didn’t come. Stefarne just kept riding. Obviously, having been the centre of attention, Stefarne had now left the command of the soldiers to Gwaine.

Gwaine shook his head after his brother and looked across to his captain who was still looking quite apologetic and confused.

‘I’m sorry, Prince Gwaine. I...’

‘Forget it, Kem. I know my brother. Let’s get these men organised so that we can go home.’

‘Yes, my Lord.’

The captain organised his men and, in no time, Gwaine was riding next to him at the head of the enlarged column. The pace, now, was more to Gwaine’s liking. Not long now and he would be in his bed at Lasatal.

‘My Lord, I have been wanting to talk to you for some time.’

‘Yes, captain.’

The two were shouting at each other over the noise of their horse’s hoof beats and of the wind around their ears.

‘The war is close now. I want to be more involved than I will be in my present position. Can you arrange for me to be transferred to the Fortress Guard?’

‘I can...’ Gwaine paused for a while, searching for the right words. They didn’t come. ‘...but I won’t.’

Gwaine looked across at his companion. The disappointment was obvious. Kem, like Gwaine and Taron, had trained as a warrior under Magnor. Kem was now in his early thirties and had spent over ten years in the Last Regiment. Gwaine realised how difficult it would have been for a trained warrior to go through the motions of Palace Guard and ornamental soldier in the court of Lasatal for all those years.

'When the battle for the Fortress has been fought, ask me again.'

Kem's reply was emphatic. 'Then I ***will*** ask you again, my Lord. ...May I ask why?'

'Yes. ...Tomorrow.' Gwaine would have liked to explain immediately but it was too difficult over the noise. He would explain to Kem tomorrow that he wanted some good officers in reserve in case the losses of the Fortress battle left him short of experienced officers.

In no time, Lasatal was in sight. The Last Regiment lined the road that led to the great gates. This time, the carriage did not stop for any banner ceremony, but continued up the hill at speed. The gates were already opened so that the column did not stop until it reached the steps of the palace.

The Royal Family of Velinon were ushered to the Throne Room of Lasatal. It was almost two in the morning, but the entire court of Lasatal was present in all its finery. Trumpets sounded as the Royal Family entered, with Gwaine following behind.

King Daroyd and Queen Lenore were seated at the far end of the massive room but, as the King and Queen and Princesses of Velinon approached they rose and walked down the seven steps to greet their visitors on their own level.

It was a warm greeting. Velinon and Arrindare were the only two countries of Amorand never to have fought against each other in war. Gwaine had long ago, during his history studies, decided that this was only because they were too far apart to make war a reasonable proposition for their small armies and small resources.

Finally, King Daroyd addressed the court. 'Now we are two. Soon we shall be seven, ...and then the Dark Emperor shall be thrown back to his evil land as he has been so often in the past. King Tyne has rushed here to tell us of the events, so far, of the war ...but, first, I shall make him rest. We shall meet here at midday tomorrow to discuss the war. You all may go to bed now.'

The court quietly broke up and moved off to their beds. Soon, only fourteen people remained in the room - the two Royal Families, Magnor and four soldiers.

'I hope you do not mind the delay, my friend.'

'No, King Daroyd. If we meet tomorrow at midday, we are still meeting much sooner than if I had spent the night in Raoul.' King Tyne tried to suppress a yawn. 'And I am exhausted. I will be pleased of a bath and a night's sleep.'

King Daroyd turned to his Queen. 'Then Lenore will show you to your rooms, where baths are already prepared.' He turned to Gwaine. 'Gwaine, ...Stefarne has suggested, that while we are meeting tomorrow, you can show Princess Tanya and Princess Susanne around the palace. Meet them here at eleven in the morning.'

Gwaine was stunned. He felt like saying 'What about the meeting? I should be there!' but he would have only made himself look even more foolish than he felt. He darted a look at Stefarne. Stefarne had obviously seen the animosity between Gwaine and Tanya. This was just his form of revenge. Why did his father always listen to Stefarne's suggestions? Stefarne had a smirk on his face. Gwaine looked at Tanya, expecting to see a broad grin and an 'I told you so' expression. Tanya only caught his gaze for a second before lowering her eyes to the floor and following Queen Lenore out of the room. He silently thanked her for that.

Within seconds only Magnor and Gwaine were left in the huge chamber.

Magnor gave Gwaine a knowing smile. He had never been easily fooled by Stefarne. 'I will tell you everything of the meeting. You will miss nothing.' He turned and left.

Gwaine suddenly felt exhaustion fall on his shoulders as he had never felt it before. He looked toward the ceiling and allowed his arms to fall limply at his sides before sighing deeply. At least the journey was over. He walked toward the far door shaking his head as he talked to the surrounding emptiness.

'I don't really give a damn. I'm going to bed.'

THE WORST TOUR

The morning was bitterly cold. Gwaine looked out of his window, across the flat land and out to sea. As he scanned the greyish blue water, his eye met the horizon and he scanned higher into the grey sky. There wasn't a patch of blue in sight, the wind was howling in gusts and sleet was falling to the ground.

He grimaced at the bleakness of the day before undressing and washing from the bowl on the corner table. The wash was as quick as the water was cold. He was drying himself as he searched through drawers and hangers. His teeth were chattering as he threw on his white trousers and white satin shirt.

As he pulled on his fur-lined boots, he thought of the all-black garments that would become his uniform in only four days. At the age of eighteen he would be proclaimed Warlord, Commander of the armies of all the Kings who would eventually join the Council of Kings. There were only two Kings at the moment, but hopefully all seven would eventually meet in this castle and combine their armies in opposing the Dark Emperor. Once proclaimed Warlord, Gwaine would wear only his black uniform until he dispatched his enemy from the land of Amorand, ...or until he died trying.

He wrapped his light blue cloak around him, knowing all too well that he had thicker, warmer cloaks in his wardrobe. They were less colourful, however, and Gwaine was determined to wear bright colours in these last days before his life turned black. Besides, he wanted to make a better impression on Princess Tanya than he had made last night.

Gwaine grabbed his sword from beside the bed, wrapped the belt around his waste and began buckling it. He suddenly stopped, undid the belt and replaced the sword in its bedside resting place.

'Why should I wear it?', he thought to himself, 'My most dangerous mission today is to show two Princesses around the castle and grounds. Princess Tanya can't be that dangerous. Besides, she already thinks I'm a boy trying to play soldier. If I show up wearing a sword, she'll cut me to pieces with her sharp wit.'

Gwaine checked himself in his mirror as he walked to the door, before heading directly to the Throne Room where he had agreed to meet Tanya and Susanne. Of course, they weren't there and he waited another quarter of an hour before they arrived.

As they entered the hall, Susanne was still making some adjustment to her fur cloak. She and Tanya were dressed simply, in yellow dresses and fur boots and heavy fur cloaks. Gwaine had been lolling about, sitting sideways in the King's throne with his legs dangling over the large armrests and his feet resting on the Queen's throne; looking absent-mindedly out of the large windows at the dismal weather. He pounced to his feet as he heard them enter, but not quickly enough to avoid being caught in this ignoble position. A faint smile flickered across Tanya's lips.

'Good morning, my Lord.'

'Good morning, my Lord', Susanne echoed from behind Tanya.

'Good morning, my Ladies. I apologise for the dismal weather that we have turned on for your tour.' He'd had a quarter of an hour to work on that one, but it still didn't sound right.

'Oh, that's all right, my Lord. I prefer the cold to the heat anyway,' Tanya retorted with a smile.

Gwaine wondered what the hell they would talk about when the subject of the weather had been exhausted. It was nice to see Tanya smiling though. Perhaps last night's cutting wit was just caused by the long journey. Susanne was still quiet and withdrawn.

'Well, you've seen the Throne Room, so we'll move on to the Banquet Hall and work our way around the castle and then, if the rain stays away long enough, I'll show you the Immortal Gardens. As you've seen, it's only living quarters above, so we'll stay on the ground floor.' Gwaine's well-rehearsed spiel was sounding to him like well-rehearsed spiel. He gulped, took a deep breath to steady his nerves and motioned to Tanya and Susanne that they should move toward the door.

Gwaine showed Tanya and Susanne the way to the Banquet Hall. Standing inside the massive room, he rattled off capacity figures and told of great receptions for great Kings and travellers. He tried to delete any reference to previous gatherings of the Council of Kings or any remarks that had connection with previous Warlords. He didn't want to give the impression that he was preoccupied with thoughts of battles and soldiers. His nerves had settled and his sentences were flowing more freely now. This was turning out easier than he thought it would be.

Tanya was bored stiff. At the age of seventeen, she had been guided around all of the other castles in the land of Amorand and most of those in the far continent of Silosus. They were all constructed basically the same and many were grander than this one, and most of the tours had been led by much more articulate guides than this boyish second Prince.

By the time they had reached the castle's main entrance, only half way through the tour, Gwaine knew that he had lost Tanya's attention. He didn't know about Susanne. She was too shy to make comment at any time. But Tanya had not remarked on anything he had pointed out for some time and he had noticed her, on several occasions, stifling a yawn.

'At least she's being polite about it all', he thought to himself. 'A lot of Princesses would have told me what to do with this tour by now.'

Trying desperately to recaptivate his audience, Gwaine stopped at the main entrance. To the right was the entrance and the hundreds of steps leading down to the castle's square below. They stood in a large foyer with a sloping wall on their left. The wall sloped backward to highlight the flags, shields and commemorative spears that decorated its face. Ahead, the corridor continued on around the castle and to the remaining half of the ill-fated tour.

Gwaine was looking to his right, about to intrigue his guests with statistics on the number of steps and their exact height above the square.

'What's that?' Tanya asked.

Gwaine spun around, pleased that a question had broken the silence, but his pleasure was soon destroyed. Of all the things to ask him!

'What's what? ... My Lady'. Gwaine's question was a stalling action designed to give him time to formulate an answer. In the next few moments, though, his mind concentrated on a vain wish that Tanya would simply forget her question.

'The plain black shield directly below your King's coat-of-arms. What's it for?'

Gwaine searched for an answer that wouldn't involve connotations of soldiers and battles, but there was none. 'To hell with it anyway', he thought. 'I've already made an awful, impression.'

'That's my shield, my Lady. It's the shield of the Warlord.' Having said it, Gwaine wondered why he had tried to avoid the conversation all morning. He wasn't ashamed of being Warlord, and he had nothing to fear from this young Princess. Even his attempts to impress her now seemed stupid. She was a first-born princess, heiress to her father's throne. She would one day marry a King. She would not be impressed by a second born Prince who was soon to become a soldier.

Tanya stared at him without answering. She appeared to be deciding whether to believe his reply, or not. If she had stared at him in this way only ten minutes earlier, Gwaine would have wilted, but his attitude had undergone a complete change. He straightened his back and returned her stare.

Obviously deciding to believe his statement, Tanya launched into a question that surprised Gwaine by its frankness.

'If no other Kings join you, can you defeat the Dark Emperor's army?'

Gwaine studied the question and the questioner. He could see no reason to lie. Tanya had asked an honest question. She deserved an honest answer.

'No, my Lady. I could not even defend the Fortress of Marsh.'

Tanya looked to the ground and bit her lip thoughtfully.

'But the other Kings ***will*** join us, my Lady, and we ***will*** defeat the Dark Emperor.'

'Thank you, my Lord', Tanya replied without emotion. She moved on, obviously intending that the tour should continue. Susanne and Gwaine followed.

At this point, Gwaine determined that he would get Susanne to say something, ...anything! He began with the comment that was most obvious.

'I hope this tour is not too boring for you, my Lady.'

Susanne was startled. Gwaine could see the panic in her eyes as she tried to find an answer. Tanya was still walking slightly in front but had turned her head to look back at her sister and Gwaine.

'Oh no, my Lord! Its not ***too*** boring', Susanne blurted out, and instantly stopped walking and closed her eyes with a grimace as she realised what she had said.

Tanya turned on the spot to face Gwaine and Susanne. Gwaine could see that she was searching for words that might lessen the severity of her sister's blunder.

Gwaine saw the humour of the situation. Grabbing and squeezing Susanne's hand, he burst into a laugh that echoed in the empty corridor.

Both Susanne and Tanya laughed with a sense of relief that seemed to break down all of the barriers.

'I'm sorry, Gwaine. I didn't mean it that way.'

Gwaine was beaming. Not only was Susanne now talking, but she had used his name rather than calling him 'my Lord'.

'That's alright, Susanne. When this tour is finished, I expect to receive an award for Amorand's worst tour guide.'

Susanne gave Gwaine a smile that told him that he had made a friend.

'Come on', he said. 'Lets get the pain over with. We'll do a whirlwind tour from here.'

'Not so quick', Tanya interrupted. 'You've missed a door. Aren't you going to show us this one?'

Her question was asked light-heartedly, but Gwaine's serious reply stopped her smile.

'No, Princess Tanya. I am not going to show you this one.'

Tanya crossed her arms across her chest. 'Why not? What are you hiding, Prince Gwaine?'

Gwaine smiled. This was a better atmosphere. 'This is the Hall of the Council of Kings. It has not been opened for two centuries. You shall see it in four days when I am proclaimed Warlord.'

The Princesses had questions to ask about the history of the Hall and about the ceremony that would take place in four days time. During the discussion, the three failed to notice the two soldiers who had appeared at the corridor's bend, about a hundred metres further on. The soldiers stood watching Gwaine and the Princesses while they had a whispered argument.

'We can't do it now. The Emperor said that she must be alone.'

'She is as good as alone. There is only the boy and her younger sister. She is as good as alone. We will never have another opportunity like this.'

'Very well. You are right. It is unlikely that she will ever be entirely alone. There are no soldiers in sight. The children will all die quickly. Let us go'.

Gwaine, Tanya and Susanne were now walking down the corridor toward the two soldiers. They were of the army of Velinon, some of whom had arrived at dawn. Gwaine hadn't had an opportunity to talk with any of the newly arrived soldiers. As was the Velinon custom, he stopped approximately three metres from the soldiers, slapped his left chest with his right fist and bid them greetings. The response that Gwaine expected never came. Instead, the larger of the two drew his sword, shouted 'Now!' and leapt forward. The other was a little slower off the mark. Before the second soldier had his sword completely drawn, Gwaine had pounced forward and placed himself between the soldiers and the Princesses.

'Run!' Gwaine had hardly screamed the command to Tanya and Susanne as the first soldier thrust his sword toward his stomach. Gwaine dived to his right and the sword gashed through his blue cloak. He kicked out at the soldier's groin and connected. As the soldier screamed in pain and anger, Gwaine saw another blade being thrust toward him. Already off balance, he could only dive backwards, reaching for the floor with his hands. As he did his first backward tumble, he felt the blade against his boot, but no pain registered.

Three backward tumbles later, he came to a standing position to see the two soldiers running full speed toward him. How he would have loved to draw his sword. At least he had given Tanya and Susanne time to get away. He turned to run and saw both Princesses standing watching him only about ten metres down the corridor.

'Run. Damn it!', he screamed at them as he ran toward them. They both turned to run. Gwaine could not imagine these two courtly ladies outrunning the soldiers over any distance. He glanced over his shoulder to see that he was only two metres outside of his pursuers' sword reach. He needed a weapon! As he neared the main entrance he remembered the ceremonial spears so high up the sloping wall. He dived up the wall, but the slope was too steep for him to take any more than a couple of strides before his foot slipped. His momentum carried him rolling forward and upward. He stretched himself to his limit, touched a spear and unseated it from its supporting brackets but then lost it as he began to roll down the wall, his momentum still carrying him forward. As he landed on his knees on the floor, the spear fell across his shoulder. Gwaine grabbed it as one of the soldiers, unable to stop on the polished floor, impaled himself on the spear's point. The other soldier dived at Gwaine and thrust his sword at his chest. Again he jumped to his right, but this time felt the pain as the sword cut through his upper left arm. Gwaine, acting now out of instinct, arced to his left and moved backward into the oncoming soldier, grabbing his sword hand with his good arm. Jabbing his left elbow into the soldier's abdomen, Gwaine jerked his head back to bash the soldier's nose as he buckled from the abdomen blow. A slight release of the grip on the sword and Gwaine had snatched it away. He arced to his left again, but this time with the sword. He felt the sword connect, saw the massive wound to the soldier's neck, lost his balance at the end of the arc and fell to the floor.

Gwaine jumped to his knees, still frantic to defend himself, but the sight that met him was one of death. One soldier, impaled on the spear, lay dying, looking blankly toward the ceiling. The other was lying in a pool of blood where his torn jugular vein was allowing his life's blood to be pumped away.

Gwaine felt sick and numb. He dropped the sword and, clutching his wounded arm, slouched back against the wall. There wasn't much pain from his arm. Only a sticky, oozing sensation as his blood flowed through his fingers and down his arm.

Soon he could hear heavy feet running. He could hear shouting. He recognised the frantic voices of Tanya and Susanne in the midst of male voices. Someone leant over him. The face seemed strangely proportioned and distantly close. It asked him how he was. He didn't understand the question. His mouth dropped open to ask something, but he had forgotten what. All went black.

***

Gwaine regained consciousness on the bed in his own room. It was some time before his eyes could focus properly and only slightly longer for a massive headache to make its presence felt. It was dark in the room. Looking toward the window, Gwaine could see that the day had not improved. The sky was darker now though, as if evening were approaching. He turned to look at his aching arm. It had been bound and was resting within a sling. Only then did he notice his mother, sitting quietly in a chair by the door.

'How do you feel?', she asked in her usual soft, warming tone.

Gwaine tried to reply but his dry throat only caught and trapped his words. He coughed to try and release his vocal chords.

'Water', he managed to croak.

The Queen pushed herself out of the deep chair, walked to the chest beside Gwaine's bed and poured a goblet of water from the pitcher that had been placed there.

She sat on the edge of the bed as she handed him the goblet. She remained silent as he clumsily wriggled himself into a sitting position, braced by the bedhead, and drank all the contents of the goblet.

'Thank you.' His voice was breathless after his long drink.

His mother made no reply. Gwaine was feeling a little unnerved by the silence and his mother's stare. He wished that she would say something. He searched for something that he could say to her to break the silence, but he couldn't think of anything except the day's events and he didn't want to discuss that. Finally, though, he decided that even that topic was better than this heavy silence and his mother's studying glare.

'What did Magnor say about my arm?' He knew that it would have been his master who treated his wound.

It took some seconds for the Queen to answer. The far-away thoughtfulness in her eyes panicked Gwaine. 'Perhaps it's really bad', he thought. 'Will I ever be able to use it again?'

After that eternity of seconds, she finally answered.

'He said that you lost a lot of blood and will need a lot of rest and good, healthy food before you can do any more training'. Her voice was full of controlled anger and sarcasm. She had never liked the way Magnor treated her son as nothing more than Warlord. To her mind, it seemed that he considered Gwaine as something non-human, something that was designed to do a job and nothing more. She wasn't happy to have 'her child' treated that way and had told Magnor so on more than one occasion. The calmness and warmth returned to her voice as she continued.

'He said that the wound would cause no permanent damage and that you will be fit for the ceremony on your birthday.'

She looked down and bit her lip. When she looked up, there were tears welling in her eyes.

'Gwaine, you frightened me!'

Her voice wasn't controlled anymore. She was fighting back the emotion in her voice and the tears in her eyes.

'When the soldiers came to the Hall and said that you had been wounded, I thought all my nightmares had come true. I wouldn't believe their assurance that you weren't badly hurt. I was sure that you would die.'

Tears were streaming down her cheeks now. Gwaine had never doubted his mother's love for him and had always sensed her helplessness and anguish at having to give up her son so that the Kings could have their Warlord. He wished that he could ease her pain, but he couldn't think of a way. He reached forward and touched her cheek to catch a tear as it fell.

'I'm sorry, mother. I wish I could help. Your lot is more difficult than mine. I must go and fight the battles, but that is a thousand times easier than waiting for news from the battles and imagining the worst.'

Gwaine felt embarrassed at what he wanted to say next. He wondered why, and then forced himself to continue.

'I love you. Thank you for caring about me. ...I'm sorry it's so hard for you.'

Queen Lenore of Arrindare straightened her back and took a deep breath. She gave Gwaine a half-smile as she searched through her cloak for a pocket and, eventually, a handkerchief. She briskly wiped her eyes and face as she stood up, and then leant over Gwaine to take the goblet. She had apparently decided, in all her strength, that the time for self-pity was over. She kissed Gwaine's forehead before replacing the goblet on the chest and walking toward the door.

As she reached the door she turned to face him.

'I'm proud of you, Gwaine. I wish you had been the first-born.'

As his mother left the room, Gwaine was still reeling from her words. He was not surprised that she felt that way, only surprised that she had told him so. Stefarne had rarely shown any love toward their mother. In fact, he had often displayed dislike and hostility toward her. Gwaine thought of those times and of Stefarne's behaviour in general and he screwed his nose up at the thought. He had no time for his stuck-up, ill-mannered, older brother and he certainly wasn't going to lay here thinking about him.

Obviously, Gwaine was expected to stay in bed and be waited upon until he fully recovered. It didn't sound such a bad idea - he quite liked the idea of getting some attention from some of his mother's pretty, young handmaidens.

Only ten minutes of sitting in his room changed his mind. His thoughts varied between the sight of his mother crying, Stefarne's behaviour and, even worse, the sight of the two soldiers as they lay dying on the floor of the main entrance foyer.

Gwaine had never killed anyone before. He kept telling himself that he should be proud. Initially unarmed, he had killed two trained soldiers and saved the Princesses from a certain fate at the hands of those two assassins.

He wasn't proud. He had taken life and, for all of Magnor's years of Warlord training, that went against his basic nature and made him depressed and sick to the stomach.

Gwaine rolled himself out of bed and, with some difficulty and pain, managed to change out of his torn and blood-soaked shirt. This time his choice of clothing was much more practical, choosing warmth before fashion.

He threw his shirt in a corner where his torn blue cloak was already laying. He took off his boots and examined the gash in the right one where the soldier's sword had almost penetrated to his lower leg. The boots, too, went into the corner. Someone would throw them away later. Pulling on a new pair, Gwaine decided to go and see Magnor. Magnor would lift his spirits by praising his abilities and his intelligent use of the skills gained from all those years of accumulated training.

Gwaine was at the door when he remembered something. He went back to the window side of his bed and picked up his sword. With a great deal of effort he finally managed to wrap it around his waist. 'From now on', he resolved, 'I'm not going anywhere without it.'

SLOW TO COOL

Gwaine had expected praise from Magnor. Upon entering the war room, he was amazed at the reception he received.

'Here he is! The stupid child who will never be a true Warlord, let alone a warrior.'

Gwaine stopped in his tracks. 'Stupid Child'? 'Never be a true Warlord'? 'Never be a Warrior'? Magnor obviously had it all wrong. He mustn't have heard the full account. He obviously didn't know that there were two of them and that he was unarmed. Or that he had saved Princess Susanne and Princess Tanya.

'My Lord?' Gwaine couldn't think of any reasonable reply to this attack. 'What have I done?'

'Yes, that's right.' Magnor was livid. 'You don't even possess the intelligence to realise when you've made an error.'

Gwaine straightened his back and took a breath. Magnor wasn't the only one in a bad mood. This had not been a good day.

'Then stop babbling, my Lord Magnor, and tell me what I have done wrong.'

Magnor was surprised by Gwaine's words. Gwaine had never stood up to him before. He had always accepted Magnor's abuse as part of his training, as part of his fate as the second prince of Arrindare.

'What have you done wrong? ...Answer me this, my foolish Prince, ...what have you done right?'

Gwaine was still formulating an answer, when Magnor continued.

'Tell me this, my young fool, ...why were you unarmed? Where was your sword?'

Gwaine had been prepared to stand up to Magnor, to argue his case, but this question stopped him cold. He could only stare at Magnor in anger and frustration.

‘Well! ...Where was it?’ Obviously Magnor was going to push this argument. Gwaine could not hope for his temper to suddenly quell today.

He looked away from Magnor, trying desperately to find a reasonable answer. There was none.

‘Well?’, Magnor demanded.

When Gwaine’s answer came, it was in a subdued, almost embarrassed voice.

‘It was beside my bed.’

‘Oh, what a wonderful spot!’ Magnor’s voice was full of sarcasm. ‘I am sure it was quite safe there. ...No chance of it being scratched or damaged while doing anything stupid, …like defending lives. ...And why was it beside your bed?’

Gwaine had found it difficult enough to answer the question of the sword’s whereabouts. It was virtually impossible to answer why it had been there, ...without sounding absolutely stupid. He wasn’t going to admit to Magnor that he was worried about the impression it would make with the pretty, young Princesses from Velinon. Gwaine decided that he was in real trouble. It was time to counterattack.

‘It doesn’t matter why it was beside my bed. I wasn’t wearing it. That is sufficient. Yes, I accept your rebuke. I should have been wearing my sword. I will wear it from now on. I have learnt my lesson.’ As Gwaine uttered those last words, he moved his left arm to indicate the physical memory of his lesson.

Magnor wasn’t prepared to give up. ‘I think you’re too stupid to learn any lesson. You should have learnt it when the assassin’s arrow flew past your ear. I warned you then of your danger. And now you are wounded as the Dark Emperor’s forces draw close to our land.’

‘The wound is not serious. ...You said yourself that I will be fit by my birthday.’

‘True. The wound is not serious, but it worries me that you have been wounded in your first fight. How many scars will you have by the time all of the battles have been fought? Do you think that you can defeat the Dark Emperor with a score of one wound per battle? ...I don't think you have the brains to survive this war.'

Gwaine's temper was at boiling point, but it was easily matched by his frustration. He had no answer to Magnor 's attack. All he could do was attempt to change the subject.

'Enough of this babbling, Magnor. Do you have news of today's meeting?'

The ploy didn't work. Magnor only became more enraged. 'Nothing that would be of interest to you, child. ...Go away, and play your games with the girls from Velinon.' Magnor turned his back to Gwaine and reached for some implement from the wall behind him.

Gwaine was livid, but there was nothing he could do. He turned and stormed toward the door.

'By the way...' Magnor's voice was quite nonchalant, as if none of the previous argument had occurred.

Gwaine stopped in his tracks. The anger in his reply was obvious.

'What?'

'I like your badge.' Magnor's voice remained calm.

'What badge?'

'Your sling. …I didn't think the wound was serious enough to warrant it. ...It must be a badge of honour, so that all the old women of the court will notice your wound and remark on what a brave little Prince you are.'

Gwaine disappeared through the doorway in a rage. Magnor's words did not warrant a reply.

Magnor replaced the implement on the wall and smiled to himself. He was proud of his young Warlord.

Gwaine stormed down the corridor. His cheeks were hot and his heart was thumping loudly in his ears. He wanted to hit something ... anything. Magnor was right of course. He should have been wearing his sword. It was stupid of him to go out without it. He knew that, but Magnor had no right to rebuke him that way. He knew he had made a mistake - why not leave it at that.

He looked down at the sling and thought of Magnor's words. He wildly pulled the sling over his head with his good arm. There was an instant searing pain in his left arm that stopped him in his tracks. He slowly straightened the arm, pain etched into his face. He hoped that he would never find out how much pain was involved in a serious wound.

Once the pain had subsided, his mind re-established its interrupted feelings of anger and frustration. He clenched his teeth, threw the sling in a corner and stormed on.

As he rounded a bend in the corridor, he walked headlong into King Daroyd, who was walking with his Queen and the Royal Family of Velinon. He hurt his arm in the collision. The look of pain on his face could not be avoided but he wiped it away quickly and bowed to his father.

'Forgive me father. I was hurrying and not thinking.'

King Daroyd did not look displeased but, if he was going to make any comment, he was not quick enough. It was Tanya who replied. Her voice was full of pity.

'My Lord, does your wound hurt badly?'

The question was asked sincerely and, at any other time, would have been greeted kindly. Right now, though, it was the last thing that Gwaine wanted to hear; particularly in the pitying tone that Tanya had used. Magnor's sarcasm was still ringing in his ears.

'The wound is not serious.' Gwaine's reply was only slightly less angry than his previous conversation with Magnor. He was tired of hearing about the wound. It, like the sling, was a badge of shame, displaying his stupidity and childishness.

Tanya was startled by the anger in his reply. The expression on her face showed confusion as she wondered what she had said wrong and what she should say next to correct her error. Finally she gave a quick curtsy and thanked him for saving her from the two assassins. It was another poor choice of a topic.

Gwaine searched for a reply that would not betray any more of his anger. After all, it was not Tanya's fault that she was raising the wrong subjects. She was not aware of his meeting with Magnor. Eventually, he replied with the only comment he could force himself to make without too much anger.

'It was my duty, my Lady.'

Tanya took offence. Her grey eyes turned to ice.

'Well, thank you, my Lord, for doing your 'duty'.' She wheeled with a flap of her cloak and walked briskly away from the group.

Gwaine dropped his head and closed his eyes. He had done it again. When he looked up at the group in front of him, only Queen Kayla was smiling. The others looked either surprised or angered, or both.

Still smiling, Queen Kayla shook her head at Gwaine. 'I can see you two are going to be very good friends, ...once you stop snapping at each other.'

Gwaine's anger had now subsided. He was pleased with Queen Kayla's comforting words.

'I'm sorry, my Lady. My anger should have been used elsewhere. I will run after Princess Tanya and apologise for my rudeness.'

'Well, heed her mother 's advice and run after her slowly. She is very slow to cool.'

Gwaine smiled. ‘Thank you, my Lady. I will run slowly.’

He bowed to the group and stepped aside to let them pass. Susanne moved forward and stopped in front of him. She threw her father a worried look, before giving Gwaine a curtsy.

‘Thank you for saving me this morning, my Lord.’ Her voice was trembling and as she finished she took a step backward, obviously expecting to receive Gwaine’s anger as Tanya had.

Gwaine felt ashamed. Tanya and Susanne had obviously been instructed on how to thank him. Tanya, for her effort, had received a rebuke. Now, poor Susanne was terrified of him. Gwaine gave a deep bow.

‘It was my honour, my Lady. I am glad that you are unhurt.’

Susanne gave a relieved smile, curtsied again and disappeared around the corner with her parents.

Gwaine began to run down the corridor after Tanya. He only ran four or five strides before deciding that the pain wasn’t worth it. He settled on a brisk walk. As he approached the next bend in the corridor, he looked through the window and saw Tanya sitting in the garden.

Night was falling. A strong icy wind was blowing the sleet at ever changing angles to the ground, ...but Tanya sat motionless on a bench, seemingly unperturbed by the cold. Gwaine was looking at her back, but he could see that she was staring at the waters of the garden pond. He imagined he could see the steam rising from her anger. Queen Kayla was right - she was slow to cool.

Gwaine approached slowly and quietly, but he was sure that Tanya was aware of his presence. He stood beside a tree, only three metres from the bench, waiting for some sign from Tanya, but she ignored him. She continued to sit motionless, staring at the pond.

He coughed.

No effect.

'Princess Tanya.'

Still no reply.

Gwaine stood for some time while Tanya sat, ignoring him, looking at the pond. Having tried the standard forms of attracting someone's attention, Gwaine decided it was time for drastic action.

'It's late in the day', he told himself. 'Almost time to get changed for dinner anyway.'

He walked to the far side of the pond. From there he checked to see whether Tanya had changed her mind about acknowledging him before striding into the knee-deep pond and wading to the centre of Tanya's gaze.

He marvelled at her concentration. She still refused to acknowledge him.

'Princess Tanya. I would like to apologise for my rudeness.'

Gwaine went down onto his knees so that the water came almost to his waist.

Tanya couldn't take any more. Her lips softened into a smile as she giggled at Gwaine's ridiculous position.

'You look silly.'

'Oh, I am silly, my Lady. ...Silly, …stupid, ...childish. You ask anybody. Everyone knows.' With those words, Gwaine scanned back over the day's events and, in particular, the argument with Magnor. He decided to accept the rebuke as it had been intended. Magnor was right. Gwaine decided to be more responsible in future.

'When are you going to show me your Immortal Gardens?'

'Come with me tomorrow morning. There is something there that I must retrieve for Magnor.'

'Very well. I will meet you in the Throne Room after breakfast.' Tanya rose and walked toward the steps that led into the Palace. She glanced over her shoulder. 'I do hope that you intend changing for dinner.' She disappeared.

Gwaine suddenly felt very alone and quite ridiculous. He stood and waded out of the pond, searching as he moved for anyone who may have seen him. Deciding that he had not been seen, he sloshed his way to his room.

THE IMMORTAL GARDENS

After breakfast, Gwaine went directly to the Throne Room. He was surprised to find Tanya, Susanne and Ellorn already there, waiting for him.

The three walked toward him as he entered, Ellorn carrying the picnic basket. Gwaine was delighted to see his sister included in the day's plans.

'Good morning, ladies.'

'Good morning, my Lord', the three replied in unison. Ellorn, who was in the centre, flowed straight into a question.

'How is your wound, Gwaine?'

She immediately received an elbow prod to the ribs from both sides and a 'Sssh' from Tanya. The surprised look on Ellorn's face, as she looked to her left and right for an explanation, was comical. Gwaine couldn't hold back a laugh.

'Thank you, Ellorn. My wound is completely healed.'

Ellorn gave him a quizzical look. Of course it wasn't healed. Why had he told her that? Why had Tanya and Susanne prodded her in the ribs and told her to be quiet? She resolved not to mention Gwaine's wound again until she had made some surreptitious enquiries as to what was going on.

'Are you ladies prepared for a long walk?'

'Oh yes', Tanya replied buoyantly. 'Ellorn has told us about the long walk up the mountain trail to the rainforest and the Immortal Gardens. It sounds beautiful.'

'Alright, then let's go.' Gwaine turned toward the door but suddenly stopped before the girls had had a chance to move two paces. He turned to Tanya.

'Does your mother know that you are going to the Immortal Gardens with me?'

Tanya looked surprised at the question. 'Of course, my Lord. I always tell my mother where I am going. She has given her permission.'

Susanne and Ellorn were already walking ahead. They had apparently become very close since Susanne's arrival. Gwaine and Tanya moved off after them.

'Actually,' Tanya continued, 'mother thinks I am very safe with you.' She paused. 'Though, ...it was her suggestion that Susanne and Ellorn might enjoy today's walk as well.' She cast a coy smile at Gwaine.

The four walked through the Palace corridors and down steps that led to the garden and pond where Gwaine and Tanya had made their arrangements for today's journey.

Tanya glanced at the pond and then turned to Gwaine with a smile.

'You're nuts.'

Gwaine returned her smile. The weather was still dismal, but it looked like being an enjoyable day.

'All warlords are nuts. You ask Taron.'

'Who's Taron?'

'He's the Commander of the Fortress Guard. You met him in the marsh. Though, you were probably too busy shivering to notice.'

'Oh no. I remember. He's very good looking. Is he a friend?'

Gwaine deliberated for a while on his answer. 'He's my only friend.'

Tanya gave him a studying stare, but he avoided her eyes by looking ahead at Susanne and Ellorn who were moving further away.

'Slow down you pair. Don't get out of sight.'

Susanne and Ellorn looked back and slowed their pace.

After some time of walking in silence, Tanya decided to reopen the conversation.

'I heard a rumour this morning that King Thale and King Bartak had arrived in your port.'

‘The rumour is correct, my Lady. Thale and Bartak sailed into Port yesterday evening.’

‘That makes four.’

‘Yes, ...but there is still no news of the others.’

‘What did Magnor tell you of the meeting between our fathers?’

‘Nothing.’ Gwaine’s reply was bitter.

Tanya didn’t know whether to continue this conversation. She didn’t want to be on the receiving end of Gwaine’s temper again, and he was sounding annoyed. She went silent.

‘Magnor isn’t talking to me’, Gwaine continued. His voice had lost its bitterness and he sounded light-hearted again. ‘He is annoyed with my stupidity.’

‘Why? ...What did you do?’

‘It’s not what I did. It’s what I didn’t do.’

Tanya waited for Gwaine to continue. She was trying to contribute as little as possible to this conversation, for fear of angering him.

‘I didn’t wear my sword yesterday, after he had warned me of the likely presence of assassins.’

‘I thought you handled the situation very well.’

‘I almost got us all killed. We were lucky. ...Magnor is right to be angry. He will tell me the news when he has calmed down. …Anyway, there couldn’t have been much of importance that we didn’t already know, or he would have told me, despite his anger.’

The path was narrow and steeper now. Up ahead, Susanne and Ellorn were already walking single file and were having difficulty pulling themselves up between two trees on either side of a particularly steep section of path. Susanne went first and then took the basket off Ellorn so that she could follow. They walked on very steadily, as the path was now becoming wet from the heavy mist that they were walking into. This was the beginning of the rainforest area.

Tanya moved ahead of Gwaine as they approached the two trees. She tried to lift her long skirt away from the muddy track with her left hand while pulling herself up with her right hand on one of the trees. It didn't work. She lost her grip and slipped down the incline, backing into Gwaine. Gwaine caught her and steadied her stance.

'You will have to use two hands Tanya. I'm afraid your dress may have to get a little muddy around the bottom.'

In mock misunderstanding, Tanya moved forward and arched her head backward to peer at her bottom.

Gwaine smiled. 'Not ***that*** bottom, silly.'

Tanya poked out her tongue before turning her attention back to the trees. Placing one hand on each tree, she, eventually, with a great deal of effort, pulled herself up the incline. Gwaine tried to picture this courtly young lady travelling down the east coast of Amorand and then wading through the mud of the Fortress of Marsh. He found it difficult to picture and even harder to believe that she had survived the journey.

Gwaine had imagined that he would now show off by pulling himself easily through the gap. It wasn't until he tried to grasp the left-hand tree that he remembered his wound. In the end, he had as much difficulty overcoming the obstacle as Tanya had.

Tanya stood on the far side and watched his painful effort. There was pity in her eyes, but she said nothing. When Gwaine was finally through, she turned and continued walking.

Conversation was limited now that they were walking in single file. Tanya and Gwaine had caught up with Susanne and Ellorn.

A short time later, they crossed an old brick bridge that arched over one of the tributaries of the Lasatal River. The four stopped and took the opportunity of talking, now that they were on a surface that allowed them more than a single-person width.

'This is beautiful', Susanne remarked. 'All those colours. Have all of those flowers been planted here?'

Gwaine was surprised. It was the first unsolicited remark he had heard from Susanne. He turned, to see that she was asking the question of Ellorn. Ellorn's reply was full of pride.

'No. They are all natural. The Immortal Gardens have been this way for untold centuries without any human interference.'

'So much beauty'. Tanya's remark was mellow and she was shaking her head with disbelief, '...when there is so much ugliness in the world.'

'That's why the Immortal Gardens are here, my Lady.'

Tanya didn't understand Gwaine's comment. 'Pardon?'

Gwaine was pleased with her confusion. 'The legend of the Immortal Gardens says that God placed the Gardens here as an apology for creating the Dark Emperor. The Immortal Gardens will flourish as long as the Dark Emperor exists.'

'And when the Dark Emperor dies?'

'Then the Gardens shall die.'

Tanya pointed at Gwaine to indicate that she was about to make a very important point. 'Then the Immortal Gardens are not really immortal.'

Gwaine replied to Tanya's perception with a forced smile. 'That depends, my Lady, ...on whether the Dark Emperor is immortal.'

Gwaine paused to allow his words to sink in.

'The legends also say that the Dark Emperor is really a demon ...That he will not die of natural causes. He can only be killed and, to my knowledge, none of his enemies have ever been able to get close enough to him to try. They say he lives in seclusion in a floating Palace in the heart of his land, protected only by his dark magic.'

Tanya didn't like this conversation. 'Your legends sound more like scary bedtime stories.'

Gwaine laughed. 'Yes, my Lady. I agree. Though, I am surprised at the number of people who believe in them. Even Magnor puts great store in the old legends.'

Gwaine pointed to a fork in the track. 'If we turn right here, in ten minutes time we will be at the waterfall that you can hear.'

Ellorn stiffened and turned on Gwaine. 'You didn't say that we were going there. ...You're not going to try again?'

'Don't worry little sister. We will have our picnic, and then I will give it one last go.'

Ellorn shook her head. She looked worried. 'I wouldn't have come if I'd known.'

'Known what?' Tanya asked Ellorn. Ellorn just looked at her with an expression that showed anger and worry. Tanya spun on Gwaine. 'What are you going to try again?'

Gwaine found himself searching for an explanation. Having just dismissed the old legends as 'scary bedtime stories', he now had to explain to Tanya that he was obeying an old Warlord legend. He was having difficulty convincing himself of the logic, let alone trying to convince anybody else.

'At the base of the waterfall, there is a deep hole, cut into the rock over the centuries by the falling water. There is a casket on the rock bottom that is said to contain the sword of the last Warlord who fought the Dark Emperor's forces. They say that Baradetch sealed his sword in the casket and placed it there for the next Warlord to retrieve.'

'It will be rusted away to nothing by now. ***Who*** says that it is there?' Tanya could sense another myth.

'The legends say', Ellorn interjected.

Tanya gave Gwaine a frustrated look that he tried to ignore.

'There is something there. I saw the casket last time I dived. I almost touched it.'

'And you almost drowned trying. ...Please Gwaine.' Ellorn was almost in tears. '...Please don't try again. It's not worth it.'

Gwaine looked down at the old stone of the bridge. 'But it is worth it. He looked up into Ellorn's deep blue eyes. 'The sword, regardless of its condition, will command the respect of all of the armies of Amorand, and of all the Kings. ...I am not an impressive looking Warlord, Ellorn. I need the power of that sword.'

'I don't understand…' Ellorn would have, perhaps, said more, but Tanya stopped her words by grabbing her hand and interrupting.

'I understand what Gwaine is saying. His world is now politics and power.' She gave Ellorn a reassuring smile and squeezed her hand. 'Meanwhile, our world is still pretty flowers and picnics. Come on. Let's go and find a nice spot.' She led Ellorn off by the hand with Susanne following.

Gwaine was amazed at how easily Tanya had got him out of that difficult situation. He was building a healthy respect for this pretty young Princess.

The four tramped along the track, and were soon at the waterfall.

The picnic conversation was light and enjoyable with no more thought of swords or warlords or the coming war. Only when Ellorn and Susanne had gone off to play in the shallows of the water did Tanya raise a serious topic.

'Why can't it always be like this, Gwaine? Why do we have wars, hatred, sickness, death...?' Her voice trailed off as if to leave to the imagination all of the other blights that faced mankind.

Tanya had been lying on her back, staring at the huge tree that spread above them. When Gwaine made no comment, she rolled onto her side to see whether he was, in fact, awake.

Gwaine was sitting with his back propped against the trunk of the huge tree that Tanya had been studying. He was wide awake, but he hadn't considered that Tanya really wanted a reply.

'Why?', Tanya demanded.

Gwaine was quiet for a while. He had an answer, a philosophy, but he wasn't sure that he wanted to tell anybody, in case they picked it to pieces and proved him wrong. He had built his survival around his philosophy. If it were destroyed, he would have nothing to cling to during the hard times.

Tanya's wide-eyed, expectant, gaze lulled him into a feeling of trust. He decided that Tanya would be kind enough to leave his beliefs in tact even if she disagreed with them.

'Why would we leave paradise to be born into this world if this world were just another paradise?'

Tanya showed instant interest. She didn't understand Gwaine's question, but it certainly had potential for an interesting discussion. She sat up and crawled over to Gwaine's tree trunk and propped herself next to him. Then she settled herself so that they were shoulder to shoulder, and moved her head so that she was looking into his eyes with their noses almost touching.

‘Please say that again.’

Gwaine was amused by her comical antics. ‘Well…’. He was looking for somewhere else to start the conversation rather than at the end. ‘There are some prerequisites to this conversation. ...First, do you believe in God?’

‘I think so’, was Tanya’s instant reply.

Gwaine accepted that answer. It just about summed up the strength of his own beliefs.

‘Alright. …Secondly do you believe in a life after death? ...Um, ...in eternal life?’

‘I think so.’ Tanya was taking some of the levity out of the questions. She had pulled her legs up and wrapped her arms around her knees like a small child.

Gwaine was pleased that she wasn’t taking him too serious. ‘Do you believe that, after death, the soul arrives in a place that we call paradise? ...Somewhere that is perfect for a rest after a hectic life ...somewhere where there is no hatred, no wars, no sickness, ...or any of that sort of thing?’

‘Um...’ Tanya was considering the clumsy question. ‘Yes, I suppose I had always imagined that sort of thing. Fluffy white clouds, harp music, lovely warm days. Yes, I think that is the sort of place that you’re talking about.’

‘Right, …they’re the prerequisites for the conversation. Now, answer me this. How many centuries do you think it would take you to get bored with fluffy white clouds and harp music? How long do you think it would be before you longed for some excitement? Don’t you think you would miss the feel of a tree, the taste of good wine, the feeling of exhilaration when you ride a swift horse?’

‘Yes, I suppose I would get pretty bored with paradise, if it didn’t have some excitement. I would miss some things from this world, but certainly not war and hatred and disease.’

Gwaine studied her answer for a while before continuing.

‘If there was no love in the world, would you miss it?’

‘Yes. ...Of course.’

‘Yes. If you had known love and then suddenly there was none, you would miss it. But what if the opposite happened? What if there was suddenly no hatred?’

‘That would be great’, Tanya responded excitedly.

‘Would it?’

‘Of course it would’, Tanya replied with certainty, but then, seeing the ernesty in Gwaine’s eyes, she doubted her hasty answer.

‘...Wouldn’t it?’

Gwaine only answered her question with another question.

‘If there was only love, ...after a period of time, hatred would be a distant memory and love would become the norm, ...the absolute. Do you think that you would still appreciate love if you had no opposite to compare it with? Would you still enjoy the love of others, if you accepted that as the only proposition, …that, without doubt, without reason, everyone would love you?’

Tanya thought for some time. ‘I see your point. ...You’re saying that we need some hatred in the world so that we can compare it with, and apreciate, love.’

‘That’s right. ...Now, if you are prepared to accept that, then you can extend it to your other woes. How could you appreciate peace unless there was some war? How could you appreciate good health unless there was sickness? How could you appreciate security unless there was some fear? For everything good that you want in this world we must have a corresponding evil so that we can appreciate the good.’

Tanya rested her chin on her knees and thought about Gwaine’s theory. When she spoke, it was in a worried tone that could have easily led to depression.

‘But, ...what about all the people who are hurt by these things. If war and hatred and things like that are just to make us appreciate the good things, then it seems cruel of God, or whoever, to let them hurt people. What about the soldier killed in the war, the child killed by disease? Why should they suffer?’

Gwaine’s voice lowered. He could have easily slipped into depression as well. ‘Because, they chose to leave paradise, ...to take their chances in this holiday from boredom. They chose to feel fear, to fight wars, to get sick ...or, at least, to run the chance of those things. They probably didn’t want to end that way. They, ...we, were probably hoping for the exhilaration of life without actually becoming involved in the drama. ...You pays your money and you takes your chances. ...Just like in the travelling carnivals. ... Anyway, what have they really lost by death. They are simply returned to paradise, where they can rest until they are ready to have another exciting holiday.’

‘But, if your theory were right’, Tanya’s brow was knotted with worry, ‘...then this is all a game. There is no point to anything we are doing ...to any of our struggles and heartache. It’s all pointless.’

‘Not at all. There is a great deal of importance in our struggles. As players, it is our responsibility to see that the bad and good are kept in their proper balance, ...that there is only just enough bad to make us appreciate the good, and no more. We can struggle for that. And, while we’re at it, we can try to help the other players, ...to try to help them enjoy their holiday without really being caught up with the bad and being hurt.’

It was some time before either made another comment. Tanya looked across at Gwaine and studied him for a while.

‘I don’t like my holiday. ...Can I get my money back?’

Gwaine smiled at her comment. It was a good way to close off a conversation that was getting far too depressing. He searched for a reply.

‘I know what you mean. They must have run out of wine in paradise. I would have been happy to stay there otherwise.’

He pushed himself to his feet and helped Tanya up.

‘When are you going after your sword?’

‘Not today. I will come back tomorrow without Ellorn. Let‘s just have a nice paradise sort of day, today.’

‘Good.’ Tanya looked relieved as they walked toward the water. ‘I’ll come with you tomorrow.’

THE SWORD OF BARADETCH

Gwaine ran into the throne room.

'Magnor has summoned me to the war room. There may be a change of plan.'

'Oh, ...I see.' Tanya was disappointed. She was looking forward to today's adventure. She looked around the room as if searching for something to do. 'I'll wait here until you find out for sure.'

Gwaine turned to leave. He was surprised at the passive way that Tanya had accepted his announcement. It was good of her to be so understanding and, particularly, to wait for him to return.

He stopped at the door and looked back at her. Why should she wait? She had priority over Magnor. He had made plans with Tanya long before Magnor's spur-of-the-moment call.

'Did I show you Magnor's war room?'

'No. We didn't get that far.'

'Well, come on. ...You must see it to believe it.'

Tanya didn't need to be asked twice. She didn't like the idea of spending an unknown amount of time waiting for Gwaine to return. She was running toward the door as Gwaine finished his sentence.

'Won't Magnor mind?'

Gwaine's voice came in a rush of anger. 'He can mind if he wants to. I'm getting tired of Magnor's moods. I'm getting tired of being at his mood's call.'

Tanya's stomach knotted with fear. She didn't want to be caught in the middle of an argument between Magnor and Gwaine. She walked silently beside Gwaine as they moved through the corridors to the lower level of the Palace.

Tanya had to peer in search of Magnor as they entered the dimly lit room. He was dusting a strangely shaped chair that reclined against the far wall. To Tanya's relief and Gwaine's surprise, he seemed pleased that Tanya had visited his war room. He bowed as deeply as his age would allow.

'Welcome, Princess Tanya, ...to my cavern of trinkets and baubles.'

The greeting was warm, so that Tanya had no difficulty in giving a warm reply. 'Thank you, my Lord Magnor.' She curtsied. 'I hope I am not intruding.'

'Of course not. I had hoped that Gwaine would bring you.' He turned his gaze to Gwaine. 'You saw Kem before breakfast and told him that you were keeping him in reserve, ...until after the battle for the Fortress.'

Although Magnor had simply made the statement, Gwaine immediately felt on the defensive.

'I believe that is a sensible strategy.'

'Yes. …I agree. …You will lose many good men in that battle.'

Magnor's reply was a surprise, not just because he had agreed. He had made the comment on loosing good men with such depth of feeling that Gwaine could have easily believed that Magnor knew which men would die.

Magnor seemed to have become engrossed in his own thoughts. His deep eyes were looking through Gwaine as if the young Warlord had ceased to exist. '...Many good men...' He re-emerged from his thoughts and sighed deeply before continuing.

'I have news of the war and the other Kings.' He walked to his model of Amorand. Gwaine and Tanya followed. 'The Dark Emperor has taken a surprising gamble. He has retained only one army in his land at this early stage. While one army, under the command of Qarad has been dispatched down the east coast of Amorand, another is now moving down the west coast. You will meet those two armies in the battle for the Fortress. Such is the desire of the Dark Emperor to win that decisive battle that he is gambling everything.'

Gwaine felt his spirits sink. It was going to be a difficult battle to win against one army, ...but two? He forced himself to ask a question, to veer his mind into something more productive than despair.

'What of the other Kings, ...the other armies?'

'King Raynor is fighting a rear guard, delaying action as he retreats down the eastern side of Barikarn. King Fenore of Tayle has joined with King Vole of Cadel and they are fighting a similar withdrawal on the other side of the mountain. I believe that they have already crossed into Barikarn.'

'Then the battle is very close.' Gwaine could feel the weight of the world falling on his shoulders as the fear and despair built up within him.

'The day after tomorrow is your birthday, ...the day of the Warlord ceremony. The following day, the court will move to Raoul so that they can be kept informed of the build up to the battle. By then, all the armies will be in Raoul and Taron will have them assembled and equipped. ...I believe the day after will be the day of the battle.'

Gwaine couldn't think of anything to say. He tried hard, but nothing came. His mind was numb with the incredible disbelief of it all. His testing time had finally come, but he wasn't ready for it.

'You are ready, Warlord.' It was as if Magnor had read his thoughts. 'If the war had held off for another ten years, you would still have this feeling ...but, you ***are*** ready.'

Magnor's voice was full of encouragement and strength. Suddenly, as always with Magnor, his mood changed. He gestured with his finger in the air as his eyes widened with mock amazement. '...Except for one thing.'

Gwaine's worries dissipated. He had to give Magnor credit. He was a master of change.

'What thing?'

Magnor regained his serious composure. 'A sword, my young prince. A symbol of your power and strength.'

Gwaine nodded. Today's plans were now more imperative than ever. Time was running short. He had to get that sword.

'Well if you have finished with us, my Lord, I was about to go for a swim under a waterfall.'

Magnor turned to Tanya. 'And you, my Lady. What are your plans for today?'

Tanya was surprised, after all this time of being a spectator, to be asked a question. It took her a short time to collect her wits.

'Um …I was going to help Gwaine.'

'Very good. ...Go then, ...and be careful.'

Tanya and Gwaine headed for the door.

'Warlord!' Magnor's call stopped them in their tracks. 'There will be less than two armies attacking through the Fortress. The Dark Emperor must man his captured cities and Thale and Bartak have made a substantial impression on Qarad's numbers. ...And remember this, ...numbers in the small area of the marsh is not a great advantage. There is a limit to the numbers who can fit in the area, and the more who come, the more the mud will be churned for those who follow.'

Gwaine nodded. He was less than convinced. 'Yes, my Lord. I would still rather be on the defending side. The Fortress of Marsh is a formidable defence.'

Tanya and Gwaine disappeared out of the room. Gwaine led Tanya through the Palace corridors to the exit that led to the track to the Immortal Gardens.

Only a hundred metres down the track, Gwaine veered off and crawled under a bush. Tanya's curiosity was aroused as he fossicked around and finally emerged with a large coil of rope.

'What are you going to do with that?'

Gwaine gave a cunning grin. 'Baradetch was a mighty Warlord, ...a strong and fierce warrior. When the war came, he was a large man of twenty-seven years. When his time came to retrieve the sword, the legends say that he merely dived to the bottom of the hole and swam to the surface with the casket. He was a mighty warrior.' Gwaine paused and gave Tanya a wink. 'Fortunately, I've got the brains.'

Obviously, Gwaine wasn't ready to reveal his plan, so Tanya let the conversation lapse. She walked on, simply enjoying the forest and its wonderful colours.

When they reached the two trees, Tanya suddenly stopped. Gwaine, who had been walking behind admiring her attractive figure, almost walked into her.

Tanya swung around with a swirl of her skirt. 'I bet I can get through easier than you.'

Gwaine shook his head. 'I'll be surprised if you can get through at all. Yesterday's effort wasn't very encouraging.'

Tanya turned back to the trees and marched toward them.

'My effort! You should talk. ...I thought I was going to have to carry ***you*** through.'

'You're a good talker, Princess. Let's see some action.'

Tanya marched up to the trees, put both arms out to secure a grip and pulled herself up the incline and through the gap with relative ease. Gwaine was impressed. Once she was on a leveller section of track, Tanya turned to Gwaine, crossed her arms and poked out her tongue.

'Of all the cheek', Gwaine yelled in pretend anger. He ran toward Tanya and took a flying leap through the trees. Tanya, seeing that he was going to easily pass the obstacle and would soon be within reach of her, turned to run. She slipped on the wet track and landed, bottom first, in a particularly slimy part of the track.

Gwaine tried to stop but it wasn't easy. He realised that, unless he did something, he was going to run over Tanya who was now lying in the slime, propped up on her elbows, watching, wide-eyed, as Gwaine came hurtling toward her.

Gwaine went down on his knees in a desperate attempt to slow his progress. It took some of the impetus out of the collision that soon followed. He slid on his knees into Tanya and finished on top of her prostrate form, forcing her deeper into the mud and slime.

Gwaine and Tanya had formed a friendship since meeting only three days ago, but Gwaine immediately realised that they did not know each other well enough for this position not to be embarrassing for both of them. He would have dived straight to his feet and apologised profusely, if his arm had not been hurt in the mêlée. He was forced to lie still for a fraction of a second that felt like minutes, until the pain subsided.

He forced himself to his knees, holding his left arm against his chest in an attempt to alleviate the pain. 'I'm sorry, my Lady.' He couldn't think of anything else to say. He watched Tanya, pushing herself out of the mud, and felt his cheeks burn with embarrassment.

Tanya clambered to her feet as quickly as she could, without saying a word. Gwaine could see the redness of her cheeks. She avoided his eyes as she inspected her mud and slime affected dress.

Gwaine was still on his knees. 'I am sorry, my Lady.'

Tanya looked down at him. She hesitated for a moment and then grinned. 'You pick the funniest places to go down on your knees to apologise.'

The ice had been broken. What was mortally embarrassing only seconds ago, was now worth a laugh.

Gwaine grabbed his rope and picked himself up off the ground.

Tanya considered asking if his wound was very painful. She didn't. Instead, she pulled her skirt so that the bottom of it was lifted away from the track and slowly turned in front of Gwaine. Remembering their conversation, near this spot, on the previous day, Tanya smiled and asked 'Did my dress get a little muddy around the bottom?'

Gwaine ignored the base of her dress and pointedly studied the wet muddy stain around her bottom. 'Yes, my Lady. Your bottom did get muddy.'

Tanya smiled. 'Not ***that*** bottom, silly.'

They laughed together before moving off, a little uncomfortably, toward the waterfall.

When they finally reached the waterfall, Gwaine became very serious. He busied himself searching the surrounds of the water for rocks of a specific size and shape. Tanya began to feel forgotten as he became engulfed in his search for the perfect rock. Eventually, though, he returned to Tanya with the last one.

He had collected a rock that was shaped like a large banana and six smaller, fist size, rocks that were roughly round.

'That should do it', he remarked as he dropped the last one on the grass near Tanya.

'Oh, yes. I think it should', Tanya replied dryly as she studied the collection of rocks. '... Do what?'

Gwaine just replied with a cheeky grin. He took one end of his rope and tied it to the banana shaped rock. He tied knot after knot around the rock. Tanya decided that it was obviously very important that the rope didn't come off.

Having finished his knots, Gwaine removed his shirt and started folding it so that it enclosed the six small rocks. Tanya noted that Gwaine's left arm was tightly bound, but a wet patch of dressing was evidence that the wound was weeping as a result of their collision on the path.

The folded shirt was left on the grass as Gwaine gathered the larger rock and his coil of rope.

'Let's go.'

'Go where?' Tanya's question was asked without a great deal of emotion. She was starting to get irritable at Gwaine's secrecy.

Gwaine picked up the warning in Tanya's lack of tone. He stopped his progress toward the water. 'This rope will pull the casket to the surface, but first, I have to get it down to the bottom of the hole.' Gwaine lifted the rock slightly to display it to Tanya. '...Hence, this anchor.'

'Oh, I see. You just throw that in, swim down to the bottom, untie the rope, tie it around the casket, and then swim back to the surface.'

Gwaine was taken by surprise. Firstly, because the basic elements of his plan were so obvious to Tanya, and secondly, because she had made the whole venture sound so simple and straightforward.

'Well, ...that's close, my Lady. ...Yes, we do drop the anchor as close as possible to the casket. Then, I ***try*** to swim down to the bottom of the hole. I have tried swimming to the bottom before and failed. It is very deep and the currents caused by the waterfall are incredibly strong and travel in all directions at once. That is why I have made that belt of weights.' Gwaine pointed to the folded shirt containing the rocks. 'I will wear that around my waist in the hope that it will weigh me to the bottom. ...Once on the bottom, I will have very little time. I will cut the rope from the rock and tie it to the casket, ...try to move the casket to break any seal that it may have formed with the bottom, and then drop the weights and swim for the surface.'

Tanya just nodded. 'Oh, yes. That sounds simple enough.' She walked past Gwaine toward the water, obviously anxious to get on with the job.

Gwaine was left dumbfounded, staring incredulously at the blank space where Tanya had been standing when he last addressed her. He shook his head in bewilderment. 'Perhaps I'm over-dramatising', he whispered to himself as he turned to follow Tanya to the water's edge.

Tanya had stopped on the very edge of the water. Gwaine walked past her into the frigid liquid. Within two strides the water was up to his chest. His senses were screaming and his breath was halted. Gwaine had forgotten just how cold these waters were. He turned to Tanya and threw her the end of the rope. 'Don't let go of this, ...no matter what', he yelled over the roar of the waterfall.

Tanya grabbed the rope and wound it firmly around her hand as she watched Gwaine wade toward the point where waterfall met water.

Gwaine was holding the large rock to his chest, uncoiling the rope as he waded further from the water's edge. He stopped about two metres from the fall of water and tried to steady himself. The force of the water was terrific. He prodded with his foot, trying to find the hole's edge. The ground just in front of him sloped away quickly. This was it. He glanced behind to check that the rope was free and then dived forward.

Gwaine's world was suddenly a blur. He felt the weight of the rock slowly drag him downward and then a blow like a sledgehammer on his back as he was hit by the full force of the falling torrent of water. Some of the air was knocked out of him with the force of the blow.

Gwaine peered around in the blurred maze of bubbles to try to find the bottom of the hole. He felt the panic rise when he couldn't orientate himself to his confused surroundings and his lungs started demanding some of the air that he had lost with the blow of the waterfall. His greatest sensation was the feeling of being pushed at great speed by an extremely strong current, but was it a downward current?

Gwaine considered dropping the rock. 'It would end up on the bottom somewhere', he told himself. He fought the urge to let go and tried to suppress the panic. His lungs were screaming now. They wanted air and they were working overtime on Gwaine's mind to make sure that he knew about it.

Suddenly, all was still. Gwaine looked around. The quiet, after the roar of the waterfall and currents against his ears, was unbelievable. He saw light in his blurry world and decided that was up. Twisting himself frantically, he pointed himself in the opposite direction, toward the bottom of the hole. What seemed an incredible distance further down the hole, he saw the rock bottom and what looked like some sort of box. He was, as far as he could determine through the blur and in his disoriented state, almost directly above the casket, if indeed that was what it was. He released the rock. The obvious thing to do now was watch where the rock landed in relation to the casket, but Gwaine was in a panic for air. As soon as he released the rock, he started swimming frantically for the surface. Looking up toward the light he saw the turbulence of the waterfall cascading into the hole. He swam to the opposite wall of the hole, as far from the water entry as possible. To Gwaine's relief, there was an upward current on this wall. By the time he reached the surface, he was in blind panic, fighting desperately against his mind's suggestion to breathe in, regardless of whether it was air or water. As soon as he broke the surface, he was gasping deeply and loudly for air.

Tanya was already in the water. She had decided that Gwaine was taking too long just to drop a rock. She didn't know what she could do, but she wanted to be in a close enough position to help if she was required. She was beside Gwaine within seconds of him surfacing, guiding him toward the rock edge and half supporting his frantic form.

When they reached the edge, Gwaine allowed himself to fall on the rock so that his upper half was out of the water. Tanya sat beside him quietly for several minutes while he fought to regain control over his breathing. Even when his breathing had returned to normal, Gwaine made no attempt to talk, ...or even to recognise Tanya's presence. He laid on his side with his forehead resting on his arm, staring blankly at the rock surface only a centimetre from his nose.

Tanya caressed his wet hair. 'What went wrong?'

Gwaine shook his head and issued forth a despairing sigh. It was some seconds before he replied. 'Nothing.' He sighed again. '...It's all going to plan.' He rolled on his back and forced a smile that looked more like a grimace.

'Well…' Tanya was looking for another way of asking her question. '...If it's all going to plan, ...how's the plan going?'

Gwaine shook his head and smiled. He was starting to recover. 'Awful! …I should have just chucked the thing in like a fishing line. I might have had better luck.' He lifted his head and placed his arms under it to form a pillow. For the first time, he noticed Tanya's condition. He noticed that she was still holding the end of the rope. He was pleased with that - Tanya was dependable. He also noticed that she was soaked. She had gone into the turbulent waters of the waterfall pond completely dressed.

'That's a dangerous way to swim in rough water. ...How many layers of clothing are you wearing?'

Tanya was surprised by his question. 'None of your business, sir.' Her reply was angry. At seventeen, she knew that wasn't a question that a gentleman asked a lady. Anyway, how dare Gwaine chastise her when she had taken the risk to help him.

Gwaine forced himself laboriously to his feet. Ignoring Tanya's anger, he offered her his hand and pulled her to a standing position. When Tanya attempted to withdraw her hand, Gwaine held it tighter. She gave him a questioning look. Gwaine's next words were in the most serious tone that he could muster.

'Don't go in the water. ...You are wearing too many clothes. ...I would rather drown than have my friend drown trying to save me.'

Tanya didn't miss the significance of his words. He had called her 'my friend'. Only yesterday he had said that Taron was his only friend. She couldn't help beaming. She leant forward and gave him a kiss on the cheek, and then, feeling embarrassed by her action, searched for a question that would change the subject.

'Now what do we do?'

Gwaine gave her an impish grin. 'What, ...after the kiss?'

'No, silly.' Tanya felt her cheeks reddening. '...After you drop the rock near the casket.'

'Oh, the casket! ...I'd forgotten about that.' Gwaine saw the exasperated look that he was getting off Tanya and decided that it was time to be at least semi-serious. 'Now, I dive down and tie the rope around the casket - nothing to it.' He walked past Tanya, toward his rock belt. This time it was Tanya who was left staring at thin air, where a conversation had been taking place. She shook her head as she turned to follow him. 'I'll kill him.'

Gwaine was already tying the shirt containing the six rocks around his waist when Tanya rejoined him. She noted that he was tying knot after knot in the shirt.

'How are you going to get that off so that you can come back up?'

Gwaine patted the knife attached to his belt. 'I cut it off.' He started walking toward the water but Tanya's next question stopped him in his tracks.

'What if you drop the knife?'

Gwaine's brow knotted. He didn't have an answer and he didn't want to think about the consequences. He started walking again. 'I pray for a sudden, localised drought.'

Tanya's blood froze at the answer. It was a joke that was meant to cover up a flaw in his plan. She would have preferred a more substantial answer, but she knew the subject wasn't worth pursuing. Gwaine was already in the water. She ran after him to the water's edge.

'Good luck!'

Gwaine didn't look back. He shook his hand in the air as a casual sort of wave that would have been better utilised if he had been going for a short bush walk rather than a dangerous, weighted swim to the bottom of a hole. Tanya saw him wade to the point where he had disappeared earlier. A slight splash of the water and he disappeared below the surface.

The nonchalant attitude that Gwaine had displayed to Tanya, was an act. Under the water, his fears rose to a crescendo. The feelings of suffocation and panic from his earlier swim were still fresh in his mind.

He was sinking quickly under the weight of his six rocks. He did have the advantage, this time, that he was prepared for the water torrent's sudden force on his back. This time, as he was forced suddenly downward, he managed to retain the air in his lungs. The blurred disorientation was not as much of a problem because he knew that he was moving downward and he would soon be in still water.

As he entered the still water, he twisted himself to face the bottom and kicked frantically to speed his descent. He could see the casket below him, with the rock sitting only about a metre away from it. Gwaine decided that he would put that down to good fortune rather than good management.

After what seemed an age, he touched the bottom and headed for the rock. In a fleeting thought, he marvelled at the strength and endurance of Baradetch, to retrieve this casket without the assistance of any of the tricks that he was using. Gwaine's lungs were starting to complain. There was still a great deal to do before he could head for the surface, let alone breath air again.

He drew his knife from its sheaf and cut the rope from its rock. Reaching across to the casket, he grabbed what looked to be a handle and pulled himself toward it. 'How the hell am I going to get out of here. I'm going to drown.' Gwaine threaded the rope through the handle and started tying a knot, but his mind was going into panic. It had done some rough calculations, based on the pain in his lungs, and decided that he had to give up now and swim to the surface or drown. Gwaine finished tying the knot. 'One will do', his mind told him. He fought the pain and panic and started a second knot. This was all in vain if he pulled the casket halfway up only to have the knot slip. He finished the knot. 'Let's go. Cut the belt.' His mind was screaming. Gwaine wanted to take a breath. The panic was rising. The suffocation and desperation were unbearable. He had been holding his knife since he had cut the rope. As he pulled the belt away from his stomach and brought the knife near it, he thought of Tanya' s question. 'What if you drop the knife', rang through the chambers of his panicked mind. It was a self-fulfilling question. The knife fell from his hand to land at his feet. Shear panic took over. He wanted to bolt for the surface. He started to stretch his legs to kick off from the bottom. 'It won't work', he told himself as he tried to gain control. He turned and groped over the blurred rock bottom for his knife. He was in agony now. His lungs were screaming. He wanted to breathe in – anything! It didn't have to be air. He just wanted to breathe. His hand touched the knife. He cut the belt and kicked with all his might from the bottom and headed straight for the wall, searching for the upward current.

After what seemed an eternity of pain and suffocation and panic, Gwaine surfaced, again gasping loudly for air. Tanya was there again to help him to the rock edge.

It was like waking after a nightmare, returning to sleep and dreaming the same nightmare. Gwaine was lying half on the rock edge, half in the water, gasping for breath, as he had after his first dive.

When he had won control over his breathing he rolled on his back, prepared to scold Tanya for disobeying his request. Only then did he notice that she had stripped down to her petticoat. Under his gaze, Tanya sat back and covered her breasts and erect nipples that were so well defined by her soaked clothing. She was obviously embarrassed.

'Sorry.' Gwaine was honestly apologetic, as he realised that he had been staring. He forced himself to look into Tanya's eyes. 'Thank you for your help.'

Gwaine stood up and waded back into the water. He pulled the free end of the rope around to the side of the hole with the upward current. Only then did he realise that he had forgotten to move the casket to break any seal that it may have formed with the bottom. He prayed that it would come easily as he started to take the slack on the rope.

The casket did come easily and Gwaine found the weight easy to lift. It wasn't long before he was clutching the long metal box to his chest as he waded back to shore.

'We've got it. ...We've got it', he screamed excitedly to Tanya. Tanya emerged from behind their tree, fully dressed in her soaked clothing and looking just as excited as he felt.

Gwaine placed the box on the grass under the tree. 'Of course, it's probably just a lump of rust by now.'

'It doesn't matter', Tanya responded excitedly. 'You've got the power of the sword. The condition of the sword, itself, doesn't matter.'

Gwaine searched the casket for a means of opening. It was a simple latch and pin arrangement. He withdrew the pin and lifted the latch, but when he tried to lift the lid of the casket it didn't budge.

'Gwaine, ...there's some sort of seal around the join.' Tanya was down on her knees studying the brown, hard compound that lay in the join of the casket and its lid. 'You'll have to prise it open.'

Gwaine's hand immediately went to the knife at his belt. The sheaf was empty. He had dropped the knife while he was frantically swimming for the surface. He crawled across the grass to his sword and used it to break the seal and prise open the box.

When the lid was lifted, the sight that met their eyes was of a bright red thick liquid. Gwaine thought, at first, that it was blood but, when he put some rational thought into it, he decided that it was more likely to be some sort of preservative.

'I wouldn't put my hand in there if I were you.'

Tanya's advice was well received. Gwaine decided that it probably wasn't dangerous but, just to be on the safe side, he went to the other side of the casket and pushed it over, spilling the entire contents onto the grass.

When the casket was returned to its upright position, there were two swords lying on the ground.

Gwaine immediately forgot his worries with the red liquid and grabbed the larger sword. The sheath was in good condition, as was the plain handle.

He stood up, holding the sword handle with his right hand and the sheath with his left. 'Behold.' He was talking to himself as much as to Tanya. '...The sword of the Warlord of the Seven Kings of Amorand.'

With those words, he began to withdraw the sword from its sheath. To Gwaine's amazement, it was in perfect condition - not a sign of rust. He went down on his knees and sat it on the ground between himself and Tanya.

Tanya studied it. 'I have never seen a metal that colour before. ...It is almost blue under that red liquid.'

'Yes.' Gwaine's absent-minded reply was partly in amazement at what he had done and partly in awe of the weapon that sat on the ground before him. '...Magnor was correct. It is a special weapon.'

Tanya was burning with curiosity as to the smaller sword, but Gwaine was obviously so awe struck with Baradetch's sword that she didn't like to change the subject. They sat in silence, staring at the sword between them, for some time. Eventually, she could take no more. 'Gwaine. ...The other sword?'

Gwaine awoke from his thoughts and peered across at the small, jewelled sword. To Tanya's surprise, his eyes became very sad at the sight of it.

'What is it, Gwaine?'.

'It's the Lady's sword.'

Tanya gave him a questioning look. Gwaine's answer hadn't helped her at all.

'Baradetch loved Princess Belanne of the land of Cadel. He gave her this sword.' Gwaine reached for the sword, removed it from its sheath, and sat it between him and Tanya, near Baradetch's sword. It, too, was perfectly preserved.

'What is it doing here?'

'The legends say nothing of the sword being in the casket. ...They say only that the Lady returned the sword to Baradetch when she left for Silosus to marry one of the Kings of that land.'

Tanya could now understand the sadness of the sword. 'I see. ...She didn't return his love.'

'Oh, I don't think that was the problem.' Gwaine stopped and looked into Tanya's lovely grey eyes.

'Well…?'

'Well…', echoed Gwaine. 'She was a first-born Princess and Baradetch was only a second born Prince, …a Warlord. They were not ...permitted to marry.'

Tanya couldn't look Gwaine in the eye. She lowered her head and pretended to stare at the Lady's sword.

After some moments of embarrassed silence, Gwaine reached for the Lady's sword, replaced it in the sheath and, after wiping the red liquid onto his trousers, placed it in Tanya's lap.

'A present for a friend.'

Tanya didn't look up. A tear ran down her cheek as she ran her fingers over the jewel-studded handle.

'...On one condition', Gwaine continued.

Tanya looked up. 'What condition, my Lord Gwaine?'

'Regardless of what fate has in store for both of us, ...I don't want it back. ...Friends don't return presents.'

Tanya wiped the tears from her face. 'Agreed. ...Thank you friend. It's a lovely present.'

Gwaine resheathed Baradetch's sword and pushed himself wearily to his feet. He put out his hand to assist Tanya who was struggling to untangle her long, wet dress from underneath her. 'Let's go and show Magnor what ***we*** have done.'

THE PROMISE AND THE LADY'S SWORD

Magnor couldn't be found that day. The next morning, Gwaine and Tanya met in the Throne Room and then proceeded to the war room.

At last they had found Magnor. When they walked into the cavernous room Magnor was, once again, cleaning his strange chair. This time he was rubbing it with a thick paste that was leaving the metal chair highly polished and reflecting images as well as any mirror.

He turned to face them as they entered. Gwaine marched to the centre of the room and drew his sword. He held it proudly with his arms extended at eye level, the sword held horizontal. Magnor's eyes gleamed with excitement as he took a hesitant step closer.

'Oh yes!', he remarked excitedly. 'Oh yes. That is Baradetch's sword.' He stepped closer to examine it. Gwaine lowered the sword to allow his master to take it from him but Magnor made no such attempt. 'And it is remarkably preserved. ...Excellent. ...Excellent, Gwaine.'

Gwaine was pleased with Magnor's reaction. During all of Magnor's training, Gwaine had done everything he could to please his old master, but, in all those years, there had been very little praise ...only more difficult tasks and greater pain. At last, with the war so close, Magnor had shown satisfaction and even excitement at something Gwaine had achieved.

'The legend was true, my Lord. The casket was there, as you said it would be.' Gwaine had disagreed so often with Magnor over the fact and myth of the legends that he felt obliged to admit that at least one of them was true.

Magnor gave Gwaine a knowing smile. 'Many of the legends are true, my young Prince. They are simply beyond your understanding at this stage. All will be revealed in time.' Magnor moved to his right and stood before Tanya.

Tanya, for her part, had been standing quietly in the background, bursting to show Magnor her sword. She had managed to contain her excitement only by telling herself that Baradetch's sword was the most important, that this was Gwaine's moment.

'And what news do you have, my Lady?' Magnor was already looking at the sword that hung from her waist.

Tanya could have kissed him for noticing and taking an interest. She withdrew the sword from its sheath and held it in front of her in the same pose that Gwaine had adopted. 'A present from Prince Gwaine, my Lord. ...It is the sword of Princess Belanne.'

Magnor stepped forward and studied the sword. 'Yes, ...it is the Lady's sword, ...and just as beautiful now as it was two centuries ago. It is a marvellous gift, my Lady Tanya. Treasure it, for there is much love and power in that sword.'

Tanya was happy with Magnor's words. If it were possible, the sword was even more treasured now than before he had viewed it. 'Yes, my Lord. I shall keep it safe.'

'Oh no, my Lady. That is not what I meant. A sword is not designed to be laid beside a bed ...', Magnor cast a sly look at Gwaine, '…for safekeeping. It is designed for the safety of the owner. Your sword has been designed with a Lady's size and strength in mind. It has been designed to protect its owner from harm.' Magnor stopped and studied Tanya. 'Have you ever been taught to use a sword?'

Tanya shook her head. 'No, my Lord. ...Though, I would be keen to learn, ...in these dangerous times.' She had sensed an imminent offer.

'Very good. I shall teach you.'

Gwaine was immediately worried. He didn't want Tanya to suffer, as he had, at the hands of this hardened old warrior. 'Magnor. I don't think …'

Magnor didn't allow him to finish. He could see the worry in Gwaine's eyes. 'And you need not worry, Gwaine. I shall not try to make a warrior of the Princess. I shall display patience in teaching her the basic principles of defence. That is all.'

Gwaine was reassured by Magnor's words. He rebuked himself for underestimating Magnor. That old warrior had been around more courts than Gwaine would ever consider counting. He knew the skills of a gentleman as well as he knew the skills of battle. Tanya was in good hands.

'But that is later.' Magnor's tone implied that he was about to change the subject. 'Right now, there is much to do. Two Kings are at Lasatal. Another two, Thale and Bartak, are at Raoul. The remaining three are now approaching the Fortress of Marsh. They will all be here for the ceremony of Warlord, tomorrow night. There is much to be done for the ceremony. The hall is now being prepared. But it is all superfluous. The only reason for the gathering is the Warlord's oath. Do you know the Warlord's oath, Gwaine?'

'Of course, Magnor. It is quite simple. ...I will drive the evil forces of the Dark Emperor from our lands. …Even I shouldn't forget that, when the time comes.'

'Can you do it?'

Gwaine was confused by Magnor's question. 'Can I give the oath?'

Magnor realised the ambiguity of his question and tried again. 'Can you drive the Dark Emperor's forces, the two armies, from our lands?'

Gwaine looked thoughtfully at the floor. 'I hope so. ...Baradetch fulfilled his oath. There is no reason why I should not.'

Gwaine wasn't happy with his reply. Neither was Magnor.

'Baradetch was fortunate. The Dark Emperor's forces were not well organised and they were surprised by the Fortress defence. Baradetch only had to chase a disorganised retreat out of Amorand to fulfil his oath. I am taking nothing away from him. He was a great Warlord, ...but his task was easier than yours. The Dark

Emperor knows of the strength of the Fortress defence, his armies are greater in numbers and more organised. If you win the battle for the Fortress, you will then have to lay siege to every fortification in Amorand. ...Can you fulfil your oath?'

Gwaine had tried optimism and Magnor had rejected it. He decided to try honesty as a second option. 'I don't know, Magnor. I will try to fulfil the oath. ...If I can win the battle for the Fortress, then I have a skeleton of a plan.'

'Associated with the legend of Martren?'

'Yes, my Lord. That will play a prominent role.'

'Very well.' Magnor sounded satisfied. 'You are aware of the difficulty of your task. That is all I was testing.' Magnor went silent for some time while Gwaine waited to be tested further.

'You have stated the oath as it is written in the history books. Do you think that you will get it right on the night?'

Gwaine thought about his answer. 'It is a very simple oath, my Lord. I do not foresee me accidentally misquoting it on the night.'

Magnor grinned. 'We will see. ...Now, go. Immediately after supper, you will go to your room. You will stay there until I call for you, tomorrow evening. I shall give you warning as the time approaches so that you can be ready for the ceremony.'

Gwaine and Tanya, realising that they had been dismissed, turned and left the war room. It was now after nine in the morning and a free day lay ahead of them.

'Well, what shall we do now?' Tanya knew there was no easy answer to the question. She had been trying, herself, to think of something to do. After the adventure of the previous day, today's lack of planning was an anticlimax.

'I don't know. ... I should know. Today is my last taste of freedom. Tomorrow, I will be proclaimed Warlord. The next day, I will be preparing for war at Raoul and the following day, if Magnor is correct, I shall be fighting in the Fortress. ...I should have great plans for today.'

They walked on in silence, Gwaine looking despondently at the floor as they moved aimlessly through the corridors. Tanya snatched an occasional glance toward Gwaine as they walked. She was looking for some sign of age, or maturity, or greatness in the young man walking beside her. She saw none. She could not believe that her friend would soon be riding off at the head of great armies to fight great battles that would determine the future of the whole of Amorand.

'Are you scared, Gwaine?', Tanya whispered, still looking toward the floor.

Gwaine didn't answer.

Tanya was annoyed with herself. It was a stupid question to ask. Of course Gwaine would be scared, but he would be too proud to openly admit it. She mentally kicked herself for asking the question without thinking more. She wasn't surprised that Gwaine was ignoring her dumb question.

They came to the steps that led to their garden. Without communication, they both veered off and walked directly to the bench.

After sitting for some time staring at the pond, Gwaine turned to face Tanya. 'That's a dumb question. Of course I'm scared.'

Tanya laughed. She couldn't help it. She knew Gwaine was serious, but she was relieved that he was still speaking to her and overjoyed that their relationship was close enough that he could tell her the truth, and even tell her when he thought her dumb questions were dumb.

Gwaine sat upright on the bench and turned his body to face Tanya. 'I fail to see the humour in the situation. I have just admitted to being scared out of my wits about going off to war, and you think it's funny.'

Tanya thought for a moment that he was seriously rebuking her, but he spoilt his act with an almost undetectable movement at the corner of his lips that indicated a stifled smile. When it was obvious that Tanya had seen through his charade, he allowed the smile to surface.

‘You’re cracked, young Lady. I pity the people of Velinon if you ever take the throne. You’re absolutely warped.’

‘Well, that would explain why we get on so well, wouldn’t it. ...That’s why we’re friends.’

Gwaine became serious. He looked into Tanya’s eyes. ‘That’s why we’re ***good*** friends.’

Tanya caught the mood. ‘Yes, Gwaine. That’s why we’re good friends.’ Tanya dropped her gaze. ‘That reminds me. ...While we are being serious. ...Mother told me that I should not have accepted your gift and that I should return the sword straight away.’

Gwaine’s spirits fell. He had thought that Queen Kayla liked him. While he did not expect her to look upon him as a prospective son-in-law, he did expect that she would allow him to be Tanya’s friend and give her gifts. He waited in depression for Tanya’s next words and the return of the sword.

‘I assured her that it was a friend’s gift and I pointed out that I had made a vow not to return it.’ Tanya found the courage to look at Gwaine. ‘It’s lucky that you placed that condition on the present. Once mother knew that I had made a vow, she didn’t pursue it any further.’

‘Then you can keep the sword?’

‘Yes. I can keep the sword. ...But, I think it’s pretty clear what the reaction would be if ...well ...’ Tanya’s cheeks grew red, ‘...if, at a later stage, you wanted to be a suitor.’

Gwaine’s spirits rose a little. At least Tanya could keep the sword. ‘Oh well, ...that was to be expected. As much as I would have liked to have been considered acceptable to your parents, I always knew that I wouldn’t be. ...Anyway, it’s rather premature to consider. Do you know that Baradetch was the only Warlord in the history of Arrindare to survive being Warlord.'

Gwaine immediately regretted his casual remark. The colour went out of Tanya's face and her eyes filled with tears. Before Gwaine realised what was happening, Tanya was running up the path that led to the Immortal Gardens. He sat in shock for some moments before running after her.

When he finally caught up with her, she was leaning against the trunk of a tree, sobbing. Gwaine slowed his pace as he approached and walked the last few metres. He placed his hands on her shoulders and turned her to face him. Tears were streaming down her cheeks and she was sobbing uncontrollably. Gwaine pulled her to him. Tanya nestled in and placed her head on his shoulder as he wrapped his arms around her.

'I'm sorry, Tanya. That was a thoughtless thing to say.'

'Is it true?' The question was only just audible through the sobs.

Gwaine couldn't think of any answer other than 'yes', so he ignored the question.

'Come on, settle down. ...Why is it, every time I go out with you I come home wet. I'll have to wring out my shirt if …'. Gwaine didn't finish. The attempt at light relief had obviously failed. He stood in silence, holding Tanya to him, until she had cried herself out. Even then, they stood for several minutes just holding each other, each gaining comfort from the nearness of the other.

Finally they broke the embrace and moved apart. Gwaine grasped her hands.

'How about a paradise picnic at the waterfall?'

Tanya freed one hand to wipe her eyes. 'Sounds good. ...Have you got a handkerchief?'

Gwaine searched through the pocket of his cloak and produced the handkerchief.

'Prince Gwaine!' Magnor was calling from the garden.

Tanya quickly wiped her eyes before they ran hand in hand down the path to the garden.

'Everything has gone wrong, Gwaine.' Magnor was yelling up the path the moment that Gwaine and Tanya came into view. 'The Emperor's forces are moving quickly toward the Fortress of Marsh. The battle may be tomorrow. The court is preparing to leave immediately for Raoul. You shall become Warlord tonight, in Raoul. We must move quickly. Princess Tanya, you had best find your parents and see what plans they have for you.'

Gwaine and Tanya stared at each other in disbelief, neither knowing what to say or do. They both felt cheated.

'Well come on. ...Come on', Magnor demanded. 'Kiss, or cuddle, or something. We have to go. Now!'

Tanya took the initiative. She threw her arms around Gwaine's neck and planted a kiss on his lips that took him by surprise.

'I expect to see you after the battle.' Tanya's bravado was spoilt by the catch in her throat. '...And I'll be very cranky if you let yourself get hurt.'

Gwaine grabbed her and pulled her to him. He gave her a bearhug and then returned her kiss. 'Look after yourself, my Lady.'

'Alright, alright. Let's go', demanded Magnor.

The three headed toward the steps that led into the castle. Magnor and Gwaine turned left and Tanya ran to her right. Gwaine peered over his shoulder to catch a last glimpse of Tanya as she disappeared around a bend in the corridor.

GOOD COMPANY ON THE EVE OF WAR

Gwaine and an escort of ten soldiers of the Last Regiment sped toward Raoul. It was almost six in the evening when they approached the city of tents that sat at the base of the Raoul mountain range.

During the journey, Gwaine had tried to sort out his emotions and fears. With every problem that he focussed on, his mind went into a confusion of despair and frustration that always ended in a simple wish to forget everything and just sail away to Parrin.

The legends claimed that this beautiful land was to the east of Lasatal, beyond the daring of the Amorand sailors. There Baradetch still lived - a life of comfort that was unparalleled by any King who had ever reined in glory and wealth.

Gwaine didn't believe the legend of Parrin but it was, nevertheless, his favourite fantasy - to leave all of his troubles and simply sail away in search of Baradetch and his new land.

He had a great deal that he would have liked to escape from. He was between problems. He had left unsolvable problems at Lasatal to travel into extreme danger in the Fortress of Marsh.

Gwaine turned his attention to Tanya and their hurried parting in the garden. Tanya obviously cared for him, and his feelings for her were not easily defined. He did know that he had never cared for any girl, or anybody for that matter, the way that he cared for Tanya. Gwaine shook his mind back to reality. He could never be any more to Tanya than just a friend and, besides, he would probably never see her again. Gwaine imagined that would, undoubtedly, please King Tyne and Queen Kayla. He was far from being suitable for Tanya. She would marry a Crown Prince. Someone like Stefarne. Gwaine shuddered at the thought.

'Hopefully, I'll be killed and long buried before there is any indication of that.'

Gwaine's mind turned to Parrin and Baradetch. It was little comfort. Baradetch had to earn his journey to Parrin by winning the battles. Gwaine's battles were still to be fought.

The first battle would probably be in the morning. Even if he could win the battle and survive the battle, it was only the first of many. He could not see any way that the Dark Emperor's forces could be expelled from Amorand. They occupied too many cities. He did not have the numbers to lay siege to all of those cities and win. Depression took over. He could not defeat the Dark Emperor on the battlefield. Parrin was a very attractive alternative.

'What a birthday tomorrow will be.'

The complaint jumped into his mind without any real thought. It was rather stupid, Gwaine decided, that with all of his problems, he was now pondering the trivial fact that his eighteenth birthday had been spoilt.

It was, nevertheless, a line of thought that he pursued. Other Princes of Amorand had magnificent parties when they turned eighteen, with banquets and dancing and all of the trappings that were associated with birthdays. The dumb second Prince of Arrindare was going to be fighting for his life in the Fortress of Marsh. Gwaine gritted his teeth with the unfairness of it. He had even heard of a custom in a Kingdom of Silosus where the Prince turning eighteen was sent off to bed with the handmaiden of his choosing. Gwaine spent some time considering the advantages of such a custom. He decided, in the unlikely event that he ever survived to have a son, that would be his son's eighteenth birthday present.

He pictured, in his mind's eye, the handmaidens of Lasatal. He could think of a number who were very desirable, but none of them were as attractive as Tanya. His mind delved deeper into the fantasy before he finally rebuked himself for thinking of Tanya in that way, but his mind would not be fully deterred. Finally, he resorted to the tactic of reminding himself, yet again, that he would probably never see

Tanya again and, anyway, he was not going to have a birthday - he was going to fight a battle.

Gwaine shook his head in frustration. The problems were unsolvable. They kept rotating in his mind, taking turns at frustrating and depressing him.

The sight of the tent city was a relief. Taron would be in the Commander's tent with his armies spread around him. Taron would talk of things that would distract Gwaine's mind from its confusion.

The soldiers took no notice as Gwaine and his escort rode among the tents. They could not have known that he was the one who would soon become Warlord. Gwaine decided that it was just as well that they didn't recognise him. He felt rather pathetic at the moment. His emotional problems and outright fear were weighing heavily on his boyish shoulders.

They reined to a halt outside of a large square tent that bore the flag of the Commander of the Fortress Guard. As Gwaine dismounted, Taron walked out of the tent. His facial expression turned from concentration to anxious surprise as he realised Gwaine's presence. He turned, immediately, to the guard who was casually leaning on his spear at the tent entrance and bellowed so loudly and suddenly that the soldier almost toppled over as he jumped to attention.

'***Wake up, soldier! Prince Gwaine has arrived. I expect to be notified of such things.***'

Taron turned to Gwaine and bowed. 'Welcome, my Lord.'

'Thank you, Commander. I could do with a drink and a talk, if you have the time.'

'Of course, my Lord. We have much to discuss.' Taron turned to the officer of the escort. 'The officer of the day is at the end of this row. He will see to your needs.'

Taron lifted back the tent flap to allow Gwaine to enter. The only furniture was a map table in the far corner, so Gwaine threw himself onto the floor and stretched himself into a lying position.

Taron rummaged through a bag and produced a crock and two goblets. 'Wine?'

Gwaine opened one eye and studied Taron. 'You soldiers have a hard life, don't you?'

'It's a frugal existence', Taron replied. 'Was that a 'no'?'

'No. It was not a 'no'.'

Taron smiled. He had already uncorked the crock. He filled the goblets and handed one to Gwaine, who immediately drained the contents in an attempt to provide some moisture for his parched throat. Taron refilled the goblet and joined him on the floor.

'Welcome to my magical world of tents.'

Gwaine sat up. He was pleased that Taron was in the mood for a light conversation. He couldn't have taken anything heavy, yet.

'Very impressive', Gwaine replied, peering out of the tent opening. 'What happens when there's a gale?'

'My world picks itself up and flies away. I told you it was magical.'

Gwaine concentrated on not laughing. He wasn't going to give Taron that satisfaction. Instead, he managed a drop-dead look. 'Magnor told me to hurry over here - that your jokes were suffering some terminal illness.'

Taron, unable to think of a comeback, topped up their half empty goblets.

'Alright, you've cheered me up. Now tell me the worst.' Gwaine's voice had a fatalistic ring to it that indicated that he was prepared for anything that Taron could throw at him.

'The armies of Fenore, Vole and Raynor have been badly mauled. While they were retreating down the coast, Qarad sent a force along the mountain range that came down at Martren, between them and the Fortress of Marsh. They had to fight a desperate battle on the flats. Luckily, they broke through Qarad's force and made it to the Fortress, but their losses are heavy.'

Gwaine shook his head in frustration. He wasn't prepared for ***this*** news. 'Where are they now?'

'The Kings and their courts are at Raoul. The armies are still coming through the Fortress. They will stay at the Fortress as our final line. I have set up medical services there already.'

'What does this mean to our defences?'

'Not much. We will just have less soldiers in the marsh tomorrow, but our final line will be stronger than I had planned.'

'Then you expect that the battle will be tomorrow?'

'Yes, without a doubt.'

'Could it be earlier?'

'No. Qarad has wounds of his own to lick, and tired soldiers to rest. It will be tomorrow morning.'

Gwaine had finished his wine. He refilled his goblet and topped up Taron's. 'Well, ... I don't know about you Taron, but', Gwaine lowered his voice to a whisper and leaned closer to Taron, '... I'm scared stiff.'

Taron laughed. The wine was starting to have a cheerful effect. 'So am I, Gwaine, but this is what we were trained for. This is our destiny.' Taron's face dropped to a serious expression. 'Or, I think it is my destiny to command the defence of the Fortress. King Vole's son came through here earlier, claiming that he had earned the right to lead the defence and that the Kings would see to it that he did.' Taron paused to study Gwaine's face. 'Their wish is my command. I will serve the Prince of Cadel, if that is the decision of the Kings.'

'The Kings can make any decision they like, Taron. I am Warlord. The decision is mine to make. You have been trained since childhood as a warrior, and you have studied the plan for the Fortress defence and improved it over years of study with Magnor. You shall command the armies of the seven Kings. Tomorrow is your destiny, not that of some upstart Prince who doesn't even know how to retreat without being outflanked.'

'Thank you, my Warlord.' The sincerity in Taron's voice was impossible to ignore.

Gwaine felt embarrassed by his friend's display of gratitude and immediately searched for a way to lighten the conversation. 'Come on mudfish, tell me a joke and we'll see if they've improved.'

Taron could always be relied upon for his instant wit. 'Have you heard the one about the warrior Prince and the pretty young Princess from Velinon?'

'No and I don't think I want to. It doesn't sound funny.'

'Oh, it's not a joke my friend. It's a constant flow of reports from everyone who has been to Lasatal in the last few days. They say that you're inseparable.'

Gwaine peered around the tent. 'She's not here. Your sources are obviously mistaken. We are not inseparable. I would find all these rumour mongers and hang them if I were you.'

Taron smiled. This conversation was obviously worth pursuing.

'They talk of unchaperoned excursions into the Immortal Gardens and a present of the Lady's sword. Is this all untrue?'

Gwaine drew his sword and placed it between him and Taron. It was partly a tactic to evade the question, but it was mainly the result of a sudden realisation that he had not shown his sword to his friend.

'Behold! The Sword of Baradetch.'

Taron was instantly distracted from his attack. He gazed in amazement at the perfectly preserved sword, at the strange metal and marvelled at the history that lay within its structure. 'Baradetch held this sword? This sword defended our Fortress and drove out the evil horde over two centuries ago?'

Gwaine was pleased with his friend's reaction. 'This is ***his*** sword.'

Taron reached forward and let his hand hover just above the blade as if he was deciding whether he would touch it or not. He withdrew his hand.

'You can touch it, Taron. Pick it up and wield it.'

'No.' Taron refilled their goblets. 'It is your sword. It used to belong to Baradetch. Now it is the Sword of Gwaine. I cannot touch it. Nor should anyone else.'

Gwaine was surprised. His friend was usually very practical. He could not understand this out-of-character reply.

'They told me that you had retrieved the sword, but I thought that it would just be a stick of rust. ...It's perfect.' Taron's voice trailed off into silence as they both sat quietly admiring the implement of war that lay between them.

Some time later, Taron broke the silence. 'Was the Sword of Belanne with this sword?'

Gwaine shook his head and sighed. Taron was like a bloodhound on a scent. 'Alright, I'll tell you. Otherwise you'll hound me to my grave. ...Princess Tanya helped me to recover the casket. As a token of appreciation, I gave her the Lady's sword.'

'That's some token of appreciation.' Taron's tone implied disbelief.

'Well what was I going to do with it? It would look pretty stupid hanging from my waist. Would you have me riding into battle at the head of the seven armies of Amorand with a woman's sword hanging from my cute little waist? I could wear a dress too, if you would prefer.' Gwaine pulled up breathless. He realised, immediately, that his little outburst hadn't helped his case at all.

The smug look on Taron's face implied that he had scored a victory. 'And who was present when you made this presentation to the pretty, young Princess?'

Gwaine did not reply. He could only give Taron an icy stare. Any reply would be futile.

Taron continued as if Gwaine had answered. 'And why were you unchaperoned?'

'Because it was unnecessary.' Gwaine went to top up the goblets but the crock was empty. He rolled it along the floor angrily and it came to rest beside Taron's bag. 'The Queen of Velinon assumed, quite rightly, that I was trustworthy. Her courtiers were put to better use in making preparations for the Warlord Ceremony. It would have been ridiculous to have people wasting their time babysitting Tanya and I.'

'Tanya?'

'That ***is*** her name, Taron, but you can call her Princess. That is, if I ever bother introducing you to her'.

Taron laughed. This was going better than he could ever have hoped. He suddenly rolled onto all fours and crawled over to his bag. After rummaging through it, he returned with another crock of wine.

Gwaine shook his head. 'It's a hard life, being a soldier.'

Taron had uncorked the crock and held it above Gwaine's goblet. There he paused and turned to Gwaine. 'Was that a no?'

'***No***. It was not a flaming 'no'. Just pour it, ...and wipe that stupid, gloating expression off your face.'

Taron laughed and shook his head. He filled the goblets. 'I don't know why you're carrying on. You're obviously smitten by the young lady. Why don't you just admit it and be done with it? After all, there is only you and I here. I wouldn't blame you for being attracted to Princess Tanya. Why are you letting me have so much fun?'

Gwaine put his chin in his hands and bent forward to stare at the floor of the tent. It was a sign of submission and depression. 'I don't mind telling you how much I care for Tanya, as long as you keep it a secret from Gwaine. He just gets depressed.'

'Why does he get depressed?'

'Because he's a second Prince and she is a Crown Princess, and because he will probably be killed in battle without ever seeing her again anyway.'

Taron's spirits fell as he realised the validity of the reasons for his friend's depression. He gave Gwaine a slap on the shoulder. 'Come on Baradetch. Belanne is better off without you anyway. You're a moody bastard.'

Gwaine forced a pathetic smile. 'Let's talk about the battle strategy.'

'Oh, garbage.' Taron was weary of discussing the battle strategy. He had been discussing it over and over for days with all of his section commanders. 'We have been discussing the battle strategy for the past ten years. There will be lines of bowmen in the swamp. As the enemy moves too close to a line, the next line will give covering fire for a withdrawal. We shall wait on the outskirts of the Fortress with a final line and will be kept informed by the bugle signals that we have established. The lines of bowmen and the sections within each line will communicate by those bugle signals. When the enemy cracks, we shall charge into the Fortress and force Qarad out of our marsh. Now, I refuse to discuss it any further. Drink your flammin' wine.'

Gwaine drank his wine. He had absolute faith in Taron as a Commander and as a friend. He didn't need to know any more.

THE WARLORD'S OATH

The Lasatal Court and the Kings had arrived in Raoul. The main reception room had been hurriedly transformed into a suitable venue for the Warlord Ceremony and Magnor had fetched Gwaine from Taron's tent.

Gwaine now found himself seated astride a black stallion in the hallway directly outside the reception room. Magnor had helped him dress in his all-black Warlord uniform. That is, after he had thrown buckets and buckets of cold water over him, in an attempt to sober him up. It hadn't worked.

Gwaine, now in a very congenial mood, despite Magnor's soaking, was occupying himself with greeting every courtier who hurriedly passed by, and by winking at every pretty girl who had to pass through the corridor. His conversation with Taron had extended into the draining of the second crock of wine.

Taron, too, was not his usual sober self. Gwaine could see him through the open door of the room. He was half seated, half slumped in a row of chairs on the far side of the room. His facial expression lacked the usual perception and intelligence that Gwaine had come to know but he, nevertheless, looked happy enough. He was flanked on either side by two attractive handmaidens who had obviously been given the job of keeping him sitting upright and from falling on the floor. This they were doing with little difficulty, apart from the occasional lapse of concentration when Taron's mobile hands had them defending their innocence.

Queen Lenore came rushing out of the room. She was obviously feeling the pressure of the moment, with so many rush preparations to be made. She hurried to Gwaine's side. 'Gwaine, I…'

She wasn't given the opportunity to complete her sentence. Gwaine was surprised and thrilled to see his mother. 'Mother! You're here too! I didn't think that you would leave Lasatal.'

Gwaine leant to his left to get a clearer view of his mother. She placed her hand on his left shoulder to prevent him falling off the horse and pushed him back a little to re-establish his equilibrium. He didn't seem to notice.

All of the stress of the frantic activity went out of Lenore's face. It was replaced by a mother's calm sternness. With her hand still supporting Gwaine by the shoulder, she looked deeply into his eyes and spoke with cold precision. 'Gwaine. Listen to me.'

'Yes, mother.'

'The floor is highly polished. …It is very slippery. ...You will have to ride very carefully.'

'Oh, good.' Gwaine's reply was buoyant. 'It's alright. I know how to ice skate. But, you might have to have a word or two with the horse.'

Lenore's face displayed a patience that only a mother could muster. Magnor had told her that Taron and Gwaine had 'had a little too much to drink'. Only now did Lenore realise just how much of an understatement that was. She carried on in the same slow, deliberate style. 'You ***will*** be careful, ...won't you?'

Gwaine could feel the concern in his mother's voice. He concentrated on supplying a sensible reply. 'Yes, mother. I will be careful.' And then he ruined it. He pointed an educational index finger at his mother as he changed the subject. 'You're very attractive, mother. Father doesn't spend enough time with you.'

Lenore was taken by surprise. She allowed a warm smile to creep across her lips. 'Thank you, son. I will mention that to your father.'

'Good.' Gwaine sat back up in the saddle. The crouched position was getting uncomfortable.

Lenore shook her head at her drunken son. How was he going to get through the ceremony without mishap?

'Do you remember the Warlord's oath, Gwaine?' Gwaine looked dully at his mother. He didn't think that he was as drunk as everybody thought he was, but he was having fun and certainly enjoying the attention. 'Um, ...tell it to me.'

'Listen carefully. …I will cast the Evil Emperor's forces from our land.'

Gwaine had nodded at every word as his mother had pronounced them. He immediately launched into an attempted repetition of Lenore's statement. 'I will casket Evil Emperors for our land.'

Lenore couldn't contain her humour. She giggled at Gwaine's recital. 'Oh, Gwaine. You're a trial. You ***do*** know. Don't you?'

'Yes, mother. I know.'

'Alright then. I have work to do. You just try to stay in the saddle. I will be back before the ceremony starts.' She moved toward the door. 'Don't forget, the floor is polished.' She disappeared through the doorway.

Gwaine resumed his self appointed duty of greeting every hassled courtier who rushed through the corridor. Some minutes later, Stefarne made a dignified entrance at the end of the corridor. He was dressed in magnificent robes, flanked by two well-dressed attendants. As he approached, Gwaine greeted his brother. 'Hoy, Stef. How are you?'

Stefarne came to an instant stop and peered in surprise at his brother. The faces of his attendants displayed more shock than surprise. 'I am well, little brother. And how are you?'

'Oh. I'm happy, as always.' Gwaine was leaning forward with his arms folded on the base of his horse's neck. He had found it tiring sitting upright. Besides, he was dizzy. 'I thought you were commanding the defence of our coastline against a surprise attack.'

'No. I relegated that authority to Commander Kem. This ceremony is much more important.'

‘Yes, I always enjoy these ceremonies. Happy Fruitfest Ceremony, brother.’

Stefarne was already walking toward the door, but he paused at Gwaine’s words. The Fruitfest Ceremony was not for another three months. He quickly decided that Gwaine was obviously feeling the effects of the pressure and the gravity of the occasion. He disappeared through the doorway.

Gwaine was pleased that Stefarne was at Raoul. It meant that he was out of the way, and Kem could get on with his coast vigilance. Poor Kem had almost been driven mad by Stefarne’s commands over the last few days.

Queen Lenore reappeared.

‘The ceremony will start any moment. When you here the trumpets, you ride carefully to the bend in the aisle, about where you can see Taron.’ At this point, Taron’s head disappeared. He had obviously slipped off his chair. Gwaine buckled over with laughter and almost slipped off the horse. Lenore put her arm around her son to steady him. She tried to remind herself of the importance of this ceremony, but Gwaine’s jovial mood was contagious. She couldn’t help joining him in laughter.

By the time they had recovered and looked back to the bend in the aisle, Taron’s two handmaidens had put him back in his seat and he was staring bewilderedly at the people who were about him, apparently wondering what the fuss was about.

‘Alright. As I was saying…’

‘I gotta go’, Gwaine interjected. His laughter had reminded him of something.

‘What?’ Lenore asked incredulously. ‘You’ve got to go where?’

Gwaine had thrown himself off the horse and somehow managed to remain upright as he landed. He leant toward his mother and whispered. ‘I gotta go.’

‘Oh no.’ Lenore couldn’t think of anything else to say.

Gwaine staggered off, up the corridor.

Lenore looked back at the horse that she had been left to mind. She didn't know whether to laugh or cry. 'Oh, no', she whispered to the horse.

The trumpets had already sounded twice when Gwaine returned. With some difficulty he remounted the large stallion. Lenore continued her brief as if there had been no interruption. 'At the bend, you turn left and ride to the table in front of the Kings' table. The seven Kings are already there.'

'Thank you, mother.' Gwaine had tried to muster a sober tone of voice in order to reassure his mother. The trumpets sounded for a third time as Magnor came rushing out of the door.

'What's wrong?' His question was full of stress.

'Nothing, my Lord Magnor. Nothing is wrong.' Gwaine's reply sounded quite sober and Magnor was immediately reassured.

'Good', Magnor replied 'Remember, Gwaine – ***I will drive the Dark Emperor's forces from our land.***'

Gwaine couldn't help himself. 'Thank you, my Lord Magnor. I shall return to Lasatal and pray for the success of your mission.' He spurred his horse forward and left two bewildered people shaking their heads in disbelief.

'The first thing the horse did on entering the room, was skid on the polished floor. Gwaine pulled it under control and slowed its speed.

All the way to the bend in the aisle, Gwaine continually reminded himself of the levity of the situation. He tried to look sober and think sober thoughts. He told himself that he had only been acting the drunk, that now was the time for seriousness.

At the bend, he broke his concentration long enough to look into the seated crowd. The first face he saw was Taron's, and the picture of him slipping off his chair replayed in his mind. He could have easily broken into laughter, but he fought the urge. By the time he had turned the bend to face the seven Kings, he had even managed to wipe the grin off his face. He decided that he was doing very well.

At this point, the trumpets blared an announcement that sent Gwaine battling to control his startled mount. As if he didn't have enough problems trying to direct a spirited horse through the haze that existed in his mind, dozens of well trained courtiers suddenly dived to the walls and snuffed out the candles that provided light to the assembled crowd. The only light in the room now emanated from the seven candelabras that sat at the table of the Kings.

'Very dramatic', Gwaine thought. 'Now, how the hell do I find my way to the Kings' table without trampling half the court?'

Slowly though, his eyes adapted to the changed situation and he moved on, down the aisle. A lone drum beat a slow march as Gwaine directed his stallion to a lighted table that seemed an eternity away, through some magical mist of yellow haze.

Bathing in that magical haze, sat seven men. Seven creviced old men, it appeared. For the light shadowed every mark on each face and gave each King a look of great age and wisdom.

Finally Gwaine reined his mount to a halt at the table, as his mother had instructed. He surveyed the line of Amorand Kings. 'Flaming hypocrites', he thought. 'If it hadn't been for the Dark Emperor chasing them to this table, they would probably be bickering and fighting over boundaries and petty insults, as their families have done all through the history of Amorand.'

King Daroyd rose and broke the silence. 'Friends, our enemy is near. Six of our seven Kingdoms have been overrun by the evil horde. As I speak, the forces of the Dark Emperor are preparing for battle. They camp just a short distance from here, on the far side of the Fortress of Marsh.'

Until now King Daroyd had been peering past Gwaine, into the darkness of the assembled court. Suddenly, Gwaine found himself eye to eye with his father. Gwaine was, with this act, the absolute centre of attention. Every eye was now focused on him. Every hope was now resting on his shoulders.

'In dark times such as these', Daroyd continued, 'our ancestors have, by tradition, turned to the second born Prince of Arrindare. Now, we turn to Prince Gwaine of Arrindare and ask the question that was asked of the great warrior, Baradetch, before him. ...Prince Gwaine, will you be Warlord of our seven armies of Amorand?'

Gwaine had expected, since childhood, to be asked this question. Nevertheless, it came as a shock. Amidst all this pagentry, this quiet, this magical setting, he had become an observer. He believed that he could have easily floated to the ceiling and laid amongst the rafters and casually watched the passing of events and time.

He forced himself down from the rafters of his mind and pushed forward the only answer that was possible.

'I will.'

And, with those two words, the realisation dawned that what he had most dread had come to pass. His world, from now on, was to be the living nightmares of his childhood.

Daroyd continued. 'The Warlord, before he is accepted by the Seven Kings, must make a pledge that will become his goal. Upon the completion of that goal, the Warlord is released from his bond to the Kings, but he cannot be released from his duties until that goal has been achieved, until the pledge has been fulfilled. What is your pledge, Prince Gwaine?'

Gwaine immediately launched into his reply. 'That I will drive the Dark Emperor's forces from our land.' Gwaine wished that he could see Magnor's face. 'And, that I will destroy the Dark Emperor.'

The silence from the court was broken as a murmuring slowly grew. King Daroyd's face dropped. Magnor had told him that his son had been drinking. Daroyd searched his mind for a remedy to this blunder as the murmuring of the court grew louder.

'Your pledge is wrong.' Daroyd's voice was no longer the strong, educated sound of a King, but rather the quiet chastisement of a disapproving father. 'What is the correct pledge?'

Gwaine was unmoved. He looked into his father's face and spoke softly. 'There is no wrong pledge, father. The pledge is mine to make and I have made it. I now stand by that pledge.'

King Daroyd stood in silence, wondering what his next move should be. It was King Radrath who interjected.

'He is right, Daroyd. He has made his pledge, ambitious as it may be. Carry on with the ceremony.'

Some of the Kings nodded or grunted their agreement. Daroyd bowed his head, realising that he could do nothing now to change the pledge. 'Your pledge is accepted by the Seven Kings of Amorand. In the name of these Kings, assembled here, I proclaim you Warlord.' Daroyd looked to Gwaine's side. 'And may the sword of Baradetch protect you from harm.'

After a short pause Daroyd raised his voice slightly to indicate a change of subject. 'There is only one other matter to dispense with before you ride to the Fortress to prepare for tomorrow's battle. Prince Soran of Cadel has earned a great reputation, already, in fighting the Emperor's forces. He has requested, and the Kings have agreed, that he be allowed to command the Fortress defence tomorrow. We acknowledge that the decision belongs to the Warlord, but we request that it be so.'

'The request is denied.' If Gwaine had not been feeling the effects of the wine, he may have been more tactful, but he had already made a decision on this point.

Besides, he could read his father fairly well and he could tell that King Daroyd was not in favour of the plan. 'I will be pleased to have Prince Soran's experience at my side tomorrow, but Commander Taron shall command the defence. He has been trained since childhood for this one battle and the defence has already taken position in the marsh under his instructions. I will not make any last minute changes.' Gwaine hoped that Taron was wearing an intelligent expression on his face at this very moment.

King Vole jumped to his feet. 'I request that you reconsider, Warlord.'

'No, King Vole. My decision is made.'

'Very well then', King Daroyd continued immediately, leaving King Vole without any further argument. 'You may leave for the Fortress of Marsh, but...', and here Daroyd lowered his tone again to that of a father, '...I suggest that you meet in the courtyard with some people who would like to wish you well'

Gwaine nodded to his father and then straightened himself in the saddle as he scanned the Kings. He bowed and then turned his horse as the court erupted into applause and cheering.

Gwaine trotted his mount back down the aisle and breathed a sigh of relief as he rode, without mishap, through the doors and back to the corridor. He dismounted immediately, left the stallion with an attendant, and tried to find his land legs and a clearer head as he strode to the courtyard.

A short while later, Gwaine and Taron and fifty soldiers stood to attention as King Daroyd and Queen Lenore, followed by Magnor, descended the steps to the courtyard.

Without uttering a word, Lenore moved to Gwaine and gave him a quick hug before withdrawing a step. There were tears in her eyes. 'I promised myself that I wasn't going to cry.' She wiped her eyes with her handkerchief. 'It was a foolish promise. I love my son too much not to be upset.'

‘That was a senseless pledge, Gwaine’, Daroyd interjected from behind. There was no anger in his voice, only concern. ‘You cannot possibly destroy the Emperor.’

Gwaine smiled at his mother as he moved forward and kissed her on the cheek. ‘Thank you for the tears.’

Only as he stepped back from his mother, did Gwaine acknowledge his father’s words. ‘It is not the pledge that I would choose to make willingly, father. It is the only pledge that I could possibly make. Over the centuries, with every assault, the Dark Emperor comes closer to victory, he learns more and becomes more powerful. Even if I can repel his forces this time, he will soon return. And, next time, he will win. If I chose the easier pledge of ‘driving the Dark Emperor’s forces from our land’, then I would only be stalling the inevitable defeat. My mission cannot be as simple as Baradetch’s. The Dark Emperor must be destroyed. Magnor knows that I speak the truth.’ Gwaine nodded toward Magnor, who was standing behind the King and Queen.

Magnor moved forward to join the group. His dark green eyes stared at Gwaine and seemed to penetrate his thoughts. ‘Yes. Gwaine speaks the truth. The Dark Emperor must be destroyed.’ Magnor turned to the King and in a less ominous voice, as was his forte, he changed the subject. ‘But the battle for the Fortress comes first. Let us wish Gwaine and Taron well in that battle and worry about the pledge later.’

‘Yes’, chimed in Queen Lenore, in a voice that made every attempt possible to be cheery. ‘I have a secret present for Gwaine from a young lady.’ Lenore withdrew a multi-coloured scarf from her cloak pocket. ‘It is a Velinon tradition for a young Lady to present a scarf to her warrior, that must be carried by him into battle in order to protect him from harm.’ Lenore’s eyes widened in a pretence of fear. ‘And if her parents ever find out that I delivered this, my life won’t be worth living.’

Gwaine laughed at his mother's acted fear and accepted the scarf. He crumpled the soft silkiness of the material in his hands and tried to picture Tanya's face. 'Thank you, mother. Please tell the young Lady that I will wear her present.'

'I will.' Lenore turned her attention to Taron. 'And just so that you won't feel left out, Taron, Princess Ellorn sent you a scarf, and a message that she expects to see you on the third day of next week for her promised riding lesson.'

Lenore had been walking toward Taron as she talked and searched for the scarf in her pocket. As Taron accepted the scarf, she surprised him by throwing her arms around his neck and embracing him. As she drew away, she increased the look of shock on his face by planting a kiss on his lips. 'You two look after each other.' The order was cast to both Taron and Gwaine.

Gwaine would have enjoyed the moment more, had he not been staring intently at Magnor's eyes. From the moment Lenore had approached Taron, all of the usual life and green depth had gone from those dark eyes. They had become suddenly dull and portrayed the deepest depths of sadness.

'Come. We cannot hold these warriors any longer.' King Daroyd had taken control of the situation. 'There is a storm near at hand and you have a long way to travel.' Daroyd made the slightest of movement toward Gwaine, but then stopped and straightened himself. 'Fight well, son. You too, Taron. I will see you both when you return from the marsh.'

Gwaine would have liked to run to his father and hug him farewell, but the mood had been set. He bowed to his King. 'Until the battle is over, my Lord.' He turned and mounted his horse, before nodding his farewell to Magnor.

'Taron.' Magnor's voice sounded more strained than Gwaine would have expected. Taron waited for his command through second after second of silence. Magnor seemed to have forgotten his words. Eventually, he almost whispered his command. 'Fight well young warrior. ...You too, Warlord.'

'Yes, my Lord', both Gwaine and Taron answered in unison. Taron bowed to the party before riding to the front of the column of soldiers.

Gwaine winked and smiled at his mother, before raising his plain black shield to his chest and his sword above his head. He screamed at the top of his voice and the soldiers immediately echoed his words.

'***To the honour of the Kings.***'

AT THE EDGE OF BATTLE

It had been almost two hours after midnight when Taron and Gwaine finally laid down in their tent. The three hours of restless half-sleep that followed had not been nearly enough. Nevertheless, here they were, dressing for battle in the morning twilight while distant trumpets sounded the alarm that the enemy had began its advance.

Gwaine rechecked his uniform and equipment and gathered his shield from the ground. Only then did he turn his attention to Taron and his preparations. Taron was looking pale, and the way that he was fumbling with his sword belt indicated to Gwaine that he was not his usual self.

'How are you?'

'Awful', was Taron's whispered reply, 'Sick. ...That wine must have been off.'

Gwaine stifled a laugh. 'It wasn't the quality. It was the quantity that knocked you around.'

'Rubbish', was Taron's dry response, 'I always drink in moderation. Not like some drunks that I know.'

Gwaine ignored Taron's attempted slur on his drinking habits. 'Anyway, it made for an interesting ceremony.'

For the first time Taron allowed a smile to creep across his lips. 'Yes', he muttered as his eyes betrayed his mind's wandering, 'You don't happen to know the names of those two young ladies, do you?'

Gwaine laughed. 'No, I don't, but I do know what they thought of your drunken gropings. You can forget about them, my friend.'

'Drunken gropings? I...'

An Officer of the Fortress Guard burst into the tent and saluted Taron. 'Commander, the battle has begun. The trumpets tell of the withdrawal of the first line of bowmen...'

'Already?' Gwaine interrupted with astonishment.

'That's alright', Taron replied quietly, 'Over one hundred thousand enemy soldiers have entered our Fortress. It is to be expected that our initial lines will withdraw quickly. As our enemy's losses become greater and the mud clings to his feet more, then he will slow down, and eventually come to a stop.'

Gwaine was impressed by Taron's composure, regardless of whether it might be real or acted.

The Officer continued. 'Columns of arrow bearers have already been dispatched into the marsh, as you instructed, and your reserve forces are now awake and preparing for battle.'

'Thank you, Raiff. I will be in the command tent shortly.' Taron had obviously meant to dismiss his Officer by this remark, but Raiff continued to stand before his commander. 'Is there something else?'

'Yes, Commander.' Raiff's perplexed state was obvious. 'Prince Soran has instructed me to inform you that he grows impatient in the command tent. He wishes me to ask how much longer you will be.'

'I see', Taron replied in a tone that implied irritation. 'Inform Prince Soran that I will be there shortly to give him his instructions.'

'Yes, Commander. He has also commanded me to organise our forces in preparation for advancing into the marsh within the hour.'

Taron turned to Gwaine with raised eyebrows.

Gwaine's anger had already surfaced with the tone of Prince Soran's first message to Taron. Soran's presumption of being able to give this sort of command to their forces was added fuel to Gwaine's growing rage. 'You will inform Prince Soran',

Gwaine roared, 'that I have countermanded his order. Our forces shall remain where they are until either Commander Taron or I give instructions to the contrary. Furthermore, you will accept no further instructions from Prince Soran. Is that understood?'

Raiff bowed to his Warlord. He could not disguise the smile on his face. 'Yes, my Lord. I understand.'

Gwaine overcame his temper and lowered his tone. 'You will have enough to do today without playing messenger for some upstart Prince. You may go.'

Raiff bowed and left.

'Speaking of upstart Princes', Taron began, 'how do ***you*** feel this morning?'

The question was such a stark contrast to the angered conversation of only seconds ago that Gwaine couldn't help laughing. 'Oh, shut up! ...Come on. Let's take a walk around the camp so that we can keep his highness waiting a little longer.'

As they moved between the lines of tents of the camp, Gwaine marvelled at the force that he now commanded. What struck him most was the difference in uniforms. The seven different uniforms of the seven armies of Amorand were once again fighting on the one side. How many times these colours had met each other as enemies on the battlefield, Gwaine could not begin to count. But now, for this brief moment of history, they were united, symbolised by the one common element of their uniforms - the black cloak that each soldier wore who followed the Warlord of the Seven Kings.

When Taron and Gwaine finally arrived at the command tent, Soran was pacing impatiently near the entrance. Gwaine had met Soran before, but as they approached the tent he was forced to shake his head and re-ask himself the question that had nagged him for so many years. Why did everybody look more like a Warlord than the Warlord? Soran was a thick, muscly character. At nineteen years of age, he looked like he could chew up, and spit out half a dozen Baradetches, he was respected by his soldiers, and he certainly lacked nothing in the line of self-confidence and gall.

'And if we're not going to advance on our enemy, what are we going to do?' Soran boomed at Gwaine and Taron as they approached the tent opening.

Both Gwaine and Taron brushed past Soran as they entered the tent.

'Good morning, Soran', Gwaine chimed happily.

'Good morning, Prince Soran', Taron echoed in an equally amicable tone.

Gwaine marched to a chair next to a map table that displayed the deployment of the armies in the marsh. He slouched in the chair and put his feet up on the table. Taron sat at the corner of the table and leant on it with a bored expression as he studied its detail.

'We're going to wait and see what happens', Gwaine finally replied.

'What sort of leaders are you?' Soran questioned with disgust. 'You should be out there cracking skulls instead of hiding away in here. You should be leading your soldiers in a charge against the Dark Emperor's forces.'

Gwaine no longer felt any inferiority to Soran. Soran obviously had the brawn and the courage to be a Warlord but, Gwaine decided, he was totally devoid of the necessary brain. 'Thank you for your suggestion, Soran, but I would rather win this battle. There will be plenty of opportunity, this afternoon, for cracking skulls.'

Distant trumpets interrupted the dispute. The second line of bowmen was withdrawing. Gwaine looked worriedly at Taron. 'It's all happening too quickly. Can't we get a clearer view of what's going on?'

'The Line Commanders will send back runners after every withdrawal. A network of runners will relay the information to us here but, from that distance, it will be at least an hour and a half before we have our first report.'

‘And in the meantime we can do nothing?’ Soran questioned incredulously.

‘And in the meantime, ***we*** can do nothing, Soran.’ Gwaine was pleased that Prince Soran was finally comprehending the logistical problems of the battle. ‘However, centuries of planning is now in play. While we do nothing, lines of bowmen are facing our enemy, columns of soldiers are delivering arrows and medical supplies, and messengers are rushing to deliver information on the battle that will allow us to make decisions and take actions. But, for the moment, ***we*** do nothing.’

Soran’s shoulders drooped a little as the sting went out of his attack. Gwaine motioned to a chair at a corner of the map table, and Soran accepted the offer. As he sat, he folded his arms across his chest and sighed heavily. He stared at the map table, boredom written over his face.

They sat in silence as the trumpets announced the withdrawal of line after line of bowmen. Gwaine’s spirit fell with every trumpet. The Dark Emperor’s forces were advancing with apparent ease. He looked across at Taron. There were no signs from Taron that gave any indication of his feelings and Gwaine was determined not to ask the obvious when the answer was just as obvious. Until the messengers started arriving, they could not judge how the battle was proceeding or decide what actions to take.

‘Alright.’ Soran broke the silence with a tone of voice that indicated submission to the inevitable, ‘If I am to sit here, helplessly passing the time, you could at least explain to me what is happening. What is the battle strategy? How do I interpret those damned trumpets? What must happen before we can ride off to battle?’

Gwaine studied Soran and his questions. The questions were reasonable, and the way that they had been asked suggested that Soran had stopped playing the high and mighty warrior Prince and was prepared to treat Gwaine and Taron at least as equals. ‘We do not go into battle until we receive the message that the enemy’s momentum has been stopped and that he is ready to be pushed back out of the Fortress of Marsh. Alternatively, we go into battle as the last line of defence when the Dark Emperor's forces have defeated our Fortress defence, and are about to emerge from the marsh.' Gwaine paused to give Soran time to absorb the implications of that alternative.

'And the Fortress defence is lines of bowmen', Soran interjected. 'Organised how?'

'The lines of bowmen are set up from the beginning of the Martren waters to this side of the Raoul waters. Each line is divided into sections with their own Section Commanders. When a Section Commander decides to withdraw, his trumpeter sounds the withdrawal and the whole line withdraws, so that no one is outflanked. The withdrawal is covered by the arrow fire of the next line.'

'And the withdrawing line joins the next line?'

'No. That would not give each soldier time to prepare for the oncoming assault. The withdrawing line joins the next back-up line. Each soldier then has the opportunity to re-equip himself with arrows and find cover from which he can fire on the enemy.'

Taron joined in. 'The advantage of a withdrawing line joining a back-up line is that, as the enemy moves deeper into the Fortress, our lines grow stronger. As his energy and numbers are depleted, our lines of defence are enlarged.'

Soran nodded thoughtfully. 'And what about the trumpets?'

'That's simple', was Gwaine's instant reply. 'As a line withdraws, a trumpeter in the back-up line announces it with a long blast which is picked up and relayed by designated trumpeters in subsequent lines, until it finally sounds within hearing of this camp.'

As Gwaine spoke, another trumpet blared another withdrawal. The conversation was broken by the sound and each warrior sank into his own thoughts and despair at the enemy's speedy advance.

Two hours after the first trumpet announced the battle's beginning, Gwaine shook his head as the trumpets announced the withdrawal of the last line of bowmen in the Martren waters. 'End of defence number one', he mumbled despondently.

Taron looked up with a start, seemingly shocked by the broken silence. He shook his head in exasperation. 'Where are the messengers? Surely, they must come soon'.

Almost as Taron completed his sentence, pandemonium broke in the camp as the assembled soldiers welcomed the first messenger. He was quickly ushered into the tent where Taron, Gwaine and Soran waited anxiously.

The breathless messenger bowed before gasping his message. 'I report from line one, my Lords. ...At least a full army ...is advancing into the Fortress of Marsh. ...There are mounted units ...and foot soldiers. ...They are armed with bows, spears, and swords.'

Gwaine knew that he could not have expected much information from the first line, but he was, nevertheless, disappointed. Taron was obviously just as deflated, as he dismissed the messenger. Logically, they could not expect to learn a great deal of the battle's progress until they had heard from three or four messengers. Messenger two arrived ten minutes later. The trumpets had already announced the withdrawal of another line. The second message was almost identical to the first. This, too, was to be expected.

Messenger three gave an encouraging report. 'Enemy advancing quickly, but sustaining huge losses. Few casualties among our ranks.' While this was good news, it gave no indication of any action that was necessary. What's more, the information was two hours old and the trumpets told them that the enemy was still advancing quickly.

The fourth messenger gave the first real indication of the reason for the rapid advance of the Dark Emperor's forces. 'Mounted troops being used to advantage when firm footing is available. Spearhead, localised attacks by mounted soldiers are quickly breaking the line forcing a withdrawal and heavy casualties.'

'That's our problem', Taron shouted. 'When they can get a solid footing for their horses, they're attacking quickly at a single point in our line, breaking through, and forcing our bowmen to withdraw or be outflanked.'

'And that also explains why their advance has been slowed. The trumpets haven't sounded the withdrawal of our second line of the second defence yet.' Gwaine leant over the map as he talked and pointed to the second line. 'Their horses won't find any firm footing in that mudhole, or in any of the second defence.'

'No', replied Taron. 'But they can still use localised attacks of foot soldiers in an attempt to break the line.'

The trumpets sounded the next withdrawal.

'I suggest that we move our forces from the Raoul waters into that second region.' Gwaine thumped the map. 'We have to keep them in the mud for as long as possible. Once they get into the Raoul waters, their mounted sections are going to run all over our bowmen.'

'I agree.' Taron was already walking out of the tent, but he stopped and turned at the opening. 'That means that we will have to move these soldiers into the Raoul Rivers now.'

'Yes. Mounted! …With some bowmen.'

By the time Taron had returned, another two messengers were waiting. Their messages reiterated the problem with the mounted soldiers, but the second of the messengers had an extra message that worried Gwaine and Taron. 'Qarad is an excellent Commander. He is everywhere, encouraging his soldiers.'

Soran finally broke his silence. 'I am tired of your style of war. I am going into the Raoul Rivers to crack some skulls.'

'Yes, Soran.' Gwaine stood up and stretched his back. His muscles were unhappy with the hours of sitting. 'It's time we all moved into the water. I'm afraid we will be meeting Qarad's forces in the Raoul Rivers. They will not be held in the mud.'

Taron shook his head. 'No. Not this time. You were right, Gwaine. If we are lucky enough to stop the Dark Emperor this time, he can't be allowed to try again. He must be destroyed.'

Soran had already disappeared when Gwaine and Taron emerged from the tent. Section by section, the soldiers were moving into the cold waters and would soon be taking up their defensive positions.

Raiff and a mounted section were waiting with Taron's and Gwaine's horses, already saddled.

'When we are in position, Taron, I want a messenger line set up to tell me exactly where Qarad is at all times and, particularly, where he is when he enters the Raoul Waters.'

Taron was baffled. 'Why, my Lord?'

'Because he is an ***excellent Commander***. I want to know where he is'.

THE FINAL LINE

The lines of bowmen, reinforced by the bowmen from the Raoul defence, had done their job. It had been five hours since Qarad's forces had entered the slime and mud and stagnant waters and quicksand of the second zone of defence. They had incurred incredible casualties and their attack had slowed to a crawl. Nevertheless, the attack continued and the lines of bowmen were still being relentlessly pushed out of the mud, toward the Raoul waters.

Gwaine, Taron, Soran and Raiff stood in knee deep water receiving messenger after messenger from the battle lines. The descriptions of the battle were much more graphic now. Weary soldiers with black rimmed, distant eyes told of the enemy attacking over layers of the bodies of their comrades, of the blood red mud and blood red waters of the Fortress, and of the relentless waves of attackers being cut down by swarms of arrows that turned the sky black and whistled death as they flew to their victims.

The wounded were now being withdrawn in greater numbers. The four watched silently as soldiers of the seven armies were carried past them to dry ground and medical treatment. Horrific wounds drifted past them in a morbid procession of pain and blood and death.

Gwaine looked across at Taron and wondered if he was feeling the same fears that were gnawing within him. He studied the faces of all of his companions. All were pale and fraught with tension. Even Soran displayed outward signs of apprehension.

'It doesn't feel like a board game any more, Taron.'

'No, Gwaine.' Taron shifted his weight in the water and searched for his words. 'No. It's all too real. Real fights. Real blood. Real death. …I preferred last night's heroic pageantry.'

Gwaine thought back to last night's ceremony and to their ride from Raoul to the camp. He remembered how high he had ridden in the saddle. He was Warlord, ...a tragic figure, riding off to save his land from the evil threat. He shuddered that he could have so easily deluded himself. He didn't feel like a hero anymore. Standing here in the Raoul waters, he felt like an eighteen year old who was out of his element. He didn't know what he had assumed a battle would be like, but this certainly wasn't it. This was too base and crude to be the sort of thing that old soldiers boasted of, ...to be the adventure that the history books painted in glowing terms of noble and fearless heroism. He felt inside his cloak pocket and crumpled the softness of the scarf between his fingers.

A trumpet sounded and each warrior reacted with a start. It was the last line withdrawing. The enemy would soon be in the Raoul waters.

'Is this where we expect Qarad to be, Taron?' Gwaine cleared his throat to try to relieve the tension in his neck muscles.

'Yes, my Lord. If he advances in a straight line, he will be here shortly.'

'Are the bowmen in the trees, ready to defend the last line's withdrawal?'

'Yes. Everything is in readiness.'

'Good. Give the command to mount, Raiff.'

As Gwaine, Taron and Soran mounted their horses, Raiff moved away shouting orders to his junior officers. Bedlam broke out behind them as orders were shouted and shields and swords clanged as hundreds of soldiers of that section rushed to their mounts.

Soran moved his horse off to his left. 'I'm going to fight by my countrymen. I will see you all at the Martren River.' He galloped off through the water without another word, to join a Cadel section only two hundred metres away.

Gwaine pulled his shield to his chest and drew his sword. He looked deeply into the water in front of his horse and took a deep breath in an attempt to quell his nerves.

Taron did likewise, but found the procedure to be just as futile as Gwaine had. 'Oh shit!'

Gwaine checked Taron's gaze and then peered in the same direction. Soldiers of the seven armies were moving out of the mist. As they ran, they occasionally turned to let fly an arrow at the still shrouded enemy. The twang of bowstrings could be heard in the trees as the bowmen defended the withdrawal of their fellow soldiers in the water. Battle screams were sounding less than a hundred metres ahead.

Taron re-adjusted his shield. 'Oh shit', he repeated even more emphatically.

'It could be worse, Taron', Gwaine shouted above the approaching battle sounds, as he prodded his horse forward.

'How, Gwaine?' Taron yelled as he prodded his horse after his Warlord.

Gwaine checked his left-hand side. Raiff was there. With a nod, Gwaine indicated that the charge was about to begin. He looked over his right shoulder to Taron. 'Some people die of old age', he shouted. He spurred his horse into a trot as the first of the Dark Emperor's forces appeared out of the mist. The mist enshrouding the muddied all-white uniforms of the enemy made them look like attacking spectres.

Taron kept pace with his Warlord and considered his comment. He had seen the old people, their active minds trapped in bodies that no longer answered their commands, sitting around waiting for death to claim them. Perhaps Gwaine was right. It could be worse. He forced his mind back to the present as he spurred his horse to even greater speed. Behind them, the trumpets blared a charge and the banners unfolded and raced to keep pace with their Commander and Warlord.

The adrenalin flowed in their veins. As they raced toward the enemy, the withdrawing bowmen were forced to dodge and weave to avoid being trampled by the charging horses. The white soldiers ahead were falling victim to the arrows fired from the trees as they hesitated and their attack faltered. These mounted soldiers had spent all day routing bowmen who were defending on foot. The sight of an attacking, mounted force was a surprise that they had not anticipated.

This hesitation was exactly what Gwaine had hoped for. He crashed into the thin enemy line at speed and was able to dislodge an enemy soldier from his saddle by the sheer momentum behind his sword blow. The edge taken off his momentum, he moved to the next enemy and threw a sword blow against the white shield as he defended against his enemy's sword.

A split second later, there was a deafening metallic roar as the bulk of Gwaine's force plummeted into the ranks of the white clad figures, swords clashing against shield and sword and flesh and bone.

Qarad's thin line of weary soldiers wilted under the onslaught. Gwaine looked around for an enemy to fight, but could only see the red and black uniforms of his Fortress Guard. The white soldier he had been fighting, only a second earlier, had been dispatched by one of his soldiers during that initial clash.

Gwaine prodded his horse from its standing position in an attempt to regain some momentum on the watery battlefield. He had been overtaken by a number of his soldiers, including Taron, and was now keen to regain his position at the head of the charge.

The enemy line had been badly broken and those still mounted were fleeing toward the mud of the Fortress. Gwaine's hopes rose at the sight of the uncontrolled retreat in front of him. The retreating white soldiers were, once again, a perfect target for the bowmen in the trees and were being quickly cut down by their marksmanship.

The battle's tide seemed to be irreparably turned until a huge soldier with a blonde, bushy beard appeared from nowhere to bark commands at his soldiers. In no time, the enemy had wheeled and regrouped to face the charge.

Once again, there was a deafening clang as the two lines met with steel against steel. Gwaine could see the enemy footsoldiers running through the water to join the battle and reinforce their beleaguered mounted troops.

As Gwaine threw sword blow after sword blow at his enemies and defended against their blows, his mind replayed the single, most important strategy of the battle as it now stood. He had to get to, and kill, Qarad. The battle would have been decided by now, except for Qarad's command of his forces. His influence over the Dark Emperor's soldiers could still mean the end of Arrindare and the end of all chance of releasing Amorand from the Dark Emperor's clutches.

Gwaine's sword blow veered off his enemy's shield and cut deeply into the side of the neck of the white soldier. As the limp form slipped from its horse into the already blood tinted Raoul waters, Gwaine searched for another foe. Finding none within reach, he took time to search for Qarad.

The huge Warlord-type figure was not difficult to find. Qarad was involved in the battle only twenty metres away. Gwaine spurred his horse in Qarad's direction, only to be stopped within ten metres by another mounted enemy. The battle seemed to be getting bogged down with neither side willing to give ground. Qarad's influence over his soldiers had prevented a major route.

Gwaine now found himself fighting mounted soldiers while desperately trying to avoid the spear thrusts of the foot soldiers. He cut down his mounted enemy and spurred his horse away from the footsoldiers, still moving in the general direction of where he had last seen Qarad. As soon as he moved away, one of the footsoldiers fell with an arrow protruding from his chest. Obviously, the archers in the trees were prepared to take the gamble of choosing targets in the mêlée of battle. Gwaine counselled himself not to move suddenly between an enemy and the trees unless he had to.

As Gwaine drew his attention away from the fallen soldier, he looked directly into the face of his quarry only half a metre from him. Qarad's sword blow was already on the way and Gwaine had to react quickly to bring his shield into position. The massive blow, delivered from Qarad's huge frame, was almost enough to knock Gwaine out of his saddle. The return blow from Gwaine's off balance position was pathetic and required little attention from Qarad. Had it not been for Gwaine arching his left arm and catching Qarad on the nose with the edge of his shield, the Warlord's battle may have ended there and then. Gwaine quickly brought his shield back into position, just in time to catch Qarad's next blow.

A spear was thrust at Gwaine from a lower level as Taron and one of his soldiers arrived and distracted Qarad. The enemy was breaking and beginning to retreat. Qarad broke away and galloped after those who were leading the retreat, yelling commands to his frantic soldiers.

Gwaine galloped after Qarad. He had to keep Qarad distracted to prevent him from controlling his forces in the effective manner that he had been. He threw a blow at Qarad's shield and was immediately answered by another massive blow from Qarad that shifted him across his saddle.

While some of Qarad's soldiers continued their retreat, others rushed to the aid of their Commander as Taron and some soldiers of the Fortress Guard rushed to Gwaine's aid.

In the ensuing battle within a battle, Gwaine found himself apparently fighting against everyone except Qarad. He looked around and found Qarad moving away from the group, barking commands at his hesitant soldiers and again restoring order to his ranks.

Throwing all caution to the wind, Gwaine broke away from his fight and arched around the group, trying to prod his mount up to speed. Straightening up, he pushed his horse to a full gallop toward Qarad, praying that his horse could remain on its feet long enough to reach his foe.

At high speed he raced through the bedlam of horses and men and flailing swords, defending against the sword blows as well as he could in the unreasonably short time allowed to react against them.

Qarad saw Gwaine coming and prodded his horse toward him. Within metres of each other, Gwaine showed no sign of reducing his speed. Qarad threw a massive sword blow at his attacker that was deflected by Gwaine's shield. Having made no attempt to strike a blow or reduce his speed, Gwaine crashed his horse into Qarad's horse and threw his shoulder into Qarad's side. Both horses and both riders went down and disappeared for an instant below the surface of the water. Gwaine, having planned the collision, recovered his footing quickly and dived across Qarad's struggling horse to deliver a sword blow to Qarad's neck and chest as he struggled to force his large frame out of the water. Qarad disappeared below the water in a flurry of air bubbles and bloody froth.

As the horses kicked and flayed around him, Gwaine was forced to jump out of the way of a spear that tore through his Warlord's cloak. Retreating white soldiers slashed at him as they raced past, forcing him to slip and re-enter the chilly, bloodied waters of the Raoul Rivers. As he emerged, though, he found himself safely surrounded by the mounted forms of Taron, Raiff and some of his soldiers.

Looking around, he saw the enemy in full retreat. Those who had been retreating had continued to retreat in the absence of contrary instructions from Qarad. Those who had seen Qarad fall, had lost heart and galloped toward the mud areas of the marsh. The remainder, confused by the lack of guidance, had simply followed the example of their comrades and had turned and run or galloped toward Martren.

Gwaine looked down at Qarad's still figure, floating face up, just below the water's surface. His open eyes displayed the sightlessness of death. Now, with the first encounter over, the adrenalin ceased to flow and Gwaine felt exhausted and physically sick. His mind scanned back over the battle and vividly displayed the face of every man that he had killed. He shook his head and water showered from his hair, as he worried over just how long he would see those vivid, dying faces.

'Gwaine?' Taron was querying his Warlord's thoughts.

Gwaine shook his head again and forced his gaze away from Qarad, to look at Taron.

'Yes. …What strategy now, Taron?'

'My officers know that they have to keep the pressure on. We cannot allow the enemy any opportunity to mount a resistance, or we will find ourselves at the mercy of our own Fortress.'

Gwaine nodded. 'I agree.' His answer was despairing. It was a grim prospect, but they had to race as fast as was possible to push the enemy out of the Fortress and hope that Qarad had used all of his resources in the attack and had none to spare in organising his own Fortress defence. 'We have to push them all the way to Martren.'

Taron nodded. 'I will take command of the right flank. You and Raiff take the centre, and I will send a message to Prince Soran giving him command of the left flank.'

Taron turned his horse and gave some commands while Gwaine remounted.

Gwaine and Taron exchanged a quick wave as Gwaine and Raiff moved forward and Taron spurred his horse toward the right flank. A messenger moved off toward the left flank.

Gwaine stopped and turned his horse as he suddenly remembered something. 'Taron!'

Taron pulled his horse to a stop and looked over his shoulder at his Warlord. 'Yes, my Lord.'

'Congratulations on the success of your defence. Your name will be carved into the history books.'

Taron laughed. 'No, my Lord. They shall remember the Dark Emperor, and Qarad, and Prince Gwaine, but no-one will remember Taron the mudfish.'

Gwaine smiled at his friend. 'Nevertheless, I will share a crock of wine with you tonight, on the far side of the Fortress.'

'Thank you, my Lord. I hope it will be better quality than the wine you served me last night.'

Gwaine and Taron shared a laugh as they both spurred their horses in their separate directions.

A FRIEND DIES IN THE FORTRESS

From the top of the embankment that formed the division between the Raoul waters and the mud wasteland, Gwaine and Raiff looked down on a scene of desolation. As far as they could see into the mist, the ground was sprawled with bodies, often layered one upon another. Death lay all around, and the mud glowed red. Not far into the mist, the sound of battle continued.

'Come on, Raiff. Let's get some organisation into this. Leave all horses for a start. They'll only slow us down in the mud.' Gwaine paused and looked behind them, at the sections of bowmen now wading toward their position. 'Get these men moving as quickly as possible. We have to pressure the enemy before they can regroup.'

Raiff soon had the force running as quickly as the mud and bodies would allow. It was almost a kilometre later, before they caught up with the sections that were pursuing the retreating enemy. They, too, had dispensed with their horses and were now moving as quickly as possible on foot.

The forces were hurriedly combined as a trumpet blared the position of the centre force. An immediate trumpet blare from the right flank indicated that it was slightly ahead. Some time later, Soran realised their meaning and a trumpet blare from the left flank indicated that his force was about level with Taron's.

Gwaine realised that he would have to push his force even harder to catch Taron's and Soran's forces, in order that the advance could be carried out without any sections of his army being outflanked. He searched for Raiff so that he could convey the urgency of their situation. When their eyes met, Gwaine knew immediately that no words were necessary. The urgency and concern showed in Raiff's eyes.

'They are well ahead of us, my Lord. We must hurry!'

‘Yes. Let’s go. All can still be lost.’ Gwaine pulled his shield to his chest and began running toward Martren, leaving Raiff to bark urgent commands as his soldiers quickly followed.

The going was much more difficult now. The mud was deepening and had been churned by thousands of feet, so that it was a thick sucking liquid. It resisted every movement and slowed Gwaine’s attempted run to a hot, sweaty, faltering trudge.

The twang of bowstrings from up ahead sent everybody diving into the mud while desperately trying to bring their shields into a position that would protect them from an unknown direction. Gwaine’s face splashed into the mud only centimetres from the bluish grey face of a dead soldier. With his shield restricting his vision and the muddy water still being wiped from his brow, combined with his concentration on the dangers around him, it took some seconds for Gwaine to determine which army the young soldier had belonged to.

A white section of uniform not covered by mud eventually revealed that he was one of the Dark Emperor’s soldiers. Gwaine looked into his young teenage face, into his blue eyes and tried to muster some degree of hatred for his enemy. He couldn’t. The handsome young boy lying lifeless beside him could have just as easily been one of his own soldiers.

‘If only they were different in some way’, he thought to himself. ‘If only they looked different, ...or were even a different colour. Then it would be easier.’ Gwaine cursed his fate and tried to find some logic in his thoughts. There was none, but he knew that they were, nevertheless, true.

His thoughts were interrupted by a loud splash as Raiff dived into the mud on the other side of the dead enemy soldier. The urgency and worry were still etched deeply into Raiff’s expression.

‘We have to keep moving, my Lord. We have to overrun this thin opposition before it grows into a full-scale defensive.’

Gwaine knew that Raiff was right. They had to keep moving, regardless of what the opposition threw at them. He shook his head despairingly. He would have liked to lay his head on the ground for just a second to regroup his thoughts, but when he stared toward the ground all he saw was mud and bloodied water. More arrows cut through the air above their heads. Gwaine looked into the face of the corpse between them as he spoke to Raiff.

'Sound the trumpets. Let Taron and Soran know that we are still behind them.' Gwaine paused for a moment, trying to think of a way out of their dilemma. 'It's always hard to get moving again.'

Raiff was speechless for a moment. Finally, hesitantly, he answered. 'Someone has to give the command and move ahead to set the example and hope that our soldiers respond swiftly enough to keep him alive.'

Gwaine could see that Raiff was prepared to accept that role. He would accept his Warlord's command and lead the renewed attack. Gwaine smiled grimly. 'Alright. We'll share the risk. You give the command to move and I'll lead the charge.' With those words, Gwaine struggled to his feet and lunged forward. Raiff followed closely behind him yelling commands and encouragement to his soldiers.

Bowstrings twanged from behind the small tuft of marsh bushes ahead. Arrows whizzed overhead as one struck Gwaine's shield and deflected to his left. Still struggling slowly forward, Gwaine peered over his shoulder to check whether his soldiers were following and to see why Raiff had suddenly fallen silent. His soldiers were on their feet and following him, but the sight that met his eye numbed his body with horror. Raiff was on his knees, falling slowly forward with an arrow protruding through his neck. Gwaine forced himself to look ahead, toward his enemy. Raiff was obviously dead. There was no point in stopping.

The six enemy soldiers were quickly killed and the advance continued. Gwaine moved forward in a numb world of mud and arrows and death. He tried to concentrate on the advance, on the positioning of his soldiers and on the dangers in front of him, but his mind continually reverted to Raiff's death. The suddenness of death and its senseless randomness were the factors that shocked Gwaine the most. At one moment Raiff had been an active, highly efficient soldier; an incredible leader of men, who could have been competently left in charge of any situation. The next moment, he was just another lifeless body, one of thousands that would decay in the mud before being dragged to dry land and buried in a mass grave.

More arrows flew overhead and momentarily disturbed Gwaine's trance-like state. He resisted the urge to go to ground, remembering Raiff's words. Fortunately, the defence was small and scattered. As each small group was encountered, it was soon overrun. It appeared that the main group of the Dark Emperor's force had given the battle up for lost and had no other thought than to reach the safety of Martren. Gwaine hoped that it was so, and that Qarad had not had the numbers to prepare a defensive line.

They were soon in the deepest section of the marsh. Little vegetation grew here, providing a respite from the hidden enemy archers. Scanning the surrounding marsh, Gwaine could now easily pick every quicksand bog. The areas of quicksand that he had memorised under Magnor's instruction were now defined, like unshaded areas of a map, by the absence of bodies on their surface. Gwaine wondered whether this meant that the enemy had recognised and avoided these areas or whether the marsh had greedily swallowed the hapless soldiers who had chosen those paths.

'Sound the trumpet', Gwaine yelled across the wasteland as he scanned left and right for his trumpeter. A blare from his right acknowledged his command. Within seconds, the right and left flanks answered almost simultaneously. They were almost level with Gwaine's centre force. Gwaine sighed with relief and eased his pace just a little. Exhaustion was taking over. His breath was coming in gasps, his heart was pounding in his chest, and he was incredibly hot.

He tripped, trying to move his heavy limbs at a greater speed than the mud would allow. The mud was in charge here. It held its victims and determined how fast they could move over its surface, it sucked the last ebbs of life out of those who fell, wounded, below its surface, and it swallowed its prey through those regions of ingestion that sucked the body ever downward to be locked forever in the bowels of the Fortress of Marsh. Bodies of centuries of soldiers lie in those unknown vaults. Gwaine's spine chilled as he pushed himself away from its surface, mud and muddied water streaming down his face and clothes.

He moved on in agony, feeling pity for his enemy, who had attacked over this terrain against an organised defence. 'It must have been hell', he told himself and then shook his head. 'No. This is hell. There is no word to describe their ordeal.'

Hours later, having met no further resistance, Gwaine mounted the ridge that divided the mud wasteland from the Martren waters. As he neared the summit, he fell to his knees, propped his shield in front of him and looked back over his weary soldiers as they clambered out of the final clutches of the bog to climb the ridge.

'Sound the trumpet', he gasped as he again searched for his trumpeter. A blare from behind him answered his command. 'And damn well stay near me!' he added as his eyes met those of the young man who had just taken the trumpet away from his lips.

The return soundings from Taron and Soran placed them both on, or about, the ridge. All was going as well as could be expected.

Gwaine signalled to his soldiers before moving over the ridge and into the cold Martren waters.

'Watch the treetops', he yelled into nowhere as he scooped a handful of water over his head, partly as a refresher and partly to wash off some mud. It felt so good that he repeated the action before taking a serious interest in the watery forest ahead of him. The mist was getting heavier and falling slowly down from the trees.

‘The sun must be close to setting’, Gwaine thought to himself. ‘An organised defence here could still turn the battle against us.’

It was only then that Gwaine took any interest in the colour of the water. His stomach turned as he realised that he had just thrown handfuls of bloodied water over his head. The water’s colour was that peculiar off-green that water adopts when it is mixed with blood. Bodies of soldiers of eight armies were everywhere. Gwaine tried to push the inevitable question out of his head. ‘Were they dead before falling into the water, or were they wounded and drowned?’

Gwaine darted from tree to tree for the next two hundred metres, cautiously anticipating the flight of arrows that would signal the enemy’s defensive line. Meeting no opposition, he threw caution to the wind and moved forward at a faster pace in a straight line. A hundred metres further on he stopped behind a large tree and turned to scan his own soldiers. He was looking for an officer who could be entrusted with some instructions, but there was no officer in sight.

‘Section Commanders, forward’, he yelled at the soldiers. There was no response as all of his soldiers searched their numbers for an officer. Gwaine waited for a while, crouched in the cold Martren waters, until it became obvious that there would never be a response. His officers were dead. He scanned his soldiers, looking for an intelligent face. It wasn’t easy. All of the facial expressions were overpowered by the look of exhaustion but, eventually, he chose a soldier who looked capable of acting out his instructions.

‘You! …Come here.’

The startled soldier waded quickly through the water and bowed to his Warlord.

‘Go to the right flank and find Commander Taron. Tell him that I want to see him as soon as possible. Tell him to sound a trumpet when he is leaving the right flank to find me and that I will have my trumpeter sound my position. Is that clear?’

‘Yes, my Lord.’

'Good. Then go quickly.'

The soldier bowed before wading off to his right.

'Where's my damned trumpeter?' Gwaine screamed as he scanned his soldiers in search of the elusive young man.

'Here, my Lord', came a hesitant reply.

'I don't want you there ***here***. I want you here ***here***', Gwaine yelled angrily as he motioned that he wanted the trumpeter by his side. 'You are my communication. I don't want to have to search for you. I want to trip over you every time I change direction. Is that clear?'

'Yes, my Lord', came the subdued reply as the trumpeter came to a halt and bowed.

'Good.' Gwaine calmed his temper. 'Now, let's go.'

It was easier going now. Without the mud sucking at every movement, the muscles had an opportunity to rest, and the cold water cooled and comforted an overheated body system. Gwaine's nerves, too, had began to resume their usual degree of activity as he became more and more convinced that the battle was over, that there was not going to be a Martren defence.

Half an hour later, a different note from the trumpeter on the right flank indicated that Gwaine's soldier had found Taron. An immediate blast from the left flank indicated Soran's position. Gwaine smiled to himself. 'We don't want to know that, Soran', he whispered to his left before turning to his trumpeter. 'Ah, here you are!' Gwaine exclaimed sarcastically before casting him an apologetic smile. 'Answer that right trumpet and keep sounding every five minutes or so until Commander Taron joins us.'

'With his ears ringing from the last four or five trumpet blasts over the last twenty minutes, Gwaine didn't hear anyone moving up behind him. It wasn't until he had recovered from the shock of having someone suddenly grab his shoulder, that Gwaine recognised and responded to Taron.

'Hell! You scared me. What did you do that for?'

Taron replied with a weary smile. I whispered your name. You mustn't have heard me.'

Gwaine cupped his hand to his ear in mock deafness as he cast an accusing look at his young trumpeter. 'Eh! What did you say?' Gwaine was pleased to see Taron. He was beginning to feel very much alone in this watery forest and he needed Taron's organised influence. By Taron's lack of emotion and seriousness though, he could tell that his friend was both physically and emotionally drained. He felt ashamed of his attempted joke and his mind turned to Raiff and all the bodies in the marsh.

'What did you want me for?' Taron queried in an attempt to awaken his Warlord from his deep thought.

Gwaine shook his head slowly and brought himself back to the present. 'I'm not meeting any resistance. Is it the same with you?'

'Yes. There has been no sign of the enemy since about the centre of the marsh.'

'Right. Same here. Given that this battle is probably over, shouldn't we start structuring some lines of defence in case of a counter-attack.'

'Yes. I suppose the enemy could be regrouping in Barikarn, ready for another attack. I very much doubt it though. They haven't got the numbers, and are unlikely to have those numbers again unless they abandon all of the cities they have taken or the Dark Emperor sends his last army from the north. Neither are likely to happen. But, it would be sensible of us to start building our defence now.' Taron looked around him at the soldiers standing in the water awaiting instruction. 'Yes. We should start our defence line here.' Taron paused. 'Where is Raiff?'

Gwaine searched for the right words. He knew Taron and Raiff had been close friends. Depression hung like a weight on his chest and made breathing difficult. 'He was killed, Taron. …I'm sorry.'

The muscles in Taron's jaw visibly tightened as he fought back the emotion. The storm passed quickly and within seconds Taron was his usual, businesslike self. 'Who is your Section Commander?'

Gwaine wondered how much damage a man could do to himself by bottling so much inside himself or, for that matter, just what a man's capacity was for the containment of grief before the container either overflowed or exploded. 'I am. I have no officers.'

Taron immediately scanned the surrounding soldiers. 'Traeg!'

A soldier about five metres away stood to attention. 'Yes, Commander.'

'You are now Section Commander. Choose two junior officers. One half of this force is to continue pursuing the enemy to the edge of the marsh. The other half is to form two lines of a defence. Send messengers to the right and left flanks to do the same.'

'Yes, Commander.' Traeg bowed before moving away, shouting orders.

Gwaine marvelled at the ease with which Taron caused things to happen and at his knowledge of his men's capabilities. 'We should get organised and put up a command tent.' Gwaine paused and looked around the watery forest. 'Um, ...somewhere!'

'Yes. You're right. There's really no need for us to walk all the way to Barikarn. We've secured the Fortress. We should stop being soldiers and start being leaders again.' Traeg hurried past and Taron yelled after him. 'Traeg, I want a command tent set up on the dividing ridge to the mud. Send messengers back to hurry our supply lines. They shouldn't be too far behind. And tell Prince Soran to join the Warlord and I there.'

‘Yes, Commander. I will.’ Traeg bowed as he moved off in an obvious fluster.

‘Do you think that he can handle all of these commands?’ Gwaine was concerned that their new Section Commander was already overloaded.

‘Yes. He’s capable’, Taron mumbled toward the water as he pulled his cloak around him and bustled despondently off in the direction of the mud. ‘Come on. Let’s get out of here. I’ve had enough for one day.’

Gwaine moved after Taron, feeling a bit like a young puppy that wasn’t part of his master’s thoughts. Eventually, he caught up with Taron but found it difficult to keep stride with his friend as they hurried back into the marsh. The quantity of bodies in the water and marsh was impossible to ignore and Gwaine soon found himself pondering the mammoth task of retrieval and burial.

‘I estimate that only about a half of the enemy’s force escaped’, Taron announced without prompting.

Gwaine closed his eyes and shook his head.

‘So that’s over sixty thousand dead of the Emperor’s army’, Taron continued. ‘And, I estimate that we lost about twenty thousand men. That’s eighty thousand that we have to find and bury.’

Gwaine fell further into his depression. He would have liked to answer Taron, but he couldn’t think of any comment that wasn’t stating the obvious. He placed his hands inside his cloak pockets and pulled the cloak around him. He felt the softness of the scarf in his pocket but it gave him little comfort and only served to remind him of a surreal world that was no longer his. He looked around the body littered water. This was his world now. This was reality.

‘If there is no counter-attack before tomorrow, I will organise ten thousand soldiers on each side of the marsh and instruct each man to retrieve and bury four bodies. We should clear the marsh in two days.’ Taron’s voice trailed off.

Gwaine looked across at his friend. Taron was empty. His organisational skills were in tact and operational, as always, but there was no emotion left. Gwaine prayed that it was just weariness and shock that was affecting Taron and that he would return to his usual self when he had rested and eventually moved out of the Fortress and back to the relative civilization of Raoul.

'I hope you won't mind', Gwaine replied, trying to take the conversation away from Taron's analytical practicality. 'But, I intend to use my position and rank so that I don't have to be involved in the aftermath clean up.'

'That's alright. I intend to use my rank to give the orders and then get to hell out of here while someone else does the dirty work. I'm going back to Raoul as soon as possible.'

'Good. You've done enough. You've saved Arrindare. Now, it's up to me to convince the Kings of my strategy to retake Amorand.' Gwaine paused. He wasn't convinced that his flimsy plan was really a strategy and he didn't think that it had any real chance of succeeding and he didn't know how he was going to convince the Kings that he should be allowed to do things his way. He looked up from the water into Taron's face. 'I will stay with you tomorrow until you have delegated your authority and then we will go to Raoul for the night. The next day, you shall come to Lasatal with me.'

A flicker of a smile showed on Taron's lips. 'If that is your command, my Lord, then I have no choice other than to obey.'

Gwaine smiled at Taron's reply. It was a faint glimmer of the old Taron. Perhaps his friend was going to be alright after all. Maybe he would never be the same as before. Gwaine paused as another thought struck him. Maybe they would, both, never be the same again. He couldn't see himself through other eyes to know whether he had changed. 'That is my command.'

Both fell silent in their own thoughts.

It wasn't until they were seated on the comparative dryness of the dividing ridge, awaiting the arrival of their tent and of Prince Soran, that their long silence was finally broken. The sun had obviously gone down and, with that, the air had turned ice cold. Both sat, shivering, in their wet clothes.

'Taron, I've got some bad news. Are you ready for it?'

Taron was seated with his arms resting on his knees, with his head nestled in his arms. A hardly noticeable shake of the head indicated that he'd had enough bad news and couldn't take any more.

'I gave the command to leave horses behind', Gwaine continued unperturbed by his friend's disinterest. 'There was a crock of wine in my saddlebag.'

For some minutes Taron and Gwaine sat in silence, so that Gwaine had long decided that he had been ignored, before Taron finally replied.

'Well, if you're not going to put on wine and entertainment, I'm certainly not going to give you a birthday present.'

A SHADOW OF A PLAN

Two days later, three pale, weary figures approached the city of Lasatal. Each studied, with some degree of anxiety, the scene that confronted them. The banners, lines of mounted soldiers and crowds of civilians indicated a full heroes welcome.

'We should have expected this', Gwaine remarked despondently as he wearily shook his head. 'They wouldn't let us just come home without putting on some sort of a show.'

'I'm not up to this', Taron announced in a strained, emotion filled voice.

Gwaine knew only too well how his friend felt. 'Don't worry, Taron. I will talk to the King. We can tone down the reception. The King will understand. I'm sure he won't want speeches or anything like that.'

The three of them had practically no sleep since the battle. They had found that every moment not spent awake was a torture of ghouls and spectres and dying faces. The horrors of the battle had replayed with every lapse into unconsciousness.

Stefarne, Kem and ten soldiers rode to meet them about a kilometre from the beginning of the throng of people.

'Congratulations, brother. We are all very proud of you.' Stefarne was repugnantly buoyant.

Gwaine forced himself to reply cordially before turning to Kem. 'Kem. Send a messenger to the King. Tell him, that I beg him to keep this to a minimum. We three are not well.' He could think of no other way of wording their condition.

'Rubbish, brother', Stefarne proclaimed excitedly. 'You shall receive full honours for your great service. There shall be no compromise in today's festivities.'

Gwaine ignored his brother and stared earnestly at Kem. Kem looked at the three faces before him and understood the exhaustion and depths of depression that were scored into them. He signalled to one of his soldiers who immediately sped off to deliver the message to the King.

They all watched the messenger speed toward Lasatal until he disappeared into the mêlée at the base of the mountain. Only then did Kem return his attention to his Warlord. He studied his Prince's face and then the faces of Taron and Soran. He had seen those eyes before, in the faces of soldiers who had seen and caused events that they didn't want to remember, but always would. When he finally spoke, it was with a quiet, calm voice that expressed understanding and sympathy.

'My Lords. We have been sent as your guard of honour. We shall fly your banners into Lasatal, as you have flown them into history. We have been given the honour of riding with the warriors who have thrown back our enemy and preserved our freedom.'

Kem's poetic words left Gwaine feeling ashamed. He didn't want this praise. He hadn't deserved it. He wasn't a hero. He was just a boy who had hacked and sweated his way through the mud of the Fortress of Marsh, feeling only fear and repulsion with every weary step.

'Thrown back our enemy?' Stefarne chirped loudly. 'You smeared his blood from one end of the Fortress to the other. The southern end of the Bay of Oracles changed colour with their blood. It was a massive route, a monumental victory.'

Gwaine glared at Stefarne. He could not ignore his brother's buoyant behaviour any longer. He was about to tear strips from Stefarne for his superficial view of the battle and its consequences when it suddenly occurred to him that he'd had a similar analytical conversation with Taron after Thale and Bartak had fought Qarad at the Radsey River. Thirty thousand soldiers had died in that battle, but Gwaine and Taron had only discussed the consequences as they affected the overall strategy of the war. Stefarne had never been in battle, as Taron and Gwaine had never been in a battle at that stage. Gwaine bit his lip and took a breath to quell his temper. 'Thank you, brother, for your welcome. We are all very tired.' Gwaine hoped, by that comment, that Stefarne would accept their tiredness as good reason to be less exuberant. 'And you must remember, Stefarne, that not all the blood that flowed to the Bay of Oracles was our enemy's.'

Stefarne changed visibly. He seemed to settle in his saddle as he took on a sombre countenance. 'Yes. Forgive me, Gwaine. I was so excited by the outcome that I momentarily forgot the cost.'

Gwaine was shocked. Was that really his older brother who had said that? Perhaps there was hope for him yet. He pondered the possibility of a changed Stefarne as they rode toward Lasatal, the banners flying overhead and the crowds cheering their return.

The corridor that led between the cheering crowds and columns of the Last Regiment finally ended at the Lasatal Gate. There stood King Daroyd with a smile that seemed to cover his entire face. Behind him stood the other six Kings, and, further back, were the Royal Families.

The bedlam of noise and movement ended moments after King Daroyd raised his arms as a signal for silence. When he was sure that all was still, King Daroyd sucked in a breath and boomed his voice to the surrounding crowd.

'The first stage is complete. Our combined armies have successfully defended Arrindare and have thrown our enemy back over our boundary. ...Today, we welcome home three weary but triumphant warriors. We ask nothing of them today except their good company. ...But, soon the second stage shall commence. Soon, we shall begin our assault on our enemy, who occupies the other Kingdoms of Amorand. ...Soon, they shall be driven back to their cursed Emperor. ...Today is a day of celebration, when we celebrate our first victory. ...There shall be many more days of celebration when we will celebrate many more victories.' Daroyd turned his attention to the three young men in front of him. 'Come. Welcome home to Lasatal. Enter our city. Greet your friends and loved ones.'

Gwaine nodded his appreciation to his father for the brief welcome as he and Taron and Soran moved through the gate to the sounds of the cheering crowds. Kem and Stefarne and the guard of honour followed closely.

They dismounted when they had passed through the gate and were immediately mobbed by family and friends. Gwaine found himself in his mother's embrace, receiving a periodic kiss and embrace from Ellorn as she alternated between him and Taron. Soran was similarly preoccupied with the attention of his own family until emotions subsided enough for the entire group to begin the walk to the castle.

Only metres further on, Tanya and Susanne stood before them, curtsied and welcomed them home, but were soon engulfed by the mass of well-wishers surrounding them.

Gwaine was disappointed by their brief appearance until he realised that, in this highly public place, Tanya and Susanne could have done no more than they had done, even if they had had the opportunity to be more familiar.

Finally at the castle, the throng was reduced to family as Taron and Gwaine were led to a small reception room attached to the main Banquet Hall. Gwaine peered through the last small opening in the doorway as King Daroyd pulled it shut behind him. Daroyd gave him a quizzical look.

'We seem to have lost Prince Soran', Gwaine replied.

'Oh!' Daroyd laughed. 'No. We haven't lost him. His family has taken him to their quarters in much the same way that we are being selfish with you two.' He threw himself into a chair and motioned for Gwaine and Taron to be seated. Stefarne, Ellorn and Lenore joined them at the end of the large dining table. 'Now, how are you both?'

Gwaine and Taron stared at each other, searching for a response that would quickly sum up their conditions.

‘Oh, ...we’re alright’, Gwaine finally answered with a shrug of his shoulders, and then as an afterthought he added, ‘We could do with a good sleep though.’ Gwaine was amazed at his blithe response. He would have liked to say much more about his problems.

Daroyd gave them both a long searching look. ‘A battle of the magnitude of the one you have just fought must be very physically and emotionally draining. ...Quite a traumatic experience, ...I would have thought.’

‘Yes, Sire’, Taron replied enthusiastically. He had perceived a sympathetic ear. ‘It is impossible to sleep without reliving the horror of the battle.’ He pulled himself up quickly and cautioned himself that this wasn’t the way for a warrior to behave.

King Daroyd nodded knowingly. ‘Yes, Taron. That is normal. You need not be afraid to express your problems. ...What of you Gwaine? Are you sleeping well?’

‘No, my Lord. I have the same problem as Taron.’ Gwaine had no desire to hide his emotional strain from his father. He needed to talk to someone.

‘Of course you have. You are not heartless. You are caring young men. Wars and battles cannot be rationalised and explained away.’ Daroyd stopped and looked around him, at his family, before returning his attention to the conversation. ‘We have other matters to discuss now, but tomorrow you shall both come to my room and we shall discuss the battle. In the meantime, I want you both to know that I am proud of you. You have saved Arrindare. Though, how we retrieve the rest of Amorand is anyone’s guess. ...Or, I should say ‘is Gwaine’s guess’. Do you have a plan Gwaine?’

‘Yes, my Lord. Though, I don’t think that you or the other Kings will like it.’

‘Well, I’m sure that I don’t like the present situation. Any plan will be an improvement. When do you want to talk to the Kings?’

‘As soon as possible. I’m keen to get it over with.’

‘Very well. There is food and wine on the way. You two enjoy yourselves. Lenore will see to your comfort, I’m sure. I will organise a meeting with the Kings.’ Daroyd was already walking to the door. ‘Taron! Be careful. I’m sure Ellorn will try to talk you into a riding lesson.’

‘Thank you, Sire. I will be on my guard.’

Gwaine’s time with his family flew all too quickly. After two short, relaxing hours, he found himself locked in the Hall of the Council of Kings facing the Kings’ Table, where the seven Kings of Amorand were seated. Only Magnor was invited into the room before the huge wooden doors were pushed closed and sealed.

An eternity later, the Kings finally stopped whispering among themselves and recognised the young Warlord standing before them. It was Daroyd who opened the proceedings.

‘Once again, our congratulations on your victory, Warlord. With Arrindare now safe from the Dark Emperor’s grasp, we anxiously await the disclosure of your plan for driving his forces from the remainder of Amorand.’

Silence fell on the large room while Gwaine tried desperately to suppress his nervousness and collect together all of the well rehearsed sentences of the speech that he had planned. Before he could utter a word, however, King Fenore interjected.

‘Before you begin any explanation of any plan, Warlord, it is necessary for us to be aware of the relative strengths of the armies, so that we can consider your plan in the light of our relative strengths and weaknesses. Do you have that information?’

‘I have the basic position as far as numbers, my Lord.’ Gwaine was pleased with the diversion. At least he could warm up with figures that he knew, before he tried to explain the rather vague and hypothetical outline of his plan. ‘As you are aware, the Dark Emperor has kept a full army of seventy thousand in the north. The two armies that he dispatched southward, totalling one hundred and forty thousand, has been reduced to below seventy thousand. A large part of the credit for that should go to King Thale and King Bartak for their magnificent defence of the Radsey. Against those numbers we now have seventy five thousand, not counting the Last Regiment who are employed in coastal surveillance of Arrindare as well as ensuring your personal safety and the safety of the Royal Families.'

'So, we now outnumber our enemy in the south', King Thale added excitedly.

Gwaine panicked a little as he wondered just what this old King would have him do now that this slight numerical advantage was known to him. The excitement in his voice indicated that Gwaine should now have no difficulty in storming every fortification in Amorand and chasing his enemy back over his borders. He searched for words that would quell King Thale's excitement. 'Only for a brief period, my Lord. I am sure that the Dark Emperor will dispatch part of his remaining army from the north to secure his grip on Amorand.'

'Why would he do that?' came King Tyne's voice in a relaxed, even tone. 'Even given our insignificant supremacy of numbers, it would appear that our enemy's grip on our land is far too tight for us to prise it open. He holds all of our major fortified cities. You could lose your entire army just by laying siege to one of those cities. The Dark Emperor is well in control of our six Kingdoms. Why would he dispatch part of his domestic force and weaken his control over his own people?'

'Because I would make him, King Tyne.' Gwaine was ecstatic. This question and answer approach to his plan was working much better than his rehearsed speech could ever have done. 'Because I want him to send part of that force south.'

'My dear boy', King Fenore interrupted in his best condescending tone. 'I would think that you have enough problems with the number of our enemy already in Amorand. Why would you want more? And, even if you did want them, the Dark Emperor is not likely to do something just because you want it to happen. He has sufficient of his soldiers in our territory. He does not need to send more. So, why should he?'

'Because, as I said my Lord, I would make him. The first stage of my plan is to make the Dark Emperor uncertain and insecure as to his ability to hold Amorand with his present numbers.'

There was visible movement at the Kings' Table. Gwaine had their interest. King Tyne leant forward across the table. 'How would you do that, Warlord?'

'Who cares!' King Bartak roared from the end of the table. 'We don't want more enemy soldiers in our land. We want less. Have you forgotten what we are trying to do, boy? We are trying to throw our enemy out of Amorand. Not invite more in.'

'That is my eventual aim, my Lord.' Gwaine was getting annoyed. This was the second King who had called him ***boy***. 'When you have heard my ***full*** plan, you will understand. But, we are getting too far ahead.' Gwaine turned his attention back to King Tyne and quelled his temper. King Tyne, at least, had shown an active interest in hearing his plan. 'The Dark Emperor's security and strength in Amorand, rests in the knowledge that he holds, and can continue to hold, our fortified cities. His largest force, as a result of his retreat from the Fortress of Marsh, is at Martren. I can take Martren.'

'Madness!' came the exasperated growl from King Bartak as he slapped the table and assumed an arms folded posture, indicating annoyance with the boy who stood before him.

The excited interest in King Tyne's eyes turned to disappointment. He withdrew back across the table and looked disappointedly at his Warlord, as did all of the other Kings. 'You cannot take Martren. ...Or, if you could, you would lose most of your army in the process and the enemy would retake the city in no time. All would be lost.'

King Tyne's quiet, controlled voice contrasted sharply with that of King Raynor's. 'You cannot take Martren', he yelled. 'My city is a magnificent fortress. You would lose your entire army on the slopes of my mountain.'

‘Your city is a magnificent fortress, my Lord, with a monumental weakness’, Gwaine replied calmly.

King Raynor’s face turned red with rage. ‘Then tell me, Warlord...’ he called in a voice that seethed with cold anger, ‘What is the weakness of my city?’

Gwaine smiled. He knew he had won. It couldn’t have gone better. ‘It has a secret underground passage that leads from the base of the mountain into the lower catacombs of your castle.’

‘Gibberish!’ came King Raynor’s angry reply.

‘Hold, Raynor.’ King Daroyd interrupted. ‘Gwaine. Are you referring to the tunnels mentioned in the legends?’

‘Yes, my Lord.’

‘Gwaine, that was five or six centuries ago. King ...um ...what’s his name? ...The King of Barikarn at the time dug the tunnel to break a long siege. The legends say that he sent some of his soldiers out through it to outflank his enemy. ...Was he at war with Cadel or Tayle? I’m not sure now. Magnor, you must know.’

‘Yes, my King’, Magnor spoke for the first time. ‘The legends say that Barikarn was at war with Cadel and that the tunnel was dug to break the siege of Martren. The manoeuvre didn’t work, but the siege eventually collapsed anyway.’

‘It’s only legend, though. Isn’t it? There were no records kept at that stage. It’s unlikely to be true.’

‘The tunnels exist, my Lord.’ Gwaine was throwing everything into his words now. He passionately wanted to convince the Kings. Everything hinged on this point. ‘I have found the opening. I have been inside the tunnels. They are huge and cavernous - natural caverns joined by man-made tunnels, chipped out of stone in most cases. I have had soldiers inside, moving rock falls and clearing disintegrated sections of the tunnels. The tunnels are there and they are now ready to use.’

King Daroyd turned to King Raynor. 'Given that the tunnels are there, what sort of defence could the Dark Emperor's force put up?'

King Raynor's reply was subdued. 'They would have little care for our meagre siege. They would go to bed laughing at us. If our force was large enough and approached with stealth, most of our enemy would die in their beds.'

'Hardly the way to fight a war', King Thale remarked disgustedly.

Gwaine understood the remark. It echoed his own disturbed conscience. 'No, my Lord. But we are desperate to win.'

'Yes. If we held Martren', King Vole remarked hopefully, '...we would be one step closer to retaking my castle in Cadel.'

'No, my Lord', Gwaine replied quickly. 'I'm sorry. We could not hope to hold Martren. If we left soldiers there, our enemy would lay siege and those soldiers would be isolated. They would be of as little use to us, as they would be dead. We would have to withdraw our force immediately, to Arrindare. Remember, we are only trying to make the Dark Emperor feel insecure so that he will send more soldiers.'

'Why!' King Bartak screamed in exasperation. 'Why would you want more soldiers in Amorand?'

'Because my Lord, ...my Lords…' Gwaine looked from one face to the next along the line of Kings to ensure that he had every man's complete attention. 'I will be in the North Continent, stirring mayhem and rebellion against the Dark Emperor.'

The room fell silent. Gwaine tried to look at all of the faces at once to see the effect of his plan. His father was smiling.

'Yes. This is a plan.' King Daroyd smiled thoughtfully and stroked his chin before turning his attention to Gwaine. 'Well done, Warlord.'

'It won't work' King Fenore dived in to de-wind Gwaine's sails. 'How is this boy going to stir up rebellion? And who would stand up against the Dark Emperor?'

‘There is a King in the far north mountains of the Northern Continent. He is called Moridare. He lives on a huge mountain plateau. His people are self-sufficient and have never been conquered.’

‘Then why hasn’t the Dark Emperor conquered them?’ King Fenore queried disbelievingly. ‘Are you saying that he can’t?’

‘No. I am saying that their mountain fortress is a strong enough deterrent for the Dark Emperor not to have bothered losing large numbers of his soldiers in conquering a King who sends him tribute and recognises him as Emperor.’

If this King is subservient to the Dark Emperor, then why would he help you to fight against him?’

‘Our spies say that he does not like being subservient, ...that he is an ambitious man who would like the title of ‘Emperor’ for himself. I will offer him the opportunity of that title. I will offer him a much-depleted army to fight against. The more enemy soldiers that I can attract to Amorand, the easier will be my task in the north. That’s why Martren is so important. If an Amorand force can take Martren, then the Dark Emperor will be left in doubt as to the security of his grip on all of the cities that he holds.’

‘But…’ King Tyne stopped, obviously trying to assemble his thoughts. ‘But, if you do stir up rebellion, the Dark Emperor will only withdraw the same number as he dispatched. We could be no better off.’

‘That is one possibility, my Lord. But, it depends on just how much damage I can cause while that force is in the south. Rebellion is a disease. Once started, it grows uncontrollably. Particularly against an evil ruler such as the Dark Emperor. If I am successful, I believe our enemy’s numbers in Amorand will be greatly reduced. If I can destroy the Dark Emperor, you will see our enemy running from our land without mounting another defence against our combined armies.’

‘And what chance do you put on your success, Warlord?’

Gwaine stood quietly considering his answer. If he answered optimistically, the Kings would laugh at him and reject him as a dreamer. If his answer were too pessimistic, then the Kings would reject his plan. He had to be careful. 'If I cannot convince Moridare of his chance to defeat the Dark Emperor, then he is likely to present my head to the Dark Emperor as his next tribute. If I can convince him, then it might well mean, at worst, a loosening of our enemy's grip and, at best, the end of the Dark Emperor. It all depends on how persuasive I can be.'

King Tyne gave a friendly laugh. 'Well if that is what we are relying on, then Amorand is saved and the Dark Emperor is as good as dead. You have convinced me of the plan.' He turned to the other Kings. 'I support this strategy. What say the rest of you?'

'No', King Fenore roared. 'This is foolishness. It cannot work.'

'We will have a vote', King Daroyd interrupted. 'There is obviously a division of opinion. Raise your hand, all those who agree with the execution of this plan.

'Gwaine shrunk at the term 'execution'. He wished his father would be more careful with his choice of words, but he was pleased to see King Daroyd and King Tyne immediately raise their hands. There was no movement from the other five and Gwaine's spirits fell. He had lost, after all his planning and persuasive talk.

Slowly, King Raynor raised his hand. 'I am keen to see my city of Martren awash with the blood of my enemy.'

Gwaine tried to force a smile. King Raynor's poor excuse for raising his hand was his way of giving support to the entire plan. But, he had still lost by one vote. Gwaine was about to concede defeat, when King Vole suddenly raised his hand. Gwaine hadn't expected support from King Vole and the surprise must have shown in his face.

King Vole gave him an amused smile and explained. 'Prince Soran speaks highly of your abilities. I will trust his judgement.'

‘Then so be it’, King Daroyd replied excitedly. ‘The plan is approved. When do you leave, Warlord?’

‘A ship waits for me at Port, my Lord. I shall sail tomorrow morning.’

‘No.’ Magnor’s voice from behind startled Gwaine and he visibly jumped. ‘I have much to tell you that may be of assistance in your endeavour. We will meet tomorrow morning. You cannot sail before the following day.’

‘Very good, my Lord. We will meet tomorrow morning.’ Gwaine would have preferred to begin his journey as soon as possible. He was disappointed that Magnor had delayed his departure.

‘Good’, Daroyd stated in a tone that implied an ending. ‘This meeting of Kings is over. Good luck, Warlord. All hope for Amorand goes with you.’

IN THE NORTH

Leaning on the ship's rail, Gwaine tried to discern the distant shoreline in the darkness. After weeks of sailing, out of the sight of land, the hardly audible sound of waves crashing on the rocks of an unknown beach heralded a renewed fear and foreboding within him. In a short while, the captain would becalm his ship, only long enough for Gwaine to slip over the side, before moving his ship further to the west, out of sight of land, to return to Arrindare. Gwaine would be left alone to find his way to shore and safety, before beginning his overland trek to the mountain castle where King Moridare would decide his fate and the possible fate of Amorand.

Gwaine groped through his pack to ensure that he hadn't forgotten anything, before throwing it onto his back and securing the straps. He then rummaged through the pockets of the cloak that Magnor had given him. Everything seemed to be in place - even the scarf that Tanya had given him before the battle for the Fortress.

With nothing more to do until the ship had stopped, Gwaine allowed his mind to stray. He thought of the battle and his meeting with the seven Kings to discuss his plan. 'What plan?' he asked himself. 'Fenore was right. It won't work. Moridare will cut my head off rather than talk to me. That is, if I don't get taken by a shark or bashed senseless against a rock and drown. Or, if the Dark Emperor's soldiers don't catch me before I reach the mountains.'

Gwaine grimaced at the morbid possibilities. He shook his head and forced his mind to move on. He thought of his last meeting with Magnor. It was Magnor who had told him of Tanya. No one else had apparently been game. 'Strange', he thought to himself. 'Magnor told me so much in that meeting. The trivial gossip about Tanya shouldn't rate a thought by comparison.'

'Her parents have offered her hand to Stefarne', he had said in his usual nonchalant manner. Only the state of the fight against the Dark Emperor seemed to interest Magnor. The lives and loves of the people around him had no effect on that fight and, therefore, rated no priority or concern. Only when Gwaine had not answered, did he show any regard for Gwaine's feelings. 'Does that affect you?' he had asked.

'It affects me', Gwaine had replied, fighting back his emotion and anger at Magnor's style of announcement. 'But, it should not. She is above my station. I always knew that. She shall marry a King, ...like Stefarne. ...That would explain why I haven't been able to talk to her without being surrounded by chaperones. I thought she would have told me, though.'

'Oh, I don't think she knows. Her parents haven't told her yet. You can be sure, though, that you will not have any possibility of talking to her before you leave.'

Magnor had been right. All attempts to contact Tanya, to get a farewell message to her had failed. Gwaine had run into a wall of guards, chaperones and tall stories before time had finally run out and he had to leave for Port. In the last, he left a note with Ellorn in the hope that she could deliver his farewell message.

'This is as close as I can safely go to the shore.' The captain's quiet announcement, over Gwaine's shoulder, startled him back to the present. The present? Magnor had even taken that away from him.

'Very well. Bring the ship to rest at your discretion. I have no better idea of this coastline than you have. Wherever you stop is a gamble.'

'Yes, my Lord. I will round this next point and see if I can find somewhere that looks promising.' The captain bowed slightly before moving away.

The present? Gwaine recalled a conversation with Magnor that now seemed an eternity in the past. Gwaine had been foolish enough to state his intention of living for the present. 'The past is only for historians', he had told Magnor. 'And no one has ever promised me a future. I could be slain tomorrow. I will live for the present.'

Magnor had smiled in reply. 'Did you just say that?' he had asked with a twinkle in his eye.

'Pardon?' Gwaine was often baffled by Magnor's questions.

'Did you just say that you ***will live for the present***?'

'Of course I did', Gwaine had replied in bewilderment.

'And when you said it, we were in the present.'

'That's correct.'

'Then why are we talking about it in the past tense?'

'Because it happened', Gwaine had replied irritably.

'Because it happened in the past', Magnor added with a wicked, winning grin. 'There is no present. It is a fleeting delusion. This is the past. In the split moment of recognition of what is called ***present***, it becomes the past. Time stampedes forward, Gwaine. Put your trust in the future, promised or not, for it is your only chance of having any control over your life.'

Gwaine thought of the change that conversation had made to his life. Magnor's philosophy may have been correct or it may have been one of his cunning tricks, but Gwaine had become a planner, a strategist, from that day.

Gwaine spun around as he heard the sails being wound down. His heart quickened in tempo. This was obviously where he got off. Two of the crew lifted a log onto the rail and allowed it to fall into the water. The short length of rope that had been tied to it groaned against the ship as it became taught and pulled the log behind. This was Gwaine's vehicle to shore. The log would provide buoyancy as Gwaine paddled toward the crashing surf. It would prevent him being pulled under by the weight of his clothes and provisions, and it could easily be discarded on the shore without raising any of the questions that an abandoned boat would have.

The captain stood at his side as the boat slowed. 'All is ready, Warlord.'

'Yes. Thank you, captain. I wish you a safe return journey.' Gwaine clambered over the side of the ship and secured his feet in the netting that draped down to the water. With his head just above the railing, he took a last glimpse of the ship and its captain. 'Tell the King that all is going well.'

'I will, my Lord. May the Gods go with you.'

Gwaine nodded his final farewell before climbing down the rope and lowering himself into the water. It was surprisingly warm, a stark contrast to what the water temperature would have been in the southern latitudes around Arrindare.

The crewmen pulled on the rope to manoeuvre the log alongside Gwaine. Supporting his weight on the log, he immediately set about untying the rope. He recalled the panic of the last time he had tied a knot - in his weight belt before entering the waterfall hole in search of Baradetch's sword. His luck with knots didn't seem to have improved. This one put up a good battle before finally giving up and releasing its hold on his log. Without looking back, he started paddling toward the sound of the surf. Seconds later he heard the sound of the winches as the ship's crew wound the sails into position and the captain set his ship to the west.

The moonless sky may have been perfect for sneaking a ship near their enemy's coastline, but it was certainly a hindrance to Gwaine as he tried to discern the location of that same coastline. In almost total blackness and in waters that he did not know, Gwaine tried to convince himself that the sound of the surf was getting louder. After a great deal of worry, it gradually became obvious that the noise was, in fact, getting louder. He was paddling in the correct direction. Some time later, the worry returned as it became evident that the noise was getting far too loud.

There were rocks nearby. The swell was getting higher and he was starting to feel some backwash from the rocks.

The rocks were obviously directly ahead, but whether safety was to the left or to the right was anybody's guess. Being on the right side of his log, Gwaine took the gamble and immediately started paddling the log frantically to the left. It was hard going with the water becoming more turbulent with the passing seconds. He gasped for breaths between waves breaking over his head as he considered the urge to ditch his log and swim. Common sense prevailed over his panic, however, and he decided that he would have little chance of survival without the log's buoyancy. His clothes and provisions were simply too heavy and waterlogged for him to survive in this rough surf.

Eventually he came upon calmer water. His breath came in gusts as he clutched his log and rested from his exertion. The sound of the waves on the rocks were now on his right and were being steadily overpowered by the surf's noise ahead of him. The swell was increasing again. 'More rocks', he told himself as he listened to the growing noise. He took a deep breath and breathed a sigh of relief as he discerned the sound as more of a gentle, rolling roar than the previous clash of waves against rocks.

He felt himself lifted and cast forward by the power of a wave. As the wave's power ebbed and it began to retreat to the sea, his feet momentarily touched the ground. A second later another wave picked him up and broke with a crash, spilling him and his log in a tangle of subaqua gymnastics. Releasing the log, Gwaine struggled to find his footing as the wave retreated to sea to regain its lost energy. Finally finding his feet, he was suddenly hit in the back by another wave and cast forward into the side of the log. This time, retaining his footing, he struggled through the water to the shore and up onto dry sand.

Gwaine peered toward the horizon in search of a sail against the dark sky. He could see none. He was on his own now, with no hope of support. Turning his back to the sea, he carefully found his way to the cliffs and sought out a small cave that would provide protection from 'the all-seeing eyes' that Magnor had described.

'Do not think yourself safe from the Dark Emperor's gaze, no matter what the distance between you', he had warned. 'He has the means to see you from the sky. His vision is blinded only in the dark of night and when you are under cover, so that you cannot see the sky, ...and it cannot see you.'

Gwaine had not believed Magnor's magician's talk and had told him so, but Magnor had become so agitated and insistent that Gwaine had finally agreed to heed his warning.

'Promise me', Magnor had insisted. 'Promise me, as a Prince of Arrindare and as a warrior, that you will travel only under cover of dark while you can, and that during the day you will not let the sky see you.'

Gwaine studied his tutor. Magnor was getting old. Perhaps his old brain had spent too long studying the ancient legends and fables.

'Promise me', Magnor screamed in frantic, desperate tones.

In the end, Gwaine had promised, in order to appease Magnor.

'Now that you have doubled, or possibly tripled, the duration of my march to Moridare, please explain to me how I will always avoid going out into daylight.' Gwaine had hoped that Magnor would see the impossibility of the promise that he had forced, and capitulate. Surely, he would see sense and release Gwaine from his vow. Magnor's reply had left him in no doubt as to his master's lost grip on sanity.

'If you have to go out in daylight, it can only be out of desperation and for a short period and …you must wear this cloak and hood.' Magnor handed him an extremely large cloak that was mainly mat black in colour with thick diagonal bands of silver. It seemed more metallic than material.

Gwaine couldn't help himself. He had to ask. 'Where's my pointed cap?' To make things worse, he couldn't control the humour in his voice. He should have died under Magnor's black stare, and his sense of humour quickly departed.

'This cloak', Magnor continued dryly, '...will protect you from his gaze. His all-seeing eyes will not see this cloak. In it you will become his blind spot. Only the two eyes in his head will be able to see this cloak.'

'Yes, and the eyes of everyone I walk within five kilometres of. Can't the colour be altered to something that will blend with my surroundings?'

'The colour and material are its active ingredients. It is they that cause the blind spot in the Dark Emperor's gaze.'

Gwaine had thought himself condemned to night travel until he struck on a loophole. 'If, in the cloak, I cannot be seen, then I can travel during daylight.'

'No. A blindspot that is always moving is soon visible. You have promised, Warlord.'

Gwaine recalled his depression at that point and his resignation to travel at night, as he had promised. He rummaged through his pack, searching for some food. This small cave would be his home for the next sixteen hours or so. Only hours to daylight, it was much too late now to strike out across country. He would have to wait for night to fall again.

Magnor's magician's talk and warnings rambled through his brain. 'Surely, Magnor cannot believe all of this', he told himself. 'A magic wand that throws lightning and kills an enemy from a distance, ...a castle that floats above a fiery pit, ...rocks and dirt that turn to flames when touched, ...unseen eyes that see an enemy that is out of sight.' It was all too absurd. Magnor had obviously dreamed up these scary stories to make Gwaine even more cautious. 'I wish he wouldn't treat me like a child. He could have just told me to be careful.'

Gwaine moved forward and peered out through the cave opening. The sky was brightening. He scanned the small arc of horizon that was visible to him and thought of the ship and its crew, on their homeward journey to Arrindare. He felt very lonely. 'May the Gods go with you', echoed in his mind. 'Funny how the mariners always have more than one god. They rely too much on the elements not to include gods of the seas and winds. Lucky Taron hadn't heard the captain's parting words though. God knows what Taron would have replied with.

'Gwaine tried to visualise Taron. He thought of the good times they had shared and the trouble they had stirred together. He wished it could have always been like that, but the battle had changed them both. Taron was still in deep depression when Gwaine had left for Port. 'How will he take his transfer?' Gwaine shook his head and sighed as he remembered the decision that he and Magnor had made. Taron's mental state had worried them both. He deserved a break anyway. Taron had done his job - he had defended the Fortress. It was only fitting that he be promoted to Commander of the Last Regiment. Kem would get his wish. He was to be transferred to Commander of the combined army, in Gwaine's absence. Gwaine hoped that Taron would accept and enjoy his new position at Lasatal. He was sure that Kem would enjoy his new responsibility.

To maintain the absolute secrecy of their plan to take the fortifications of Martren, Magnor had taken charge of arrangements. Without even Kem's knowing, a section of the Last Regiment would have entered the passages and hopefully surprised their enemy. It frustrated Gwaine that the battle would have been fought and decided by now, but he had no way of knowing the outcome. If the plan had not worked then he was sitting, soaked to the skin, in this cave for nothing. He would walk into Moridare's castle with no bargaining point. He would die.

Gwaine shuddered. This line of thought was getting him nowhere. He drew his pack under his head and tried to settle down for a day's sleep. Tonight he would begin his march toward Moridare's mountain plateau.

THE CURSE OF THE SWORD

After ten nights of torturously slow progress, Gwaine was finally on the slopes of Moridare's mountains.

Crawling from sparse cover to sparse cover, he weaved his way tenuously, slowly, up the mountain toward the large fortified city above him.

Only halfway to his goal, covered in mud and grime, Gwaine was forced to come to a halt. It wasn't the weariness of the long, difficult journey that had pulled him up short, though the pain in his groaning muscles had certainly reached a level that demanded a rest. Above and beyond that pain and weariness, though, two spears hovering ominously above his head, suggested the wisdom of a halt to all movement.

Gwaine lay motionless on the ground, staring up into the grim faces of the two mountain warriors. They had obviously studied the pattern of his ascent and waited in silence for him to move into the cover that they had occupied.

For some moments, only Gwaine's erratic breathing disturbed the silence on the mountain. Finally, he decided that it was up to him to break that silence. He took a deep breath to gain control over his breathing and his nerves.

'I am Prince Gwaine of Arrindare', he stated in his most royal voice. 'I seek an audience with your King.'

His captors weren't impressed. Gwaine wasn't surprised. It was an absurd comment to make, given the situation. He searched for another way to explain his presence on their mountain, but couldn't think of a plausible excuse. It didn't matter anyway. Without a word, the mountain warriors soon had his arms tied behind his back, Baradetch's sword was taken from him and he was marched up the mountain, toward the city.

'At least I've been captured by the correct army', Gwaine consoled himself. 'If I had to be clumsy, it is better for it to happen here than in the Dark Emperor's domains.' And it felt good to be able to march upright after all those nights of crawling and, at best, darting in a stooped run between cover.

He was marched, in silence, up the mountain and through the city gates. Gwaine looked above the city toward the night sky. The mountain continued ever upward. Perhaps the plateau was above them. It was certainly a very defendable mountain. No wonder the Dark Emperor had left these people to their own devices, so long as he received tribute and their pledge of loyalty.

Gwaine was taken to the castle and brought before the warrior's officer.

'We found him sneaking up the mountain, sir', the larger of the two warriors reported. 'He claims to be a Prince, seeking an audience with the King.'

The officer broke into laughter. When he had recovered, he turned his attention fully on Gwaine. 'Pardon me, my Lord Prince' he begged sarcastically. 'We don't have many royal visitors here. Though, I have always imagined that, if we were visited by royalty, they would ride up to our city on fine horses, dressed in fine robes.' He scanned Gwaine's form, slowly, from head to toe. 'While, on the other hand, you sneak up our mountain like an assassin, dressed like the local pig farmer.' His mood suddenly changed for the worse. 'Now, tell me who you are, before I lose my patience.'

Gwaine wished himself home. ...There was nothing he could do but put on a bold face and try to bluff his way through. He straightened his back and stared the officer in the eye.

'I am Prince Gwaine of Arrindare, Warlord of the Seven Kings of Amorand. I seek an audience with King Moridare. Are you the senior officer?'

The officer was obviously perplexed. Gwaine's manner was certainly not that of a pig farmer, but he was far from convinced. 'You have gall, assassin, but the truth will make your death simpler and less painful. We have special deaths for silver-tongued liars.'

Magnor had warned Gwaine of the code under which these people lived. Their word was their honour, and any person found lying was considered to be without honour. Banishment or death was not uncommon punishments for lying. Magnor had warned 'Beware that you are not found out if you tell Moridare anything that is untrue. He will kill you, no matter how great his desire to be Emperor.'

Gwaine fought to maintain his composure as he stared coolly at the warrior before him. 'I am Warlord', he retorted in feigned anger. 'Now, fetch your superior officer so that I may arrange a meeting with your King.'

The officer stood his ground and returned Gwaine's glare. 'Very well', he finally conceded. He motioned to one of the warriors who immediately left the room. 'You shall meet my superior officer. I warn you, though, he does not have the same friendly character as I. You shall regret having him called.'

Gwaine waited in silence for at least five minutes while the officer sat at his desk playing with his dagger and idly studying his strange captive. Finally, the soldier reappeared with a large, red-haired man who looked to be well into his fifties.

The younger officer rose from his seat and bowed to his superior. 'My Lord Harn. I apologise for disturbing you. This boy has been caught sneaking up our mountain. He claims to be the Warlord of the Kings of Amorand and demands an audience with our King.'

Harn studied the captive before uttering any word to his officer. 'I have no time for this foolishness', he remarked almost casually. 'Kill him.'

The hair stood up on the back of Gwaine's neck. This was it. It had all been for nothing. In desperation, he searched for something that would alter the decision. Harn was already at the doorway. 'Your King shall have your head when he discovers your stupidity.'

Harn stopped at the doorway and turned. It appeared that he was about to reply to Gwaine's abuse, but thinking better of it, he turned to leave, before stopping again and facing Gwaine. 'If you are truly the Warlord, then answer me this. Where did your army first resist the Dark Emperor's invasion?'

Gwaine's reply was immediate. 'At the Radsey River, the border between Radrath and Seyldrek.'

Harn nodded almost imperceptibly as he acknowledged the correctness of the answer. He took a single step back into the room.

'Who were the opposing Commanders in the battle for the Fortress of Mud?'

Gwaine smiled at the subtle trap. 'In the battle for the Fortress of Marsh, Qarad led the Dark Emperor's forces. My Commander of the Fortress Guard was Taron.'

Harn's eyes narrowed. He moved further into the room. 'Who slew Qarad?'

'I did', came Gwaine's instant, cold reply.

Harn studied Gwaine in silence, while Gwaine stood unflinchingly and returned his gaze. Finally, Harn nodded thoughtfully and uttered, as if to himself, 'Yes, you could be the Warlord. This information is not easily obtained.' In a louder voice that was obviously meant to finalise the issue one way or the other, Harn asked 'Can you prove your identity?'

'I carry a letter that is signed and sealed by the seven Kings of Amorand. If your King can recognise any of those seals, then my identity is proved.'

'He may be able to identify them', Harn remarked less than convinced. 'Do you have any other proof?'

Gwaine had only one card left to play. 'My tutor, Magnor, tells me that your warriors were so impressed by the Warlord, Baradetch, that they gathered together every detail they could find on his life and legends and armoury. We are told there exists a small library and museum to his honour as a warrior.'

'That is correct', Harn replied. 'How does this help you?'

'In that library, his sword is drawn and described in minute detail.'

'Yes.' Harn was getting impatient.

'Then you need only compare that detail with that sword.' Gwaine nodded toward the sword in the hands of the soldier who had disarmed him. 'That is the sword of Baradetch.'

The soldier let out a blood-curdling scream that sent a chill through Gwaine's bones. The sword fell to the floor.

Visibly perspiring, the soldier looked ashamedly at his officers. He bowed his head. 'Forgive me. I...' His voice trailed off. He was searching for an explanation. Finding none that was satisfactory, he bowed again. 'Forgive me.'

He received no reply. All four warriors simply stood and stared at the sword that lay on the floor.

It was Harn who finally disrupted the eerie silence. In a low voice, that was less than convincing, he instructed the soldier to pick up the sword. The soldier only looked pitifully at his Commander with a face that pleaded for a release from the command.

'I said, pick it up'. Harn had regained his composure and his authoritative voice. 'Are you some child, frightened by tales of magic and curses? ...Are you a mountain warrior?'

The derision had its effect. The warrior straightened his back before stepping forward and quickly swooping the sword from the floor. Once in his grasp, however, the sword, or the tales of its curse, exerted an influence over the man that turned him pale and stooped in posture. He turned to Gwaine. 'Is it true that whoever takes Baradetch's sword, dies before the next daybreak?'

The voice was so pitiful that Gwaine felt sorry for the warrior. He had heard tales of the curse but had always put them down to fanciful stories, part of the pagentry of the legends. He would have told him so, given the opportunity.

'Enough of this', Harn commanded. 'We have not proved this boy to be the Warlord. He may yet die an assassin's death before midnight.' Harn turned to Gwaine. 'Where is this sealed letter?'

'In my backpack.'

Immediately, the other warrior began undoing the straps of his pack. After rummaging through its contents, the warrior found the letter and presented it to Harn.

Harn studied the seven seals while he addressed his junior officer. 'You will take our 'Warlord' and your two warriors to the anteroom of the Throne Room. You will talk to no one! I shall meet you there with the King and his ministers. They shall confirm or deny the authenticity of these seals and that sword. Now go!'

Gwaine was led out of the room and through a maze of corridors and stairways. They marched in silence through the most magnificent castle he had ever been in, until finally they entered a room with large embroidered lounges, silk tapestries and gold statues.

They did not have to wait long before the two large wooden doors were flung open by an ageing man in black robes. He motioned for them to enter the Throne Room.

As Gwaine walked into the large hall, he scanned the small gathering that surrounded the throne. Harn was there with two warriors of similar age and build. Two men in black robes (presumably the King's advisers), similar to the old man who walked before them, were standing just below the throne, talking to King Moridare. One of them held Gwaine's sealed letter.

'I hope at least one of our Amorand neighbours has traded with this castle in the last few centuries.' Gwaine's thoughts represented his slim chance of acceptance as the Warlord of Amorand. If King Moridare's advisers did not have any records of any of the seals, then there was little chance of proving his identity. Baradetch's sword was unlikely to prove anything. After all, apart from its peculiar colour, it was only a plain sword.

The old adviser brought them to a halt about five metres from the throne. Harn and his two warriors moved between them and the throne, while the old adviser took up a position behind Gwaine. Gwaine bowed before the King.

'Greetings King Moridare. I am Prince Gwaine, Warlord of the Seven Kings of Amorand.'

'Yes', King Moridare replied with a touch of surprise in his voice. 'That does appear to be so. My advisers have recognised two of the seals on your letter.'

Gwaine quietly breathed a sigh of relief and found himself wondering which two seals had proved his identity. Without command, the warrior on Gwaine's right leant forward and placed Baradetch's sword on the floor. Moridare only smiled at the action before continuing.

'You must forgive my surprise.' Moridare's air was very casual. 'I do wonder why the Warlord of the seven armies of Amorand has left those armies in the midst of war to travel the expanse of two continents to visit me.'

'Because I believe, King Moridare, that we can be of mutual benefit to each other.' Gwaine quickly glanced at the assembled group. 'But, ...perhaps it would be better if we could talk with a little more privacy.'

Moridare casually waved his hand in the air. 'I am confident that no one in this room will repeat what we say here. You may speak in absolute security.'

Gwaine wasn't convinced. Moridare could probably trust his advisers and senior military officers, but Gwaine wondered at the security of these talks before the young officer and his two warriors.

'First, tell me how I may be of benefit to you, Warlord, and then we will discuss your benefit to me.'

Gwaine tried to dismiss the almost bored, casual attitude of this King, but it was very disturbing when the fate of Amorand, and his own life, depended on the success of these discussions.

'My armies have repelled the Dark Emperor's attack on Arrindare.'

'The Emperor's attack', Moridare interrupted.

'I beg your pardon, my Lord', Gwaine replied in bewilderment.

'The Emperor's attack. ...You are in the North Continent now. We do not refer to our beloved Emperor as 'The Dark Emperor'. He is our esteemed ruler, the father of our united nation. But, …forgive my interruption. Please continue.'

'Um, thank you, my Lord. Gwaine was unsure of the sincerity of the remarks, but he was suddenly very nervous and more unsure of his mission than he had ever been. 'My armies have repelled the Emperor's attack on Arrindare, and reduced the number of his soldiers in Amorand to a level that approximates our own force. However, the Emperor's force holds most of our fortified cities. It would be very difficult to take all of those cities by force, so…'

'Virtually impossible, I would say', Moridare interrupted once again.

Gwaine bowed slightly to acknowledge his correction. 'It would be virtually impossible to take all of those cities by force, so what I need is a distraction in the north that would encourage the Dark Emperor ...um ...the Emperor ...to withdraw his army from Amorand.'

'I see', Moridare replied thoughtfully. 'And what sort of a distraction did you have in mind?'

'Oh', Gwaine shrugged as he searched for the right words. 'Civil unrest, rebellion, a challenge to his authority and position.'

Moridare grinned good humouredly at Gwaine's words. 'And you expect me to begin this chain of events?' he asked incredulously. 'Are you mad? The Emperor would have my head on a plate.'

'If the Emperor could have had your head on a plate, he would have had it by now', Gwaine replied calmly. 'You have a strong army and a very defendable mountain range. The Emperor's army is only a third of its usual size. Besides, you don't have to go to war against the Emperor in order to achieve these aims. There are more subtle ways.'

'Enough. Stop.' Moridare was trying to control his humour. He was close to laughter. 'You have travelled a long way to ask this sacrifice of me, Warlord. One presumes that you have something to offer to entice me to commit this suicidal act. What is your reward for my absurd behaviour?'

'I shall cause you to be Emperor', Gwaine replied immediately.

The humour disappeared from Moridare's face. 'You think me a fool, Warlord.'

'No, my Lord. I think you powerful enough to control this North Continent. I have plans that will cause chaos and destabilise the Emperor's power. As a result of our actions, he will be forced to withdraw his army from Amorand. My armies will then be free to enter his territory and help you take control. I shall destroy the Dark Emperor for you and place you in his castle, on his throne.'

Moridare was quiet. Gwaine took some comfort in the fact that he was at least considering his plot.

The hall was in silence for minutes that seemed like years. King Moridare sat casually on his throne and stared into the emptiness of the hall. When he finally straightened himself in his throne, he turned his attention to the three standing just behind Gwaine.

'Are you the ones who captured the Warlord?'

One of the warriors replied, indicating his comrade. 'We caught him on the mountain, my King.'

'Did anyone else see him on the mountain?'

'I do not think so, my King.'

'Did anyone in the city see him?'

'The streets were deserted. If anyone did, by chance, see us, then I don't think there would have been any reason for them to be suspicious of our actions.'

'Very good. Has anyone in the castle seen him?'

'Only my officer, here, my King.'

'I see.' Moridare turned his attention to the young officer. 'Are you aware of anyone who knows of the Warlord's presence here?'

'No, my King', the officer replied proudly. 'Only we three saw him before Commander Harn was called, and we have spoken to no-one.'

'Excellent', King Moridare replied, obviously pleased with the behaviour of his soldiers. 'Well, Warlord. The situation is this.' Moridare paused as he studied Gwaine and allowed him to sweat on his decision. 'I am tired. ...Therefore, I will go to bed and, tomorrow, I will consider your proposal. Though, I warn you, I am very likely to reject your plan and have you killed. I do not consider you a threat to the Dark Emperor. You will remain my guest though, until I have made my final decision.'

Gwaine's spirits sank. He needed a miracle. His words obviously hadn't been enough.

'In the meantime', Moridare continued, 'we need to ensure the secrecy of this meeting and the words we have spoken. Harn!'

Harn nodded to his King as he and his two senior military officers drew their swords and moved toward Gwaine, the officer and the two warriors. Gwaine watched in horror as the three beside him were driven through and fell to the floor, dying.

A moment later, a heavy blow from behind him, thudded dully through his head and everything went black.

MAGNOR'S LESSON ON LEGENDS

Magnor was busy with some old scrolls when he heard Tanya's voice in the corridor. He immediately dropped the scrolls on his desk and rushed to pick up the cloth on his, now shining, metal chair. By the time she entered the War Room, he was busily polishing the already glimmering reflective metal surface.

'You do spend a lot of time on that strange chair of yours, my Lord Magnor.'

'Yes, Lady Tanya. It will be proved to be time well spent, I expect.' Magnor slowly straightened himself and turned to face Tanya. His eyes were immediately drawn to the sword at her waist. 'Ah! Sword lesson. I had forgotten.'

Tanya looked disappointed. 'Oh! Is the time inconvenient then?'

'No, my Lady. Not at all. Though, my old bones would appreciate a small rest before we begin any physical exertion. Will you join me in a glass of juice before we begin?' Magnor motioned to a table in the corner of the room with a pitcher of juice and two glasses already waiting.

Tanya smiled. She had got to know Magnor fairly well over the past few weeks. He was a schemer. She turned to her chaperon. 'You may wait in the corridor for me.'

The chaperon hesitated, obeying her duty to stay with the Princess. But, then, obviously considering Magnor's advanced years, and her mistress's temper, she curtsied and left the room.

Tanya watched her exit before moving toward the table, followed closely by Magnor.

'And what is it that you wish to talk to me about, my Lord Magnor?'

Magnor saw her seated and poured the juice before heeding the question.

'I was just hoping for your pleasant company, my Lady. Your sword skills have developed well over the last few weeks. You are well skilled for a lady in your position and, certainly better skilled in the basics of defence than most young soldiers. I see no need to continue the lessons.' Magnor shuffled a little and displayed a twinkle in his eye as he always did when he was changing the subject of conversation to his own choosing. 'Tell me. How are the wedding preparations going?'

Tanya screwed her nose up as a sign of disgust and exasperation, before answering Magnor in a voice that displayed uncontrolled irritation. 'The wedding plans are going very well, thank you, despite my outright refusal to marry Stefarne, and despite Stefarne's stated intention of not marrying me unless I am in agreement. Both sets of parents are apparently convinced that we will change our minds before the wedding day arrives.'

'And why won't you marry Stefarne?' Magnor queried in placid tones. He had always been an expert at asking direct questions regardless of the emotional state of the person being questioned.

'Because I don't love him', Tanya replied emphatically and loudly.

'But surely', Magnor continued undaunted by Tanya's growing anger. 'Surely, you would not be the first Princess to marry for State reasons rather than love. Surely you expected that this might be asked of you.'

Tanya crossed her arms tightly across her chest and seethed. She had heard this argument over and over from her parents. It seemed that they had now recruited Magnor into their marriage drive. She hadn't expected that Magnor would become involved in such a lowly pursuit as marriage arrangements.

Seeing the resolve that had set in Tanya's facial features, Magnor did not bother waiting for a reply to his questioning. 'It would appear to me', he continued, 'that the problem is not that you don't love Stefarne, but, that you love someone else.' Magnor sat quietly, allowing time for his words to be digested.

Slowly the hard resolve and anger in Tanya's glare melted. She unfolded her arms and leant forward to take her glass from the table. She dropped her gaze to the rough wooden surface of the table as she sat in silence.

When she finally replied, it was in a pitiful, child-like voice that conveyed her worry and helplessness. 'Have you heard anything of him? Can you tell me any news?'

'Only what I have told you in strictest confidence, of his plans. And I have done that in peril of my life. If the Kings found out that I had told anyone of the plan, then my days would be numbered.'

'Your confidence is safe with me, Magnor. I appreciate your trust, in telling me. But, have you heard, or do you know, anything of him since he sailed from Port?'

'His ship is not expected to return for days, my Lady. Even then, we will only be told that he was dropped safely within swimming distance of the coast. You will not hear any news, my Lady.'

Tanya's look was distant. 'I will never forgive my parents for not letting him see me to say 'goodbye'. I will never see him again.' She was whispering to herself, almost forgetting Magnor's presence. 'Or, even worse, I may greet him sometime in the future as a brother-in-law.' She looked up with a start. Both thoughts were more than she could bear. 'Magnor', she implored. 'You've got to help me! I know you can. You know ...things. Things that haven't happened yet. Things that have happened at a distance. Please!' There were tears in her eyes as she begged. 'Please, help me. Tell me. ...Please!'

Magnor was embarrassed and bewildered. He looked away to avoid her pleading eyes. 'You give me too much credit, Tanya. I am just an old warrior.'

Tanya jumped to her feet and ran toward the door. Halfway, she stopped and stared back toward Magnor through tear filled eyes. Tears streamed down her face as she sobbed and shouted. 'You're lying to me. I thought you were my friend, but you don't care about anyone. All you care about is the war. You don't give a damn about me or Gwaine or any other pawn of yours who gets hurt in your little war games.'

She had almost reached the door when Magnor called her name. It was a pleading, emotional call that Tanya felt obliged to answer. She turned and listened through her sobs for Magnor's response to her outburst. He stood at the table, his shoulders drooped, now looking twice as old as he did only minutes ago. Tanya was surprised at the emotion in his face and the compassion in his eyes.

'I do care about you and Gwaine, and many others who have suffered because of the Dark Emperor's dreams of power. ...Close the door and we will talk.'

Tanya obeyed immediately and returned to the table. She didn't want to cut her link with Magnor. Her belief in some undefined ability that he may possess was her only grasp on what she wanted in life, rather than what everybody else wanted for her.

When Tanya was seated and had regained some of her composure, wiped her eyed and forced an apologetic expression, Magnor reached across the table and patted her hand. Tanya found the act comforting and ignored the lack of protocol of the situation. Despite her outburst only minutes ago, she did feel a warm affection for this old warrior.

'Now. This is the first thing that you must understand', Magnor began in a low, warming voice. 'I am not a magician or, even, a seer. Sometimes I believe that I see things that are a little distance into the future. I often believe that I can see things happening over a distance. I say 'believe', because sometimes what I see isn't true. For instance, I was almost certain that young Taron was going to die in the Marsh. Happily, I was wrong.' Magnor's mind drifted away from the point. 'I have a great affection for that boy. I hope he will soon recover from his melancholy and regain his usual humour and temperament.'

After Magnor had sat in silent thought for some seconds, Tanya re-opened the conversation and tried to steer it back on course. 'I have been too well chaperoned to be able to talk to Taron. Though, I have seen him at a distance. ...Have you seen anything of Gwaine, Magnor?'

'I have been trying to see Gwaine ever since he sailed out of Port. I believe I saw him swim to safety on the beach, and then travel safely inland to Moridare's castle.'

Tanya waited impatiently before questioning further. 'And then?'

'And then nothing, Tanya.' Magnor looked into Tanya's eyes with an expression of concern and frustration. 'Now I can see nothing. I can only feel a terribly intense feeling of foreboding and fear. Though, I believe that they may be my feelings rather than Gwaine's. But, I am worried. Something is wrong. I think Gwaine may need help, but I don't know what danger he is in, or what I should, or could, do to help him.'

They sat in silence, holding hands, trying to gain some comfort. Tanya didn't want to end the conversation here. This ending was of no more help or comfort to her than when Magnor had been unwilling to tell her anything. She tried desperately to think of a question or strategy that would keep the conversation alive and give some ray of hope.

'Can't we send another ship? I mean …I know it will take a long time, but if we send soldiers they may get there in time to save Gwaine.'

'Have you ever heard Gwaine refer to Baradetch as ***flying like an eagle***?'

'Yes', Tanya replied somewhat bewildered by the change in direction. 'When he was laughing at some of the sillier legends.'

'Yes', Magnor replied dryly. 'Gwaine was often mocking the legends. It was one of his downfalls as a Warlord, his lack of belief in things that he did not understand.'

Tanya's heart jumped at Magnor's use of the past tense when referring to Gwaine. 'We have to do something, Magnor. You must have some skeleton of a plan.'

'I have a shadow of a plan, my Lady. It is not solid enough to be called a skeleton. ...Anyway, getting back to Baradetch flying like an eagle…'

'No!' Tanya snapped in anger. 'Tell me your plan.'

'No', Magnor replied firmly. 'First you listen to the particular legend that gave rise to the story of Baradetch's power of flight.'

Tanya sat in irritated silence. Why did Magnor always have to be so frustrating?

'Baradetch was at Lasatal', Magnor continued. 'The armies of Velinon, Tayle and Cadel were retreating down the west side of Amorand to take up the defence of the Fortress of Marsh, when the Barikarn army arrived with a report that a large force of the Dark Emperor's army had arrived by sea and were waiting to meet the retreating armies at the border between Barikarn and Cadel. The Barikarn King was a stupid, petty little man who had often been at war with all three armies. Anyway, what it came down to was this; he had withdrawn his Barikarn army without sending any warning to the other Kings that they were retreating into a trap. When Baradetch heard of this, he was furious. He was about to lose almost half of his army and there was nothing he could do to warn them of the trap. Even if his messengers could have got through, there just wasn't time to travel that distance.'

'Magnor', Tanya interrupted. 'This is very interesting, but…'

'The legends say', Magnor continued regardless of Tanya's attempted interruption, 'that Baradetch raced down to this room, and the very next time he was seen was when he rode into the Fortress of Marsh at the head of the three armies. He had reached them in time to warn them of the trap and lead them over the mountains to avoid the waiting enemy.'

'It's a good story Magnor', Tanya conceded, pleased that the ordeal was over so that they could get on with business. 'Now, what is this shadow of a plan?'

'The legends say', Magnor continued, completely ignoring Tanya's question, 'that after Baradetch had disappeared from this room, the only thing that had altered was that the chair...' Magnor motioned to his well-polished chair. 'That the chair had changed from a gleaming, polished, mirror reflection to a black, charred finish as if it had been in a fire.'

'Oh!' The connection between the legend and their present problem had dawned on Tanya. 'Now I see why you have been spending so much time on that chair. You're hoping that someone will sit in it and fly to Gwaine.' Tanya was disappointed. If this was Magnor's shadow of a plan, then there was little chance of helping Gwaine.

'Yes', Magnor replied excitedly. 'Baradetch said that he sat in the chair, pulled the arms upward and commanded it to send him to his army in Cadel.

Tanya allowed herself to slouch a little in her chair. This was an anticlimax. She hadn't expected a great plan, but she wanted more than folk stories. For the sake of politeness, she forced herself to ask a question. 'What magic makes it work?'

'The magic of the stars, my Lady. Though, the legends say that it uses so much power that it can only be used once in every hundred years.'

Tanya's spirits had dropped as low as she could stand. She covered her eyes with her hand and allowed a few tears to run down her cheek. She bit her lip to try to prevent herself from breaking into sobs. Her pathetic attempts to hide her misery were nowhere near enough. Magnor's excitement faded away as he realised that his tale and plan had been less than convincing. He took Tanya's hand from her eyes and squeezed it comfortingly.

'There are many things that we cannot understand, Tanya. That does not make them untrue. The unknown is always the most exciting.'

Tanya wiped her eyes once again. 'What do you intend doing with the chair?'

'I will ask the Kings to allow Taron to try it. If it works, then Gwaine will have assistance. If it doesn't, then I will merely look like a doddery old fool.'

Tanya forced a smile and squeezed Magnor's hand. 'You're not an old fool. You're just trying to help Gwaine.' Tanya looked at Magnor and tried to imagine him attempting to convince the Kings of his magical seat. 'You won't convince the Kings.'

'They have nothing to lose by the experiment.'

Tanya withdrew her hand and left the table to study the chair. After a quick glance she turned back to Magnor.

'They won't let you tell Taron the plan. It's top secret.'

'I can convince them that Taron is a good security risk. He is a senior officer.'

Tanya smiled at Magnor's ready replies. He had obviously spent some time planning this. She decided that he deserved a better reaction than she had so far given.

'Taron's not mentally well. You said yourself that he is not himself.'

'If Taron is judged not to be capable, then someone else may have to try. I am not convinced that Taron is the right person to send anyway. He has much the same abilities as Gwaine. If Gwaine is in trouble, then I would rather send someone with different abilities that may give a different solution to whatever problem he is facing.'

Tanya leant toward the chair, putting her hand out to touch some round protrusions underneath the right armrest.

'Don't touch that!' Magnor yelled, with such force and panic that Tanya visibly jumped and stepped back a pace from the chair. Seeing her shock, Magnor tried to remedy his overreaction. 'I'm sorry, my Lady. It's just that I don't know what they're for. They may be important to the operation of the chair.'

‘I see’, Tanya replied, still shaking from the shock. She went back to studying the chair, more in an attempt to steady her nerves than to gain any information on its operation. She tried to remember where the conversation had been up to. ‘If you want different abilities to Gwaine’s, what abilities did you have in mind?’

‘Not knowing the problems that Gwaine faces, it’s hard to say, my Lady. In general, I would be looking for intelligence, ability to use a sword, someone of a rank that would be accepted by a King and, importantly, someone who loves Gwaine enough to risk their life for him.’

Tanya knew that she could fill the first three requirements. She was only waiting on some clue from Magnor, that he wanted her to be the one to go. The fourth requirement was the clue. It was obvious that Magnor wanted her to try the chair. She immediately turned around and backed onto the chair, pulling the arm rests up and back toward her.

‘Take me to Gwaine’, she commanded in a loud, royal voice.

Magnor jumped to his feet and turned his back to the chair. He clenched his eyes closed before a flash as bright as lightning lit up every corner of the room. The thundery sound was still reverberating off the walls as Magnor turned and ran toward the chair. Tanya was gone and the chair was as black as charcoal and still sizzled with the heat.

The chaperon burst open the door and searched frantically for the cause of the commotion and for her young mistress. Magnor only brushed past her, leaving her bewilderedly searching for another exit that Tanya may have used.

As Magnor marched quickly through the corridors a wicked grin appeared on his lips as he gleefully rubbed his hands together. He would have to rush to tell the Kings this terrible news.

MORIDARE'S DUNGEON

The morning light had been shining through the barred window onto the dirty sandstone floor for hours. Gwaine had lain quietly on the cold floor for much longer than that, though. When he had first regained consciousness, sometime during the night, he had tried to move, but had ceased all efforts when he discovered that the chains joining his wrists were actually imbedded into the stone wall of his cell. His head hurt too much anyway. The pounding within his skull was accompanied by a sticky sensation on the right side of his face. In the daylight, he could now see a large stain of dried blood on the floor where he had lain while unconscious.

Gwaine tried to drag himself out of his stunned semiconsciousness as his pained senses alerted him to approaching footsteps and voices. The large door was unbolted and pushed inward, revealing the now familiar forms of Harn and King Moridare.

'Good morning, my young Warlord', King Moridare boomed exuberantly as they moved into the room. He towered over Gwaine as he studied his captive. 'My, we do look pitiful. Not the sort of boy that I'd send on a dangerous mission, like destroying the Emperor. What say you, Harn?'

'No, my King', Harn replied instantly. 'Should still be in a crib, if you ask me.'

Gwaine could tell from their attitude that his mission was a failure and that this was his last day alive. He slowly forced himself up into a sitting position leaning, for support, against the brick wall, and studied King Moridare. This large, bearded man in his late thirties, dressed in the gold embroidered robes of his office, had been the fulcrum of the plan to destroy the Dark Emperor. That he had listened to Gwaine's plan with such an air of boredom, was both an infuriation and a frustration that Gwaine could not come to terms with.

‘Good morning, King Moridare’, Gwaine finally replied, coolly. He assumed his privilege of rank in not even acknowledging Harn’s presence, and took some comfort in Harn’s obvious anger at the insult. ‘And who do you intend sending on the dangerous mission of destroying the Dark Emperor?’ Gwaine’s head hurt. He would rather have not been involved in argument at this point in time. ‘All of your brave warriors seem to have avoided the task for the last few centuries. At least this ‘boy’ has the guts to try.’

‘No-one shall take arms against the Emperor’, King Moridare replied.

‘Then you shall lick his boots for the rest of your days. Or, at least, until he is strong enough to ride up here and knock you off your little hill.’

‘Enough!’ Moridare roared angrily. His face was glowing red. ‘My decision is made. You cannot destroy the Emperor. You are just a boy with no power that could destroy, or even challenge, the Emperor.’

‘I can destroy him and make you Emperor’, Gwaine shouted emphatically.

‘You cannot’, Moridare retaliated in just as determined a tone. He took a deep breath and calmed his temper before continuing. ‘If I thought for one moment that you might be able to do as you say, then I would follow. I have grovelled to the Emperor, as my father before me grovelled, just to ensure our survival on this mountain. I would dearly love to destroy him. I would be Emperor.’ Moridare stopped and, once again, studied the blood stained boy at his feet. His tone dropped to an almost apologetic whisper. ‘I admire your bravery in coming here. You shall die quickly, later today.’

It appeared that King Moridare and Harn were about to turn and leave. Indeed, they had both half turned toward the door, when they froze and stared, mouths gaping open, at the far wall. Gwaine was spell bound for an instant by their seemingly frozen forms, before turning his attention to the direction of their gaze. There, on the far wall, was the glimmering shadow of some ghostly form. It throbbed into focus, showing the outline of a woman, before becoming blurred and shadowy once again. It vibrated in and out of focus for seconds before finally settling on a solid form.

'Tanya!' Gwaine screamed incredulously as he jumped to his feet. Tanya looked just as stunned as King Moridare and Harn. She shook her head in an obvious attempt to clear the cobwebs from her mind, before drawing her sword and assuming a threatening posture.

Moridare and Harn moved backwards, away from the sorceress in front of them, their mouths still gaping in horror.

'What is this magic?' Moridare yelled to Gwaine in a fear filled voice.

For all that Gwaine wanted to reply and turn this dramatic entrance to his advantage, he could think of nothing. Moridare's words, ***what is this magic?*** just echoed over and over in his mind.

'Release Gwaine or die', Tanya demanded in the most authoritative voice that she could muster. It was a valiant effort, but the tremble in her words couldn't be helped. Magnor's chair had worked. The shock of being with her old friend in the safety of Lasatal one second, and the next in danger in a distant land, was more than she could cope with.

At the sound of Tanya's voice, the fear had been quelled in Moridare and Harn. This spectre was flesh and blood after all. How, or why, it was here could be dealt with later. Now they could fight against it. They both drew their swords.

'Hold, King Moridare', Gwaine screamed. His shock at Tanya's arrival had now turned to concern for her safety. 'You wanted proof of powers that could destroy the Dark Emperor. Surely, if you seriously wanted to be Emperor, this is proof enough that I am not just another boy. I repeat. I can make you Emperor.' Gwaine stared earnestly at King Moridare and summoned the most serious and pleading voice in his final attempt. 'Join with me. Help me destroy the Dark Emperor. Release your people from fear. I will put you on his throne.'

Moridare stared at Gwaine thoughtfully. He straightened himself from his defensive stance and leant on his sword as he studied Tanya, still holding the Lady's Sword as a threat to the two unknown men on the far side of the cell.

Finally, Moridare allowed a warm smile to drift across his lips. He replaced his sword as he slapped Harn cheerily across the chest. 'Come. Put your sword away, Harn. These people are our friends. Undo the Warlord's chains.'

Harn immediately followed his King's commands, and, seconds later, Gwaine was free, wringing his wrists to restore the circulation of blood to his tingling hands.

'Perhaps you will be good enough, Warlord', King Moridare continued, 'to introduce me to your very attractive friend.'

Gwaine smiled. Moridare was a very polished character and he obviously had an eye for the ladies. 'King Moridare, I would like to introduce you to Princess Tanya of Velinon. Princess Tanya, King Moridare and his Commander, Harn.'

Tanya felt ridiculous. Gwaine had just introduced her to a King, and she was still standing, pointing her sword threateningly at that King and his Commander. She took an embarrassed step backward and quickly replaced her sword in its sheath. 'Forgive me, my Lord', she exclaimed as she gave a low curtsy.

'It is a pleasure to meet you, Princess Tanya. One day, you must explain to me how you perform that magical trick. Where have you come from?'

'From Lasatal, my Lord.'

'No. I don't mean that, my Lady', Moridare replied with a grin. 'Where did you come from today? Were you in hiding on the mountain?'

'No, King Moridare. Today, I came from Lasatal.'

The smile disappeared from King Moridare's lips. 'I see', he replied unconvincingly. 'I do not pretend to understand and I see no point in trying. Tell me, Princess Tanya, do you believe that the Warlord can destroy the Dark Emperor?'

For the first time, Gwaine turned his attention completely to Tanya, and Tanya saw the gash above his temple and the blood stained side of his face. She took several paces to join the group and obtain a clearer view of his wound. She forced her attention back to King Moridare. 'Gwaine has been trained since childhood in all forms of combat and strategies', she explained calmly. 'I believe the Dark Emperor has met his match. Gwaine will destroy him.' And then, in a dry, accusing voice, she added, 'That is, after I have treated his wounds.'

Moridare was taken off guard. In his Kingdom, it was unusual to be rebuked by a woman. He was noticeably flustered. 'I shall send women to treat his wound. You shall take your place, as your royal rank dictates, in my court.'

'No', Tanya replied. 'I shall treat Gwaine's wounds.'

Gwaine hastily intervened, in an effort to avoid a clash that could have damaged their newly formed alliance. He could understand Tanya's reluctance to be entrapped in Moridare's court. 'With respect, King Moridare, your customs do dictate that a woman shall reside with her man rather than within the court.'

'Your understanding of our customs is correct, but I do not see its relevance. Surely, you're not suggesting that this young Princess is your woman.'

Gwaine could see danger in this course. He was on the verge of lying to King Moridare. Magnor had warned of the ethics of these people. To be caught lying to Moridare would mean death, but he could not allow Tanya to be sent off to Moridare's court. An attractive young woman with no power base and no friends would find life very difficult in that environment. Moridare, himself, obviously had designs on Tanya.

'I would not admit such a thing in my own court, King Moridare, but, under your code of ethics, I believe it is correct and proper of me to make that statement.'

Moridare was obviously agitated. He studied Tanya for some sign that would indicate that the statement was true or false, but she had already suppressed her wide-eyed, surprised look at Gwaine. In an attempt to validate his claim, she moved forward and nestled into his side.

'Very well', Moridare finally conceded in anger. 'You shall stay together. But, I warn you, if I discover that you have lied to me, you shall both die.' He strode toward the door, followed by Harn. At the door, he turned. 'You shall stay here. I shall send attendants to show you to your room, and prepare baths and clothes and whatever else you need. Today, I will allow you to rest. Tomorrow, we shall discuss our strategy.' He and Harn disappeared through the doorway.

Tanya and Gwaine listened for their footsteps to disappear, before Gwaine took Tanya in his arms and held her to him.

'What the hell are you doing here? This isn't a safe place for a Lady.' And then in an even more questioning, incredulous voice, he asked, 'How the hell did you get here?'

'Oh', Tanya shrugged. 'I flew.'

THE DANGER OF A LIE

Tanya had washed the dried blood from Gwaine's face and was in the process of cleaning the wound when an attendant arrived at the door of their quarters with Baradetch's sword and Gwaine's backpack.

Tanya placed the delivered articles beside the bed and returned to treating the wound. Gwaine flinched at the touch of the warm water.

'Oh, don't be a baby. It's actually nowhere near as bad as it looked. All that blood on your face made it look like some horrific gash, but now that it's clean, it's just a small cut.'

'It still hurts', Gwaine replied impishly. He was pleased to have Tanya's company, though he was still having some trouble comprehending her story of how she came to be here. He nodded toward the sword. 'It's lucky that poor fellow didn't know what he was delivering or he would have gone berserk. They have a legend here, that whoever takes Baradetch's Sword will die before the next morning.'

'He wasn't taking it', Tanya replied logically. 'He was bringing it back.'

Gwaine ignored her comment. He was preoccupied with thoughts of the warrior who had taken the sword on the mountain. His stomach turned as he thought of the fate of the three who knew too much.

'He's very dangerous, you know', Gwaine stated, almost absent-mindedly.

'Who? The attendant?' Tanya queried.

Gwaine wondered if she was being deliberately irritating. 'No. Of course not. Moridare is dangerous.'

'Oh, yes. I agree', she confirmed calmly as she applied the healing cream to the wound.

'He had three of his own soldiers killed, just because they knew who I was.'

Tanya finished her treatment and studied Gwaine. Lying on the bed, he looked like a young boy who had been hurt at sport and who needed an early night so that he could play again tomorrow. That image was easy to believe until she looked into his eyes, distant, dark eyes that had seen far too much. She wanted to put her arms around him and mother him better, but, instead, she slapped him on the shoulder playfully. 'Come on, doldrums. There's a hot bath in the next room, clean clothes and some brunch. Let's get comfortable and enjoy the rest of the day.'

Gwaine followed instructions. He climbed off the bed and headed toward the bath. He wondered if Tanya realised their danger in having lied to Moridare, and then decided that there was no advantage in talking about it. With his shirt halfway off, he stopped in the doorway. 'Do you want to go first? I'm pretty grubby.'

'Have a look at the size of the bath', Tanya replied with raised eyebrows.

Gwaine gave her a quizzical look before moving through the doorway. A surprised whistle emanated from the room before Gwaine poked his head around the door. 'It's not a bath. It's a swimming pool.'

Tanya nodded. 'You would need twenty Warlords to get that much water dirty.'

Gwaine disappeared back into the room. 'Twenty Warlords. Now, that would be handy.'

'No thank you', came Tanya's instant reply. 'One is enough of a problem.'

'Thank you', Gwaine responded before splashing into the pool.

Tanya looked for something to do in the small living quarters. The attendants had done it all. 'Can I come in and start brunch? Or, would that be too indecent?'

'No. That wouldn't be indecent in this depth of water. You're welcome to come in.'

Tanya moved quickly into the room and dived for the food tray. She had only had a very small breakfast, with the intention of having something more substantial after her sword lesson with Magnor.

'Tanya. Why did Magnor send you?'

'Because you needed help, of course.'

'He didn't know that.'

'He did. I don't know how. But, he did know.'

'Then why didn't he send a warrior?'

Tanya gave him a cross look. It sounded like Gwaine wasn't happy with Magnor's selection. 'I'm sorry if I'm not up to expectation', she replied tersely.

'No, don't get angry. I'm pleased to see you. It's just that I would have expected Magnor to send a warrior. I'm just trying to work out his logic.' Gwaine doubted that his reply would have appeased Tanya.

'Well, his logic is really quite sound. He knew, somehow, that you were in trouble and, that if a warrior's skills were needed to get you out of trouble, then you would already be out of trouble.'

'Pardon?' Gwaine decided that he had missed something, somewhere in that statement.

Tanya took a deep breath to show her exasperation. 'You are a warrior. True or false?'

'True.'

'Right. Then, if Magnor had sent a warrior, he would only be duplicating your skills. True or false?'

'True.'

'Right. You already had those skills and you were still in trouble. So, therefore, there was nothing to be gained in sending someone with the same skills. You needed someone with entirely different skills.'

‘I see’, Gwaine replied before lapsing into silence. He was searching for a tactful way to ask his next question, but he couldn’t think of one. ‘Tanya.’

‘Yes.’ She knew what was coming.

‘What are ...um ...your skills?’

‘I, dummy, in case you hadn’t noticed, am a woman. I think that is going to count for a lot with our King Moridare.’

‘I see’, Gwaine replied thoughtfully. ‘That is a fair comment’, he finally conceded. ‘I had noticed, by the way.’

Tanya smiled. ‘Thank you.’ She bit into a second bread roll.

‘But, your sex is also our greatest peril at the moment. King Moridare was quite serious when he said that he would kill us if we were caught lying to him.’

‘I know. We will have to be careful.’

They lapsed into silence. Gwaine was content that Tanya realised their danger and would be on her guard when they met with selected members of Moridare’s court.

Gwaine quickly finished his bath. He was keen to get to bed after the long hours spent on the hard, cold floor of the cell.

‘Would you pass me a robe please, Tanya.’

Tanya left the tray and grabbed two robes. She dropped one at the side of the pool and walked toward the doorway. ‘While you’re getting out, I’ll get undressed and into my robe in here.’

Gwaine clambered out of the pool and put on the towelling garment. ‘Give me a yell when you’re ready and I’ll move the brunch into there so that you can have your bath.’

‘Alright, I’m ready.’

Gwaine grabbed a roll and placed it between his teeth. He couldn’t eat it while he was pushing the trolley, but at least it felt like he was getting closer to eating.

When he moved through the doorway, he found Tanya snuggled up in bed.

'I thought you were going to have a bath' he asked in surprise, replacing the bread roll on the side of the tray.

'I don't need one yet. I had one in Lasatal this morning.'

'Alright. We had better sort out sleeping arrangements.' Gwaine had been trying to sort this out ever since they had arrived in the room. He couldn't see much of an alternative, but he had been too embarrassed to discuss the problem with Tanya.

Tanya allowed him to stand in uncomfortable silence for several seconds before she made any comment.

'I don't see any alternative. There's only one bed.'

'Oh, well ...um...' Gwaine's embarrassment was growing. With every attempt to solve the problem, he came up with the same sole solution. 'Um ...I could sleep on the floor I suppose.'

'Gwaine, you know we will have to sleep in the same bed. There's no lock on the door. If Moridare walks in and finds you sleeping on the floor, then we're dead.'

'Alright', Gwaine conceded. 'I know. We will have to sleep in the same bed. I just didn't want to be the one to say so, in case you thought I was trying to take advantage of the situation.' Gwaine's voice trailed off. He had never been so embarrassed in his whole life.

'I know you're not trying to take advantage.'

'You have my promise that I will behave like a gentleman.'

Tanya shook her head and growled in exasperation. 'I don't believe this.' She looked away and laid quietly staring at the wall while Gwaine stood in embarrassed silence. He would, perhaps, have said something to rectify his statement, if only he'd known what he had said wrong.

When Tanya returned to the conversation, she had tears in her eyes. 'I don't want that promise', she said quietly in a strained, tearful voice. 'Now, will you please take off your robe, hop into bed, and make love to me.'

Gwaine was stunned. He considered what she was saying and found himself having to move behind the brunch trolley to hide his reaction to the thought of making love to this attractive young woman.

You don't have to do that, Tanya. We only have to pretend. I mean, ...I'm not saying I wouldn't like to ...but you don't have to. I mean, Princesses aren't allowed to do that. Your parents would kill us both.'

'Gwaine, I appreciate that you're thinking of me. That's sweet of you. But, Moridare is going to kill us before our parents get a chance. And what do you think would have happened to me if we hadn't lied and I'd gone off to his court?'

'What you're saying is quite right, Tanya. But, we only have to pretend we're lovers.'

'No!' Tanya interrupted vehemently. 'I will meet selected ladies of the court. You don't know what these women are like. They will talk to me about sex and find out that I don't know anything. Some of the older ones will know just from looking at me. I've got 'virgin' written all over me. And if Moridare gets suspicious, then he only needs to send his physician up here to force me into an examination.'

Gwaine leant his elbows onto the trolley with his chin in his hands. He tried to think of a reply, some solution that would allow them to just pretend. He wondered why he was trying so hard. He had fantasised about Tanya, almost since their first meeting.

'Gwaine', Tanya implored. 'You know that there's no alternative. We either become lovers or we're dead, and the Dark Emperor wins. Besides', she added with a coy smile, 'apart from all the logical reasons, I'd really like to make love. Wouldn't you?'

Gwaine forced a smile. 'Oh, yes. There's no doubt about that.' He shook his head and stared at the shapely young woman in his bed. 'You're absolutely gorgeous.'

Tanya bit her bottom lip and gave an impish expression. 'Then take your robe off and come to bed.'

Gwaine surrendered to Tanya's calm logic. He moved the trolley out of the way, removed his robe and dived under the covers, brushing her warm nakedness as he pulled the covers back into position.

He rolled across and extended his arm over her trim waist as he settled himself into a position that allowed him to comfortably place a quick kiss on her lips. He withdrew to speak, but she wrapped her hands over his back and pulled him down for a more passionate, extended kiss.

'This probably sounds dumb', he finally got to say. 'But, before we make love, I want to say that I love you.'

'Alright. Say it', she responded playfully.

Gwaine laughed. 'You sure know how to hurt a serious comment, don't you.' He looked into her grey eyes. 'I love you, Tanya.'

The eyes filled with emotion. 'I love you too, Gwaine. I'm glad I'm here in danger with you, rather than being safe at Lasatal without you.'

A mixture of feelings swept over Gwaine. He was glad that she was here too, but he would die if anything happened to her. He kissed her lips, softly at first, but extending into a hard passionate kiss as he ran his hand over the firmness of her young breasts and down over her waist to her inner thigh. His hand moved slowly, firmly over her nakedness as his lips explored her face, neck and breasts. She writhed with pleasure as Gwaine took the time to prepare her for the union that they both yearned for. Knowing that she could wait no longer, Tanya closed her eyes and groaned softly as she motioned for him to move on top of her. Moments later they were both locked in a brief frenzy as they shared their love.

Their passion satiated, Tanya gasped deeply for breath as Gwaine supported himself on his elbows above her and studied, with concern, her attempts to control her breathing.

The door burst open as a familiar voice yelled 'Warlord'. Gwaine peered over his shoulder, in startled surprise, to see Moridare, Harn and another member of the court who carried some medical instruments.

'What the hell', Gwaine demanded. He could think of nothing to say that expressed his feelings.

Moridare was obviously surprised to find Gwaine and Tanya in bed and turned somewhat bewildered to Harn and his physician.

Tanya swallowed her embarrassment and slowly pushed the covers down Gwaine's naked back so that she had a clear view of Moridare and so that she was sure that Moridare had a clear view of her flushed cheeks and her naked shoulder and breast. She returned the covers to hide herself from view.

'Forgive us Warlord, ...Princess Tanya', Moridare exclaimed through his embarrassment. 'This is obviously an inopportune time. We shall meet tomorrow.'

Gwaine still couldn't think of anything to say. He heard the door closed as he returned his attention to Tanya.

'Are you alright?', he asked. It didn't sound the correct thing to ask, but it was all he could think of.

'I'm fine', Tanya replied in an afterglow tone. She groaned as she wrapped her arms around Gwaine and pulled his weight down onto her. 'Not only have I just made love to the man I love, but I've found the greatest way in the world to avoid execution.'

Gwaine smiled and kissed her neck. 'Oh, yes. The only moral dilemma about what we just did, is that we almost didn't do it soon enough.'

CHAOS, HYSTERIA AND REBELLION

Gwaine shook his head and yawned and wondered why Moridare had summoned them so early in the morning. The sky was still dark when the attendant had roused him and Tanya from their sleep.

They had bathed and dressed as quickly as possible and had almost had to run to keep up with Harn as he lead them to the antechamber to the Throne Room.

With a simple command of ‘Wait here’, Harn had disappeared almost half an hour ago, leaving Gwaine and Tanya trying to make conversation through their drowsy stupor.

Gwaine looked across to Tanya and studied her composure. In the short time available, she had managed to arrange her appearance to perfection. Every curl of her dark, shoulder length hair was in place and her dress was draped over every curve of her young body in a way that highlighted her femininity without distracting from her regal bearing.

He smiled as he thought of the time they had spent together yesterday. Even had they not made love, Gwaine would still have considered it as one of their ‘paradise days’. They had enjoyed each other’s company, as they had in Lasatal. The rapport and banter had returned as they romped and bathed and joked together during the day. They had both been sad when night had fallen and their free day had come to an end. Even the joy of snuggling up together to say goodnight and holding each other as sleep encroached, could not totally dispel the emptiness of finalising such a perfect day.

Gwaine leant across and tapped Tanya on the hip to attract her attention and break her obvious deep thought. She smiled and slid along the lounge as he lifted his left arm to indicate that he wanted a cuddle. He pulled her closely to him and kissed her cheek.

‘Thank you for a wonderful day.’

Tanya didn't answer, but merely snuggled deeper into Gwaine's side and grinned as she remembered the fun of the previous day.

Gwaine felt as if a weight had been lifted from his shoulders. He thought back to the melancholy and depression that had afflicted him and Taron after the battle for the Fortress and marvelled at his sudden recovery.

'You know. Taron probably needs a day like that. He could bounce back.'

Tanya looked up at Gwaine in pretended surprise. 'He'll have to find another girl. This one's spoken for.'

Gwaine laughed at her quick response. 'You bet you are', he announced as he squeezed her quickly to his side. 'I wasn't planning on renting you out. Anyway, Taron has never had any serious problem finding girlfriends. He should be able to make his own arrangements.'

'You could always give him Ellorn.'

'I beg your pardon?' Gwaine queried in surprise.

'Ellorn', Tanya repeated. 'You know. Your sister.'

'Yes. I know who she is', Gwaine retorted quickly. But, why would I give her to Taron?'

Tanya smiled coyly. 'Because it would make her very happy. She's very interested in him.'

'Oh, is she?' Gwaine replied with all the protective intonation that an older brother could muster. 'Well, she had better behave herself, and Taron can look elsewhere.'

'Hypocrite', Tanya proclaimed dryly. 'You're lucky I haven't got an older brother.'

'Yes', Gwaine conceded, climbing down off his high horse. 'I suppose you're right. You don't need an older brother to scare me, though. I'm worried enough about ***my*** older brother, who is supposed to be your husband in the near future, not to mention the fear that your parents put into my soul.'

Tanya giggled. 'It's a real mess, isn't it.' She looked into Gwaine's face. He had turned serious with the thought of the problems their relationship would cause at home. 'Anyway', she announced in an attempt to change the topic and his sudden serious mood. 'It's alright by you, then, if Ellorn chases Taron?'

Gwaine smiled. 'Yes. It's all right by me. Though, any relationship they have, has as little chance of approval as ours has.'

'That's alright', she stated, thinking back to the previous day. 'It's amazing what lengths a relationship can go to, even without approval.'

Gwaine only grunted a reply. His mind was obviously still on the serious implications of their relationship. Tanya thought in silence for a while, searching for another conversation.

'I still haven't been introduced to Taron. I was overly chaperoned when you returned from the battle.'

'I will have to remedy that when we get home. You two would get along very well.

'Tanya went silent. It was her turn to be serious, as she thought back to a conversation with Magnor.

'What's wrong?' Gwaine asked, realising her changed mood.

'Nothing', she lied.

Gwaine looked down at her. Her head was resting on his chest and she was staring into the emptiness of the opposite wall.

'Magnor has been known to be wrong, you know.' Gwaine was only guessing, but Tanya's instant response proved his guess to be correct. She sat up with a start and stared disbelievingly into his face.

‘Magnor said that he doesn’t tell predictions. He wouldn’t have told you’, she stated emphatically, and then, overwhelmed by doubt, she added, ‘Did he?’

Gwaine studied the seriousness and concern in her beautiful young features. ‘No. Magnor has told me nothing, but your concern has just told me everything of what he told you.’

Tanya felt miserable. She had slipped. She had allowed herself to be tricked into revealing something that Magnor had told her should never be spoken of. ‘You said yourself, Magnor has been known to be wrong’, she pushed forward in an attempt to alleviate her error.

Gwaine forced a smile. ‘Of course he has. I’m sure that he expected Taron to die in the Fortress. He was wrong. I don’t believe in his powers of prediction.’ Gwaine paused, wondering if he really wanted to ask the question that had formed in his mind. ‘What did Magnor predict for me?’

‘Oh! It’s silly really’, Tanya replied in an attempt to lighten the conversation. ‘I earbashed Magnor into telling me what he thought your future was. I asked him about mine as well but he said that he never reveals a prediction to the person it applies to.’

Gwaine waited for further information, but Tanya had apparently ended her part of the discussion. ‘And what did Magnor predict for me?’

Tanya’s face took on a pained, thoughtful expression. She obviously didn’t want to impart the information, but she could find no way to avoid the direct question.

‘Promise me’, she replied. ‘That you won’t take it serious, and that you won’t dwell on it.’

‘I have already told you that I believe Magnor to be fallible.’

Tanya allowed her shoulders to droop as she slipped back along the lounge to get a complete view of Gwaine, but then, unable to look him in the eyes, she stared at her hands as she spoke. 'Magnor said that you would never return to Lasatal.'

Gwaine forced a smile. 'Of course not. I'm going to set up lodging outside of the castle of Velin so that I can see you every day.'

Tanya grimaced at his quip. She looked into his face, concern written all over hers. 'He said', she continued, 'that you would fall in a distant land.'

'Of course I will', Gwaine replied light-heartedly. 'I'm the clumsiest traveller that you've ever met. I tripped over three times just finding my way from the water to the caves, when I first arrived in this land.'

Tanya shook her head with frustration. She was about to have words with Gwaine about his casual attitude when the large wooden doors were flung open and they were summoned into the Throne Room by one of Moridare's advisers.

As they moved through the doors, Gwaine squeezed Tanya's arm. 'Don't worry about Magnor's predictions', he whispered. 'I'm not.'

The gathering around the King's throne was similar to what Gwaine remembered of his last visit to this large room, except that the King, his three advisers, and his three military commanders had been joined by two senior looking ladies of the court.

'Welcome Warlord. Good morning Princess Tanya', Moridare boomed as they approached. He was obviously in an excellent mood. 'Good news. The Emperor has dispatched thirty thousand more soldiers to the south continent. He now has only forty thousand soldiers in the whole of this continent.' As a casual remark, Moridare added, 'Oh, I'm so pleased I didn't kill you. This is a heartening sign.'

Gwaine smiled to himself and bowed. 'It is good news, King Moridare. It will aid our cause.'

‘Yes. Though, why he would want to weaken himself to this extent is beyond me. He should have had enough of his army in the south continent to hold your armies. It is a foolish move.’

‘It is the move I had hoped for and planned for, King Moridare.’ Gwaine was in his element. He knew things that Moridare couldn’t, and he could now explain his strategy to Moridare in the light of strategies that had already succeeded. ‘The Dark Emperor has dispatched more soldiers to Amorand because he is no longer confident of his ability to hold the fortifications of that continent against my armies.’

‘Nonsense!’ Moridare interjected. ‘You take too much credit, Warlord. How could you have caused this movement of troops?’

Gwaine beamed with confidence. ‘When I left Arrindare, my armies were planning to lay siege to the fortifications of Martren, in Barikarn. It was the Dark Emperor’s strongest defence, a magnificent mountain fortress. Princess Tanya has reported that Martren has fallen with only two or three hundred of the Dark Emperor’s force escaping. Thousands of his soldiers have perished. The first part of my plan is complete and successful.’

‘And how much of your armies are left, Warlord? Do you still have an army after this great battle?’

‘My army is similar in size to the Dark Emperor’s southern force.’ Gwaine waited, for effect, before adding, ‘...Counting the thirty thousand that has been dispatched.’

Moridare was visibly impressed. If possible, his good mood had been improved. He rubbed his hands together with glee. ‘Come to my map room, all of you. Warlord, we have much to discuss.’

Moridare led the small gathering through the doorway behind the throne into a dimly lit room that was mainly table. On the extremely large table was a relief model of the northern continent. The first item on its relief to take Gwaine’s attention was a mountain tower in the middle of a large expanse of desert - the Dark Emperor's castle.

'Yes. That is your goal, Warlord.' Moridare, too, was studying the mountain and its tower. 'Though, how you will get to it, I don't know. From his mountain tower, the Emperor can view every movement in the surrounding desert. You could not approach in daylight without being seen. Even if you could, there is no entrance to the tower. It is said that it floats above a fiery chasm and no one can enter unless the Emperor lowers a drawbridge. It is my belief that the Emperor is beyond our reach. We would be better rewarded by plotting the destruction of his army, so that he has no further power on this continent. He will become a prisoner in his impenetrable tower.'

'No King Moridare. I must destroy the Dark Emperor.' Gwaine moved closer to the table and peered over the entire map before returning his gaze to the desert mountain and it's tower. 'Though, there is no reason why we cannot plot both the destruction of the Emperor, and his army.' Gwaine looked at Moridare and raised his eyebrows questioningly.

Moridare smiled cunningly in reply and clapped his hands together with excitement. 'I like your attitude, my young Warlord. How shall we do this?'

Gwaine was surprised by Moridare's question. He was only putting forward a basic theory that they could have two aims rather than choosing between them. He certainly had no idea of how to achieve those aims. He felt the panic surge through his veins as he searched for a stalling tactic.

'Uh, ...Well. First, we need more information before we can finalise on any strategy. ...I am interested to know where you have gained your information on the Emperor's castle. Who told you of the fiery chasm and the drawbridge?'

Moridare grinned wickedly. 'We have our spies', was his only response.

Gwaine waited for more information, but none came. He was reticent to ask questions on such matters, but he needed to judge the validity of the information and whether there was more to be known. 'Where are your spies, King Moridare, and how have they gained this information?'

To Gwaine's relief, Moridare did not seem to be concerned at the delicacy of the subject. 'They have infiltrated the ranks of the Emperor's own garrison.'

'Then they are inside the castle', Gwaine stated with a degree of satisfaction.

'No', Moridare corrected. 'No-one goes inside the castle except the Emperor.'

Gwaine was startled by Moridare's statement. 'Surely he has soldiers and servants.'

'No', Moridare replied emphatically. 'No-one but the Emperor, has ever been inside the castle.'

Gwaine was about to interject when Moridare had a change of mind. '...Except perhaps his provisions officer', Moridare added.

Gwaine shook his head and put his hand forward to indicate to Moridare that he should stop talking. 'Hold. Let's go back for a minute. You are saying that the Dark Emperor lives alone in his castle. No soldiers. No servants. Is that correct?'

'Yes. That is what we have been led to believe.'

'You are saying', Gwaine replied slowly, emphasising each word, 'that he lives alone and does his own cooking, cleaning, washing, etcetera. Is that what you are saying?'

'Yes. That is correct.'

Gwaine was disbelieving. 'That does not sound like much of an Emperor. It is certainly not the life style that one would expect of an Emperor.'

'Obviously, he trusts no one', Moridare replied.

'What about provisions?' Gwaine continued. 'You mentioned a provisions officer.'

'The Emperor's garrison is based to the east of his castle, at the base of this mountain range, between the two rivers that you can see on the map. Each month, they deliver a cartload of provisions to the castle. The drawbridge is lowered and the provisions officer drives the cart into the castle storeroom. There he unhitches the horses, attaches them to the empty cart from the previous delivery and drives out. Presumably, the Emperor unloads the stores as he needs them.'

Gwaine looked at Moridare in surprise. 'Then its simple', he stated incredulously. 'You have spies in that garrison. Instruct them to poison the food.'

Moridare's shoulders slumped noticeably as he looked at Gwaine in disappointment. 'Do you think us fools?' he demanded angrily. 'Of course, we have tried that. The result is, that the Emperor still lives, and every soldier who went near the food that month, including our spy, is dead; put to the sword at the Emperor's command. He has some method of detecting the poison. If this is the best you can do, Warlord, you can go back to the dungeon.'

Gwaine took a deep breath and sighed in an attempt to cover up the panic that Moridare's outburst had caused within him. 'Forgive me King Moridare. It was the excitement of gaining new information that caused my rash suggestion.'

Moridare quelled his temper. 'Very well. But remember, Warlord, I will not suffer foolish plans. You are asking me to put my Kingdom and my life at stake. If I am not convinced that you can plan this coup, then you will feel my blade.'

Gwaine returned his attention to the map and pretended to be studying its contours, and formulating a strategy, while he concentrated on bringing his nerves under control. He rubbed his palms discreetly over his hips to wipe away the sweat that had formed there, as he cast a look toward Tanya. Since entering the room, she had been swept away to the far corner by the two ladies. Obviously, it was not their place to talk in this gathering. Tanya bit her bottom lip to convey to Gwaine her concern at Moridare's sudden change of temperament.

'Um ...My Lord', Gwaine pushed forward hesitantly. 'If the Emperor's garrison is so far away, what has stopped an army attacking across the desert and besieging the castle?'

'The fact that there is no way into the castle', Moridare replied dryly. 'There is little point in sending an army to camp outside the Emperor's castle in anticipation of being destroyed by the Emperor's army when it finally arrives.'

Gwaine did not comment. He was waiting to see how Moridare's temperament was developing. 'Besides', Moridare continued, 'The desert itself holds death. There is only one safe path, and that is the route that the provisions cart takes from the mountains to the castle. Those who stray into the desert, die. Even careless soldiers have strayed off the safe path and died.'

'How do they die?'

'The ground below them erupts. There is a deafening noise, I am told. When the noise stops, there is a large hole in the sand and all that remains of the victim is scattered pieces of burnt flesh.'

Gwaine shook his head as he pondered over the map. How was he going to formulate a strategy on this sketchy mixture of second hand reports, legends and superstition? His mind felt overloaded on the subject of the Emperor. 'Let's change the subject for a while', he announced.

Moridare gave him a wide-eyed surprised stare. 'And what subject would you prefer to discuss, Warlord?'

Gwaine smiled, as confidently as he possibly could under the tense conditions. 'Chaos, King Moridare. Hysteria. Rebellion. The overthrow of the Emperor's power base.'

Moridare smiled warmly displaying the sudden changes that his temperament could undergo. 'This sounds like my type of subject. Carry on Warlord. Tell me about it.'

Gwaine looked beyond Moridare, to his still silent advisers. He hoped that they would be displaying the same enthusiasm as their King, but they weren't. They looked bored, obviously having heard most of this conversation before. Harn looked more than bored. His dark expression displayed a degree of animosity toward Gwaine that Gwaine could not reconcile. He forced his attention back to Moridare.

'On my trek from the west Coast to your mountain, I spent much time crawling through farmland. I noticed that most of the crops were close to maturity. Would this be correct for most of the Northern Continent?'

'Yes', Moridare replied with bewilderment. 'Our main crops will be harvested within weeks.'

''And where are they mainly grown? Is there any sort of concentration of crops?'

'Not really. They are grown along the northern and eastern coasts. Why are you interested in our crops?'

'Because, King Moridare, people become irrational when there is not enough food to go around. They blame their leaders. Shortages of food have lost many a King, or Emperor, his throne.'

Moridare scratched his chin in thought. 'You want me to burn the crops, ...don't you.'

'I know that the rainy season came too early last year, and there was no surplus.' Gwaine studied Moridare before deciding to continue. 'If fires destroyed this year's crop, it would be disastrous for your beloved monarch. The people would panic and irrationally blame the Dark Emperor for their woes. They would revolt, and the army would be hard pressed to quell any riot with their reduced numbers.'

‘Think of the effect on the people, my King’, Harn interjected loudly. ‘There would be starvation and civil war. Surely, this boy’s ambition is not worth that.’

‘This boy’s ambition’, Moridare replied angrily, ‘is to make me Emperor. I shall decide what that is worth. If this decision does not sit easily with your conscience, then I shall give the commands myself. Summon your senior officer to the Throne Room. I shall meet him shortly.’

Harn bowed angrily, obviously unhappy with the course of events. He cast Gwaine a murderous look before storming from the room.

Moridare turned his attention to Gwaine. ‘The Emperor will not necessarily be forced to withdraw any of his southern force, but I would like to have your word that your army will come to my aid as soon as it is able.’

‘You have my word, King Moridare.’ Gwaine’s reply was instantaneous. ‘I shall see you made Emperor, and there will at last be peace between the northern and southern continents.’

Moridare was obviously happy with the reply. ‘Very good. My warriors shall ride today. The crops shall be cinders within the week.’ Moridare returned his gaze to his large relief map. ‘Now tell me’, he questioned without raising his attention to Gwaine, ‘what is your plan for the Emperor?’

Gwaine stood in silence, wondering what reply he could offer, and sweating more with every passing second. Finally, the non-answer occurred to him. ‘I will need time to consider what you have told me. May I talk to you this afternoon about my strategy?’

Moridare gave a wry smile. ‘I did not really expect you to have a plan already formulated.’ He looked up into Gwaine’s eyes and spoke with obvious sincerity. ‘But, ***I will expect it*** this afternoon.’

BETRAYED

'Well? What will we tell him?' Tanya's voice conveyed her stress and concern. 'We are going in circles and our time's nearly up. He'll call for us soon.'

Gwaine was unmoved. He sat, despondently, in the centre of the bed, staring at his toes.

'Gwaine! Are you listening?' Tanya yelled in frustration at his lack of response.

His shoulders and chest heaved with a sigh. 'What do you want from me?' he mumbled almost inaudibly. He looked up into Tanya's grey eyes. 'Second hand information and superstition.' He unfolded his crossed feet, straightened his legs and threw himself backward into a prostrate position. 'How?' he yelled, and then, realising the secrecy of their discussion, lowered his voice and began again. 'How can I formulate a plan on that basis?'

'It doesn't need to be a final plan', she whispered and pleaded. 'As long as it's plausible.'

Gwaine closed his eyes as if in pain. 'Alright. You tell me a plausible plan, based on the drivel that we've been told.'

Tanya was taken by surprise. She stood in silence and studied Gwaine's motionless form. 'Alright', she answered resolutely. 'We've already decided that the only glimmer of hope was in the delivery of provisions. We could use that to get inside the castle.'

'Yes', Gwaine replied in a tone of boredom. 'It's obvious, isn't it.'

Tanya's temper was rising. 'So what? It's a way.'

'Yes. But don't you think that it would be obvious to Moridare too. Not to mention the Dark Emperor. Don't you think that the delivery of provisions will be heavily guarded and its arrival at the castle viewed with suspicion and heavy security.'

Tanya stood in silence. Her first impulse was to allow the depression to sweep over her and allow her pent-up frustration to flow in the form of tears that were already welling in her eyes. Her second impulse was to bash Gwaine until he was black and blue. How dare he criticise her attempts when he had so obviously given up. She jumped with fright at the sound of a knock upon the door.

Gwaine dived to his feet and strode to the door. He cast Tanya a worried glance as he flung open the door.

'King Moridare', he exclaimed in surprise. 'This is unexpected. We were just putting the finishing touches on our plan.'

Tanya felt her knees turn to jelly.

'I must talk with you, Warlord. All is lost.' The depression in Moridare's voice rivalled the depths that Gwaine and Tanya had reached over the last few hours.

Speechless, Gwaine motioned for him to enter.

'You must leave this castle immediately and speed back to your homeland', Moridare instructed as he entered the room. Noticing Tanya for the first time, he nodded in greeting before continuing. 'I have been betrayed.'

Gwaine's blood ran cold at the news. 'How my Lord? ...Who?'

Moridare shook his head slowly, almost disbelievingly. He sat on the edge of the bed and put his head in his hands. Gwaine and Tanya immediately fell to their knees so as not to be higher than the King.

Looking up and seeing their kneeling position, Moridare only waved a dismissing hand. 'Forget all that. Arise. I won't be King for much longer. The Dark Emperor's army will soon be on my doorstep.'

Gwaine regained his height but Tanya opted to retain her position, walking on her knees, with difficulty in her long dress, to the end of the bed. 'What has happened, my Lord?' she whispered compassionately.

'My closest friend. My most noble warrior', Moridare muttered, almost to himself, in disbelief. He dragged himself out of his misery to force himself to look at Tanya. 'Harn has disappeared. He was last seen riding down the mountain, at speed.'

'Perhaps on some important errand, my Lord', Gwaine offered hopefully.

'No!' Moridare replied emphatically. 'He is on no errand. He left no message with anyone, no orders to his subordinates. The only explanation for his unusual behaviour is that he is racing to the Dark Emperor to relay our plans. He was my best friend.' Moridare returned to his misery and self-pity. 'My most trusted adviser.' With sudden anger in his eyes, Moridare glared at Gwaine. 'You see the strength of our cursed Emperor. No conversation is safe from his ears. No friend is out of reach of his black talons.'

'Tell me, King Moridare', Gwaine questioned, trying to bring the conversation back to its subject, 'What of the soldiers who were dispatched to burn the crops?'

'As good as dead', Moridare replied with a catch in his throat.

'A messenger should speed after them', Gwaine suggested hopefully.

'No. He would not catch them in time. I would be sending just another corpse into the Emperor's trap. No, they will all die on their return trek.'

Gwaine straightened with surprise. 'Then they ***will*** burn the crops?'

'Yes. Harn shall not reach the Dark Emperor in time for soldiers to be dispatched to stop them burning most of the crops. The soldiers on the north coast may even return. It is the ones on the east coast who shall perish by Harn's betrayal.'

Gwaine felt hope resurging in his veins. 'Forgive me, King Moridare. I know that you are suffering the betrayal of a friend, and the loss of many good soldiers. But, apart from those losses, heavy as they are, our plan is still intact. The crops shall be burnt. The people could rebel. The Dark Emperor, if he is to lay siege to your castle, must withdraw at least some of his force from Amorand. All is not lost.'

'Think, Warlord', Moridare responded angrily. 'Harn will tell him that you and the Princess are here.'

'Excellent!' Gwaine replied buoyantly. 'The Dark Emperor will believe that we are trapped on this mountain while we will, in fact, be somewhere else. His army can only lay siege to your mountain. You are invulnerable to the size of force that he can muster. As long as you allow him to believe that we are here, then we have the element of surprise in our favour. Harn cannot expect that you would have discovered his absence so quickly.'

Moridare sat in silence, studying the boy who stood in front of him. When he finally spoke, it was in a slow methodical style. 'I have been blinded by grief. Our plan is still healthy. Though, you cannot hope to destroy the Emperor now. He is forewarned of your intention. You must return to your army and bring it to my aid.'

'We have a plan, my Lord', Gwaine replied, obviously intending to contradict the King's instruction.

Tanya stared open-mouthed at Gwaine and panicked at his insolence.

'Then do not tell it to me', Moridare roared. 'Or anyone else. There has been too much discussion already. Begone from my castle while you are able.'

'Moridare was already to his feet and walking toward the door when he stopped and turned to Tanya. He offered her his hand as support while she struggled with her dress in an attempt to regain her feet. 'I am sorry, my Lady, that I shall not have your company in my court.'

Tanya smiled in reply. She could still see the twinkle in his eye that had always been there when he addressed her. For all his harshness and sudden changes of mood, she could not help liking this bright eyed tyrant. She leant forward and kissed him on the cheek.

The smile that Tanya's kiss had brought to his face lasted only a fleeting second. As he strode past Gwaine he issued a harsh warning. 'I have accepted your word that you will return with your army. If you fail to do so, you may only look to the north when you are looking for enemies.'

ESCAPING THE SIEGE

Despite the possibility of a section of the Dark Emperor's army being closer than Moridare anticipated, Gwaine and Tanya waited until the last rays of light had disappeared over the horizon before venturing outside of the castle. The fear of being entrapped in the siege of Moridare's mountain was far less than the fear that Magnor had implanted in Gwaine of ***the all-seeing eyes***. 'I don't believe in it, but I promised Magnor that I would only travel at night. That's all!' he had told Tanya defensively when she had attacked his ***silly superstitions***.

As darkness fell, Gwaine, Tanya, and Moridare rode up the mountain onto the plateau. Once on the high, level ground they headed east, travelling firstly along the plateau and then down the eastern side of the mountain. At the base of the mountain, Moridare had bid them farewell without questioning their strategy or their peculiar choice of direction. They were now travelling even further away from the Dark Emperor's tower.

Moridare had outfitted them in local garb in the hope that they could travel swiftly without their movement being questioned. He had supplied them with horses that had obviously been bred for endurance and had packed their saddlebags full of food and water and medical supplies.

His only comments at the base of the mountain had been a direction to stay to the south of the large lake and a final warning plea to return with an army that would break the siege. Their last sight of Moridare was a large silhouette disappearing at speed into the foliage of his mountain.

Gwaine regretted the little time that he'd had to know this legendary warrior. Tanya felt haunted by his departing words even before he had disappeared from sight.

'You ***will*** return to help him, won't you Gwaine?' she had asked as soon as the sound of hoofbeats had died in the eerie darkness.

'I made that promise', Gwaine declared before spurring his horse eastward toward the great lake.

By daylight, the next morning, Tanya and Gwaine were well hidden, high on the mountain range that ran from north to south of the Northern Continent. From their vantagepoint, they saw the force of at least ten thousand of the Dark Emperor's army racing toward Moridare's mountain.

'He's in real trouble', Tanya commented gravely.

'Nonsense. He can hold that force at bay for years. It's only a siege force. They can't hope to take the mountain. They can only hope to keep him bottled up. What it does mean, though, is that the Dark Emperor must bring some of his force from Amorand. He can't handle his domestic problems with the number of soldiers he has now.' There was an obvious note of satisfaction in Gwaine's voice. 'The plan is still healthy.'

Tanya looked solemnly at Gwaine and studied his profile as he studied the army below with obvious glee. She wrinkled her nose in disgust before turning and climbing down into their foliage bedding. 'You're as bad as Magnor', she told him as she wriggled down under the cover of the thick fern leaves in preparation for a day's sleep.

'How?' Gwaine queried absent-mindedly as he continued to watch the Emperor's army.

'You use people', Tanya replied.

Gwaine turned his full attention to Tanya, hurt by her serious comment.

'You don't give a damn', she continued. 'You don't give a damn about Moridare. His ambition and ruthlessness were just part of your plan. He has done his bit now, so you leave him defending his little hill against a large army while you run off to the next stage of the plan.'

'I am trying to save Amorand', Gwaine interjected, less than convincingly.

‘You don’t give a damn about the soldiers who will die defending the mountain’, she continued, ‘...or the ones who have already died while burning the crops. It doesn’t worry you that innocent men, women, and children will go hungry as a result of your plan or that many will die in riots as a result of their hunger.’

‘I do care’, Gwaine replied in a quiet, subdued manner. He wasn’t used to being attacked by Tanya. He had always considered her to be one of the few people who he could rely on to be on his side. ‘But, caring doesn’t help. No matter how much I cared, my actions would be the same. It is my pledge to save Amorand and destroy the Dark Emperor. This is how I must do it.’

Tanya ignored his reply. She was at full speed now and wasn’t prepared to stop for anything. ‘You even used Taron.’

‘Rubbish!’ Gwaine replied hotly, his anger suddenly jumping to the fore.

‘He was a good manager. So you used him to save the Fortress and then you threw away the shell and moved on to the next part of the plan.’

Gwaine could feel the blood pumping through his temples. He felt his face flush as he fought to control his rage. ‘Taron is my friend’, he pushed forward through clenched teeth.

Tanya looked up, startled by the anger in Gwaine’s voice. She realised that she had gone too far.

‘Go to sleep’, Gwaine commanded. ‘You’re overtired.’

Tanya snuggled down and closed her eyes, pleased to obey the command in order to escape Gwaine’s temper.

As night returned, they rose from their uneasy sleep and prepared to move southward, along the mountain range. The air was heavy with the smell of smoke and the view to the east was marred by a thick black cloud.

‘That part of your plan has worked’, Tanya remarked casually as she mounted her horse.

‘Yea’, Gwaine replied caustically, taking the comment as a sarcastic attack on his attitude toward the people who would suffer as a result of the fires. He threw himself onto his horse. ‘Are you ready?’

‘Yes.’ Tanya’s reply was subdued. She hadn’t wanted to cause a fight. ‘Gwaine. I’m sorry for what I said regarding Taron. I realise that isn’t true.’

‘Is that all you’re sorry for?’ Gwaine queried aggressively, without looking back.

Tanya straightened her position in the saddle and strengthened her will. She wasn’t prepared to apologise for anything else. ‘Yes. That’s all I’m sorry for.’

Gwaine spurred his horse forward. ‘Let’s go’, he yelled over his shoulder.

Hours of slow, weary progress, of faltering in the darkness, led into more and more hours. The night seemed to go on forever as they plied their way through the thick underbrush and timber of the mountain.

Finally a dark star dawned through the black cloud that hung heavily over the sea. Gwaine immediately began searching for a well-covered spot that would provide protection during the daylight hours.

The horses hidden as well as was possible on the side of a mountain, Gwaine and Tanya settled among the ferns for some breakfast and a sleep.

After a period of failed attempts at sleep, Tanya raised herself onto her right elbow and looked across to Gwaine. ‘Gwaine. Are you asleep?’ she whispered.

‘No’, Gwaine replied reluctantly.

Tanya was quiet for some time, trying to formulate her question. ‘Gwaine, do you have a plan yet?’

‘No’, was Gwaine’s simple reply.

Tanya grimaced at his sulkiness and wriggled closer to him. ‘Come on. Forget for a moment that we’ve had a tiff and talk to me about the Dark Emperor.’

Gwaine opened one eye and stared at Tanya. Forcing the other eye open, he rolled onto his left side and studied the legitimacy of her suggestion. 'Is that all we've had, …a tiff?'

'Yes', Tanya smiled her reply. 'That's all.'

'Gwaine smiled with relief. 'I didn't think you liked me anymore.'

Tanya allowed her head to fall softly to the ground as she rolled off her elbow, onto her back. She looked back to Gwaine with an expression that conveyed concern. 'Of course I still like you. I just don't like what we're doing.'

'Neither do I, but that doesn't mean that I can avoid doing it. You can, but I can't. I've made a promise to the seven Kings and to all the people of Amorand. I must fulfil that promise or die trying.'

'Alright. I accept that. ...Now, do you have a plan?'

'Not as such', Gwaine replied slowly and thoughtfully. 'We are now within a few hours ride of the city that houses the Dark Emperor's Guard. The supply route leads from there. I want to see it. If I can find a way, I will plan to destroy the Dark Emperor. If I cannot see a means of doing that, then we will continue south to our armies and try to push the remainder of the enemy out of Amorand.'

'Not much chance of that.'

'No'. Gwaine agreed readily. 'That's why I want to see the supply route and, perhaps, the edge of the desert.'

'And what do you hope to see there?'

Gwaine shook his head despondently. 'I don't know. I don't expect that there will be an obvious track to the Dark Emperor's tower. Only the soldiers who ride the supply route will know the safe path.'

'Then we need to follow the supply wagons', Tanya offered hopefully. 'Moridare said that one should be due within this week or next.'

'Yes. We need to follow the supply wagons', Gwaine repeated thoughtfully. 'The trouble is that we have to do it at night so that we won't be detected. The wheel tracks in the sand won't be easy to follow in the dark. On top of that, if a storm comes up, we'll be stranded with no tracks to follow and no way of finding our way back.'

They both fell silent, overwhelmed by the obstacles. Tanya finally broke the silence.

'I don't think that plan will succeed.'

Gwaine shook his head in agreement. 'I haven't told you the worst part yet.'

'Well, do tell me', Tanya suggested sarcastically. 'I'm dying to hear the worst.'

Gwaine looked across at his attractive companion and wondered whether she really wanted him to tell her. He decided that he was enjoying Tanya's company despite the depressing topic, and that the conversation was worth continuing. 'Well, we have to follow the supply wagons but, by some miracle, we have to arrive at the tower just before them so that we can dive inside when the drawbridge is lowered.'

'Oh, that ***will*** be a good trick', Tanya giggled. She grinned across at Gwaine. 'I can't wait to hear how you're going to do that. Do tell me.'

Gwaine studied Tanya's attractive young face and her bright grey eyes. He was glad she was his companion. Without her, he would probably be in the depths of depression by now. He slid himself into a position beside her and placed a kiss on her lips.

She gave him a surprised stare. 'What was that for?'

'That's for keeping me sane ...and for trying to keep me and my emotions from parting company.' He ran his fingers admiringly through the loose curls that rested on her shoulder. 'I do care about the people, you know. I'm sorry that they'll go hungry.'

‘Yes, I know’, Tanya replied sympathetically. She felt ashamed of her attack on Gwaine. After all, he was just as much a victim of the war as everybody else who was being hurt by it. She searched for some consoling remark. ‘Anyway, we can at least be satisfied that the monster who started this war will be just as hungry as everybody else.’

‘Yes’, Gwaine grinned as he moved closer to Tanya’s lips, intending to steal another kiss.

Tanya closed her eyes and waited, willingly, for Gwaine’s lips to press upon hers. Having allowed sufficient time for something to happen, she re-opened her eyes, to see Gwaine staring thoughtfully toward the ground. She gave him a questioning look.

‘No he will not’, Gwaine contradicted. ‘He’s the Emperor. He won’t go hungry.’

Tanya shook her head. Gwaine obviously wasn’t thinking properly. ‘He’ll have to, if there isn’t enough food around.’

‘There’s still food around’, Gwaine argued. ‘The crops weren’t ready for harvest. There’s still the usual amount of food around for this time of year.’

‘So?’ Tanya was bewildered. ‘There won’t be enough food around soon. He will go hungry.’

‘Of course he won’t. He’ll stock up. He’ll rush to fill his tower with all the food he can find. As far as he’s concerned, he’s under siege. ...He’s at war. There’s a faction of his own land that has proved hostile. His army is reduced to below a safe level for maintaining the peace, and his people will soon be hungry and ready to revolt.’

‘So’, Tanya asked impatiently. ‘How does that help?’

‘Shh! ...Be quiet’, Gwaine whispered. A distant, almost imperceptible, sound had gradually risen into the now distinguishable sound of horses tromping through the thick underbrush.

Tanya watched Gwaine as they lay silently listening to the approaching riders. His mind was obviously calculating something as the lines on his forehead deepened and shallowed and his eyes narrowed in thought. Finally, he moved his index finger to his lips to indicate that she should stay silent and then moved away.

Her heart pounded as she lay alone listening to the close sounds of leaves and twigs being trampled by a large number of heavy hoofs.

'Hello, friends', she heard Gwaine yell. Her heart leapt into her throat. What was he doing? He should be back here, beside her, hiding from these strangers.

A deep, amiable voice replied to Gwaine's greeting. 'Hello, young fellow. What are you doing here?'

'I'm just travelling from the north coast to the city to visit with relatives. Where are you all going?'

'Oh, we're going to the city too. Our crops have been burnt. We're going to have a few words to say to our officials about...'

'Who burnt your crops?' Gwaine asked with an incredulous tone in his voice.

'Don't know', another voice replied.

'The army reckons', another voice interjected, 'that Moridare's soldiers done it, but I reckon it was soldiers from down south. Damn wars. Why can't they just leave honest people alone to live their lives?'

'Were the crops up north attacked?' another voice questioned.

'Don't know', replied Gwaine, trying to sound as much as possible like a native of the north. 'Not when I left. Everything was alright.'

'Well, be careful, lad', the first voice warned. 'There may be still some of the scoundrels around, trying to escape the army.'

'It doesn't sound good', Gwaine replied with a well-effected tremble in his voice. 'Do you mind if I travel with you?'

Tanya panicked. What was he doing? It was still daylight.

'Not at all, lad. Grab your horse and join us.'

'Thank you. I must admit, though, that my sister is with me. I put her in hiding when I heard you approaching.'

'Very wise, lad. These are uncertain times. Just as well to be safe. Bring her along. She's safe with us.'

Tanya heard Gwaine scurrying back to her position. She gave him an amazed, incredulous look as he stood over her.

'Come on, sis', he said loudly. 'It's alright. We've got company to ride with to the city.'

Tanya obeyed Gwaine's instruction and moved out from cover. She was stunned by this sudden turn of events. As they moved toward their horses she studied the collection of twenty or so farmers and cast them a worried, hesitant smile. The farmers waited patiently as they saddled their horses.

'It's daylight, Gwaine', Tanya whispered worriedly. 'What about the all-seeing eyes?'

'What about them?' Gwaine whispered jovially. 'We are dressed like locals, and riding with a bunch of farmers. Now that we're not just the two of us, we aren't going to raise any suspicion. The Emperor doesn't know what we look like. He was just looking for a boy and a girl. We can now ride safely into the city and blend in with the crowds.'

Gwaine and Tanya mounted.

'What if they ask me any questions about where we came from?' Tanya's worry showed in her face.

'Oh, just pretend to be shy', Gwaine replied buoyantly.

Tanya cast him a black look.

'Sorry to have kept you', Gwaine shouted to the waiting farmers. 'We're ready now.'

TO THE CITY

Tanya needn't have worried about being questioned by the farmers. Apart from the occasional polite remark, the farmers tended to ignore their young companions. They were preoccupied with their own discussions.

With their crops burnt and their livelihood lost, these men had left their families to survive on what small amount of crops had escaped the fires and were now travelling to the city in search of work. But most of their conversation surrounded the secondary task. They were emissaries, sent by their farming community to take an abrupt message to the officials in the town. They were unhappy with the degree of protection that they had received from the army. They were disgruntled with the extended war and the sacrifices that were being made for dubious reasons, and they wanted to know, in straight terms, just what sort of assistance their families would receive to help them through the difficult times to come.

Gwaine marvelled at their inability to grasp the situation. They were talking about food relief for their families, without even the slightest consideration being given to the fact that all of the crops may have been burnt, and that there just wasn't going to be any food. 'Perhaps', he thought, 'they have considered it but just don't want to accept it.' Gwaine's spirits sank as he realised the full, human implications of his plan. He looked around at the amicable farmers who had so readily accepted him and Tanya into their company. They weren't his enemy. They were just like the farmers of Arrindare. As he listened to their conversation, to their stories of families left behind, he found himself hating himself and the Dark Emperor with equal intensity.

'It's our war', he told himself. 'The Dark Emperor's and mine. No-one else should be involved. No-one else should be hurt. It should be just the two of us.'

Gwaine felt little excitement when they finally reached the base of the mountain range and gained their first view of the city. The misery that was drowning him from within was too great to allow either exaltation or fear.

A column of soldiers overtook them on the gallop without paying the slightest heed to the bedraggled band of farmers.

When the column was well past them, Gwaine moved his horse closer to Tanya and settled into a position at her side. They all rode in silence to the city gates and through the bustling, crowded streets, until the farmers stopped at an intersection of the stone pathways.

'We must leave you now', one of the farmers announced.

Tanya couldn't restrain herself. She cast a worried glance at Gwaine.

'Don't you worry, little lady', the farmer said reassuringly. 'You'll be safe. There's plenty of soldiers for protection. Just yell for them if anyone bothers you.'

Tanya forced a smile. However, in his attempt to console her, the farmer had only confirmed her worst fears. There ***were*** soldiers everywhere.

'We have to go up this path', the farmer continued, addressing Gwaine. 'The city's administration is in that direction. You should continue on this path. It will take you into the living area of the city. Do you know how to find your relatives?'

'Oh yes', Gwaine replied confidently. 'I've been there before, but this is the first time that I've brought my sister with me.' Gwaine had hoped to explain away Tanya's obvious fear.

'Well, we'll wish you goodbye then.'

'Yes. Goodbye and thank you', Gwaine replied. 'I hope your mission is a success and you soon see your families again.' The words almost died in his throat as he tried to utter them, but the farmers didn't notice. They were already moving along the path toward the administration area.

‘Gwaine. We’re alone’, Tanya whispered with concern. ‘We’re the boy and girl combination that the Dark Emperor is looking for.’

Gwaine only smiled.

‘We’ve got to get under cover, Gwaine.’

‘No we don’t’, Gwaine replied casually. ‘Look around you. The place is like a beehive. We’re just part of a large crowd. Let’s go and look over the market. I’m hungry.’

‘No money’, was Tanya’s terse reply. She was far from happy with Gwaine’s ideas as to their safety.

Gwaine dismounted before tapping his cloak pocket. ‘Moridare is buying lunch.’ He tied his horse to a rail among the horses of other market-goers and headed off toward the food stalls. Tanya was forced to dismount, secure her horse, and follow, shaking her head visibly as she struggled to keep up with him amongst the crowd.

She caught up with him in front of a stall where Gwaine was already involved in a discussion with the seller. They had chosen some vegetables and bread and Gwaine was about to hand over the money when three covered wagons, surrounded by soldiers, thundered down the stone path toward the city gate.

‘What’s that?’ Gwaine queried as he handed over the money.

‘Emperor’s supplies’, the old seller barked in reply. ‘He won’t go hungry’, he added scornfully, and then, realising the danger of his unguarded remark, quickly bustled off to serve another customer, casting Gwaine and Tanya a fearful glance as they moved away.

‘We have to find somewhere to sleep’, Gwaine told Tanya as they moved out of the market area and up the path that led to the residential area. ‘We’ve got things to do tonight.’

‘You’re not thinking of following those wagons are you?’

‘I certainly am.’

‘Why?’ Tanya asked incredulously. ‘What can you hope to do? You said yourself that you had to follow the wagons and arrive before them, to be able to get into the tower.’

‘I did …and I will.’

Tanya was fed up with Gwaine’s behaviour. He was being too sure of himself, and she couldn’t see any reason to be anything but scared. She shoved him with all the strength she could muster into the brick wall that lined the path, forcing him off balance. He fell into a sitting position at the base of the wall with Tanya, hands on hips, leaning over him. He stared up in shock, into Tanya’s angry grey eyes.

‘What the hell…’

‘Never mind that’, Tanya roared. ‘You had better start explaining yourself or you’ll find yourself without a partner.’

Gwaine searched nervously amongst the passing crowd, for any signs that anyone was taking an interest in Tanya’s behaviour. A faint, amused smile from a passing old man was the only sign that he found.

‘Alright. Settle down. Keep your voice down’, Gwaine replied as he tried to console his companion.

‘What’s going on here?’ a voice roared from behind Tanya.

Tanya looked around to find a burly soldier towering over her. Her mouth dropped open and she backed up to the wall.

Gwaine dived to his feet immediately and placed himself between Tanya and the soldier. ‘It’s alright, Sir’, he pushed forward as fast as his lips would move. ‘Just a little tiff with my sister.’

‘Not good enough’, the soldier roared. Gwaine’s heart jumped into his throat. He was onto them. He had guessed who they were.

‘I expect’, the soldier continued, ‘better behaviour on the paths. Carrying on like this will get someone hurt.’

‘Yes. I apologise’, Gwaine offered, relieved that his worst fears hadn’t yet come true.

‘I’m sorry’, Tanya added pitifully from behind him.

The soldier stood for some seconds, studying them both, holding eye contact in a successful attempt to unnerve them both. ‘Alright’, he finally added quietly. ‘Just don’t let it happen again.’

‘No sir’, they both replied in unison.

The soldier gave them a last stern stare. ‘Alright.’ He moved away down the path, leaving Gwaine and Tanya transfixed and visibly shaking.

‘I’m sorry’, Tanya whispered before bursting into tears.

Gwaine turned and put his arm around her shoulder and gently guided her further up the path. ‘Come on. We’ll find an inn and I’ll explain before we get some sleep.’

‘No. I don’t want to go anywhere where we have to talk to people. Tell me as we’re walking. We should be able to find a garden or something where we can sit and relax until it starts getting dark.’

‘Alright. If that’s what you want, it’s fine by me.’

‘Tell me how you’re going to follow the wagons and get there before them.’

‘Simple. We saw three wagons, didn’t we?’

‘Yes. So what?’

‘Well, it’s not enough. If the Dark Emperor is going to stock up for a long period, he will need at least four times that amount.’

‘Keep talking’, Tanya urged, failing to see any connection.

'He will need more than the delivery of goods that we saw. So, if I follow that delivery, I will be waiting on the Dark Emperor's mountain for the next delivery to arrive.'

'Unless that's the fourth delivery', Tanya added dryly.

'Pessimist', was Gwaine's only reply.

They walked on in silence, searching for somewhere unobtrusive to sit and pass the hours to nightfall. Eventually they came across a garden setting, off one of the paths. The seats were occupied so they moved directly to the only tree in the garden and took their positions under it, leaning against its trunk.

Tanya wiped her eyes as Gwaine divided their bread and vegetables into two portions.

'Don't you mean 'we'?', Tanya queried.

Gwaine gave her a puzzled look. 'Pardon?'

'You said, 'I will be waiting on the Dark Emperor's mountain'. You meant 'we', didn't you?'

'Um ...no I didn't. I was going to find somewhere for you to stay.'

'Why?' Tanya was forcing back the tears.

'Because it's too dangerous.'

'Too foolhardy you mean', Tanya interrupted sarcastically.

'Perhaps that too', Gwaine conceded. 'But, definitely too dangerous. I would rather find somewhere safe for you to stay.'

'There's no such place, Gwaine, and you know it.'

'There might be. We haven't looked yet.'

'Well if you find it', Tanya commented stubbornly, wiping the tears from her cheeks, 'how do you intend keeping me there? How are you going to stop me coming with you? You'll have to kill me.'

Gwaine sat in silence staring at his lunch. He wasn't hungry anymore. Tanya was right. Where could he leave her that was safe? How could he make her stay there even if such a place existed? As much as he disliked the idea, he would have to take her across the desert to the Dark Emperor's tower. He would have to try and refine his plan a bit more, seeing it was more than his life that was at risk.

'Alright, you win. I guess you will have to come'. Gwaine's tone was full of defeat and despondency.

'Of course I will, silly', Tanya added in a tear filled voice that was attempting to be cheerful. 'There was never any doubt of it. Now, let's get some rest.'

'Good idea. You go first. I'll wake you when it's my turn.'

Tanya handed Gwaine her untouched lunch and he rewrapped all of the food as she snuggled up against his shoulder and the tree trunk in preparation for sleep.

ACROSS HIS DESERT

'Tanya ...Tanya. It's time to wake up.'

Tanya stirred and opened her eyes to a chilly, twilight world. The daylight was fading.

'What happened?' she questioned groggily. 'You didn't wake me.'

'Yes I did', Gwaine replied defensively. 'Just then.'

'Rat! You need sleep too.'

Gwaine leant across and kissed her forehead before forcing himself stiffly to his feet. 'I'm tough', he offered in a mock-serious tone.

'No you're not. You're just a good actor', Tanya countered as she pushed herself to her feet.

Gwaine forced himself into an upright stance and tried to waken his stiff limbs. 'Come on. Let's get the horses and get moving.'

With the horses quickly fed and watered, they mounted and moved back down the path. Gwaine studied the crowd. It was thinner now and was mainly moving away from the markets toward the living quarters of the city. No one paid them any attention, though, as they moved against the main flow, back toward the market place.

The market place was closing. Only a few stalls were still open for business with most of the business people either packing up or already loaded and preparing to move their carts.

Tanya was prepared to ride directly through the market place and through the city gates, but Gwaine suddenly veered off and down a side path to one of the remaining stalls. She followed, reluctantly.

As they approached the stall, two men, possibly farmers, rode away with hunting crossbows and arrows strapped to their backs. Gwaine studied the crossbows closely as the two men rode past, before moving to the stall where they had been purchased.

'How much for a crossbow and a quiver of arrows?'

The old man behind the stall eyed him carefully before answering. 'Ah, well, very popular these. Now that there looks like being a food shortage. A lot of the crops have been burned you know.'

'Yes. I've heard', Gwaine answered, quietly studying the old man's salesmanship. 'How much?'

'Well...' The old man hesitated as he scratched his hairy chin and studied his crossbows. 'It's late in the day, and I don't want to take all of these home just to bring them back again tomorrow...'

'How much?' Gwaine enquired again, impatiently.

The old man eyed him up and down before answering. 'Four coins for you, lad. That's the best I can offer.'

Gwaine looked thoughtfully at the collection of bows on the counter.

'It's too much', Tanya commented calmly from behind Gwaine.

'It's the best I can do', the old man barked. 'Take it or leave it.'

A stifled look of satisfaction swept over the old man's face as Gwaine placed his hand in his cloak pocket. He fumbled around but only found three coins. The old man's face turned to stone again as Gwaine withdrew his hand, empty.

'My sister's right. It is too much', Gwaine commented calmly. 'I wouldn't pay any more than two.'

The old man gave a harsh, hollow laugh. 'Two? That wouldn't cover the material to make it. Why, I'd just be covering the material for the crossbow and arrows with three coins.'

Gwaine smiled. There was obviously an opening for negotiation. 'What if you only gave me a couple of arrows?'

The old man gave him a surprised look. 'And what good would only a couple of arrows do you?'

Gwaine forced a most sincere expression. 'I am an excellent shot', he proclaimed with pride.

The old man was obviously taken aback. He stood in confusion, alternating his stare between the bow and the young braggart in front of him. Finally, he came to a conclusion. 'The crossbow and two arrows', he stated. 'Nothing more?'

'Nothing more', Gwaine echoed in reply.

'Three coins. No less', the old man proclaimed.

'Done.' Gwaine reached into his pocket and produced the three coins.

The transaction completed, Gwaine and Tanya joined the business people as some drove their cartloads of goods and others rode their horses through the city gate. There, the crowd dispersed to the north and south and west.

Gwaine threw the crossbow over his shoulder and pushed the two arrows into his saddlebag as he and Tanya rode among the throng that was heading to the west.

It was dark now, but the road was well defined as they rode over the river crossing and into the western farmland. A bright moon threw enough light in the night sky to reflect off the slowly moving water that was now on their left.

As they travelled, the number of people on the sandy road slowly dwindled as family said goodnight to family and turned off the road to their farmhouses.

Within an hour, there was only a handful of people on the road, and the remainder were staring questioningly at the young couple who had fallen about a hundred metres behind them.

'We're in trouble, Gwaine', Tanya whispered. 'This is their road. They know we don't belong here.'

Gwaine rode another hundred metres before answering. 'Whatever happens, just keep riding. I'll do the talking, but we'll keep riding.'

Ten minutes later, the small group stopped and veered off the road to farmhouses on either side. They said their noisy farewells and moved away from the road, leaving two mounted men waiting at the side of the road for Tanya and Gwaine.

'Good evening', Gwaine greeted them when they were within ten metres.

'Good evening', the older of the farmers replied. 'Where are you two going?'

'Oh, just out for an evening ride', Gwaine said casually. He and Tanya were still riding at their casual speed.

'An evening ride?' the man echoed incredulously. 'You two had better get back to town. You're not safe out here.'

Gwaine and Tanya were past the two men. Gwaine had to look over his shoulder to reply. 'Oh, well be all right. We'll turn back soon.'

'Well you make sure you do. It's not safe to go much further. Your parents will have your hides when you get home.'

'Yes. I think you're right.' Gwaine had to raise his voice to yell back to the farmers. 'We'll turn back soon.'

'Alright. Goodnight then.' The farmers rode off the road toward their homes.

Tanya breathed a sigh of relief. 'Whew! You made that look easy.'

‘Well’, Gwaine grinned his reply, ‘I’ve had a lot of experience in disregarding instructions in the politest possible way.’ Gwaine leant forward and peered, toward the road. ‘Wagon tracks’, he proclaimed gleefully.

‘And as deep as could be expected in this sandy road’, Tanya added just as joyfully. ‘Even I could follow those tracks by this moonlight.’

‘Well, let’s get moving then. We don’t know how far we have to travel tonight.’

‘No!’ Tanya’s reply caught Gwaine about to spur his horse forward. He gave her a questioning look.

‘Look up there.’ Tanya pointed into the distance and to the left of the road. ‘There’s another farmhouse. We had better wait until we get past there.’

As they peered toward the farmhouse in the distance, they were startled by movement only a couple of hundred metres ahead. Three mounted figures moved onto the road from beneath a tree on the right.

‘What do we do?’ Tanya queried, the fear rising in her voice.

Gwaine felt for his sword and adjusted his cloak so that he was sure the sword was covered from view. ‘We’ll find out who they are and what they want.’

They rode on in silence, studying the figures that barred their way. As they narrowed the gap between them, the uniforms of the Emperor’s soldiers became discernable.

‘They’re soldiers’, Tanya whispered fearfully.

‘Shh’, was Gwaine’s only reply.

‘Who goes there?’ a deep voice demanded.

Gwaine didn’t reply. Instead, he leant himself forward in an exaggerated peering position and kept riding at the same casual speed.

‘I said, ***who goes there?***’ the voice boomed again after a short delay.

‘Oh, I’m sorry, sir’, Gwaine answered. ‘I couldn’t see that you were a soldier.’

Tanya and Gwaine reined their horses to a halt, five metres from the soldiers.

‘We live on this road’, Gwaine continued. ‘We’re just out for an evening ride.’

‘An evening ride?’ the old soldier replied disbelievingly. ‘And just where are you riding to?’

‘Oh, just to that farmhouse up ahead, sir.’ Gwaine pointed to the distant farmhouse.

‘Do you know the occupants of that dwelling, do you?’

Gwaine considered his answer. He decided that it was too easy for the soldier to check his answer. ‘No sir. I don’t know who lives there.’

‘Just as well you gave me an honest reply, lad, or you’d be in real trouble. That house has been deserted for over ten years. Now…’ the soldier gave Gwaine a dark, warning stare. ‘Tell me what you’re really doing out here.’

Gwaine looked dumbly at the soldier. He moved his left hand to the sheath of his sword, to hold it still, in readiness for withdrawing the sword. He cast a darting look at Tanya, to see if she had any words to offer, but only found her looking down at her reins with a coy, embarrassed expression.

A laugh from the soldier returned Gwaine’s attention to the burly old man and his two younger companions.

The soldier’s attitude had completely changed. He gave Gwaine a jovial, friendly grin. ‘Well, lad. You’ve been sprung, haven’t you? Caught with your pants down, so to speak.’ He threw Gwaine a wicked wink. ‘Never mind, though. We were young once, weren’t we lads?’

The two younger soldiers laughed in reply.

‘You take your young lady to the farmhouse’, the soldier continued. ‘If anybody asks, we haven’t seen you.’

The soldiers moved their horses forward, with the elder moving between Gwaine and Tanya. As he passed Tanya, he slapped her playfully on the thigh. 'Have a good ride', he offered sarcastically, the three soldiers breaking out in immediate, riotous laughter.

Gwaine and Tanya sat immobile until the sounds of the soldiers' horses had died in the distance.

Gwaine's heart was still pounding in his chest but he couldn't help commenting. 'Tanya ...So that's why you've brought me all the way out here. You little devil, you.' He heard the whistle as Tanya sucked the air between her teeth in obvious frustration.

'Oh, shut up!' she ordered as she jolted her horse forward.

They rode at speed now. The wagon tracks were easily visible, the farmhouse was deserted, and the soldiers were behind them, prepared to cover for them if anyone happened to mention the young couple riding toward the desert.

They rode beside the river until it turned suddenly southward. Not much further on, they entered the Emperor's desert and saw his mountain rising in the distance. They travelled at speed, following the deep, grooved, wheel tracks until Gwaine called a halt sometime around midnight.

'What's wrong? We're making good speed', Tanya argued.

'Yes. We are', Gwaine replied thoughtfully. 'But we've got a problem.'

'What?'

'If the wagons return as soon as they unload, then we're going to run into them.'

Tanya's blood froze. If they were caught in the desert, then there would be no easy explanations. 'They would not,' she suggested unconvincingly, and then, gaining in confidence, she added, 'They're not as stupid as we are. If a sandstorm came up, they would be lost in the desert and lose their safe path. They would not run the risk of perishing that way.'

‘Yes. You’re probably right’, Gwaine agreed thoughtfully. ‘Still. It doesn’t really matter. There’s nothing we can do anyway. There is only one path. If they travel back at night, then we’ll run into them. If they don’t, we’ll be on the mountain in two hours.’

‘That’s right’, Tanya agreed jovially. ‘Not worth a second thought.’

Gwaine gave her a quizzical look. ‘What are you so buoyant about?’

Tanya laughed. ‘I saved our lives back there. Magnor made the right choice in sending me to help you. I’d like to see Taron or one of your warriors save you the way I did.’

Gwaine laughed at the comical thoughts that Tanya’s suggestion placed in his mind. ‘I don’t think Taron or any of those warriors would have passed the physical.’ He leant across and dragged Tanya half off her horse, to hold her and kiss her passionately, before replacing her in her saddle.

‘You know. When this is all over…’, he whispered, still holding her firmly.

‘What?’

‘I’m going to take you for a ride.’

‘Sounds great, she responded, placing a kiss on his lips. ‘But, right now...’, she changed the subject as she pressed him away, ‘we’ve got a desert to cross and a mountain to climb.’

‘Alright. Let’s go.’

THE EMPEROR'S TOWER

The first rays of light found Tanya and Gwaine huddled together for warmth under a rock outcrop on the side of the Emperor's mountain.

As Gwaine sat shivering in the near freezing temperature, he pictured this so-called mountain. Their first view of it had been in darkness but it was obvious, even then, that it was not a living mountain but a huge collection of boulders bundled onto, and around, a mountainous rock outcrop. Only the hardiest of desert plants grew on its sides, finding nutrient somewhere in its scarred and creviced features.

They still hadn't had a clear view of the Emperor's tower. In the darkness, they could only discern from its dark silhouette against the dark sky, that it was indeed a tower. It stood tall and slender like a finger pointing toward the distant stars.

They had stumbled almost three quarters of the way up the narrow rock path before Gwaine had found the hiding place they wanted. A larger cave-like overhang had been used to hide the horses while they had taken the smaller outcrop for their own shelter. It faced east but was partially obscured from sight of the desert by a large boulder some ten metres away.

As they sat soaking up the little warmth provided by the early morning rays, the empty wagons passed only five metres to their right and negotiated a sharp right turn in what was probably the narrowest part of the rock path.

Now began the long wait. If there were to be another delivery of stores today, then the wagons would not arrive for at least another four hours, even if they had left the city before daylight.

In fact, it was six hours later when Gwaine and Tanya finally heard the sound of wagon wheel grinding and bumping against rock. The heat beat down from directly above them and they were drenched with perspiration. They had long grown weary of the desert heat and were thinking longingly of the frigid cold that they had been cursing only six hours earlier.

Gwaine reached into his pack and produced the silvery cape that Magnor had given him.

'Don't ask any questions that I can't answer', he cautioned Tanya as he threw the cape over both of them. 'Blame it on the legends and Magnor.'

With the cape covering them, they darted to cover of a boulder at the side of the track just before the first wagon, led by a number of mounted soldiers, negotiated the sharp bend.

'The next one', Gwaine ordered. Tanya only nodded nervously from below the shimmering cape.

They watched the second wagon make the turn and waited until the driver was obscured from their view before darting to the side of the wagon. They walked beside it for several metres while judging its height above the ground and pacing its speed.

Gwaine looked forward and saw the tower coming into view. He quickly darted a glance backward and saw the horses of the next wagon. There was no more time for judging and deciding. He bent as low as he could and stepped under the wagon. Tanya quickly followed.

It was a backbreaking height. Gwaine's back screamed as he tried to keep pace with the horses on the uphill climb while stooped to a height that allowed him to touch the ground with his fingertips. He looked across to Tanya and saw the pain of her exertion etched into her face.

As quickly as he could in these cramped conditions he whisked the cape off Tanya and wrapped it around himself, before diving for the running rail under the driver's feet. The relief was instant. While there was some strain on his arms as he was dragged over the rocky surface, the pain was insignificant compared with the previous pain in his back. He stared over to Tanya and saw her still struggling with her crouched walk. 'Come on', he whispered, motioning with a head movement that she should join him. She replied with a worried grimace, but when she finally joined him she signalled with a relieved sigh that the new position met with her approval.

The wagon dragged them over a distance that seemed twice as far as they had believed the tower to be, but, finally, the rock path gave way to the wooden surface of a drawbridge.

The heat rose out of the gaps in the timber and struck Gwaine and Tanya with an intensity many times greater than the desert's heat. Through his almost closed eyes, Gwaine peered down between the timbers to a bright yellow glow that appeared to be an incredible distance down in the heart of the rock mountain.

Almost as quickly as it had appeared, the heat was gone as the wooden drawbridge gave way to a metal surface, and the intensity of the underground fire gave way to a milder, more artificial light. They were inside the tower, in some cavernous room. Gwaine and Tanya stared at each other in wide-eyed amazement. They were in!

The soldiers yelled instructions as the wagons were ordered to drive in certain directions. Gwaine saw the first carriage roll through huge doorways into a room lined with boxes and barrels. Their wagon waited in the doorway, while the third wagon moved to the left through a similar huge door, probably to another storeroom.

It was no longer safe here. Gwaine could see the soldiers busily unloading the first wagon. They only needed to look toward the second wagon to discover him and Tanya.

The officer barked his commands at his soldiers. 'Come on. Move it. We want to get unloaded and back to the city for the next load.'

The driver of the second wagon jumped to the ground and ran into the storeroom to help with the unloading.

Gwaine couldn't believe their luck. The soldiers weren't staying. He motioned to Tanya to move off to their right. They scurried out from under the wagon and ran as quickly and as quietly as they could across the large room to hide behind an assortment of metal boxes under a metal staircase.

Having found relative safety, Gwaine studied his surroundings and shook his head in astonishment. 'It's all metal', he whispered incredulously to Tanya. 'The floor, the walls, the ceiling ...It's all metal!'

'Shhh!' Tanya hushed irritably. 'Be quiet ...And take off that silly cape before someone sees it reflecting the light.'

Gwaine started removing the cape, motioning for Tanya's assistance when it caught on his crossbow, strapped to his back. 'Yes, the lights', he whispered in amazement. 'Look at them. They don't seem to be candles. The flame is too constant and too bright.'

Tanya punched him as quietly as she could. 'Shut Up!' she whispered irritably.

Gwaine took the hint. He laid in silence, prostrate on the floor, watching for activity around the wagon. Finally, the driver returned and drove the wagon into the storeroom while the other two carriages drove out the other door and outside onto the mountain. Gwaine leant across to Tanya, intending to tell her of his discovery that the two doors led into one big room, but the black stare that his intended conversation raised from Tanya stifled the words in his throat. He returned to his silent vigil.

Finally, the last wagon was driven out of the storeroom and out of the tower. The soldiers mounted and rode after them while their commander rode toward Tanya and Gwaine. He stopped only metres from their position and looked up to the staircase above them as he slapped his chest in salute.

‘We have unloaded, my Emperor. Are there any commands before we return for more stores?’

Gwaine looked up in shock. The Dark Emperor was only metres above them, on the stairs, obscured from their view.

‘No. ...No commands’, came the quiet reply.

Gwaine was surprised at the gentle sound of the voice and its mellow, youngish tone.

‘But, tell your commander’, the Emperor continued, ‘that I require news of Moridare and the Warlord.’

‘I will, my Emperor’, the officer replied. ‘He did tell me, before I left, though, that Moridare was well trapped on his mountain. We have him completely surrounded, so that no one can leave the mountain without being captured by our forces. And there has been no sighting of the Warlord and the Princess, or anyone fitting their description. It appears they are trapped with Moridare.

‘Excellent. But I will not be content until your commander can guarantee that they are of no more danger.’

The officer bowed and saluted and, obviously seeing some sign of dismissal that Gwaine could not, turned and rode out of the tower. Immediately, the huge metal main door and the two large storeroom doors rumbled shut, apparently of their own volition, and a hissing sound, that could have been a thousand snakes in unison, emanated from the storeroom as a white smoke drifted from under the storeroom doors.

Gwaine laid in fear as he listened to the sound of the Emperor’s footsteps climbing the stairs and disappearing into the distance. Gwaine admonished himself for not spending more time studying the legends. There was too much that he didn’t understand.

Tanya leant across Gwaine, searching wide-eyed for the terrible monster that could have made that terrifying sound. White smoke was still wafting under the door.

'I think that's to stop anyone who tries hiding in the supplies', she suggested with a tremble in her voice.

Gwaine stared at the storeroom door and wriggled further out into the large room for a better view.

'We should be safe to leave. It seems to be locked in. Let's see if we can find the Emperor.'

Gwaine stood up, unstrapped the crossbow from his back and loaded it. 'Come on', he whispered as he moved toward the base of the stairway.

It wasn't until he reached the first step that he realised that Tanya wasn't behind him. In a sudden panic, he rushed back to see if she was in trouble.

'Are you alright?' he whispered frantically, even before he had reached their hiding place.

There was no answer.

By the time he had reached Tanya he was in a cold sweat, only to find her laying where he had left her, staring into space with tears welling in her eyes, and looking all of her very young age.

'What's wrong? ...Are you all right?'

'I'm scared', she stated pitifully. 'And…' she added, the tears now running down her cheek, 'I'm not sure, but I think today is my birthday.'

Gwaine leant forward and gently brushed a tear from her cheek. 'Happy birthday, Tanya.'

‘Gee, thanks’, she replied in an impish blend of emotion and sarcasm, as she wiped the tears with the palm of her hand.

‘If you want, you can stay here. You’ve done your part. It’s between me and the Emperor now.’

Tanya looked nervously at the storeroom door and shook her head violently. ‘No way. I’ll come with you.’

‘Alright. Let’s go then.’

Tanya accepted his outstretched hand and climbed to her feet. ‘Why are you always saying that to me? Can’t we ***not*** go somewhere, sometime.’

Gwaine only smiled as he led her to the stairway and in the direction of the Dark Emperor’s exit.

DEATH IN THE TOWER

Gwaine led Tanya, hand in hand, tentatively up the stairs. He pointed his crossbow anxiously in front of him, expecting, at any moment, to be confronted by the demon Emperor or one of his magical beasts. He fought to overcome his fear and to listen for any sounds of danger, but the thumping of his heart in his chest and the coursing of the blood past his ears, overcame all other noises.

At the top of the stairs was another cavernous room, only slightly smaller than the one below and full of large metal boxes that emitted strange humming noises and lit up in reds and greens and oranges. There was no Emperor in sight.

Gwaine and Tanya knelt at the top of the stairs for silent minutes that felt like an eternity. They scanned the room for any sign of life. There was none. Another staircase on the far side of the room was the only clue to the direction of their quarry.

'He'll be at the very top of the tower', Tanya whispered over his shoulder.

Gwaine nodded his agreement. There was no logical reason for that conclusion. It just seemed to make sense. 'We'll move carefully anyway. There's no way of knowing what's in these boxes.'

They crept quietly across the room trying to tread soundlessly on the metal floor. A sudden whirring noise sent them spilling over each other as they dived to the floor. Gwaine fought to disentangle his crossbow from beneath him as Tanya crawled behind him and away from the sound. He pointed his weapon at the offending box, but the only movement that was visible was a spinning wheel, behind a transparent cover, that had apparently started of its own choosing. The wheel wound on the final metres of a shiny brown ribbon before coming to a sudden stop. The whirring sound also stopped.

The two lay on the floor in shock. Tanya put her head to the cold floor and sucked in a lung-full of air in a vain attempt to quell her nerves. 'I don't like this place. It's alive.'

'Nonsense!' Gwaine replied with false bravado. He wiped the sweat from his brow with his sleeve. 'It's just a thing for winding ribbon.' He hoped that Tanya wouldn't question him any deeper on that subject. 'Come on. Let's get out of this room.'

Tanya was quick to follow as Gwaine jumped to his feet and moved quickly to the base of the stairs.

The stairs led to a smaller room that was very similar to the last, even to the point of having yet another staircase on the far side. Again, they knelt in silence trying to methodically study the room while their hearts thumped loudly and their breath came in quick gusts.

'Hell, I'm scared', Tanya admitted in a whispered, fearful voice.

Gwaine only nodded. He had come all this way to face the Dark Emperor but, right now, it was the thing that he hoped, most, would not happen. So much effort and planning had gone into getting here and so little thought had gone into this showdown in what was, up to now, an unknown tower inhabited by a faceless enemy.

Gwaine clenched his crossbow until his knuckles turned white and moved slowly among the now familiar boxes. This time though, halfway across the room, a metal box suddenly lit up with flashing red lights and emitted an ear-piercing scream. Gwaine stopped in his tracks, his blood chilled, and panic overtook his brain. He probably should have dived for cover, but all he could do was turn and stare, wide eyed, at Tanya.

Tanya overcame her panic first. 'It's a warning.' Her voice was strained with fear. 'He knows we're here now.'

Gwaine took a deep breath and shook himself out of his petrified state. 'Damn!' He ran full speed toward the stairs and bounded up them two at a time. Reaching the summit, he dived immediately to his right and crawled behind yet another metal box.

Once settled behind cover, he turned to see Tanya scale the last step and move to behind a box on the left side of the room, only three or four metres away.

'Welcome, Prince Gwaine and Princess Tanya.'

Gwaine recognised the mellow tones. It was the Emperor. He tried to control his breathing and fought to control his fear as he considered their predicament and what their next action should be.

'There is no need to hide', the gentle voice continued. 'I will not harm you, ...and you cannot harm me.'

Gwaine lay in silence, wondering what he should do. In the end he decided that the voice seemed far enough away not to be a great threat. He could chance a peak around the box and dive back to cover if the Emperor had a spear or bow.

Placing his crossbow on the floor behind the box, he moved to his left and glanced around the room.

The small room sloped away, down a metal ramp, to a figure draped all in white, and bathed in blinding light, only ten metres away. It stood with its back to Gwaine, staring out the huge windows that completely circumnavigated the room. Everything within the room was flooded with the intense light of the midday desert rays.

Squinting to recover a reasonable degree of vision, Gwaine tried to simultaneously study the figure and inspect the room with as scanning a view as possible from his hiding place. It was far from satisfactory but there appeared to be no immediate danger.

Gwaine was tempted to grab his bow and dispose of the Emperor while he could, but he was loath to shoot even the Dark Emperor in the back, and he was surprised by their casual reception. There had to be some sort of trap. There must be some imminent danger that was not yet evident. The Dark Emperor was obviously, by his casual nature, not caught off guard. He glanced across to Tanya and motioned for her to move back behind cover.

Gwaine and Tanya kneeled in the relative silence of the room, muscles tensed for action and perspiration running down their faces as they peered cautiously from their cover. The quiet was only disrupted by the low background hum that seemed to emanate from all of the metal boxes, by the distant warning scream from the floor below, and by their own irregular breathing.

Finally, the Emperor turned and gazed calmly up the ramp.

Gwaine's eyes widened with amazement.

The Emperor pushed back his white hood to reveal a young man, who looked to be in his late twenties, and certainly bore no resemblance to the demonic monster that they had been stalking up the stairways. He had shoulder length curls and handsome features. The expression on his face was one of mild surprise at seeing Gwaine.

'My, you are young. Aren't you?' He looked across to Tanya's location and smiled warmly. 'And the Lady Tanya is as beautiful as I have been told.'

Gwaine's attention was jolted toward Tanya. Her curiosity had brought her back out of hiding. 'Get back!' he commanded in a stern voice.

Tanya instinctively moved back behind her cover.

'Now, now', the Emperor calmly and quietly consoled, as if quieting a frightened animal. 'You're in no danger from me.' He moved to a box and touched a protrusion on its surface. The background scream, from the floor below, ceased.

'That's better', he announced. 'My instruments make enough noise, without having to put up with sirens too.' He casually pulled up a stool and sat next to the box. 'Though, it's just as well that I had that sensor activated. You've both shown a great deal of initiative to reach my control room. And you've shown that my security has become lax over the centuries. I have had no report of you since Moridare's castle. Nor did I see you cross my desert, or climb my mountain, ...or ***even*** cross my drawbridge. You have even eluded the vision of my satellites. Yes, ...you ***have*** shown great initiative.'

Gwaine was having some difficulty with the young man's conversation, but the word 'centuries' immediately struck a chord.

'What do you mean 'centuries'?', he replied sarcastically. 'You're not the original Emperor. You're too young.'

'Oh, quite the contrary, my young Warlord. I ***am*** the one and only Emperor, and you could not begin to comprehend my age or how long I have been on your planet.'

The panic and fear had completely subsided now. This handsome, amiable young man was quite a pleasing anti-climax to the fearful foe that had been imagined. ...Gwaine's eyes narrowed into a piercing, disbelieving stare. This young man was treating him like a fool. And what did he mean by 'on your planet'? 'Rubbish! You're not the real Emperor.'

The young man laughed. It was a light-hearted, merry laugh that echoed through the room. 'I will take that as a compliment, that I hold my age well.'

Gwaine had heard enough of this gibberish. He meant this likeable young man no harm, but he wasn't prepared to waste any more time. He drew his sword and stood up. 'Well, regardless of how old you are or who you are, you are now my prisoner.'

Without a word, the young man took a stick from a pocket of his cape. Its end blared a yellow glow and the metal wall above the staircase erupted into bright sparks as a deafening roar filled the room. Gwaine was thrown against the metal box by the force of the eruption before falling numbly to the floor with blood streaming over his right eye from a cut to his forehead.

Tanya scrambled back under cover.

'Now', the Emperor stated, the merriment vanishing from his voice. 'You see that it is ***you two*** who are ***my*** prisoners. I have no reason to harm you, but I will not suffer your foolishness.'

Gwaine rolled himself further behind the box. He wiped the blood from his eye with his sleeve and replaced his sword in its sheath.

'Are you alright?' Tanya's concern was evident in her voice. She could see the blood streaming down his face.

'Yeah', Gwaine replied angrily, admonishing himself for his carelessness. 'It's just Moridare's cut, re-opened.'

'Have I hurt you, Warlord?' a concerned voice queried.

'Don't be stupid', Gwaine retorted, shaking his head in an attempt to clear the cobwebs from his pained mind and to stop the deafening ringing in his ears. 'It will take better than you to hurt me.'

The Emperor laughed jovially. 'Ah! That's the fighting spirit that has thwarted my plans in the south and got you into my ship.'

'And will see you dead', Gwaine added in the most menacing voice he could muster.

'No. That wouldn't be a good idea. Killing me will not serve any purpose, and it will lead to the destruction of this ship, with you and Princess Tanya in it.'

Gwaine wasn't sure what to believe anymore. It sounded like a hollow threat, but he couldn't be sure. He only puzzled momentarily on why the Emperor was calling his tower a 'ship'. Too much of this conversation wasn't making sense.

‘And I no longer have reason to kill you’, the Emperor continued. ‘We have all served our purpose in this war. Its final conclusion will now eventuate regardless of our collective, or individual, fates.’ The Emperor paused and chuckled to himself. ‘Though, mind you, I would have been pleased some months ago if my assassins had been a little better at their profession.’

‘Then it was me that the assassin’s arrow was aimed at, inside the gates of Lasatal.’

‘Why, of course, Warlord. Who else did you think?’

‘We thought it may have been meant for the King.’

‘Oh, dear!’ the Emperor replied in a disappointed tone. ‘Was his marksmanship so bad that you couldn’t even tell who the intended victim was?’

Gwaine tried to ignore the Emperor’s disappointment. He sounded like an archer who had missed the bull’s-eye at a country fair. Gwaine shivered as he pictured himself as that bull’s-eye. ‘And you failed again the very next day.’

There was some malice in Gwaine’s statement, but the Emperor’s reply remained casual.

‘Yes. Those fools didn’t bide their time. It should have been so simple for them to dispose of Princess Tanya.’

‘What?’ Gwaine was confused. ‘Tanya?’

‘Yes. Of course’, the Emperor replied bluntly. ‘Don’t tell me you couldn’t pick the intended victim, again. I did send blunderer’s, didn’t I.’ As an afterthought, he comically exaggerated a peer in Tanya’s direction. ‘No malice intended, my beautiful Lady. Just going through the motions of warfare.’

‘Thank you’, Tanya replied softly, though she wasn’t sure why she had said it.

‘Why? …Why Tanya?’ Gwaine asked incredulously. ‘I thought I was the main target on that occasion.’

‘Oh, she posed a threat, that’s all.’

‘No she didn’t’, Gwaine countered emphatically. ‘Not at that stage.’

‘Oh, no. Not at that stage’, the Emperor agreed, almost apologetically. ‘I should have said, ***she posed an expected threat***.’

‘What ‘expected threat’?’ Gwaine’s blood was boiling. He saw no reason for Tanya to have been endangered by the Emperor’s assassins.

‘My dear young man’, the Emperor replied in an almost condescending tone, ‘the expected threat that she could in some way aid you to harm my cause.’

‘You couldn’t know that.’

The Emperor shook his head silently in a disappointed manner as he stared in Gwaine’s direction. ‘You give Magnor the credit of some degree of ‘knowing’. Why would you not offer me the same courtesy?’

Gwaine sat dumbly, considering the suggestion. This discussion was going nowhere.

‘I will have to kill you’, Gwaine warned in a matter-of-fact voice, ‘unless you are prepared to surrender.’ Having issued the warning, he immediately wondered how he could possibly carry through his threat. The Emperor’s thunder weapon certainly countered his own puny arsenal.

‘Why do you wish to kill me? We should be working together to restore peace on this continent and to put an end to wars.’

‘That’s a wonderful goal, ...but it’s not ***your*** goal. You’re a maniac. You want to be Emperor of Amorand.’

‘Why don’t you come out, Warlord. I find it difficult having a conversation with a control panel. If I wanted to kill you, I could have easily done it by now.’

Gwaine considered the Emperor's words. He was right. He obviously didn't aim his stick to kill. It was only a warning. He dragged himself to his knees and peered around the box, keeping his right hand on his crossbow.

'Oh dear!' the Emperor exclaimed. 'I have hurt you. I'm so sorry. It is not in my nature to inflict pain.'

The apology appeared sincere, but Gwaine could not restrain his fury at the hypocrisy in his words. 'Liar!' he yelled. 'You have inflicted pain and suffering and death on hundreds of thousands over the centuries. You and your bloody wars. All for your own glory and ambition.'

'No!' the Emperor retaliated in anger. 'I have devoted my life to bringing order to this continent. When my companions and I arrived on your planet, it was divided into tiny warring kingdoms. Do you think that I have caused any more suffering and death through my wars than would have occurred anyway, through the petty wars of petty little Kings?'

'Yes', Gwaine replied emphatically. 'You have waged massive wars over centuries.'

'To achieve peace! I have succeeded in the north. Until you encouraged that fool Moridare, we had not had an uprising in the north for over eight centuries. How often do you have wars in the south? Those petty old Kings go to war over any petty squabble.'

Gwaine could think of no answer.

'If you really want someone to blame for the centuries of wars', the Emperor continued angrily, 'then blame Magnor. He has opposed me at every turn. This continent could have been at peace centuries ago, if not for him.'

'With you as supreme Emperor, I presume.'

'What does it matter? Look around you. Does it look like I crave the life of an Emperor? I crave nothing more than peace and security for the inhabitants of your planet.'

Gwaine was confused. He had expected to creep in, kill the monster called 'the Dark Emperor', and possibly escape alive. He wasn't prepared for this argument, or for the possibility that the Emperor may have had good intentions all along.

'If your intentions are so pure, why does Magnor oppose you?'

'Philosophical! ...Purely philosophical!' the Emperor retorted forcefully. 'When we began our journey, the entire crew took an oath not to interfere with any civilisation that we found. All right, ...I admit that I broke that oath. But I saw so much suffering on your planet that I just couldn't turn my back on it and leave. As the mother ship was leaving your galaxy, I stole this shuttle and returned. My absence was detected somehow and Magnor was sent to bring me back, but we only argued. He couldn't understand what I wanted to do and he vowed to oppose me. It's his fault that the wars have gone on so long.'

The room fell silent. Gwaine's mind reeled in confusion. 'Magnor is not one of us?' He looked across to Tanya for some inspiration. She was sitting with her back against the metal box. The look of worried thought displayed clearly her own confusion at what they had heard.

'You and Magnor are not from this planet?' Gwaine asked incredulously, trying to absorb this incredible statement.

'No', the Emperor replied. 'But that does not mean that we are the same. The difference between us is that I care about your planet and its inhabitants. Magnor is that sort of individual who is only concerned with philosophy.'

Gwaine's mind was reeling. 'I agree with Magnor', he pushed forward, more for an argument than for any valid reason. 'You shouldn't interfere with our civilization.'

‘You had no civilization when I arrived’, the Emperor shouted mockingly. ‘You only had wars. And you still only have wars, because of Magnor’s obstinacy.’

‘Regardless of whether you call it civilization or not, you should not have interfered.’

‘Trying to bring peace, is not interference. It is not the ‘interference’ that was implied in our vow.’ The Emperor growled with frustration. ‘If I had been prepared to interfere with your planet’s development, I could have destroyed all my enemies within years of arriving here. My technology is centuries ahead of yours. Your swords and shields could not have stood against the weapons that I could have created. I can build weapons that would move a mountain. Your foolish little Fortress of Marsh would have evaporated and blown away within the blinking of an eye. Why do you think that I have not built those weapons?’

‘Because Magnor could have countered anything you did.’

The Emperor growled again, in frustration, and pounded his fist on the metal box. ‘No! Magnor is an old fool. I didn’t build those weapons because it would have advanced the technology of this planet dangerously beyond its years. That would have been interference.’

‘And’, Gwaine added, ‘because you would have given the peasants a technology equal to your own. You would have lost control.’

‘Alright. Enough! You are obviously as obstinate as Magnor. You are determined not to believe my motives, but I swear that I have worked for the best interests of the inhabitants of this planet.’

Gwaine tried to clear his mind, to come up with something that would prove or disprove the Emperor’s story. He saw the marsh, turned red with the blood of the soldiers of both sides of the conflict. He saw the dying faces of Raiff and Qarad and heard the cries of the wives and children of the men who hadn’t returned from battle.

‘I don’t believe you’, he only whispered. ‘If you really cared about the people, you couldn’t have caused that much hardship and suffering.’

‘Ha! Hypocrite’, the Emperor boomed. ‘Aren’t you the mastermind who planned the starvation of thousands of men, women and children? Wasn’t it your idea to burn the crops?’

Gwaine lifted the crossbow from the floor and then put it back. The Emperor was right, but he would have liked to kill him for saying it.

‘I am, but I don’t claim to be any saviour. I’m just trying to save Amorand from a power-crazed maniac.’ Gwaine paused and took a deep breath, to calm his anger, before bringing the conversation back to his goal. ‘I will have to kill you unless you surrender.’

‘Killing me wouldn’t help’, the Emperor stated in a very matter-of-fact tone.

‘It wouldn’t hurt’, Gwaine countered good-humouredly.

‘That’s easy for you to say. You wouldn’t be the one being run through by Baradetch’s sword.’

Gwaine smiled at the sudden relaxed banter. This young man, with his sudden changes in mood, reminded him, very much, of Magnor. He could have easily grown to like this side of the Dark Emperor. Suddenly it struck him. The Emperor was talking about the sword, not the crossbow. Possibly he wasn’t as secure as he seemed to believe.

‘Anyway, it wouldn’t do ***you*** any good either’, the Emperor continued. ‘This ship floats above its power source.’

‘I saw the yellow fire in the heart of the mountain’, Gwaine interrupted.

‘What a quaint way of putting it. Yes.’ The Emperor smiled as he ran Gwaine’s description through his mind. ‘Yes. This ship floats above ‘the yellow fire’ by my power alone. If anything happened to me, the ship would fall into the pit and explode. You and Princess Tanya would die. If you don’t care about yourself, I’m sure that you wouldn't want anything to happen to the Princess. Harn reports that you two are very close.'

'We both knew the dangers before we set off', Gwaine proclaimed in a fatalistic tone, ignoring the reference to his relationship with Tanya.

The Emperor raised his eyebrows in astonishment. 'Well, regardless of that. There's no point. Our deaths would achieve nothing. My army is retreating northward and setting up a trap in Velinon. You have lost the war, whether we were to live or die.'

'What sort of trap?' Gwaine's interest had been heightened.

'Part of my army is in the mountains. Commander Kem will lead your army along the flatland and into a trap, with half my army on each flank. It shall be the end of the centuries of wars.

Gwaine laughed. 'It's a pretty basic trap. Kem wouldn't be so stupid as to fall for that.'

'Oh, Commander Kem isn't stupid. On the contrary, he's one of my best soldiers.'

Gwaine's blood froze. There was no reason to disbelieve the Emperor. He was supremely confident that he had the upper hand. Gwaine had trained with Kem. ...He had believed him to be a friend. 'I promoted him to that position', Gwaine drawled, trying to comprehend the meaning and repercussions of what he now knew.

'Yes. You have helped me bring peace to your land.'

'No! I have helped you achieve your ambitions for power.'

'No, Warlord. You haven't been listening. That is not what I want.'

Gwaine's anger peaked with the frustration of betrayal and the loss of the war. He dived to his left and let loose an arrow that pierced the Emperor's heart.

'***No!***' Tanya screamed from above him. '***No!***'

A look of astonishment flickered over the face of the Emperor before he fell to the floor, dead.

Gwaine looked around. Tanya was sobbing. 'No, ...No ...What have you done?'

Gwaine tried to find words, but none came. He forced his mind to try to answer Tanya's question, but he wasn't sure what he had done.

'That was too easy. Something's wrong', he shouted in bewilderment. 'He couldn't be killed that easily.' Gwaine regretted his hasty, angry action.

The tower suddenly began to creak and Gwaine felt a sinking feeling as pieces of metal began breaking free. The tower began to shudder violently.

'Now what?' Tanya queried vehemently.

'He wasn't bluffing', Gwaine replied weakly. 'We'd better get out of here.'

Tanya turned toward the stairs, but Gwaine called her back.

'It's too late. The doors will be below ground level, even if we knew how to open them.'

Tanya looked around in desperation until, seeing no solution, she accepted her fate and assumed a calm resolve. 'Well, while we're waiting to die, could you please explain to me why you killed him.'

'No. I can't. ...Sorry.' Gwaine strode over to the body and searched the pockets for the Emperor's stick.

'That's not good enough, Gwaine', Tanya yelled in frustration. 'I'm about to die. I want to know. He made sense to me. What decided you that he was lying?'

Gwaine returned with the stick in his hand. 'I couldn't decide. So, I did what I came here to do.'

Tanya ran her hand through her hair in disbelief. 'Surely, you're not serious. He might have been the greatest man you ever met.'

‘He might have been.’ The shuddering had reached a level that was making standing difficult. Pieces of metal were moving around the room and falling off the walls while Gwaine fiddled with the Emperor’s stick. He pressed the three buttons. He stared through the hole that ran down its centre to try to see how it worked. He bashed it against the wall but, still, nothing happened. ‘I put my trust in Magnor’, he finally admitted. ‘He allowed me to come here to kill the Emperor. So, in my confusion and anger, I did what Magnor allowed me to come here to do.’

‘Your nothing more than a mindless assassin.’

Gwaine had been trying to ignore the true depths of what he had done, but Tanya’s words stung. Not only that, they coincided with his own thoughts on his action. He gave up trying to work the stick. ‘Are they to be your final words to me?’ he asked despondently.

‘I hope not.’ she retaliated, snatching the stick out of his hand. ‘I’ve got a lot of things that I intend saying to you. The first one, is that you’ve been holding this stick back-to-front.’ She pressed the green button and the window exploded into glass fragments.

Gwaine stared in amazement. ‘I think you just saved our lives again.’

‘You just might regret every second of it.’ Tanya’s warning reeked of sincerity.

When they reached the window, it was only four metres above the ground, and it fell another metre while they waited for the tower to lean to that side so that the fiery gap was reduced to a jumpable distance.

‘The horses’, Gwaine instructed as they picked themselves up from the hard rock surface and rubbed their bruises from the jump.

They had only ridden two kilometres from the base of the mountain when the explosion threw their horses to the ground. The ground rocked and sand blew over them in waves as a massive black cloud billowed above what was left of the mountain.

When all was still and the sand and dust had settled, Tanya and Gwaine forced themselves up out of the sand that had partially buried them.

'You alright?' Tanya queried, spitting sand from her mouth.

'Oh, great.' Gwaine coughed, trying to clear his throat and mouth of sand. He wiped his hand over his eyes in an attempt to clear them of the painful granules.

'Look at that.' Tanya pointed across the desert.

'Can't see a thing', Gwaine replied with his hands still covering his eyes.

'The desert has got big craters all through it.'

Gwaine opened his eyes as best he could and studied the craters. 'The explosion has set off the Emperor's traps.'

Tanya gave Gwaine a worried stare. 'All of them?'

'Of course', Gwaine announced with certainty. 'Probably.'

Tanya nodded resolutely. 'We're going over the desert', she told herself.

'We've got to', Gwaine added. 'We have to stop Kem.'

Tanya only sat in silence and stared thoughtfully at the desolate mountain and the billows of smoke that indicated where the tower had once stood. After a long delay, she forced her attention to her companion, sitting beside her, still wiping the sand from his eyes and hair. 'I don't like you anymore, Gwaine', she stated bluntly. 'I'll come with you to see this through, but that's all.'

Tanya moved away to retrieve her horse, leaving Gwaine sitting despondently, running sand through his fingers. The so-called Dark Emperor was dead, but there was no joy in the death of the likeable young man, and the war was probably lost anyway. It was unlikely that they would be able to travel fast enough to save their armies from destruction.

TO FALL IN A DISTANT LAND

Gwaine looked across to Tanya and studied the anger and hurt in her features. She had been a joyless companion since they began their trek southward from the base of the ruins of the Emperor's tower. But now, as they rode through the burnt-out and deserted shell of her city of Velin, her mood blackened to a new level of cold, simmering anger.

She had made it clear from the beginning that their relationship had changed, but Gwaine had accepted it only as a mood that would pass with time. It didn't. She was obviously as disturbed as he was by what they had been told at the tower's summit and she was disillusioned by the lack of reasoning that had gone into his assassination of the Emperor. Gwaine didn't blame her for that. He wasn't sure that he had done the right thing either. He only knew that he had done what he had set out to do, though he hadn't realised until after the event that his aim, by its basic nature, had made him just another one of the war's assassins. He had always seen his quest as much nobler than that. The real truth had now fallen on him like lead.

They had no problems in travelling from the destroyed tower to the decimated city of Velin. The desert sandstorms had erased any signs of them riding away from the tower after the explosion. Once out of the desert, it was only a night's ride to the coast where they finally washed away the uncomfortable desert sands.

It was on the coast that Gwaine first realised the true depths of the rift that had formed between them. During the desert crossing he had been able to attribute the lack of conversation to the heat, to the discomfort of the sand, and to the draining effect of their narrow escape. But, on the coast, the rift became obvious. Tanya remained silent and sulky even when the fresh salt air blew in their faces and Gwaine remarked good-humouredly on the beauty of the morning. The final proof of a permanent damage to their friendship came when Tanya insisted on bathing alone, further up the beach. This degree of modesty had not existed between them since their first night in Moridare's castle.

They had followed the southwest coast of the North Continent into Velinon, and made the crossing from the coast to Velin under the cover of darkness.

Now, by the morning light, they made their way cautiously up the mountain slope - the shattered cobblestone pathway leading them between rows of burnt-out homes and shops. There wasn't a soul in sight.

'It will only take a few years', he told Tanya. 'It will be far greater than it was before.' Tanya didn't reply. The anger in her face had been replaced by a grim look of acceptance. She rode upright in her saddle; a tragic Princess returning home, regardless of the state of the home and regardless of the fact that no one was there to greet her.

They approached a juncture in the path. Upward was the castle gate. To the left was another path that eventually led outside the city and into the mountain range.

'There's no point in going into the castle', Gwaine suggested. He had long grown weary of this one sided conversation. 'We should move into the mountains before the Emperor's army passes through the flatland. Time is growing short.'

It wasn't until they reached the juncture that Gwaine knew that Tanya had accepted his reasoning. Tanya turned her horse onto the left-hand path beside him.

He shook his head disgustedly. 'You're behaving like a child. Stop sulking and talk to me.'

Tanya ignored him. A kilometre of silence later, within the shadowy greenness of the forest, she finally spoke.

'I preferred being a child', she stated quietly. 'It seems like a hundred years ago. The world seemed so secure and warm when I was on my mother's lap or on my father's shoulders.'

Gwaine nodded in agreement. There was no answer.

They had reached the next summit before he found a reply. He smiled to himself as he tried to picture an outsider listening to their protracted conversation.

'Did you ever work out when your birthday was?'

'No. I thought it was the day we were in the tower, but I'm not sure anymore. I've lost all track of time.'

The path was becoming smaller and more difficult to follow now and it began to drizzle as they moved deeper into the rainforest area of the mountain. In a saddle of the mountain range, Gwaine was forced to move slightly ahead of Tanya as the path suddenly narrowed between two trees. He scanned the area before turning in his saddle and calling his horse to a halt.

'This reminds me of part of the Immortal Gardens.' He pointed to his right where the ground sloped away rapidly to a heavily treed and ferned incline which led to a dark shadowy grove some twenty metres down.

'The Gardens will be dying now, if the legends are true.'

'Oh, Shut up!' Gwaine growled angrily. He couldn't bear to think of such beauty passing away, especially as a result of something he had done. He turned on Tanya. 'You've been a wretched torture of misery since the tower. How you can accept that degree of martyrdom, just by being an onlooker, evades me.'

'An onlooker?' Tanya began to protest.

'Yes, an onlooker. You didn't kill the Emperor. I did. I'm the one who has to live with that and wonder for the rest of my life whether I killed a villain or a saint.'

'You use the term ***killed*** fairly easily', Tanya responded in anger. 'Why don't you try ***murder***. You're nothing more than an assassin.'

Gwaine wheeled his horse and moved it beside Tanya's as she flinched away from him in fear. He didn't know what he intended in his anger, but he was sure that he could never hurt her. 'Alright. I'm an assassin. I have no argument against that. What did you expect …a romantic dual with a dramatic end, ...good vanquishing evil. In the midst of a war, I murdered my enemy. There's no honour or glory in that. Neither is there honour or glory in war. There's only blood and suffering and death. It's time you climbed out of your fairytale images and realised the truth.'

Tanya sat quietly, staring wide-eyed at the boy who had been yelling at her only moments earlier. His meaning had not escaped her, but what was uppermost in her mind was the fact that he had been yelling.

'What makes you think that there aren't any enemy soldiers in these mountains?' she queried calmly.

Gwaine visibly tried to quell his temper, realising the implications of Tanya's question. 'There will be, but they will be behind the force retreating along the flats. We haven't seen any enemy on the flats yet.'

'We may have passed them last night. We were on the western side of the mountain. They may have moved along the eastern side last night.'

'It's possible', Gwaine conceded. He stared calmly into Tanya's grey eyes. 'I'm sorry I yelled.'

Gwaine was facing down the path, so that Tanya's fearful expression and the twang of bowstrings were the only warning he had of the coming arrows. He dived to his left, across Tanya's horse, pushing her with an outstretched arm as he tried to release himself, in full flight, from his stirrups.

Tanya's light frame dislodged easily and quickly from the saddle as an arrow flew to Gwaine's right. A blow, like a hammer, to his left shoulder sent him reeling forward and downward.

He hit the ground solidly between the horses, their hooves thrashing around him as he tried desperately to regather his wits and his breath. He tried to force himself off the ground with the intention of diving down the slope after Tanya, but his left arm didn't respond. He only threw his weight onto his left side, screaming in agony as the arrow's shaft hit the ground causing its tip to dig deeper into his shoulder. An arrow whistled in the air just above his head as yet another landed within centimetres of his outstretched right arm. He tried again to raise himself quickly off the ground, this time with the knowledge that his left arm was useless, and dived with all the energy he could muster into the green wall of ferns and trees that studded the long slope.

Fern after sapling after tree stood in his way as he careered uncontrollably down the wet incline, every projection from every plant torturing him as they swiped the wooden shaft that projected from his back, moving the metal tip violently within his wound.

By the time he had come to an abrupt halt in the cold mud and moss of the grove, all sense of pain had gone. His body was now overwhelmed by an intense numbness. The cold floor of the grove felt soothing against his face as a heavy drowsiness fell on him like a leaden blanket.

'***Gwaine!***' Tanya screamed as she crawled through the mud and moss from where she had come to rest after her graceless fall from the path well above. Her concern over the scratches and cuts she had incurred had vanished at the sight of the arrow and blood and Gwaine's still form.

Tanya had only just reached his side when the sound of crashing plants and falling forms became audible close above them. Gwaine tried to look up, to see where the commotion was coming from but he only managed a glimpse of two enemy soldiers landing several metres away, before his energy ebbed and he allowed his head to fall back to the cold earth. He willed his hand to reach for his sword but nothing happened. There was no response.

A blinding light flashed above him and thunder echoed in the small dark grove, and then the lightning and thunder repeated itself before all went silent.

He laid in his silent numbness as if lost in some magical dream. Time seemed to have no further meaning. The soldiers should have been upon them by now.

Tanya's sobs finally broke the spell. That, and a sickly burning smell that reached into Gwaine's dream and pounded at his nostrils.

Arms around his chest pulled him gently from his lying position in the mud until he was resting partially in Tanya's lap. Her face was streamed with tears. The pain was returning to his shoulder.

'We've got to get you back to the castle', she whispered through her sobs. 'Can you ride?'

Gwaine considered the question slowly. It took some time to comprehend its meaning and even longer to force his head to shake a negative reply.

Tanya studied the grove in desperation. 'Well, you'll just have to. You can't stay here.' Her voice overcame the sobs and she summoned the strength to force forward a command. 'You will have to ride! I'll go and get the horses.'

She laid him gently onto his right side and started up the slope, but she stopped to stare to her right as a disgusted, sickly expression covered her face. Gwaine forced himself to look in the same direction. There, on the grove floor, lay the charred dismembered bodies of the two soldiers who had attacked them.

Tanya dropped something heavy onto the ground. 'It's a foul weapon', she whispered to the shadows, before climbing out of sight.

Gwaine recognised the Dark Emperor's weapon lying in the mud. 'All weapons are foul', he tried to whisper, though he was sure Tanya couldn't have heard him.

Tanya shook him back to consciousness. 'Come on Gwaine.' Her voice was frantic. 'You're losing a lot of blood. We've got to get back to the castle. Please, ...get up.'

Gwaine closed his eyes and sighed. The numbness was decreasing now but the weariness was all consuming. 'Leave me alone', he mumbled. 'You don't owe me anything. Leave me here.'

'Oh, don't talk rubbish', she pleaded. 'I'm not going to leave you.'

Gwaine didn't respond.

'Gwaine!' she yelled sternly. 'Get up! Get up and try! Do you want me to carry you all the way to Velin? Do you want me to carry you?'

Gwaine shook his head wearily and made a pathetic, token attempt at moving but Tanya's arms were immediately around his chest, supporting him and encouraging him to his feet. He gritted his teeth and tried harder, pushing the ground with his right arm while his left shoulder responded with agonising pain.

He somehow found himself on his feet, though the world was spinning around him and most of his weight seemed to be leaning on Tanya.

'That's good', she encouraged. 'I've found one of the horses, and if we follow this gully for a while, it finally rises fairly evenly back up to the track.'

Tanya supported him over to the horse and leant him against it while she gathered the reins. Gwaine closed his eyes to the giddy world and gritted his teeth with the pain and effort.

'You have to get on, Gwaine.' Tanya had learnt better than to ask questions. She was giving desperate commands now.

More from Tanya's effort than his own, Gwaine managed to end up in the saddle. Tanya seated herself behind him, steadying him while trying to guide the horse with the reins.

The ride was uncomfortable. Every slip of a hoof was like a dagger blow to Gwaine's shoulder. He occasionally fell into unconsciousness, despite the pain, only to be jolted awake by Tanya as she fought to keep him in the saddle.

Blood saturated the back of his shirt as the wound allowed his last reserves of strength to ebb away. By the time they had reached the castle, Tanya's top was also saturated with blood from her desperate efforts to hold him in position on the horse.

Tanya rode the horse up the castle steps and through the corridors. It proved painful for Gwaine, but she reasoned that it would have proved practically impossible for him to dismount and walk.

The time for caution had passed. There was no checking for any hidden enemy; no careful study of their surrounds. Tanya rode directly into what had once been her bedroom and helped Gwaine dismount onto the bare bed. Other than the bed, the room was totally empty. Everything had been taken.

'I'll go and get some sheets or something to pack the wound', she frantically explained to Gwaine as she moved away from the bed, but she stopped in horror as she passed the window. 'Gwaine, your army is on the flatland', she yelled even more frantically, realising that they were too late to stop Kem's deceit.

There was no audible or visible reply from Gwaine. Tanya stood in silence, the stress fading from her face. She folded her arms nervously across her chest before moving back to the bedside.

'Gwaine, please don't die', she whispered pleadingly as she ran her hand gently over his clammy brow and studied his deathly pale skin and blood soaked shirt. 'Please don't die. ...I'm sorry.'

IN THE TUNNEL

The narrow tunnel was dark and hot. Gwaine crawled and wriggled his way through its confinement, his claustrophobic fear rising to a crescendo. Combined with his fear though, was an unnerving feeling of weightlessness. The pain had gone from his shoulder and limbs and a renewed vigor and energy had replaced his exhaustion.

He peered into the pitch darkness, searching frantically for some sign of Tanya and tried to yell, but no sound passed his lips. He crawled on, groping his way through the dirt and mud, pulling himself through narrow rock holes that led only into more confined darkness.

Time was immeasurable. A faint red glow replaced the blackness in the distance, as the tunnel gradually became wider and allowed Gwaine, firstly, to rise to a crouched walk and, eventually, to walk upright toward the, now, intense redness of the corridor.

As he reached a bend in the tunnel he placed his hand on the rock surface for balance. He recoiled in horror as the red glow showed an old bony hand that rivaled Magnor's in age. He studied both hands by the red light and then felt the creviced leathery skin of his face. He cried noiselessly as he realised the change that had overcome his body. He tried to scream for Tanya or Taron or anybody who could help him, but despite his effort, the red passageway remained silent.

Gwaine sat in self-pity and confusion. Where was he? What has happened to him? Why was he alone? ...Alone? He had to keep moving. He had to find Tanya. Tanya was all-important now. If it wasn't for her, Gwaine could have easily laid down and died. Death held no fear. He was Warlord. He had been bred to die. That was his mission in life, ...to fight and die as Warlords before him had fought and died. If not for Tanya, he would have been content to lie in the tunnel and wait for his time.

After all, he had won the battles, he had met the Dark Emperor and destroyed him and his tower. He could die now and still be regarded as the greatest Warlord, the hero martyr who died trying to save the lands of the Seven Kings. Perhaps it would be better not to live. He was now a hero, but if he returned to Arrindare, he would suffer life's greatest anticlimax. He would be old, ...an old relic of the court. Just another dottery old soldier. Maybe he would even do something in later life that people would disapprove of. People remember wrongs much easier than rights. They would forget his exploits and call him a 'politician', a 'bureaucrat', or something equally repulsive. Yes, it would be best to die here.

Tanya! ...He had to find Tanya! The peace that had overcome him at the thought of dying was gone and the desperation returned. Magnor had obviously sent Tanya for more reasons than just to save him from Moridare's dungeon. His mission wasn't over until he returned his Princess to the safety of her court. He had to survive long enough to ensure her survival. Tanya was his will to go on. She was Magnor's insurance that Gwaine would not settle for martyrdom. 'That cunning old fox', Gwaine thought with the mixed emotions of admiration and exasperation. Magnor knew the strength of his affection for Tanya.

He forced himself forward and around the bend. A blazing fire raged in the middle of the pathway. There on the far side of the fire sat Tanya, with two beautiful, blonde-haired children. She cuddled them and kissed them lovingly as she scooped a handful of wheat out of a bag and threw it onto the fire. The fire raged higher and obstructed Gwaine's view of Tanya and the children. He tried to yell to them, but his voice would not issue forth any sound. He sat impatiently waiting for the fire to quell its fury so that he could see Tanya again and the two beautiful children.

Eventually, he could see them again. The sight of Tanya filled him with a warm glow. She was as beautiful as ever. Gwaine moved closer to the flames to gain a better view of the children on her lap. They looked unwell. They were still the same beautiful children, but they looked paler and their cheeks were drawn. Tanya reached back into the bag and produced another handful of wheat that she threw on the fire. Gwaine was driven back by the flames and was forced to wait impatiently for the fire to die down again.

As soon as he could, he moved forward to see Tanya and the children. He waved his arms to try to attract their attention, but they did not see him. The children looked sick. They lay limply against Tanya, their cheekbones prominent and their stomachs bulging. She reached into the bag. Gwaine tried to scream to stop her. He was forced back from the fire again as it feverishly ate the handful of wheat.

With every ebb of the fire Gwaine tried desperately to attract Tanya's attention, but he was continually forced back as she ignored his presence and fed the wheat to the hungry fire.

Only when the children had obviously died of starvation, did she acknowledge his presence, and then the hatred in her eyes and face froze him with fear. She allowed the small figures to fall from her lap as she stood and stared at him with cold hatred. She picked up the bag of wheat and threw it onto the fire. The fire exploded and immediately extinguished itself. The small amount of light that shone from the smouldering embers revealed only an empty cavern. Tanya and the small, lifeless children had gone. The glowing embers and a pale blue light in the distance gave the only clue to the path he should take. He moved toward the blue glow, tears in his eyes, sobbing uncontrollably and silently at the death of the children and Tanya's disappearance.

He seemed to float down the roughly cut corridor. He careered uncontrollably toward the blue glow as if attracted by some form of magnetism. As he rounded a bend his blood froze and his neck and face tensioned into a terror that he had never known before. He dropped softly to the ground in front of the source of the glow. It was Qarad. Gwaine tried to scream and then crawled backwards, away from the horror before him. Qarad still wore the water and blood soaked uniform of the Dark Emperor's army and the wound to his neck and chest hung open.

‘Welcome to my tomb, Warlord.’ Qarad’s empty voice rang inside Gwaine’s head. ‘Have you come to join me for an eternity of boredom in this pit?’

Gwaine could only shake his head frantically. He knew that words would not come.

‘Who loves my children, now that you have killed me?’

Gwaine continued to shake his head. He had always considered Qarad as a General and a warrior. He had never considered him to be a person, a husband, or a father.

‘Who killed you, Warlord?’

Gwaine shook his head even more frantically. He tried to tell Qarad that he wasn’t dead, but with the first soundless movements of his lips, Qarad erupted into loud, echoing laughter and disappeared.

In the darkness, Gwaine relived Qarad’s death. He thought of the suddenness of it, and of Raiff’s death. ...One moment a living legend, the next, just another corpse.

The blue glow returned. The Dark Emperor walked up to Gwaine with Tanya at his side. Tanya looked lovingly into the Emperor’s eyes and cuddled his arm. Gwaine could understand her feelings. The Emperor looked like a god. Dressed in long flowing robes, his young handsome features and long blonde hair were bathed in a cool blue glow. Tanya drew her gaze away from her companion to stare at Gwaine with a disgusted grimace. His leathered old body must have looked repulsive, and failed miserably in comparison to the splendid beauty of the Emperor.

As Gwaine stared up at them, the Emperor’s saintly features suddenly transformed to the head of a dragon-like serpent and silvery white light sprayed from his red eyes and stung Gwaine’s body.

Gwaine screamed a pained guttural scream that emanated from the depths of his tortured soul.

BY THE SEA

The silvery rays of light had danced on the ceiling for hours, changing in intensity with the slowly increasing brightness of the morning. The shimmering, silvery display combined with the shrieking of the sea birds was a bewildering phenomenon. This was not Velin.

Gwaine felt the heavy bandages that wrapped firmly around his shoulder and chest, and studied the small puncture wounds to his arm and hands. This was Magnor's medicine. Magnor must be near at hand. But where was he? ...And where was this place? He studied the style of the building and tried to imagine somewhere like this, that was very near the seaside. He could only think of Port Oracle. No other place fitted the criteria, ...not in Amorand anyway.

'It can't be', he whispered to himself, 'I haven't been unconscious that long.'

'It is, and you have.' Magnor's voice was unmistakable, emanating from somewhere behind Gwaine's bedhead.

Gwaine visibly jumped with the surprise answer to his question. He peered over his bandaged shoulder to see Magnor leaning in a doorway to another room where he had obviously taken up residence.

'How do you feel, young Gwaine?'

Gwaine took stock of his feelings and was surprised by the result. 'Not bad, my Lord Magnor, ...surprisingly.'

'Oh!' Magnor intoned with a hurt expression. 'It doesn't surprise me. After all, you had an excellent physician caring for you. Though, I wouldn't try to jump out of bed if I were you. You would probably fall flat on your face. ...Your well being, at the moment, is attributable to your medicines.' Magnor pointed to a container of water and an empty satchel beside Gwaine's bed. 'There will be much pain when they wear off.'

While Gwaine soothed his parched throat with the cool water, Magnor walked to the door and called in a guard. 'Tell the Commander, that Prince Gwaine is awake.' He re-shut the door as the guard hurried off down the corridor.

'What's going on, Magnor?' Gwaine queried with a shake of his head. When he had been wounded in the Velinon mountains, a great deal had been left unresolved. There was so much that he needed desperately to know, that 'What's going on?' only summed up his general confusion and thirst for information. Then the full implications of Magnor's command dawned on him. The 'Commander' was coming. 'Magnor. I must tell you about Kem.'

'Hold, Warlord', Magnor laughed good humouredly, holding his hands in front of him to protect himself from Gwaine's barrage. 'One thing at a time.'

'But this is important, Magnor.'

'It can wait until after I have answered your question.'

'No Magnor!' Gwaine answered forcefully, trying to push himself up from his pillow. A stabbing pain shot through his shoulder and forced him back to the bed in agony.

'Do I have to tell you not to do that?' Magnor asked with compassion.

Gwaine shook his head, his eyes still closed with pain.

'Now, I assure you that whatever you have to tell me about Kem can wait, no matter how important you feel it is. May I now answer your question?'

Gwaine opened his eyes and stared at Magnor. He wasn't satisfied, but he was sure that any further argument would be a waste of time. 'Please continue', he replied dryly.

'Very good. You are in Port Oracle. It has been over a week since we found you close to death at Velin. You lost a lot of blood and had everybody very worried for several days. Not to mention poor Tanya. She was at her wits end when we arrived at the castle.'

'Is Tanya all right?' Gwaine interjected with concern.

'Yes. Tanya is very well. She has had some trouble coming to terms with having killed those two soldiers, and with the ordeal in general, but she seems to be on the improve.' Magnor stopped in thought and then decided to continue. 'I even noticed, yesterday, that she was taking more interest in the wedding preparations. ...Yes. She seems quite well.'

Gwaine's spirits fell. He had almost forgotten Tanya's betrothal to Stefarne. Though, it didn't really matter. Gwaine still cared deeply for Tanya, but she had made clear her disgust for him. There was no reconciling the rift between them now.

Gwaine forced his mind back to the original topic. 'What of the war. How did you escape the trap in Velin?'

Magnor raised his eyebrows in a surprised, questioning gaze. 'What trap, my Prince?'

'Why, …the trap, my Lord.' Gwaine was dumbfounded. 'The enemy was in the mountains waiting to outflank you.'

Magnor gave a hearty laugh. 'My dear Warlord. After all I have taught you, how could you think that our army would allow itself to be outflanked? That was no trap!'

Gwaine stared at Magnor in bewilderment. 'But…' He groped weakly for an explanation as the door opened and Taron entered the room.

'You see, Commander Taron', Magnor boomed, pointing at Gwaine. 'I told you that the Warlord was repairable.'

Taron was beaming. He strode to the side of the bed and searched for a way to embrace his friend. Finding none that wouldn't cause him pain, he settled for ruffling Gwaine's hair. 'Welcome back to life, Gwaine. I thought for sure that you would die.'

Gwaine beamed in reply. 'It's good to see you, Taron.' Gwaine studied the brightness of his friend's eyes. 'And you look well. Much better than the last time I saw you.'

Taron's face displayed a flicker of sombreness before returning to a grin. 'Yes, I'm well. I have my problems, but I am much better than I was at our last meeting.'

Gwaine was pleased with his friend's improved mood. 'You will have to tell me your recipe for returning from depression.'

To Gwaine's surprise, his flippant remark embarrassed Taron and forced him to break their eye contact. Taron stared at the floor as he answered. 'I would like to talk to you in private, my Lord, about that. I have much to confess to you as a friend.'

Gwaine's surprise ebbed as the words 'Taron needs a day like that' raced to the foreground of his mind. Ellorn's name followed quickly after. Gwaine fought to suppress the urge to smile as he imagined the fun he would have while Taron sweated through his confession. 'Very well Taron. It sounds serious. I look forward to our discussion, as soon as possible.'

'Thank you, my Lord.' Taron's reply was subdued.

'Anyway', Gwaine began buoyantly, trying to restore the happy mood. 'I now know why you weren't outflanked in Velinon. With Taron as Commander, there would be no possibility of the enemy pulling anything like that. I was worried that Kem was in command.'

Taron jumped to the defensive. 'Oh! I'm sure that, if Kem had not been killed in Seyldrek, he would have commanded the army at least as well as I did.'

Gwaine stared at Taron in disbelief. 'Kem was killed?'

'Yes, my Lord.' Taron, realising his blunder, turned to Magnor for help. 'I'm sorry. I thought you must have discussed that.'

'No Taron', Magnor answered dryly. 'We haven't discussed that yet.'

'I'm sorry, Gwaine. That was a foolish way for me to tell you.'

'That's all right Taron. ...How did it happen?'

'Kem and I were Stefarne's senior officers. Kem was encamped in Seyldrek, near the mountains, when the enemy counter-attacked. The attack failed but Kem was struck down by an arrow. He died quickly, my Lord.'

Gwaine only nodded in shock. The tragedy of the war was that, for all their planning and scheming, the final outcome had probably been decided by an unlucky arrow. The Dark Emperor's final plot had been undone by one of his own bowmen.

Magnor gave a poor imitation of a cough, in an attempt to drag Gwaine's attention back to their previous conversation. 'You wanted to tell me something about Kem.'

Gwaine couldn't see the point anymore. 'Does Tanya know that he is dead?'

'Yes. She knows. Like you, she expressed surprise that he was not leading the army when we arrived at Velin.'

'What did she say when she learned of his death?'

Magnor looked surprised at the question. 'Nothing my Lord. I don't think that she knew him very well. Why do you ask?'

'Oh, no reason. ...I suppose she didn't know him very well.' Gwaine had always been impressed by Tanya's common sense in always knowing what to say and when to say nothing. She still had an unblemished record. 'It's a shame. He was a good friend and a great warrior.'

'Yes', Taron agreed readily. 'He shall go down in our history books as one of the great heroes of this war.'

Taron and Magnor stood in silence while Gwaine tried to absorb all that he was being told. He tried to formulate more questions. Suddenly, he reacted with a start and looked quizzically at Taron. 'Did you say that you were ***Stefarne's*** senior officers?'

'Yes, Gwaine.'

'Oh my God!' Gwaine laughed sarcastically. 'How did that happen ...and how the hell did you survive it?'

To Gwaine's amazement, Taron was immediately on the defensive. 'Prince Stefarne led the counter-attack out of Arrindare and all the way through Amorand. He has earned a great reputation and a great deal of respect among the soldiers of all the armies of Amorand.'

Gwaine was taken aback by Taron's mild rebuke. He looked to Magnor for assistance. 'Surely we're not talking about the same person.'

Magnor smiled warmly and nodded. 'You said yourself that you saw a change in Stefarne when you last met. The war has matured him. He saw the suffering and the tragedy around him and stopped thinking about himself. You will see a different Stefarne when next you meet. ...Tanya has certainly noticed a difference.'

Gwaine's spirits fell. He felt a fool. 'Yes. She has chosen correctly. ...And what do the people of Amorand think of ***me***, Magnor?'

Magnor lowered his eyes and puffed his cheeks in thought. 'I'm sorry, Gwaine. Your mission was secret. They wonder where you went. They wonder why their Warlord left them in their time of need.'

Gwaine gritted his teeth. His emotions swayed between frustration and anger and depression. He thought of all that he had been through, ...Moridare's castle, the plot to burn the crops, the Dark Emperor's desert, the murder of the Dark Emperor, and those last angered words with Tanya. All that pain for nothing. His people believe that he merely ran away.

Seeing the anger in Gwaine's thoughts, Taron tried to lessen the severity of Magnor's words. 'But now that you have returned, Gwaine, we can tell the people of your successful mission and the part it played in the winning of the war.'

Gwaine slowly shook his head. He ran the events in the North Continent through his mind, over and over. There was nothing there that he was proud of. 'No. Leave well enough alone. I don't know which is the greater shame. Let the people believe that I ran away. Maybe I did. Maybe I never expected my plan to succeed. Maybe I ran away to die, ...to escape.'

'Your success will be known, Gwaine', Magnor interjected. 'It is part of your history, but it will always be overshadowed by the tails of great battles and bloodied warriors. How much detail of your exploits becomes known, is up to you.'

'Then I choose, …none', Gwaine replied vehemently. I only wish that I could be as easily ignored by the historians of the North Continent. God only knows what sort of monster I will be described as by them, for centuries to come.'

'Very well', Magnor consoled as he searched for a change of subject. 'And now that you are no longer Warlord, what shall you do?'

Gwaine stared in bewilderment at Magnor. This conversation was moving too quickly. Yes, the Dark Emperor was destroyed and the enemy had been driven from Amorand. His pledge had been fulfilled. He was no longer Warlord. 'I will ask my father to allow me to join our armies in the North Continent. There is still much to be done.'

Taron looked at his friend in horror. 'Our armies aren't in the North Continent, Gwaine.'

Gwaine's reply expression was just as horrified. 'Why not? ...Where are they?'

‘They’ve been dispersed, my Lord’, Magnor chimed in. ‘They’ve returned to their homelands.’

‘Impossible!’ Gwaine shouted in anger. ‘Get them back. We have to rescue Moridare and restore order. I’ve promised that our armies will aid Moridare.’

‘Yes. I know what you’ve promised. I have listened to Tanya and Stefarne argue for hours on end with the Kings who remain at Port Oracle. They want to restore order so that the effects of the famine can be overcome and so that we can bring peace to the two continents. I agree with them, but the Kings do not.’

‘But they are making a liar of me. I promised!’

‘Yes. Tanya has already placed that argument before them. They are unmoved.’

‘Why? We could unite the two continents. There could finally be peace.’

‘They don’t want the north united. They see a divided north, at war with itself, as preferable to a united north that could threaten Amorand.’

‘The old fools. We could bring peace.’

‘They don’t care about peace. They are only interested in the security of their own realms.’

‘The fools! We’ve got to change their minds. We’ve got to talk to them.’

‘Stefarne and Tanya have already tried and failed.’

‘We could convince them, Magnor. They will listen to your wisdom.’

Magnor stared at Gwaine in silence, his old shoulders drooped and despondent. ‘No, Gwaine’, he whispered in an old, tired voice. My interference in the affairs of this world ended when you killed Rycon. I was only here to counter his effect.’

‘Then our opportunity for peace will be gone. Wasted!’

‘Gwaine’, Taron interrupted in a quiet tone. ‘It’s too late. The armies have already returned home. Kings Vole and Fenore are already warring with each other, over some petty insult. There’s nothing more to be done.’

Gwaine slumped further into his bedding. He felt like lead. Moridare would despise him for the rest of his days and the petty wars would now be waged in the north as well as in the south. His voice came in a gust of despondency. 'Then if I cannot return to the North Continent, what career do you suggest, Magnor, for a retired, failed Warlord?'

Magnor bowed his head. It was an unanswerable question. 'I do not know, my Prince. For my part, I have asked the King for a ship to sail in search of Parrin. It leaves from here in three days, provided I can find a crew of volunteers.'

Gwaine studied Magnor's plan. It was obviously an invitation. 'Show me Parrin, my Lord Magnor.'

Magnor smiled a sad, wry smile. 'You are very welcome, Gwaine.'

'And I, my Lord Magnor', Taron added.

Gwaine looked, in surprise, at Taron. His face must have displayed the question, for Taron answered it immediately.

'I love the Princess Ellorn, too greatly, to ever be happy in this land.'

A VIEW OF LASATAL

Gwaine shuffled slowly down the dock to the waiting ship. On only his second day out of bed, he couldn't have wanted for an easier, leveller walk, but his breath, nevertheless, came in gusts with the exertion. He clutched his shoulder as he walked, in an attempt to stop his awkward movements reverberating through his wound. He could see Magnor watching him from the ship's rail.

'Old bugger', he complained to himself. 'He wouldn't think to offer some help.'

As he reached the gangplank a supporting hand suddenly appeared, steadying him by his right arm.

'Can't have my Prince taking a swim this early in the morning', Taron quipped with a broad grin on his face.

'Thank you, Taron. ...Though, once we're aboard this ship, I'm no longer your Prince. ...Just another member of the crew.'

'Oh, that's alright then', Taron replied good-humouredly. 'Once we're aboard ship, I'll turn you around and push you into the drink.'

Gwaine laughed. 'I warn you, I'll be forced to drown.'

'Well in that case, I'd be forced to pull you back out again.'

Gwaine was warmed by Taron's reply. At least their friendship had survived the war, even if there was little else to be cheerful about.

With Taron steadying his movements, Gwaine found the gangplank much less of an exertion than he had anticipated.

'Good morning, my Lords.' Magnor's voice was full of cheer. More so, than Gwaine could ever remember.

'Good morning, Magnor', Gwaine and Taron replied in unison.

Having negotiated the step down to the ship's deck, Gwaine immediately scanned the area around Magnor, searching for somewhere to sit and rest his overheating frame.

Magnor stepped backward and bowed as he gestured to a chair, already set up near the rail. 'I thought you might be in need of this, my Lord.'

Gwaine smiled with relief and immediately regretted his dark thoughts of Magnor. The 'old bugger' wasn't too bad after all. 'Thank you Magnor. I am certainly in need of that.'

Gwaine settled into the chair as Magnor produced a blanket and draped it over Gwaine's lap.

'Thank you, my Lord Magnor', Gwaine said in genuine surprise as he stared up into Magnor's creviced old face.

'I trust that you and Taron have said goodbye to everyone. We will be sailing at any time now.'

Gwaine tried to find a satisfactory answer to Magnor's question. Taron beat him to the reply.

'To everyone we could, my Lord.' Gwaine looked into Taron's sad face and repeated his reply despondently. 'To everyone we could.' Gwaine had been refused any contact with Tanya and he could well imagine that the same barrier would have existed between Taron and Ellorn.

The three fell into a silence as they stared, lost in their thoughts, toward the Port Oracle Lodge. Taron finally broke the uncomfortable quiet.

'Thank you, Gwaine. Your mother told me that you pleaded my case for Ellorn.'

'Oh, that's all right, Taron. No thanks required. I failed miserably. My father apparently has some grand plan for a convenient marriage between Arrindare and Cadel. He was most impressed with Prince Soran, ...and he seems obsessed with the idea of forming an alliance with another Kingdom that is in dispute with Barikarn. He doesn't trust the security of the Fortress of Marsh now that all of the armies of Amorand have marched through it.' Gwaine was desperate for a light-hearted comment to end the conversation. 'Besides, my motive wasn't all that honourable. I was looking for a way of leaving you behind.' He turned to Magnor. 'How long, my Lord, is this voyage to Parrin?'

Magnor only smiled toward the dock. Coming along the main dock area were Stefarne, Queen Lenore, and four attendants who were having some difficulty carrying an extremely large crate. Stefarne's voice was clearly audible over the distance. 'Be careful with that', he commanded. 'It's most fragile'.

Gwaine smiled to himself as he watched the attendants visibly trying harder to be more careful with the weight, which was obviously too great for their number. Stefarne was definitely in command. They respected him and were trying desperately to obey his difficult command. To Gwaine's surprise, the crate was successfully manoeuvred up the gangplank and delicately placed on the ship's deck, two metres behind where he was sitting. The red faced attendants bowed deeply to Stefarne and Queen Lenore before departing wearily.

When Gwaine had boarded the ship to sail to the North Continent, Stefarne had delivered to him a small crate of wine from his private cellar. Upon hearing of Gwaine's plan to sail in search of Parrin with Magnor, Stefarne had promised an even greater gift.

Gwaine stood and bowed as Stefarne and his mother boarded the ship.

'You see', Stefarne boomed as he pointed to the crate. 'My gift grows with the distance you travel.'

'Thank you, Stefarne.' Gwaine was overawed by the changes in his older brother. He had always been very selfish with his wines. 'Your present shall comfort us and warm us on the cold nights at sea.'

Stefarne's wide grin seemed to double with Gwaine's words of gratitude. 'Yes. I'm sure it will. I hope you enjoy my selection.'

'Your good taste in such things has always been renowned, brother.'

Queen Lenore brushed past Stefarne and embraced Gwaine. Gwaine immediately winced but tried not to betray the pain to his mother. 'I helped Stefarne with the selection and packing, so that you will think of me, too, when you're being warmed on those cold nights.'

'I will think of you mother, and during the day as well.'

'Good.' Lenore kissed him on the cheek and stood back. 'I'm not going to cry this time. We've argued about you leaving, so that's over now. I just hope that you will return to us one day.'

'That may happen, mother. I cannot say.'

The captain's voice boomed from the command deck. 'We're ready to cast off, my Lord Magnor.'

Magnor merely waved in reply.

'Very well', Lenore continued. 'I'm not going to stay and wave. It takes so long for a ship to disappear from view.' She kissed Gwaine's cheek. 'Goodbye. I love you.'

'I love you, mother.'

Lenore kissed Taron's cheek as she passed him and then hurried down the gangplank and along the dock without looking back.

Gwaine, Taron, Stefarne and Magnor stood in silence and watched her stride quickly along the dock while searching for her handkerchief, before she disappeared into the building.

Stefarne strode forward and gave Gwaine his hand. Gwaine noted that his handshake was stronger and more confident than it had ever been. 'Little brother, if

I can't offer you sufficient incentive to stay, then I will promise you justice after you have gone. Our history books shall record the truth of your feats in the North Continent. It was your deeds that caused our enemy to retreat, not mine. I will not accept glory that is rightfully yours.'

Gwaine's spine chilled with Stefarne's words. While he was pleased with his brother's display of honour, he had grown to value the anonymity of his actions in the north. 'No Stefarne. I am not proud of my deeds. I would rather that you accepted the glory and used your esteem in Amorand to bring peace between all of the Kingdoms.'

'And to the North Continent', Stefarne added. 'I will try to honour your promise to Moridare, in your name.'

'Thank you, brother. It would please me to think that there was still a chance of peace on these continents.'

The noise of ropes being released attracted everyone's attention.

Stefarne turned back to Gwaine, obviously feeling the strain of their parting. 'I'm sorry, Gwaine, that we weren't closer brothers.'

Gwaine embraced his brother. 'We are now. The past means nothing.'

Stefarne returned Gwaine's embrace before turning and walking to the gangplank. Stopping at the top of the plank, he turned and bowed. 'My Lord Magnor, my Lord Taron, brother, ...I wish you success in your voyage. Like my mother, I will not stay to wave, but unlike my mother, I will not be so ambitious as to promise not to cry. I will miss you all.'

Stefarne turned to leave, but Gwaine couldn't restrain himself any longer. 'Stefarne!'

Stefarne turned in response.

‘Stefarne. Please say goodbye to Tanya for me. I wasn’t allowed. And please take good care of her.’ Gwaine hoped that his last comment would not be taken as an insult.

Stefarne smiled sadly. ‘I will look after her in a way that would please my younger brother. Tanya shall be well cared for. I promise you that.’

‘Thank you Stefarne. Goodbye brother.’

Stefarne bowed and strode away without looking back. Before he had disappeared from sight, the gangplank had been removed and the last ropes had been unleashed. The ship creaked as the crew used large poles to push it away from the dock. Large sails billowed and flapped as they were hoisted into a position to catch the offshore breeze.

Magnor disappeared to the captain’s deck, leaving Taron and Gwaine silently watching the shore and the lodgings at Port Oracle moving away from them.

The ship was manoeuvring among the Eleven Isles when Magnor finally returned. Taron and Gwaine were leaning on the railing, admiring the rich greenness of the islands.

‘Isn’t it a beautiful day’, Magnor chirped cheerfully.

Taron just ignored the comment as he sulkily watched the Amorand shoreline, but Gwaine couldn’t ignore Magnor’s exuberance.

‘You’re in a surprisingly merry mood, my Lord Magnor.’

‘Of course, my Lord’, Magnor replied buoyantly. ‘I do apologise for being out of mesh with you two, but while you are sad at leaving your home, I am delighted at returning to mine.’

Taron immediately straightened and joined in the conversation. ‘Parrin is your home?’

‘Well, my Lord, the answer to that question depends on which Parrin we are discussing.’ Magnor stared questioningly at Gwaine. ‘How much did Rycon tell you about me?’

‘The Dark Emperor told me a great deal about both of you.’

‘Then you know that I am not from this planet?’

‘Pardon?’ Taron interjected worriedly.

‘Yes, Magnor. I know that.’

‘Pardon?’ Taron repeated, this time to Gwaine.

‘Did he tell you that Parrin was the name of our home planet?’

‘No my, Lord. I didn’t know that. I thought Parrin was a place on this planet.’

Taron had given up questioning. He fell heavily into Gwaine’s chair, dumbfounded, his mouth hanging slightly open as he tried to follow the conversation.

‘It is’, Magnor continued. ‘I named the place where I landed, Parrin, after my home planet. We are sailing to the Parrin on your planet. From there, I shall voyage to my home. You may all come with me if you wish, or return to Amorand, or wherever you want to go.’

Gwaine turned to Taron. ‘What do you say, Taron? Do you want to travel with Magnor?’

Taron shook his head in amazement. ‘I have no other plans’, he replied weakly.

‘Good’, Magnor replied excitedly. ‘I shall show you the stars, my young friends.’

Gwaine gave a disinterested nod. ‘All the stars in the sky cannot replace Tanya’s sparkle but, since I have lost that, the stars will do as a second option.’

The ship was now passing through the strait between the two most western islands of the Eleven Isles. From their position at the rail, the three could clearly see the cliffs of the northern coast of Arrindare.

'Goodbye, my home', Taron whispered.

'Tell me, Magnor', Gwaine boomed with renewed vigour and resolve, 'While I can still see my homeland. Am I a success of a failure? Did I murder a monster or a saint? Was the Emperor's intention evil or good? ...Was the war worth winning?'

Magnor stared in the direction of Arrindare, in silence, for some time before bowing his head and heaving his chest with a huge sigh. 'I have asked myself that question for centuries. I cannot answer it. Perhaps Rycon's aim was truly to bring peace to this land, or perhaps he wanted to be supreme ruler and his story of peace was just a lie. I don't know, Gwaine.'

'Then I shall never be at peace within myself.'

'You are too hard on yourself, Gwaine. You are looking for good or evil in their purest forms. They don't exist. Good and evil only exist in degrees of mixtures of both. Rycon wasn't purely evil anymore than he was purely good. He was some mixture of both, just like you and I. We just don't know what the mixture was, which ingredient was dominant. I could never let him have supreme power because I could never know which ingredient would win under those circumstances. Forget your black and white world. Look for different shades of grey.'

'Thank you for your honest wisdom, Magnor, but I would have been happy with a short lie. If you had told me that the Emperor was evil, it would have given some reason to this destruction, to the famine I created, to the friends and love that Taron and I have lost, and to the uncertainty and emptiness of our future.'

Silence fell as the three returned their attention to the Arrindare coastline.

'We can never return, Taron.'

'No, Gwaine. I wouldn't want to return to greet Ellorn and Soran as wife and husband, anymore than you would want to greet Tanya and Stefarne.'

‘And can you imagine returning to the petty wars. Soldiers dying, defending the name of some old fool of a King. In all our depression and uncertainty, we are better leaving than staying.’

‘Oh, you poor boys. Do you want us to carry you all the way to Parrin?’

Gwaine and Taron spun in surprise at the familiar voice, to see Tanya and Ellorn climbing out of Stefarne’s crate.

‘What the hell?’

Tanya was in Gwaine’s arms in a flash, forcing a kiss on his lips as he winced in pain. He could hear Ellorn and Taron laughing while Taron spun her in circles as they embraced.

‘What about Stefarne?’ Gwaine found himself asking.

‘Oh! He and Susanne are all right’, Tanya replied buoyantly.

Gwaine laughed and hugged her to him.

Magnor moved away from the excited group and disappeared below deck, a cunning satisfied smile on his lips.

www.ingramcontent.com/pod-product-compliance
Lightning Source LLC
LaVergne TN
LVHW081315110826
845149LV00006B/1510